All' Acqua, the debut novel of Kerrville resident Hans Schlunegger, is a compelling invitation to take a ride. The plot pulls you forward, while the style of writing invites you to enjoy the journey. The smart dialogue provides road signs for this story of dangerous love and ambition. Enjoy the ride.

> —**Kathleen Hudson** is an English professor at Schreiner University, director of the Texas Heritage Music Foundation and author of *Telling Stories, Writing Songs: An Album of Texas Songwriters*, published by UT Press in Austin, Texas.

Every time Schlunegger describes an object or place, I want to touch it or go there.

> —**Andy Rich**, director, Hill Country Arts Foundation and Point Theatre

A delicious and intriguing tale that follows a naïve hero, Herman Schuller, who is swept into a torrent of deception by a duplicitous vision named Angelina. Richly textured for time and place, this story is best savored over many nights with roaring fires and fine wines.

> —**Terri Spaugh** is an author, a journalist for Creative Screenwriting and President of Texas Flix, Inc., an independent film production company

The debut novel by Swiss author Hansueli Schlunegger is an adventure and love story. It is quite a page-turner, as we follow the adventures of Corporal Schuller on his hunt after the villain Giulio and always meeting up with Angelina. Is she real or is she just a dream? We also suspect that part of the story has autobiographical undertones!

—**Jacob Baur & Wal Baur**, editors, Regional pages USA *Swiss Review*

All' Acqua is an intriguing tale, spiced by personal and social passion and grounded in human reflection on the experiences and choices that we make. The story pulls us toward affirmation that life, in all its complication, is both an exciting adventure and filled with cosmic and personal purpose.

—**Sam M. Junkin,** President Emeritus Schreiner University

A story of star-crossed lovers, thrown together in suspenseful action, irrepressible love, strained by success, duty, and honor. Masterful description puts you into the romance, amid the beauty and culture of Switzerland and Italy. You can't let go of the characters until the last sentence.

—**Danny Edwards**, author of *Double Crossover*

In his first novel, *All' Acqua,* Hansueli Schlunegger interweaves a tale of romantic love and adventure while guiding the reader across landscapes—geographic and culinary. At the heart of his tale of conflicted love stand two men who are obsessed with the same woman. The story unfolds in sleepy Alpine villages, in the brilliant salons of Milan's high fashion, on cliff-sides, and in candlelit mountain cabins. Schlunegger offers up an adventure for the heart and palate. "What one man sought, the other was about to toss aside."

–**Sylvia M. Shaw, Ph.D.,** Boston University

ALL' ACQUA

All' Acqua

a novel by

Hansueli Schlunegger

BROWN BOOKS PUBLISHING GROUP
DALLAS

For information please contact Brown Books Publishing Group
16200 North Dallas Parkway, Suite 170, Dallas, TX 75248
972-381-0009   www.brownbooks.com

First Printing 2002
ISBN 0-9720574-0-4

ACKNOWLEDGMENTS

The writing of All' Acqua, a novel based on real life experiences, would have come to a dead halt had it not been for the assistance and encouragement—freely offered and gratefully received—of close friends and family.

I owe particular thanks to Lois Schlieter, a former librarian at Schreiner University and a long time friend of my family. Her undaunted belief in the project, her encouraging words, and tireless advice—from the first pages through the last—were essential factors to conclude the novel successfully.

My gratitude goes to two gracious ladies, Sally Rich and Lois Raymer, who have offered their literary talents most generously.

I'm grateful to Walter Keiser and Walter Murer of Stans and Beckenried, respectively, who, at my side, have walked and explored the difficult mountain trails of southern Switzerland and Italy. Their efforts have rewarded the novel with richness and great realism.

I have also been very fortunate to engage the talents of a first-rate editor, Jeff Putnam (a multilingual former opera singer and published novelist who has lived many years abroad—as Mr. Putnam put it), whose experiences in European travels have added color and genuineness to the story.

My sincere appreciation goes to the publisher, Milli Brown, and her editorial director, Kathryn Grant (mille grazie, Kathryn!), whose faith in the novel brought about its publication.

The illustration on the dust jacket, and the drawings on the inside covers were beautifully done by artist Lois Raymer of Kerrville, Texas. The talented Alyson Alexander, of Brown Books, created the cover design and the interior layout.

Above all, I want to thank my family, particularly my wife, Annemarie, for their patience and understanding . . . . And I want to apologize to them for my long absences (in mind and body) during those long, late-night computer sessions. Let us hope that the sacrifices in time and personal attention will be richly rewarded with renewed love and harmony.

PROLOGUE

FRIDAY, OCTOBER 16, 1959

Thick clouds were boiling across the Zürich flatland, turning day to night. The DC6 banked sharply to the left, hail pounding the wings and fuselage. Herman Schuller held his breath and gripped the armrests with both hands; a cramp twisted his stomach, and his knees trembled. He bit his lip—this was his first flight, and he was going to enjoy it no matter what.

"Ladies and gentleman, this is Captain Keiser. I apologize for the unexpected roughness. I'm altering our course to the south where skies are clear . . ." and moments later, the clouds gave way to a cloudless sky.

Herman Schuller calculated that this change of course would take them over the Ticino, the southernmost part of Switzerland where, across the mountaintops with their eternal snow, there were citrus groves and chestnut trees in the warm valleys far below. He loosened his seatbelt, and with his nose pressed against the cold glass of the window he thought of the child he had once been, pressing his nose against the glass of the local merchant store, praying for the little train set he knew his parents could not afford to buy. He thought of the tales told by his dad about beautiful hotels in far-away countries, Egypt and England, where he had worked as a young man serving the wealthy and the famous. Herman Schuller began dreaming about going to those places and meeting its people, knowing that the time would come when he would follow his father's footsteps, making his mark in hospitality. And this flight was the first step to fulfill those dreams.

The mountains were rising from beneath the wings. Yes! There was St. Gothard with the road winding across the legendary pass. His throat tightened, his heart pounded, his eyes filled with tears as the landscape he knew so well began to emerge where, at the end of the valley far below—an insignificant speck to those who had no knowledge of it—All' Acqua lay in the lap of a rugged mountain pass, forgotten by the world.

How could he forget that beauty and desire, leave behind the warmth and hope he had found—all because of a few glorious days, beginning at the Grand Central railway station in Zürich on a gorgeous day in spring just a little over four years ago. He was in his Swiss Army uniform, on the way to exercises near a little town in the Ticino he'd never even heard of up to then . . . All' Acqua . . .

CHAPTER 1

SUNDAY, MAY 15, 1955

*T*he conductor raised the green-striped signal disk and blew his whistle. Eight powerful electro-motors sprang to life, the drive-wheels turned, and with a screech and a growl the Gotthard Express began to roll.

A lone soldier made a dash for the departing train, his cap askew, his heavy pack bouncing. There was a rifle in his hand.

"Help him with the rifle while I grab his rucksack!" Corporal Schuller shouted, leaning from the platform with one hand on the rail, the other groping for the soldier's pack. Ruedi Frei rushed to help.

The train was gaining speed.

The soldier jumped and the edge of his boot barely caught the lower step. He grabbed the railing with one hand, tossed his rifle to the platform with the other. Then his foot slipped and he would have been lost beneath the wheels of the train if a strong yank from above hadn't pulled him to the platform, nearly ripping the rucksack from his back.

"That was close," recruit Rüegg said, out of breath. "Thanks for the hand, Corp!" He lifted his left boot and stared at it, wondering if all the nails were still in place. "Who would have thought these spiked infantry boots would have saved my ass just now!" He hooked his rifle on his shoulder and walked into the compartment behind his friends.

The men stored their rucksacks and helmets and hung their rifles and ammo belts on sturdy brass hooks located to each side of the seats. Frei sat down on the inside seat and let his spider legs, with feet the size of snorkeling fins, protrude into the gangway. He was tall and stringy, and not suitable to lead the squad, since his long stride quickly outpaced the average man. He was the battalion Goliath, though there was no cruelty in him and his voice was high-pitched and weak.

The soldiers settled in their seats. Boot camp in Zürich was over and they were headed south to the Ticino on a train full of vacationers. The soldiers weren't on leave, however; they would be engaged in field maneuvers where they would show off their new skills. No more running through city traffic, no more monotonous barracks food, no more exercises on asphalt under a hot sun. Field maneuvers would be held in the mountains with real bullets. Corporal Schuller was counting on the three men with him to perform well: they were already his closest friends; he respected them and they, him.

Herman loosened his necktie, leaned back in his seat, and closed his eyes. He thought of Margrit, his girl in Basel. "Take care of yourself and come back in one piece," she had said at the railroad station. And as he had kissed her goodbye, she'd whispered, "I love you" —her last words before the train rolled from the giant hall. I *love you, too. I'm so lucky to have you my sweet Margrit—so lucky.* But did he deserve her love? Was he worthy of her beauty? "You're a fortunate fellow," his friends had been telling him. It was true, she'd had a lot of suitors—why had she chosen him?

The thought of their first kiss sent shivers from the top of his head to the soles of his feet. She had taught him how to move his lips teasingly. She'd taught him to be gentle, not to rush her, to nibble her neck, to kiss her ears! She'd taught him how a woman feels, what she wants from her man. The reminiscence of that first kiss made him burn with new desires. He opened his eyes.

Herman was average in height, build, and education. His eyes were a bright blue, and his gaze was wide open and steadfast. His smile gave a certain whimsy to his expression and girls liked him at a glance. Even so, his feeling of mediocrity led him to brag occasionally about girls he had not kissed or adventures he had not had. In life as in school he'd advanced quickly in subjects he liked but was held back in those he didn't; in his mind, homework was the most trivial of all things. He hated fights, but he'd been dragged into them, and was respected for his tolerance of pain as well as his punching ability. In spite of his weaknesses Herman was well liked by the men in his command, and he knew that he was.

"It's true!" said Spiller, loosening the first button on his shirt, "it's no longer just gossip—we're going to conduct the sharpshooting demonstration and—"

"You're fantasizing again," said Frei, butting in. "I'm usually the first to hear and I haven't heard."

"No, it's true! No shit!" said Rüegg, sounding even more certain. "And this time it'll be in front of the whole battalion. Tell him, Corp!"

Corporal Schuller nodded weakly. "It was supposed to be a secret."

"So it's true."

The corporal shrugged, "Nothing specific has been said to me; I guess I'm the last to know."

Spiller shook his head and opened a second button on his shirt. "I hope we won't be chosen this time."

"Why not?"

"Spiller's right," Frei put in, tickled to find a common cause. "Each time we get a task like that, we end up doubling with guard duty that same night."

"You can count on it," said Rüegg.

The corporal shook his head. "That was just a coincidence."

"Twice in a row?"

Herman Schuller half rose from his seat. "Men, where's your spirit? You're supposed to enjoy the service, proudly protect the fatherland and stand up to the foe. Where's your pride in the red flag and white cross? Anyway, whatever your thoughts—I'm going to depend on you!"

They responded as one: "We'll think about that one, Corp!"

The train roared down the eastern shores of Lake Lucerne through the very heart of Switzerland, then followed the River Reuss, which was master in these parts, twisting and churning. Giant clouds of vapor arose where it crashed into cliffs and foamed through gorges to the lake below.

Herman was drowsy but could find no rest. He was not himself. The sting in his side was making him uneasy. It couldn't be the rumor of the exercise—true as it was—as no such task had ever troubled him before. He opened the window to the halfway notch and inhaled the air in long, deep breaths. The fresh air felt good, but the thought of that "something" lingered.

Did it have to do with that dream he'd had the night before? No chance of that—he never paid attention to such dreams. Except . . .

except this one had kept him awake till dawn. Did it carry some sort of prophecy? He shook his head decisively. An old wives' tale! Even so, sweat was building on his forehead and upper lip—the dream was stuck in his mind like an omen. He looked at the snoring trio; one of them had been in that dream but he couldn't tell which one. He closed his eyes and let the air stream over his face.

The train passed through a series of switchback tunnels to gain altitude. The steeple of Wassen's church, brilliantly white in the midday sun, came into view above the tracks. It appeared twice more below and on opposite sides as the train climbed and reversed direction deep inside the granite mountain. Captivated passengers kept crossing the aisle to watch.

With an earsplitting bang, the train roared into the lengthy Gotthard Tunnel. Then the rhythmic sound of the wheels echoing off the tunnel walls cast a spell on Herman Schuller. His eyelids drooped and closed.

The corporal tripped in the dark over rocks and fallen trees as the cry for help grew more faint. By chance he had shone his flashlight on the body of a soldier in full uniform lying curled up on the ground. He dropped to his knees . . . and leapt up again stunned. There was a giant, hissing serpent coiled around the soldier's chest. The corporal raised his dagger . . . then held back confused, for the serpent's head was that of a woman with shiny hair and dazzling eyes.

The train's sudden jolt wiped the image from his mind. Schuller woke drained of strength, his clothes soaked in sweat.

"Airolo, Airolo," shouted the conductor walking from car to car, ripping the foursome from their sleep. They grabbed their rucksacks, rifles, and ammo belts.

"Where to, Corp?" Spiller asked, strapping down his gear.

"I know where I'm going," groaned Rüegg, pointing to a nearby kiosk. "I'm thirsty for a beer."

"Me too," added Frei, taking the lead. They tagged along as best they could behind his long strides.

They dumped their packs and leaned the rifles on them. After huge gulps of cool beer, the noise and confusion around them abated somewhat. They hardly noticed the whistle of the departing train.

Herman Schuller asked the storekeeper for help finding the way to All' Acqua. The man puffed on his pipe, then opened the pewter bowl and tapped it on his raised heel. After filling his pipe and lighting it with a series of rapid puffs he closed the tiny lid and nodded thoughtfully. "The main road would be one way to go, soldier." He took a long puff. "But you'd save time by going through the village there." He pointed with the bowed ebony stem toward a cobblestone street crowded with houses on both sides. "It's a little steep for those heavy packs, but you'll make up for it in time."

"Great," said Herman, shaking the man's hand. The soldiers buckled up and began the trek.

From the onset, the road was steep and winding, but lush meadows dotted with buttercups soon made them forget their pain and renewed thirst. When Airolo's distant church announced the hour of three the soldiers stopped to hear the bells echo off the far side of the valley, mixed now with the sound of thunder and lightning from a nearby peak. The distant downpour was creating waterfalls falling from cliff to cliff that changed to strings of pearls, and short of the valley floor, to clouds of mist. The soldiers absorbed the spectacle silently, hearts pounding under their thick coats.

After the second hour, while crossing a creek, a small village came into view across the valley. Rüegg, always ready to take a break, rested his pack on the safety wall of the bridge. "How much longer?" he complained.

Corporal Schuller unhooked the knapsack. He pushed aside the rolled tarpaulin tied to it, flipped the flap open, and removed a topographical chart. He unfolded it on the wall and flattened the pleats with the back of his hand.

Spiller shook his head. "Why do you always attach the tarp to your knapsack?"

"Just a habit," said the corporal. Spiller was right, of course—the tarpaulin belonged on the rucksack. But he'd be damned if he was going to get caught in a downpour again with the tarp strapped to the rucksack back at the barracks snug and dry. He quickly pointed to the chart. "The town up there is Bedretto and we're here at this bridge. As you can see, it ought to be easy going from now on. Two hours, max."

"Is that open for debate?" teased Spiller.

"Or is it one of those courage-building schemes we've heard time and again?" barked Rüegg.

"Cut it out, guys. Have I ever failed you?"

"Do you want to try two out of three?"

"I'll carry your rifles if I'm wrong!"

Rüegg jumped to his feet and shouted, "It's a deal!"

"Not so fast," insisted the corporal. All eyes turned toward him.

"I just knew there'd be a catch," speculated Frei.

"Damned right there is!" said the corporal steadfastly. "If I'm right, you guys pay for the wine in that village."

They looked at each other—"It's a deal"—shook hands, then burst into laughter, and slapped each other on the back.

Sturdy houses crowded the cobblestone road, amplifying the soldiers' steps so that they sounded like a battalion on the march. Windows opened here and there and young girls, watched by their mothers, waved white handkerchiefs to welcome the soldiers. Charmed, though their lips were cracked from thirst, the young men blew kisses.

Rüegg motioned to a place across the street. "A good place to have that wine!" There it stood, whitewashed and half-timbered, with bushy, red geraniums jutting from the windowsills and cascading from a giant basket above the tavern's massive door. The soldiers, Rüegg in the lead, climbed the steps, opened the door, took off their packs, and turned them sideways to fit through the narrow frame.

It was the typical Ticino ristorante: oiled parquet floor, walls with knotty-pine wainscoting, and rustic, hand-hewn beams holding up the ceiling. The unconventional sturdy tables and chairs had presumably been brought in from Italy. A *Fussballtisch* was the main attraction, and beyond it, at the wall facing the valley, two windows with long cranks, and sheer curtains fastened to the side with red ribbons. A modern jukebox blared, "*Ticinesi son bravi soldà* . . ." Soft red neon lights shimmered against the wall, and above, in their glow, was the dusty trophy of a chamois with hooked horns. Across the tavern was a ceramic stove, a masterpiece of hand-painted tiles with a shiny brass door, and the usual cozy bench up front.

The tavern was deserted save the waitress busy removing a batch of bread from the oven. She glanced at the soldiers, gave them a small smile, then thrust the long spatula back into the opening to push the last loaves of bread closer to the embers.

The foursome settled on a table next to the jukebox. Rüegg

seemed in charge, as usual. "Bring us your best Barbera," he ordered loudly. The waitress, in a pleated skirt and white blouse with puffy sleeves, brought four tumblers, and a bottle of wine. It was deftly opened and one glass poured. She waited as Rüegg took a sip, buttoned his lips expertly, then showed his acceptance with a huge grin. Soon there were shouts of "Prosit" and the sound of clinking tumblers. After mere minutes the owner, a sturdy woman in her late fifties whose dress was too short, was proudly opening the second bottle of her homemade wine.

Stirred by the aroma of the baking bread, Frei waved to the young waitress. "Hey, beautiful," he cried, "we're hungry for some good cheese and home-baked bread."

The girl dashed across the room with the order, which now included still another bottle of Barbera wine. Before long, she was back with a hunk of cheese on a wooden plank and a loaf of bread so hot still that the air above it made the room shimmer. She put a serrated knife and a small plate in front of each man.

The soldiers ate quietly. "This is great cheese," remarked Corporal Schuller after a while, taking a second wedge, and another slice of steaming bread. The cheese had the flavor of a first-grade Parmesan, but softer.

The waitress heard his comment. "We get it from a dairy farmer who lives in Val Formazza just beyond San Giácomo Pass," she said with pride. "He makes the trip twice a year on foot. It's the best around."

Corporal Schuller asked her name.

"Bernadette," she said, bashfully.

"That's a nice name . . . Are you the daughter of the owner, the woman who brought the wine?"

"Yes, signore. Mamma owns the tavern, as you said."

The soldiers turned away from her and looked through the window, alerted by a rattle like tin cans pulled on strings. A VW delivery van with wide cargo doors drove up and stopped in front of the tavern, blocking the road to traffic. They watched a slight man with a neighborly smile walk up the steps and through the door. He greeted the soldiers with a nod and headed down the corridor to a back room.

In a flash, the soldiers' eyes were once more upon the road below as a red Fiat with its top rolled down backed into the parking space below their window. By itself the two-seat Topolino would have turned the young men's heads, but the driver made them forget to close their mouths.

As she slid from the driver's seat they saw she was wearing black slacks, tight around her waist and legs, stuck into high-heeled boots like skiers' pants. She straightened the rounded collar of her white silk blouse, snugged it about her waist, and tightened the knot on her scarlet scarf that hid her hair completely. An unzipped blue jacket made of fine leather was draped sportily about her. She slid it off with a movement of her shoulders and folded it over her arm. From the passenger seat, she grabbed a blue canvas bag that she carried instead of a purse.

The soldiers stared at the door impatiently . . . then there she was in all her charm, so beautiful, elegant, shapely . . . As she passed the soldiers' table, she nodded, a slight smile on her lips. She draped the jacket over the backrest of a chair at the table beyond the jukebox and sat down with her back against the window. Dumbstruck, the young men followed her every move.

She turned toward the waitress, and when she spoke, her voice was deep and . . . sexy, there was no other word for it. "The parked van wouldn't let me pass," she said protesting mildly. "Oh well. While I'm waiting, I'll have a *boccalino* of your red wine. And bring me a platter of prosciutto and some salame sardo as well. Is that fresh-baked bread I smell? I'll have a slice of that, too."

Her eyes were big, set wide. She had long, narrow brows and a trim nose with tiny nostrils. Her lips were full and moist but finely bowed and expertly painted. A faint smile played about them. She had so many beautiful qualities it was impossible to say what was so tantalizing to Herman and his men. Herman himself couldn't have uttered two words out loud and was trying, silently, to judge her age. He was usually good with ages but the best he could do with this beauty was: younger than thirty, because of her fine skin; older than twenty because of her poise while she was stopping traffic. And because of her easy way of moving and talking and ordering, and the way she could wear simple clothes and make them look like they cost a fortune . . . Not a day past twenty-six.

She slid from her chair and walked to the jukebox. Not really knowing what he was doing, Herman rose and met her there.

"I have—I have a twenty-cent coin," he stuttered, holding out his hand. He was looking straight at her, unblinking, but his face was as red as a fresh-boiled lobster.

"How nice of you, soldier. Thank you," she said, and her voice seemed deeper and even lovelier. She took the coin from his hand.

Was it her voice or the sparkle in her eyes, the closeness of her incredibly slim body, or the electrifying touch of her hand that made him back up? He couldn't tell. Anyway, it was a sudden shyness that he could neither understand nor overcome. She said nothing, just smiled at him with wide-open eyes. Finally she winked, turned to the jukebox, and fed the coin into the slot. And as she leaned forward to read the song-labels and engage the play-buttons, the red neon glow silhouetted her well-formed bosom.

"*Sul mare luccica / L'astro d'argento, / Placi da e l'onda . . .*" filled the air, a melody Herman knew as "Santa Lucia," the song their Italian maid used to sing back home. He hummed along. Surprised, the signora turned her head to him. She adjusted her scarf and gazed at him as if searching for something without knowing what. When her eyes met his there was a moment of tension, and her cheeks, already a lovely tan, blushed darker.

Herman stumbled backward toward the table and dropped into his chair, unable to take his eyes off her. He expected her to make a funny face and laugh. But she didn't. There wasn't even a smirk.

Frei put down his glass. "Corp, what's going on; are you dreaming or what?" he said.

Rüegg let out a high-pitch chuckle. "Man, you're out of your league, big-time."

"Come on, Corp," Spiller added quietly. "Forget that woman. Besides, we're people too." And when the corporal did not react, he shook his arm.

"I . . . I'm here," stuttered Herman. His friends burst into laughter. Undeterred, he kept staring at the woman, encouraged by the mere memory of her smile.

The delivery driver came from the back room. He turned to the woman, "Sorry for blocking your way, signora. I'll be out of here shortly." Then he stepped up to the soldiers' table. "I'm on my way to All' Acqua and can take two, maybe three of you with me," he said warily, twisting his mustache. "That's all the space I have in my van."

"That's awfully nice of you, signore, but we'd rather stick together," said Spiller.

"Nonsense," said Herman. "You guys take the van. I'll walk. You'll have it hard enough during the next two weeks. Trust me, I'll make sure of that!" He grinned. "Besides, you three have overstayed your welcome here. Oh, and aren't you forgetting something?"

"What's that, Corp?" wondered Frei.

"He wants us to pay for the wine, dummy," said Rüegg bleakly.

"Oh!" The soldiers settled their tabs and left the tavern.

At the threshold, Corporal Schuller turned around and looked at the woman by the window. He made a parting gesture, raising his hand (like an Indian in a Western movie, he thought) and started blushing again. She smiled a little uncertainly, and again there was that feeling of something unresolved between them. "Have a nice day, soldier."

The corporal had to shove his men in before the cargo door could be latched, but finally the van was on its way, swaying under its heavy load.

After a last look at the tiny Fiat, Herman swung his rucksack over his shoulders, his rifle across his chest, and faced the slope. He tried to imagine the woman's face in front of him, but could only see her wide-set, dark-blue eyes and inviting lips. He started up the road with a lump in his throat.

CHAPTER 2

_T_ he sun had moved between two mountain peaks, again flooding the land with its warmth. The road was curving steeply away from the river. Under his heavy pack Herman heard only his rhythmic steps and the loose rocks he trod underfoot from time to time. Once he heard the screech of a small animal in the distance—perhaps the prey of a hawk.

The woman at the tavern was a continuing presence in his mind—her smooth face, her hair tight under her scarf, her voice deep and clear. He imagined being with her, holding her hand, looking into those large blue eyes, his arm around her tiny waist. What if he tried to kiss her full, moist lips—?

A car was overtaking him at great speed. The Fiat! Herman wanted to shout, but his throat was dry. He wanted to wave, but his arms were numb. He wanted to run, but before he could make a move, the Fiat vanished beyond a bend in the road. Slowly his reflexes came alive, and he continued one step at a time, marionette-like, until he was back to his routine pace.

He had just crossed to the inside curve when he heard, "How about a ride, soldier?"

There she was, standing next to the open car door, her left foot on the floorboard, leaning on the window frame.

"Come on—don't just stand there with your mouth open," she said in flawless German.

Herman rushed toward her, unhooking gear and his rifle as he ran. The car was too small for the pack and rifle. He walked around the Fiat to the other side, noting the Italian license plate. "Uh . . . um,

I'll remove the knapsack. Maybe . . . If I could . . . " His stammering made her chuckle. Unruffled, he put the smaller pack behind the seat—a perfect fit—and the rucksack on top of the backrests. The rifle went between his legs.

They were silent, driving off. She was concentrating on the curves in the road, while the corporal found nothing to say. He felt as if he were in a trance and was blaming the hot sun on his face.

This could have been a dream except that his shoulder was rubbing against her soft leather jacket and her fine skin was close enough to be touched. He thought she must feel his eyes upon her but he couldn't stop drinking in her smooth shoulders, her slender neck, and her face. Without makeup the skin there was as smooth as silk. Tiny punctures in her earlobes suggested earrings, but she wore none; there was not a single stone or piece of gold on her.

She must be Italian. There was the evidence of her license plate, her full lips . . . But her eyes were a deep blue. A faint whiff of sweet perfume was adding fuel to the fire.

"I heard that your outfit will be spending two weeks in the territory."

He wasn't startled by her voice, but the warmth of it meant more than her words, and he could only nod when she glanced over.

"It must be exciting to use the real thing . . . I mean, real ammo for the exercise."

How did she know so much? The lump in his throat was still giving him trouble and again he just nodded when she looked at him.

"Are you married?" She didn't give him the chance to reply, quickly adding, "You're too young for that, though, aren't you? Besides, you don't wear a ring."

He managed something like a laugh. "I'm not married."

"So you *do* know how to talk," she said, smiling. "How about your girlfriend? You do have a girlfriend."

He just looked at her.

"I never met a soldier who didn't have at least one girl," she insisted.

His answer was a bashful smile.

"Tell me this," she said, sounding a little frustrated. "How can commanders order young soldiers to play war games during the day, then send them to stand guard all night? Seems rather cruel as well as unnecessary!"

He faced her squarely, surprised by her outpouring. "It's all in a day's work for my men. They learn to catnap while standing guard, and get away with it most of the time, so it's not really all that bad."

She shook her head. "I guess you can talk that way because you're a corporal and don't have to stand guard yourself."

"You've got that all wrong," he said, sounding like himself for a change. "I've done my share. I know what standing guard is all about!"

"I didn't mean to ruffle your feathers. All I meant—"

"It's okay. Okay?" he said, surprising himself. It was the tone he would have taken with his men.

After a silence she took a deep breath and said, "Is it true that your sentries carry loaded guns while on guard? With real bullets, I mean?"

His response was quick this time. "Not that I know of. That's never been the case when I pulled guard duty. I've heard that we do sometimes at border crossings—international boundaries."

"Not even when you're protecting weapons and ammunition?"

"I don't know. We might. It's possible."

"I've heard there's such a place in All' Acqua, but I can't imagine where. Keeping that stuff around sounds risky."

She looked at him and winced as if she too was at risk.

"I'm sure they've found a secure cellar or an old bunker with sturdy locks."

He was glad of the ease of his explanation, but he was also glad that she had no more questions because he really didn't know anything.

All' Acqua was in full view. She suggested she should let him off before they met a patrol. But before he could respond, she left the road and stopped on the shoulder. She killed the engine and offered him her hand in the sudden silence.

Her grip was firm as a man's, and the touch of her hand made his neck tingle. He thanked her for the ride and tried not to show the turmoil of his emotions. Nothing else came to mind, though she seemed to expect it. He could tell she was amused by something.

"Uh, Corporal, you can let go of my hand now," she said, and then smiled at how quickly he pulled away. "My name is Angelina." Once again their eyes met and he sensed they were both ready for something, but couldn't think what.

She untied her scarf and shook her head.

"Wow!" he exclaimed as her hair flowed over her shoulders and reached almost to her waist—hair so red she'd set the car ablaze. "Your hair's red and your eyes are blue. How . . . how is that possible in an Italian? Aren't you supposed to be all black? I mean, black hair, black eyes, uh . . . I don't know what I'm saying!" The rush of blood to his cheeks had no doubt made them turn redder than her hair.

She burst out laughing. "You've got some imagination, soldier," she said. "What makes you assume that all Italians are the way you describe? Are all Swiss girls blonde with braids? Do all Swiss boys have curly hair like yours?"

"Well no . . ."

"Perhaps you're right," she said quickly. Her voice had softened. "I *am* an exception. My grandfather was from Sweden—Stockholm, to be exact—where he had an import business dealing in citrus, olive oil, and pasta. He met my grandmother on one of his trips to Milan."

"But Swedes are blonde," said Herman persistently. "I lived in Stockholm for six months and ought to know. Come to think of it, there were some redheads, too. Swedes from the north, I think."

Angelina laughed. "You sound like you were doing a scientific study."

"I . . . I didn't mean to."

"It's okay, Corporal. You're not the first to wonder about my red hair and blue eyes. Even Mama had some explaining to do at times."

"So your mother's Italian?"

"I lost her. But yes, she was Italian."

"I'm sorry."

"It's okay soldier," she repeated. She put her hand on his arm.

He wondered if her hand was faintly trembling. She had closed her eyes and was gripping his arm a little more firmly than he thought she should. Then she relaxed her grip, opened her eyes, and the smile was back on her lips.

"My grandparents lived in Stockholm for a few years, but the northern climate was too harsh for my grandmother. They settled eventually in Milan."

"Good for them!"

"I'm sorry?"

"Or we wouldn't have met today!"

She laughed outright. "Are you always so . . . Never mind. Anyway, my grandparents had a boy—my father, and a girl—my aunt. Both were typically Italian: black hair and all the other traits you have described so scientifically, not a touch of blond or red." She let go of his arm and gave him the half-smile that had stayed with him since the tavern. "By the way, all of me is real, but you'll have to take my word for it."

He didn't have time to digest this remark because she was clearly ready to say goodbye. He opened the door and took his pack from the backrest—slowly, to gain an extra minute. He put the pack on the ground behind him and leaned the rifle against it. "Well, goodbye. My thanks again for the lift."

"The pleasure was mine. I enjoyed the chat, Corporal."

He took a step back and tripped over the pack but kept his feet. He walked to her side of the car and leaned on the doorframe. "My name's Herman."

"I know. I heard it at the tavern. Do you have a last name? Mine's Bianci."

"Schuller," he said. "Bianci? Like the ten-speed racing bike? I always wanted one. That'll be easy to remember. Wait—I thought your grandfather was from Sweden! Shouldn't your name be something like Larsson, Bergman, Lagerlöf—"

"You've made your point." She laughed. "You're clever. Yes, my grandfather was an Ericson but gave his children his wife's maiden name to make their life in Italy easier."

"Your grandfather must have been very wise."

An uneasy quiet followed.

"Will I see you again?" he asked, finally.

"I live in Milan." She touched his arm again. "I'm not sure about this, Corporal, but I have the distinct feeling that we *will* see each other again someday. Goodbye for now, and take care." She took her hand back and started the car.

He took a step back. "Has anyone ever called you Angel?"

"Yes, but I hate it! Ciao!" The Topolino quickly sped ahead.

"Ciao," he said, long after the car was gone. After he'd swung the rucksack to his shoulders and started off, he remembered his other sack. "My knapsack!" He frantically waved his arms, but she was far ahead by now.

"Angel." Much too obvious, he could see that now. Still, that might have been his only big mistake.

Angelina felt good about herself. The corporal's obvious affection had not surprised her, she was used to men's reactions. Sure, he was young and somewhat clumsy, but he seemed solid at the core. If he were a few years older . . . The notion made her smile. She glanced in the rearview mirror. Far back on the road the corporal was waving his arms.

Had he forgotten something? She looked behind the seat. His little pack! Her foot moved to the brake, but she held back. It would be a nice excuse to see him again.

At the moment there were more important things to occupy her mind. Everything had seemed so simple, had run so smoothly. Until now it hadn't occurred to her that someone could get hurt, but now she wasn't sure. If something did go wrong it could very well involve this soldier.

Angelina thought of her partner in Milan. They'd always talked things out between them, shared ideas, and helped one another in time of need. Why had she been so reserved about asking her advice this time?

At the military barracks, she turned right into a side road that was separated from the barracks by a thin line of pines. After a minute she stopped the car at a white picket fence where the sun was very bright. Beyond it was a two-story farmhouse surrounded by a well-kept garden. The setting was so tranquil! A thrush was singing on a privet shrub, and in the flowerbeds, pushing through the peaty soil, were daffodils, clusters of them, and snowdrops with their droopy blooms. She could hear the bees collecting nectar.

Stop stalling. She walked along the rock path and knocked on the door.

A woman in her sixties, dressed in a thick, cotton brocade housecoat and fur-lined slippers opened the door hesitantly. Her face changed quickly to a surprised smile. "Angelina! What . . . I'm so surprised!"

"Hi, Monika. Of course I thought of you when I was up this way. I need a favor."

"I told you, anytime! Anything you want from me. By the way, my motorbike was fine—I was simply out of gas. Thanks again for the lift. Come on in! I have some linden tea brewing."

Monika took off her apron and straightened her hair. She brought the tea from the stove and the two women sat at a table in the kitchen.

Angelina took longer and longer sips.

"It's good, isn't it? I'm so glad that you dropped by. It's been lonely here since my husband died. It's three years, you know."

"I'm sorry."

"Oh, I'm getting used to it. The soldiers keep me company. I converted half of the barn into a garage, thinking I would own a car someday. Instead, I settled for a motorbike, and since it takes up so little space, I figured I would let the army use the place as a guardroom. But you mentioned a favor, Angelina. What can I do for you?"

"Could I use your telephone? I need to call my partner in Milan. With all the soldiers arriving, the one at the *gasthaus* will be tied up for the rest of the day."

Angelina put on a carefree front while she dialed. What would she tell her partner? As the phone rang and rang she became increasingly jumpy. *Come on, answer!* She was already late to meet her contact—"Captain" Giulio, as he expected to be called, was waiting for her on the slopes of Passo di San Giácomo. She hung up and accepted Monika's offer to try again after she'd had more tea.

Marie Theresa reached for the phone, then reconsidered and let it ring. She was tired of talking to clients; a lot of her partner's work had fallen to her today. Finally the ringing stopped and it was quiet again. The shops in the Galleria had closed and the office was dark except for a spear of light shining through where the curtains met. Dust particles were dancing in the narrow beam. She'd have Maria start dusting in the afternoon as well.

She went to the window, pulled the curtain aside and leaned on the glass. She shielded her eyes against the sun's reflection in a window across the street. It was a lively Sunday evening with cars and trucks returning from the first spring market. The sight of the shouting men pushing their two wheeled carts and the sole traffic cop whistling and waving his arms—like a coryphée, she thought—consoled her sometimes. Tonight she was tense. A feeling of foreboding had plagued her all day, ever since she had bid her partner goodbye that morning. "Take care of yourself and stay out of trouble!" she had shouted as the Fiat pulled away.

Marie Theresa still didn't understand why her partner had left—her second mysterious trip in as many weeks. They had always expressed their feelings, discussed the difficult situations right along with the pleasant. Was there a new man in Angelina's life, the making of another doomed affair? Marie Theresa had demanded an explanation when she had surprised Angelina preparing for another quick departure, but all she was given was an unemotional, "Trust me, partner, just this once—I'll have to do this on my own."

Marie Theresa returned to her desk, sat in the wide wingback, and let out a painful sigh. *Oh, Angelina, why the mystery?* She stared at the dimly lit, black-and-white photographs on the wall across the room. Elegant as they were, these weren't mere fashion poses. They represented a phenomenal success story, depicting the rise of one of Milan's most sought-after models. They told of a woman Marie Theresa had tutored for six long, beautiful years—a woman she had made a full partner and come to love.

She had lost her husband—the only man she had ever loved—in the war almost a dozen years ago. And when she buried him at the Cemetery Monumentale on the outskirts of Milan, she buried her desires with him. Or so she had thought . . . .

The Grand Hotel Puccini dining room had been Marie Theresa's daily luncheon stop. Not because of its convenience to her shop, the great food, the rich decor. She had been drawn there daily by the young waitress with the tight skirt, by the gracious smile on her full lips, the sparkle of her dark-blue eyes, and the fiery hair that flowed over her shoulders. Without giving a name to her feeling for the girl, but sure of it nevertheless, Marie Theresa had tutored her to become the finest fashion model of Milan.

Marie Theresa had rewarded her long hours and unselfish dedication to her job with a partnership. And it was the night they celebrated their partnership—at Ruffino's, the elegant restaurant close to the Duomo—that their relationship had reached a crisis. They had both been tipsy . . . .

Marie Theresa had told herself a million times that she wished it had never happened, but in some ways, then as now, she was glad it had. Later both women confronted what had happened. With the honesty and directness she had come to expect from her protégée, Angelina had acknowledged that she had been flattered at first by the caresses that Marie Theresa had lavished on her.

"I've always felt your love. It was no surprise, really, though I haven't been as open to such things as other women my age." But she also said that she hadn't felt right about it afterward. She'd come to think of Marie Theresa as a mother, and to love her that way.

In one of the sweetest talks they ever had, Marie Theresa acknowledged her maternal feelings, and she had treated Angelina like a beloved daughter ever since. Still, especially when the younger woman was away, images of her returned as she had been the night of the celebration. It was especially hard to let go of them now that Marie Theresa, too, was keeping something secret. True, Angelina knew about the problem with her partner's heart, but she had never been told its seriousness. Marie Theresa had just learned from Dr. Turati that her heart was responsible for the weakness and shortness of breath she had been experiencing lately; her condition had indeed gotten worse.

The phone rang again, pounding her ears like a shower of hail bombarding a metal roof. Lunging for the apparatus, Marie Theresa knocked it to the floor, and the ringing stopped. Then regrets set in. Maybe it was her partner seeking help. *Angelina, my sweet love, I worry for you.* She closed her eyes and folded her hands in prayer. *O God. Angelina is all that I have left in this world. If she gets lost, show her Thy way. If she gets into trouble, give her Thy divine guidance. But please, please protect her! Amen.*

Herman Schuller turned off from the main road and into a large clearing amidst tall pine trees. Four barracks arranged in a wide arch surrounded the grounds on three sides. In the center of the arch was a platform with a long folding table and a wooden chair. Typewritten sheets of paper, some smudged by dirty fingers, were strewn about next to a black monster of a typewriter from prehistoric times.

"I'll be a monkey's uncle!" said Feldweibel (staff sergeant) Ott, his usual phrase when excited or stirred (though he had a bad lisp and said "monkeesh"). "Itch Schuller! Welcome to All' Acqua, Corporal." There he stood with his foot on the wooden chair, his chest puffed out—with one pencil sticking out below his cap, another on top of his ear, and a third in his hand.

The corporal saluted hard enough to hurt himself—one of the many techniques he had devised to keep from laughing in the feldweibel's face.

"At e-e-e-sh, Schuller. Good to schee you again," said the feldweibel with authority. As if rehearsed, he put his hand on the proper page beside the black monster, made a checkmark next to Schuller's name, looked at his watch, and wrote down the time in the column beside the checkmark. Then he stretched out his hand. "Alwaysh a pleasure to have you on board, Schuller."

"The pleasure's mine," said Herman.

"You will share a room with two sergeants at the gasthausch; it'sch the inn farther up the road. Let me schee . . . you're with Lieutenant Stucki?" Herman Schuller nodded. "Ah. Hisch platoon isch in Barracks C," he continued, pronouncing every word with great care. "Three of your schquad checked in a quarter of an hour ago, but I am almoscht sure they are at one of the two tavernsch up the road by now."

"Thanks," said Schuller. He saluted again fiercely.

"No need for that, Herman; take care, you hear?"

Just to make sure his friends weren't there, Herman entered

barracks 'C,' the third in the row. Field beds lined the wall to the right. Benches stood across the aisle at the windows, and between them were gun racks. Three rifles were in the rack closest to the door, and three bulky field packs were stacked on the bench beside them. *Yes, they were in a hurry for beer.* He stepped outside.

Wooden troughs between the barracks served as washbasins. Galvanized pipes with holes at even spaces and flow-control valves at the ends ran above the troughs. Corporal Schuller chuckled at the standard army setup that guaranteed almost every comfort for an early-morning scrubdown—except for hot water. The barracks were painted with broken patches of green and brown that blended well with trees and shrubs. Additional barracks, barely visible through the trees, hugged the steep mountain slopes beyond.

Herman swung the rifle over his shoulder and set out for the *gasthaus* at the other end of town. Even if he wanted to, he couldn't have rid his ears of the jukebox tune. He was walking in rhythm with the melody he was humming, tapping his nailed boots on the hard pavement as though in competition with the noisy splatter of the creek below the road. This was the kind of bliss that mountaineers enjoy after a rewarding climb.

And why shouldn't he feel this great? After all, he'd just sat beside the most beautiful woman he'd ever seen, shook her hand, smelled the sweetness of her skin, swum in her shiny eyes, and brushed against her shapely figure. There was the matter of his knapsack, but . . .

He was so lost in thought he almost ran into the lone, earth-bound sentry at a bunker by the road. The young soldier snapped to attention.

"At ease, soldier," said the corporal. "You look a little tired; how long have you been standing guard?"

The sentry relaxed at the corporal's calm voice and glanced at his watch. "It'll be an hour soon."

"Carry on, soldier, and," Corporal Schuller leaned closer, "don't let the captain catch you with those open shirt buttons." With an embarrassed grin, the soldier quickly buttoned up.

Like a hen over her brood, the bunker watched over the valley and a distant mountain pass. Built into the hill beside the road and camouflaged by shrubs and small trees, the bunker was invisible from the air. It had obviously outlived its defensive purpose, Herman thought, as a doublewide, triple-hinged wooden door had replaced the firing slits and cannon ports—and the sentry in front of it meant that it stored more than paper clips. His gaze moved to the two mountain peaks beyond the creek and the pass between them rising to the horizon. That was one steep pass!

He picked up his pace for the last stretch to the *gasthaus*.

Well up the slope Angelina sat down on a rock, took off her shoe, and got rid of the pebble that had been tormenting her. She had left her car in the valley by the barrier beam with the large sign warning motorists of snowdrifts blocking the road to Novena Pass. All' Acqua was spread out below, and from here the *gasthaus* at its western end was no bigger than a dollhouse.

Indecision was making her thoughts swim. After her role had been explained, she had thought that her mission would be a relatively simple and painless way to avenge her parents. How different it seemed now that she had been face to face with real soldiers, men whose job was to do what they were told. They didn't have the luxury of questioning the meaning of their work any more than she had when she'd worked at the Grand Hotel Puccini. Whether the arms they carried were just for show or useful in self-defense, the decision wasn't theirs.

The unanswered call to her partner kept stirring in her mind. Marie Theresa would have helped her to understand what was going on. Was she going to go through with this?

She slipped the shoe back on, gave herself a push, and continued up the path. Except for the grinding of her shoes on granite, it was quiet. The quiet frightened her because it was too easily filled with memories—memories of the war, the bombings, the German troops marching in the streets; quiet memories of her parents and two graves with simple, stone crosses. Ten years, it had been . . .

In 1945, there had been nothing luxurious about the Bianci apartment on the fifth-floor of the building on Via Bertini, a quiet neighborhood almost in the country. The dwelling was nothing like the single-family home at the corner of Via Ozanam and Ponchielli, where Angelina had been born, where they had lived for as long as she could remember, and where they had escaped the allied bombs by the sheer grace of God . . . until October 16, 1940. That was the day the sirens had sounded and her mother, clutching her *borsa dei valori* stuffed with money and documents tightly under one arm, grabbed Angelina and rushed her to the air-raid shelter. It was the first air raid since Italy had declared war on England and France.

That bomb, undoubtedly meant for the nearby railroad station, had robbed Angelina of everything: her home and her dollhouse with the little stove, the tiny pots and pans, and the carved dining table with the little chairs. The books she had been reading were still smoldering when she returned. Her butterfly collection was gone, and the rare coins her dear Aunt Virginia had given her last Christmas had melted into a clump. Anna, her best friend, had been killed (it turned out) and many others, like themselves, had moved to the country, or to new neighborhoods on the outskirts of Milan.

No, Angelina thought. The apartment with the wooden floors that squeaked, sparse furniture that was old and used, a scratched and chipped gas stove, and windows that leaked had nothing in common with her former home. Yet, it was home. It held the warmth of family and the promise of better things. Photos on the rosewood buffet depicted a past when life was bountiful, and on the wall above it, there was an antique Neuchâtel clock that had miraculously survived the bomb.

The father she loved had become a chauffeur for Mussolini, and, because petrol had become a rarity, her papa had plenty of time to spend with her. He took her to the park where they strolled by the pond and the giant camellia trees, their steps in rhythm and her hand firmly pressed in his. He had taught her how to toss pebbles over the glassy water and make them skip four, five times. And there was that fatherly smile when he pushed her on the swing, and his giggles when they rolled on leaves piled high by the wind, and the sparks in his eyes when they dreamt about the promises of life. Papa had taught her how to fish for trout, how to split them open and clean out the guts, and how to cook them over an open fire on wooden spears that he cut from hazelnut bushes.

Angelina remembered sitting secretly in the darkness of the upper step to their basement and watching her father assemble her birthday present: a bicycle made from salvaged parts.

Then the war for Italy was over; the Germans were gone and their troops were no longer marching in the streets. In spite of widespread devastation—Allied bombs had destroyed two-thirds of Milan—there was an air of hope and a will bordering on fanaticism to rebuild their city. Angelina's father was prepared to do his part.

But it was not to be. It ended at midnight, the night before Angelina's sixteenth birthday. She remembered being awakened by the noise of army boots pounding up the steps and screeching on the ceramic tiles. Then she had heard the blows of rifle butts against the door and shouts demanding entry.

Angelina's father had opened the door and stood fearless before the officer who was in a dark blue shirt with white sash and a red stripe on his black pants—the feared uniform of the Carabinieri. Without explanation her father was hauled off by two young solders in shabby uniforms with helmets that lacked the straps to keep them in place. It was the last time she saw her papa.

News, and the cause of his death—supposedly from war wounds he had sustained in North Africa in 1942—came two days later. It was little comfort when he was buried with full military honors. Then the truth came out—admissions of tortures and executions of political prisoners by revenge-seeking guerillas who had infiltrated the government. Signora Bianci could not bear the injustice or understand the biases of the very people entrusted to protect the citizens. She fell ill almost overnight and died three months later in her daughter's arms.

Angelina had climbed up the last steep stretch. When she arrived at the place of rendezvous, there was no sign of Giulio or his men. She dropped onto a grassy knoll, folded her legs below her, and waited. She was still shaken by her recollections of the war, and any doubt about her mission had now vanished. If her contact did not show, she would return tomorrow, as agreed.

✥

The white stucco walls and red-tiled roof of the four-story *gasthaus* appeared from among tall pines. Moments later, Herman Schuller entered the tavern that was to the right of the front corridor.

He removed his cap before greeting the chubby woman behind the glass-topped buffet counter.

"Good afternoon, Signora. I'm Corporal Schuller; I've been told to check in with you."

The woman barely looked up. "Your room's upstairs and to the left." After he'd stood there a bit longer, motionless, she looked up again. Smiling suddenly, she unhooked a large key from a nail board and came around the counter. "I own the Gasthaus and this tavern," she said, the little smile frozen to her lips. Her black skirt was too tight and much too short. She handed him the iron key that must have weighed a pound. "You're in number five. I have only this one key to your room." Now the little smile was gone. "So don't put it in your pocket, you hear? Bring it back when you step out, or leave it in the lock for the others."

"Thanks, Ma," he replied insolently, and after bowing deeply, climbed the steps that were just wide enough for his pack. He found the room on the second floor. A third bed, quite out of place, made it so crowded that he had to leave his rucksack and rifle in the hall. The bathroom down the hall was much larger than he'd expected, however, with a wood-burning boiler in the corner that promised plenty of hot water.

Everything was clean and shiny, but home for a dozen soldiers? After cleaning up in the bathroom, Herman opened a window in the bedroom before he went out to find his comrades.

The small tavern by the road was empty except for the three soldiers drinking beer. This was bound to change in view of the young waitress who had just tapped a fresh keg of beer and filled the racks with glasses. A hundred soldiers were expected shortly in All' Acqua.

The soldiers were just leaving when Corporal Schuller came in.

"Wow, Herman," said Spiller. "You made it up the valley a lot faster than we thought." The corporal just nodded.

"I'll bet that princess gave you a ride in her red Topolino as soon as you got rid of us, right Corp?" teased Frei.

The corporal shook his head and grinned.

Rüegg couldn't stand it any longer. "Well, did she, or didn't she?" he cried.

The corporal wasn't talking and they dropped the subject.

They chose a long table with ten chairs in anticipation of other arriving comrades. They ordered wine, dried beef, smoked ham, and cheese, and Rüegg asked for four glasses. The bottle was uncorked with a pocketknife and poured.

"Hey," said the corporal, "this cheese tastes familiar. What do you think?"

The waitress heard him. "We dry our own beef and chimney-smoke our ham," she said. "But the cheese comes from a farmer who lives across the border."

"This isn't the first time we've heard about the Italian who brings the cheese," said Spiller, looking over the young black-haired waitress and leering. "Why do all you girls talk of him so favorably?"

In spite of the red ribbon in her hair and the puffy white blouse the young woman had begun to look very much like the owner's daughter. But nothing was stopping Spiller.

"Is it true that the Italians are such hot lovers?"

The waitress gave him an ice-cold look and fled to the back.

The small tavern was already livening up with more soldiers and the bosomy woman in the short dress had twenty pairs of eyes focused on her as she came from behind the buffet with a half-dozen beer mugs in each hand. She replied to the men's stares with good-natured nods and caring smiles as she whisked between tables on her towering high heels, and there were bold displays of cleavage when she bent to distribute the mugs.

"I'll be a monkey'sch uncle! The thick-asch-thievesch four! May we join your table?" Feldweibel Ott was accompanied by Lieutenant Stucki, the platoon commander. The soldiers jumped to their feet to salute.

"Settle down, men, it's too late for that sort of thing," said the lieutenant with a wave of his hand. The soldiers nodded, and the new arrivals sat beside them.

Lieutenant Stucki was liked by the men in his platoon for his leadership style. He was tall and handsome, and looked younger than his age. He liked the service. As a high-paid architect in civil life, however, he wasn't interested in a military career: "Three weeks once a year is all I can stand," he had told Herman, who thought of him as a friend.

They waited for the rest of the squad to arrive, killing time by telling jokes and gulping down Barbera wine. Herman felt that he alone was holding back, and not just because of the pain in his side and the lump in his throat, both of which had made their appearance at about the same time the image of Angelina had come to occupy his mind. He was convinced that there was nothing ordinary about his encounter with that beautiful woman, and that All' Acqua was no ordinary place. Looking back, he didn't feel that he'd let the soldiers go on ahead because there was only room for three in the van, or because he felt it was his duty as a leader to take the more difficult assignment. In spite of the chance nature of so many things that happened that afternoon, he clearly felt that he'd been singled out. Something important was going to happen here in All' Acqua, and whether he wanted to or not, he was bound to play a part.

CHAPTER 3

*C*orporal Schuller shot from bed, awakened by a commotion in the far-off barracks. He had overslept. He was alone, and the two beds beside his had not been slept in.

As he turned the corner of his bed, he stubbed his toe on an object on the floor—his knapsack, leaning against the mattress. As he stared at the bag, the woman with the red hair came to mind as vividly as she had been in his dream, a dream so real he'd heard her voice and smelled her perfume.

He shaved, washed, brushed his teeth, dressed, and rushed to the tavern. The chubby woman, yawning, coffee cup in one hand and a croissant in the other, just shook her head when Schuller asked about "the beautiful young woman in tight black pants with long red hair . . .?" She hadn't seen her.

The waitress's eyes were even droopier than her mother's. She hadn't seen the dream woman either.

Herman hurried to the field kitchen, bolted his breakfast, drank his coffee scalding hot, and brooded over the changes in his way of thinking since yesterday afternoon. Before yesterday there had not been anything special about this place, about his feelings— no special awareness. But this had changed since then, suddenly. Was he the only one seeing something strange, something ominous in the motion of events? True, there was nothing he could do to slow them down, but still, it unsettled him to see his friends and fellow soldiers acting as if nothing that happened here in All' Acqua could be anything but commonplace.

⊲⊱❄❁⊰⊳

The troops assembled on the grounds in battle uniforms, steel helmets on their heads and rifles at their sides. They lined up by squads and platoons, their officers up front waiting patiently. Minutes later, the captain arrived in stiff cap, bright uniform, and jodhpurs stuffed into tall boots. The troops came to attention with a synchronized click of two hundred boots. Captain Roth saluted, gave his orders of the day, and dismissed the company to the leaders of each platoon.

Lieutenant Stucki singled out Corporal Schuller. "Herman, the captain wants to talk to us."

"Yes, sir!" Schuller told Spiller to take over the squad and "do with them what they like the least." With a grin, Spiller saluted and marched the men out of sight behind some trees, his voice tailing off soon thereafter.

Herman asked the lieutenant, "Is it what I think it is?" The lieutenant nodded, put his hand on the corporal's shoulder, and the two started toward headquarters.

Here he was, the man of destiny yet again, Herman thought. His team would be doing the shooting demonstration. They entered the farmhouse-turned-headquarters.

The captain waited behind a desk of two sawhorses and a sheet of plywood. He puffed on a thick cigar that was tilted toward the ceiling. He looked Schuller up and down like an elementary schoolteacher evaluating a student. "Are you up to it?" he asked. He put his right boot against a sawhorse and pushed back on the chair until he was balancing on two legs.

"Yes, sir!" said Schuller confidently.

"Your team has got to be the best. Do I have your promise, Corporal? We've got some fine sharpshooters in this company. Try replacing your weakest men with them. The choice of which I will leave to your discretion."

"I prefer my own men," said Schuller. "We work well together and don't like adjusting to new attitudes."

The captain had expected such an answer. "Okay," he said. "You know what's at stake. The whole battalion will be watching! Don't let me down!" He sucked in his lips, a habit when reaching a decision. Then he sighed, walked out from behind the desk, and put his hand on the soldier's shoulder. "Remember, Schuller, this is not only a big deal to the colonel—his guests are high-ranking officers."

"Yes, sir! You can count on us!"

"Dismissed!"

Schuller and Lieutenant Stucki saluted and left together. On the way back to the barracks the lieutenant confided that he had been put in charge of setting up the targets. "I thought that you and your men should be the ones to set them up."

"I was hoping you'd say that, Lieutenant. Gives me a chance to fine-tune the release-mechanisms on the silhouettes. Nothing's worse than hitting a target that won't drop. I'll have the squad ready whenever you . . ." he stopped short. "With your permission I'd like to check out the automatic weapons first, if there's still time."

The battalion walked single file up the steep pine-bordered road to a meadow nestled between two peaks. Soldiers with red armbands directed them to both sides of a low hill. The officers scaled the hill up to red ribbons strung below the top. Two four-by-fours drove up from behind, circled the troops, and stopped up front. The battalion snapped to attention. The colonel stepped from the lead car with men in strange uniforms.

The helmeted soldiers stood up straight in their dusty uniforms, arms stiffly pressed against their sides. The officers took their places in front of them, right hand to their caps.

The colonel walked between the lines of soldiers, reviewed his troops with keen eyes, spit the cigar butt from his mouth, and ground it into the dirt with his heel. "At ease," he shouted.

A soldier brought folding chairs for the men in unfamiliar uniforms. The guests-of-honor declined the offer, and the soldier took the chairs back.

Chin high and back straight, the colonel stood taller than usual in an attempt to impress his guests. He took a few steps away from the troops, his sharp, unforgiving eyes on every soldier's face. "You're a little too close, soldier! Yes, you over there at the right flank," he thundered. Finally he explained the drill. They would be using live ammunition and armed hand grenades; they were not to ignore commands to hit the dirt or he could not guarantee their safe return to camp. Then he described the battle plan.

There was a whistle—the battalion perked up—followed by the sput-sput-sput of a light machine gun.

"Two fingers up, two fingers right!" shouted Corporal Schuller, helmet low on his face and binoculars at his eyes. The gunner fired a second burst and, half a kilometer away, the first targets dropped as if touched by a magic wand. The corporal shot tracer bullets trailing smoke, the gunner aimed after the tracers, and new targets fell like flies.

The surprise was complete. No one had spotted the squad—not the officers on the hill, or the soldiers with chills in their necks standing at its base. The distance narrowed each time the whistle blew, and rifles joined the action—then submachine guns with rapid bursts. Targets fell, split, or tumbled down the slope. Above the pounding the corporal shouted his commands.

Binoculars in his left hand, trigger in his right, the hard rifle butt at his shoulder, tracers in the sky, gun clatter in his ears, the powder fumes in his nose, Herman Schuller made this his fight. And he felt at home with the acrid air in his lungs and the smell of battle in his nostrils. The targets—the artificial enemy—moved closer now, close to the hill . . . two hundred meters . . . one hundred meters, and the guns spread bloodless death.

"Wow—all right—right on!" came from the ranks.

"Barrel change!" shouted the corporal. "You're wasting time. No! You've got to do it! We don't need a jammed machine gun now."

Rüegg had already pulled the pin and jerked back the lever. The red-hot barrel slid to the grass, where it hissed and blew smoke. Roncari squinted through the smoke, shoved the fresh barrel through the vented ribs, and the sput-sput-sput that was music to the corporal's ears once more filled the air.

Schuller shook his head in disbelief: *Must be a new record!* "Hand grenades!"

On the count of one, the first soldier pulled the firing lanyard; on two, the second followed suit, then the third.

"Hit the ground!" The command was not a moment too soon. Three flashing blasts echoed through the valley as dirt, rocks, and grass rained on those who were too close. But the "enemy" advanced with each new shriek of the whistle. Twenty-five meters now—spitting distance—the second barrage of grenades tore through the air.

"Reload, fix bayonets!" Click-click-click: the cold blades that stuck in the ground in front of them snapped to the barrels.

"Attack! Attack!" The soldiers jumped to their feet and stormed the basin yelling at the top of their lungs. Down the hill—yelling—firing—yelling—firing from all barrels.

Then there was silence.

Spent by the fight wherein they had given their all, the squad climbed back to the top of the hill. There, officers shook their hands and patted them on the back.

"I'll be a monkeesh . . . you did it!" cried Feldweibel Ott.

Then the quiet valley erupted again, not with guns or TNT but with the cheers of the men. Only now did the weary soldiers look at their work on the ridge. Split and shattered targets littered the mountainside, and others had piled up below the slope. Few were left standing on the top.

"This was the finest job I've seen in my career," cried a beaming colonel. After shaking the hands of the tired and dirty men and saluting them, he stepped into his four-by-four with the NATO officers.

"I want a beer," said Rüegg, sweating through his coat.

"Me too," said Spiller, brushing back his thin hair.

"Fall in!" shouted the corporal hoarsely. The men lined up in single file. "Attention!" The men stood straight, puzzled by the corporal's intentions. "Unload your guns; empty all magazines," he said. He walked from man to man holding out his helmet, collecting the shells that clinked as they hit the steel. He counted only eighteen shells left from the fight, two of which were his own tracer bullets. They had used their resources wisely.

Lieutenant Stucki was proud of the squad and the men he called his friends. He took the flatbed truck and helped the soldiers to the top. Then he drove them past the long column of cheering men and down the steep slope to All' Acqua.

At the bunker by the road, Corporal Schuller joined Feldweibel Ott. They stored the few shells that Herman still had in his pocket. They inventoried the cases of machine gun, rifle, and 9-mm submachine gun ammunition. Last, they accounted for the long-handled grenades.

Numb and tired, the corporal walked to the *gasthaus* for an hour's rest—the upcoming night of guard duty would be tiresome for his squad.

On the little bed he twisted and turned, kicked and fought. The target was clear and sharp. As he squeezed the trigger, it blurred. Astonished, he wiped his eyes, wiped them again—out of the target jumped two bright blue eyes, coming toward him at lightning speed. There was a loud report and they were gone. Herman bolted from bed drenched in sweat. He swallowed. The knot in his throat, that crazy sign, was choking him.

Late that same afternoon in Lainate, northwest of Milan, a crowd was gathering for the first week of Spring Bazaar. The month of May had never been more beautiful: chestnut trees were in bloom, migrating cranes flew north in V-formation, and the air was damp with midday showers. It was one of those early hot days Milan was famous for.

Vittorio Zanardelli sighed, stretched his legs, rolled his shoulders, and yawned discreetly into his hand as he would with company present. But he was alone and bored. Sweat formed on his forehead and upper lip. He dabbed them with a wet towel and took gulps of wine from a Chianti bottle.

His high-ceilinged, airy office, once an artist's studio, faced out over the great piazza. The sun had breached the great arched windows with pillars of fire.

"How can it be so goddamned hot!" Zanardelli swore.

But this was Tuesday afternoon he thought, the beginning of Spring Bazaar, the week when Lainate came to life. Colonnello Vittorio, or Vitt, as his friends knew him, pulled his chair to the window. The women in flowery gowns, men in dark suits, and kids strolling by eased his boredom. And attractive girls who were strolling below his window more by design than chance were making him feel at home.

Tall and broad-shouldered, with a rugged face, Vitt Zanardelli was a womanizer—to those who knew him best almost as legendary as was Don Juan. He had a bright military mind, but his morals caused even his closest friends to raise their eyebrows now and then.

He had been ordered to Lainate two short weeks before. There had been repeated sightings of an armed band, among them a woman, along the international border to the northwest. Vitt leaned back in his chair, crossed his bare feet on the windowsill, and rubbed his neck. There was not much truth to these sightings as a rule. But he had his orders: "And don't even think about coming back without their wicked leader!"

Zanardelli grinned as he looked from his window at the lovelies who were mingling in the crowd. *Lainate isn't all that bad.* He just had to make the best of it.

But why Lainate? It was strategically important because of the two major roads that connected it with Como and the Swiss border to the north and Lago Maggiore in the northwest, both within a couple-hour's drive.

He looked around his meagerly furnished office—the desk in disarray with charts, pencils, and a smelly ashtray full of cigar butts. Vitt rolled the chair back to the desk with a thought to cleaning up the mess. He took a rag from a side drawer and wiped away the scattered ashes. He sniffed the ashtray and then emptied its contents into the wastebasket.

He swiveled around and faced the wall behind him. Enlarged black-and-white photos in thin black frames hung on the wall with military uniformity. He stared at them as he often did when bored. They depicted a military career to which he had devoted the best part of his life. He unhooked the first picture and looked at it at arm's length.

Vitt had been a hero, and when heroes stop fighting they feel let down, forgotten by those whom they have served. He held no grudge, but deep inside he felt antipathy for those who had profited but hadn't served. Looking at these pictures boosted his morale. They were like a change of scenery—what others might have expected to get by going to the park.

There was the photograph of his first promotion to *caporale*. Another had been taken during the war—of a burning English tank he had disabled at the battle of Tobruk—an act of heroism that had hastened his promotion to *sergente maggiore*. Most prized was the picture taken when he made colonel, right on that bloody beach in Sicily.

I'm a hero for doing what soldiers are supposed to do. He took a framed newspaper clipping from the wall. It was his counterattack, skillfully planned and executed, that had pushed the Allies back into the sea. But as heroically as he had fought alongside his men, the course of war had not changed. It didn't amount to a hill of beans, but his army needed a boost, a hero, and his commander had made the most of it.

They made him a colonel, took his photograph, and sent it to every Italian newspaper still in existence. Vitt was proud of this clipping—not necessarily for his heroism or the medal or the photograph that had shown him at his best. Rather, it was for the man who had signed it at the bottom right: "My sincere tribute to you, my good friend. Dino Buzzati—Corriere della Sera."

No single event or idea had steered young Vitt into the Army. However, for a boy to make good in his family meant to succeed in the military. That meant to be an officer, a leader, and a hero. His father was a colonel who had made his mark in the First World War; his grandfather had been a general, and *his* father had been Italy's head of state. It was therefore no surprise that Vitt had made the military his career. And at the time of his rise to colonel at that beach in Sicily, he was the youngest officer holding that rank.

"You could be a general if you'd learn to keep your mouth shut!" his superior had shouted more than once. Vitt was blunt, always saying it the way it was. He had despised the Fascists for their deal with Hitler; had spoken out against the Axis and didn't care who listened. In spite of his ideology, however, which angered family and friends, he was a great soldier in the field.

He was injured by shrapnel during that last battle in Sicily and later joined a band of guerillas, or *patrioti*, as they preferred to be called, fighting to throw the Germans out of Italy.

Then Italy's war ended at Villa Belmonte on that dark April day when Mussolini was executed by vengeful *patrioti*. There were no more battles, no enemies to subdue, no chance of pride or glory, no adventures to make his heart race. After much thought, Vittorio Zanardelli had joined the secret service of the newly organized state.

Vitt Zanardelli's wife Catalina came from a respected family of great wealth and was exceptionally beautiful. They had a daughter, and he kept a recent picture of the two on his desk. However, it was anything but a picture-book marriage. At war's end, Catalina confessed to an affair she'd had with a German of the high command while her husband was away fighting. She didn't elaborate, and he didn't push for the whole truth—a romance, he figured, couldn't have been voluntary on her part. But it left deep scars nonetheless, and the marriage endured chiefly because of Catalina's exceptional beauty— and wealth—and because of their daughter, who was now fourteen. And her betrayal served as an excuse for his own adulterous proclivities, which were frequently indulged.

The phone shook him from his thoughts.

"This guy Giulio has something up his sleeve, " shouted his superior, out of breath. "It's coming down in the next few days, I'm told." The caller cleared his throat noisily. "Now listen, Zanardelli, I want you to catch this scoundrel and bring him in . . . I don't care what he's charged with . . ."

"Consider it done."

Zanardelli burst out laughing as soon as his superior hung up. It was the memory of the riot that day last summer at the Fascist-organized demonstration in the Piazza del Duomo.

A patrol by plainclothes officers of the secret service— among them the regional commander— had been intercepted, their Opel surrounded, its tires slashed. Sitting dead on the cobblestones it had become the target of old shoes, broken umbrellas, rotten eggs, and foul tomatoes the *fascisti* had originally intended for a rival group. The call for help went to the police precinct at Corso Venezia in Milan just moments before the antenna had become a demonstrator's attack tool.

When Zanardelli arrived with a squad of policemen, the crowd melted away and their comrades, the "sitting ducks," were

rescued. From their account, the gentleman who was being carried
out of the plaza on the shoulders of the crowd wielding a bowling
pin—with which he had moments ago demolished the Opel's windshield—was none other than the infamous Giulio, the self-proclaimed
"capitano" of the fascisti. As he appeared to Zanardelli then, Giulio's
clothes were pure Sicilian: A skimpy denim shirt of a bluish color,
sleeves rolled up half, faded charcoal slacks held up by gray suspenders,
and dark brown espadrilles; he sported a field-green beret that he
wore askew, and a silvery silk scarf was tied loosely around his neck.
As Zanardelli remembered him, there was an air of youthful energy
about him enhanced further by his mannish, sun-tanned chest showing
between the hems of his unbuttoned shirt.

A pebble hit the window glass, then another.

"Colonnel-l-o—it's me-e," sang a lovely voice. Vitt Zanardelli
went to the window and opened it. The shapely girl waved her arms.
"It's Patricia-a-a," she crooned. "May I come u-up?" The colonnello
mused for a second, then beckoned. He closed the window, pulled the
curtain, unlocked the door, cleared the desk, and tossed the portrait
into the center drawer.

CHAPTER 4

$\mathcal{T}$he evening was multihued and vivid, washed clean by the brief fury of a downpour. When the sun dipped behind Passo della Novena, the few lingering clouds became a fiery spectacle of bright orange and deep red. With the sun gone, the air turned crisp and still, the birds fell silent, and the pines stood calm. Only the splatter of the creek below the road and the laughter of some soldiers gathering at the field kitchen disturbed the quiet.

Schuller's squad arrived at the guardhouse at 1900 hours, right on time. The garage and converted hayloft would be the soldiers' living quarters for a full twenty-four hours. The corporal, field glasses slung about his neck and rifle butt by his foot, brought them to attention. He saluted. The lieutenant walked from man to man checking for loose buttons, tucked-in shirts, and shiny guns, then stood aside and watched the formal change of guard from one squad to the other. This done, Corporal Schuller told his men, "Make yourselves at home."

He assembled a small detail (Frei and Spiller) and led them down to the main road and then right for half a kilometer to the bunker. There, Schuller ordered the soldier on guard to unload his rifle and hand over the six shells to Ruedi Frei, his first man to pull guard duty. He watched Frei loading his rifle and said, "Keep the chamber empty and the safety on." Schuller was strict when ammunition was involved, and figured that the extra second needed to load a cartridge into the chamber was time to rethink a situation. *After all, we're not at war!*

"Stay alert, Ruedi, you never know what might come along. Remember—two shots to get our attention, three for an immediate emergency. Don't hesitate to use that rifle to signal us, but for Christ's sake don't shoot anybody."

Herman ordered Spiller to accompany the relieved sentry back to the guardhouse, and then went up the hill that housed the bunker for a look around. Brush and bramble had overgrown trenches that were, at one time, the bunker's outer defense. Amid the overgrowth was a metal airshaft, and beside it a well-hidden metal chimney. Below the road a narrow trail followed the noisy creek. Schuller raised his field glasses and scanned the trail to the point where it crossed over an arched, narrow bridge. From there, the trail separated from the valley as it took to the mountain on the left, and then only an unnaturally disturbed landscape here and there hinted of its winding course.

Schuller opened the button to his breast pocket and pulled out the chart. The trail, marked as fine dots, wound back and forth until it reached San Giácomo Pass and the Italian border at its summit. The close contours left no doubt of the difficult terrain—slopes too treacherous for anything but pack animals.

He slid down the bunker and crossed the paved road. Against the perfect cover of dwarf trees and man-size boulders the little creek ran its course, splattering noisily from rock to rock. It was a peaceful setting, truly beautiful, but also a perfect approach if someone wanted to sneak up on the sentry.

Herman went back to the bunker and told Ruedi, "I don't like what's below the shoulder."

Ruedi told him he'd keep his eyes peeled. He thought the worry in the corporal's voice was highly unusual, but . . . Herman hadn't been himself ever since their war exercise had been interrupted by that Italian bombshell. He saluted and watched the corporal walk back to the guardhouse.

Frei stood straight until the steps faded, then leaned his rifle against the bunker, opened the top buttons of his coat and jacket, and let his helmet drop to the ground.

The guardhouse felt tidy in spite of its rusticity. Piles of straw kept in place by wooden planks covered the left half of the room, and pillows made of straw-filled burlap bags promised some small degree of comfort. Red-checkered cloths, which might have covered a breakfast table at one time, draped the small windows in the wide sliding door. A single light bulb, a piece of cardboard attached to it to divert the glare from the sleeping area, dangled from the ceiling. The bulb swung with each opening of the door, throwing ghostly shadows against the walls. Below the bare light was a rustic table and an equally rough, hand-hewn chair. Large hooks on one wall served to hang the heavy packs, and below them were wooden rifle racks. The way the setup had been thought out gave the room a touch of home, evidence that someone cared.

But it wasn't the straw's extra depth, or the comfortable burlap pillows, and certainly not the rugged writing table that first caught the soldiers' eyes. A BMW motorbike looking barely used was tucked away in the back corner—any young man's dream and for many of the soldiers, perhaps, a lifelong desire.

Fortunately there was no one sitting on the bike when the door opened. A woman, probably in her early sixties, introduced herself simply as "Monika" and gave the soldiers a welcoming smile.

With a button nose, a hard little setback chin, and a slightly bent jaw that warped her smile, she was no beauty queen. Her hair, neatly tied behind her head, had been tampered with, obviously, to cover graying strands. But she still had a figure, and the sight of a woman in such surroundings wearing a green satin robe and bedroom slippers . . . the men were following her every move with interest. Also of interest was the pot of coffee in her hand that had already enriched the air with its aroma. The walnut cookies she'd brought were so warm they were steaming.

"Here we are," she said, putting the cookies and coffee on the table. "Just knock on my front door if you run short of the goodies or for whatever else you might want of me." The soldiers just looked at her with gaping mouths and widening eyes.

Spiller jumped to his feet. "'Ten-tion!" he cried.

The squad, the corporal included, saluted passionately. Spiller introduced the squad. "Signora Monika, if I may, this is Recruit Rüegg. If you need some venison, he'll get it for you with his machine-gun. Hunk Müller there will give you all the muscle-power you'll ever need, and ol' Seelos can be your stepladder to gather those hard-to-reach walnuts. Um, uh . . . you'll be out of luck with Corp, though, as he dates only convertibles. The rest of us are mere pussycats, as you can . . ."

"All right, Spiller, that's enough," said Herman.

The signora was smiling goodnaturedly, but she was also holding her robe shut with both hands.

"As for me," she said jokingly, "I'm famous for my nosiness. So if you're lonely and want to pour out your heart . . . come see me. And, just because I live by myself, don't be scared." She whisked out of the room then, her robe flapping open when she reached for the door.

At her words "by myself," the young men's stares snapped back to the corner, wondering now who was driving that classy BMW.

Schuller sent the men in pairs to the field kitchen, where they received the special treatment extended to guards. With the sun gone, a chill had set in. The men brought back canteens full of steaming stew, and ate it on the floor between their legs, savoring the warmth as well as the taste.

After eating, the soldiers, tired from the demanding day, bedded down for short periods of rest. While they snored, the corporal worked out the flow of guard relief. Seelos was on schedule for the next hour, then Rüegg, then Spiller and so forth; he tacked the list to the wall behind him. He shoved his chair closer, put his elbows on the table, and leaned his head in his hands.

What is it with me? Why the anxiety? He closed his eyes, letting his mind float in search of a clue, anything that would hint at what troubled him.

"Is it true that your sentries carry loaded guns while on guard? With real bullets, I mean?" He leapt from the chair—the voice had seemed so real.

Angelina stood for a moment, tightening her purple scarf, gazing up into the clear western sky, over sparkling trees that had been washed clean by a shower just before sunset. She felt empty, purposeless, unable to respond to the loveliness of sky and landscape. This was her third attempt trying to meet with her contact, and the climb up the wet trail had seemed longer and more tiresome than ever.

The sudden snort of an animal made her stop. In the little clearing she'd just entered three small donkeys were tied to a tree, stomping their hooves. At last! Now she could make out three men and a young woman stretched out under a group of pines close by, who seemed determined not to notice her. She planted herself in front of them and waited till one of the men raised his head. Without saying a word, he gestured toward a small rise in front of them. Angelina nodded and made her way to the top, holding on to shrubs and dwarf trees to keep from sliding back.

Once at the top there was a place to sit on the edge of a flat rock. From this vantage Angelina could see the stream and the *gasthaus*, though it was faint in the fading light. Tall pines hid the bunker. Giulio wasn't on the rise as she had expected, but she wasn't going out of her way to look for him. Was she having second thoughts again? Back in Milan she had been able to think of a number of reasons for being here. Now it was hard to think of one.

She buried her head in her arms. The young corporal kept stirring in her mind; she couldn't help thinking of him. After her fruitless wait for Giulio that first night, she had returned his knapsack before driving back to Airolo. It had been late by the time she entered the *gasthaus* tavern. Some of his buddies had been there, carrying on happily and drinking wine and beer. Corporal Schuller had retired, she was told. But she had quickly gained a soldier's confidence, and was pointed to the corporal's room above the staircase.

"It's about time you showed!"

The sharp voice shocked Angelina from her reverie. She raised her head. Giulio towered above her, hands on his hips, an aggressive expression on his face.

"Do you always have to scare people?" she snapped back. "I'm here on time, as agreed. And it's my third trip up here!" She stood to confront him and met his stare without blinking. He looked away.

"What do you have to report?" There was disgust in his voice.

"The ammunition is in the bunker, as you guessed."

"What do you base that on?"

"There's an armed sentry standing guard."

"That's it? You base your conclusion on that?"

"Not entirely. A squad of soldiers removed several boxes yesterday afternoon, heavy boxes that had to be ammunition for the exercise." Her voice was collected now, almost indifferent.

"What's that about an exercise?"

"A sharpshooting action early this morning. You should have heard the racket when you crossed the pass."

"Well, I didn't. What else?"

"I picked up a young corporal Sunday afternoon. I . . . I talked to him, asked questions on what they were doing in All' Acqua . . . ."

"Go on, go on!"

"I . . . he . . . there's really nothing to report. He didn't have much to say."

"How many guards at the bunker?" asked Giulio, his voice harsh. "Come on, be specific!"

"There's only one, the best I could tell. The guardhouse is less than a kilometer from the bunker, and the guards are changed every hour on the hour." Suddenly, Angelina was reluctant to pass on information.

Giulio, a good judge of people, sensed her hesitancy. "You aren't having second thoughts, are you?" he asked, his tone more pleasant now. She avoided his eyes and kept silent. He put his hand on her shoulder, as he had when they first met. "Think of your parents," he said warmly. "Think of what they have done to them; it's time to get even."

For a moment, Angelina saw the former Giulio: soft-spoken, persuasive, a friend.

It didn't last. His voice turned harsh again, "Get going now. You have your orders. We'll meet tomorrow morning at that barn beyond the pass."

Angelina did not say another word as she slid down the hill.

"I haven't finished yet," Giulio shouted after her. "Keep your eyes open for a possible military presence at Formazza Valley!"

Angelina walked down the slope toward her car, parked at the same spot at the barrier west of the *gasthaus*. Giulio had changed.

Gone were the courtly, kindly words. This wasn't the same man who was buying gowns for his girlfriend two months ago at the Galleria fashion house. Angelina remembered having been impressed by his certainty of purpose. He'd been very persuasive telling her about his cause during a follow-up get-together at a café.

Giulio had a way of getting people to open up, and before long she'd poured out her life story. As she talked of her father's arrest and her mother's grief, he must have sensed her desire for revenge. She'd thought of him as a kind of big brother in the way he had encouraged her. Angelina had longed for a brother—someone with the courage to stand up for the outrage to her parents. Her thoughts of how she might be able to even the score had become too heavy to bear alone.

Distracted by her thoughts of Giulio, Angelina slipped on the moist ground, and fell hard. She just sat there, unwilling to get back up. The air had a fresh, pleasant smell and the view across the valley was calming. *Why can't I just sit here for a while and enjoy the quiet?* But she couldn't stop thinking of the war's end. *Damn you, Mussolini! Damn you for having brought so much grief to my country, so much sorrow to my family!*

She thought of how her father, after recuperating from a battle injury, had served the dictator faithfully, and how this connection, together with his innocent link to a relative, General Bruno, had ultimately led to his death at the hands of his own countrymen. Angelina thought with some satisfaction of Mussolini's execution at the hands of *patrioti*, and the picture of him and his mistress, Claretta Petacci, in the Corriere della Sera hanging by their feet at Piazza Loreto in Milan, spat upon and defiled by an angry populace. She thought of the two graves, her mamma's and her papa's, with the simple stones, and she thought of all the reasons—right and wrong—that had brought her to this valley. There was no question in her mind that revenge was right, but she knew right from wrong, and she'd never consciously broken the law.

Angelina moved on with every intention of getting quickly to her car, but before very long she stopped to think again, this time about the young corporal. His face kept coming back to her. Something was hidden deep in his blue eyes, as if he knew something she didn't. Although she was quite sure he knew nothing of Giulio and his plans, she sensed he was with her in some way, the way a brother might be . . . or even a lover. He had looked so peaceful in his sleep when she returned his knapsack and set it at the foot of his bed. As she watched while he slept she had been tempted to run her fingers through his curly hair, and wake him just to talk, nothing else. But she couldn't get herself to do it. Somehow, in the back of her mind, she thought of him as too young, too immature, in spite of everything about him that contradicted that image.

She paused, looked across the valley and the road below. She began to walk, then stopped again, fascinated by the lovely prospect of the *gasthaus* set back beyond the lively creek, washed pure in the day's last light. Her bright-red Fiat at the foot of the pass, a mere toy from where she stood, contrasted sharply with the verdant background. Her heart pounded.

It's not too late to back out, she thought. But—her lips quivered; her eyes grew hard—wasn't revenge her lifelong goal? How was she to turn her back on those two graves with crosses of cold granite? In spite of all her good fortune, and great friendships, she had never been able to picture herself living a happy, carefree life.

The bunker was silhouetted against a dark blue sky as Corporal Schuller watched the changing of guard. His instructions, from loading the rifle to the emergency signal shots, had become routine. This time Rüegg heard them.

"Don't worry about me, Corp, I can handle this rifle as well as anyone," he shouted after him. He was baffled, though, to see the Corporal troubled and concerned when nothing, absolutely nothing ever happened around this outfit. He listened to his steps until they were lost in the emerging dark.

Giulio's plan could not have gone better. He'd bought six surplus submachine guns from a friendly fascist group in Genoa that was funded by a wealthy collaborator, whose identity he had yet to learn. However, Italy's strict gun control, enforced by the Carabinieri, made obtaining the 9-mm ammo almost impossible.

This was about to change. After a two-day delay, donkeys and three of his trusted men were in a clearing below the ridge waiting for his signal. Darkness would be upon them rapidly. Giulio paced, clenching and unclenching his hands. He looked at his watch—a quarter to nine; the time had come. Giulio roused his men. The attack was planned for 9:15.

Benny, swift and silent as a cat, was the band's top spotter. Besides Giulio, he was the youngest of the men. Clean-shaven, his hair neatly trimmed, he stuck out from the others like a peacock. Skilled in mountain climbing, assignments like this were right up his alley—besides being a profitable change from penny-pinching jobs. He slid from the river trail across the road, up the slope, and behind the bunker. The sentry was below him now, close enough for Benny to hear his breathing and smell his body odor.

With a cat-like jump, Benny dropped in front of the soldier and pressed the barrel of his automatic gun to his chest. In a flash and with great strength, the sentry stripped the gun from Benny's hands and swung it across the road, where it slid below the bank. He gripped Benny's arms in a vise. Groaning and shoving, the two men fought fiercely.

Benny was strong, but as the test dragged on, he realized the sentry's superior might. Then, just when he felt himself giving in, he felt the soldier stiffen and his grip weaken. Benny gave him a stiff blow on the chin. The sentry dropped to his knees, fell to his side, and rolled onto his belly. Then Benny saw the knife sticking out of his back.

Benny jumped at Giulio and grabbed him by the throat. "You promised that no one would get hurt!" Grinning, Giulio brushed Benny's hands aside. "So what?" Then he bent to retrieve his knife.

This time Herman had to do something. What did it matter if he was the only one who felt the tension in the air; he'd trusted such feelings before and had been proved right. He shook Spiller from his sleep.

"Wake up, Hanspeter," he whispered. "I'm going to take Hans some coffee and make sure he's okay. It might just be my nerves, but just in case, listen for my signal, should it come to that. And stay awake!"

Spiller asked, "Do you want me to come along?"

"No. Stay here and tend to the men. Hans knows how to handle himself. It's only—I've had this feeling all night."

"As you wish, Corp."

Herman filled his thermos with hot coffee, added some condensed milk, and stirred it with a long straw. He placed the thermos and a handful of cookies in his knapsack with the tarpaulin still strapped to it. From habit, he hooked on his field glasses and slipped the compass into his pocket. He attached a flashlight to his belt, grabbed his rifle, and rushed out the door.

It was freezing cold. Before he had gone far he was sorry for having left his coat behind. But he didn't brood for long—his anxiety grew stronger with every step. He closed in on the bunker, and his steps quickened until he was on the run.

The click of the massive bolt cutter broke the silence. The door squeaked so much as it opened it threatened to wake the entire valley. The men strapped ammo cases onto wooden racks mounted on the donkeys, which were bucking under the heavy loads. With a loud thump, a case hit the floor, scattering its contents.

"Leave it!" said Giulio fiercely.

"Someone's coming," It was Sofia, the young woman on lookout who called herself Giulio's mistress. She'd met him at a bazaar a few months ago and had an instant crush on him. Tonight a silver scarf, a gift from Giulio, bound her long black hair. What she enjoyed in beauty she lacked in common sense, and it was no surprise to anyone that she was insanely jealous of the Bianci woman.

Benny strapped down the last of the donkeys, then slid down the bank to look for his gun.

"Forget the automatic; let's get out of here," urged Giulio. He took the first donkey by its halter, all but dragging the spooked animal down the slope to the river trail. The other men followed with the two remaining donkeys, and Sofia, re-tightening her silver scarf as she ran, was close behind. They vanished into the dark, their steps muted by the stream.

⊰⭒⊱

The flashlight trembled in Herman's hand as he ran back and forth in front of the bunker. "Hans! Where are you?" he cried, panicky and out of breath. Then the beam of his flashlight found the body on the ground, the hand stretched out in search of the rifle.

"Hans, for heaven's sake, what happened?" He dropped to his knees. "Talk to me!" When he tried to raise his friend he felt his warm blood on his hand. Hans was moving his lips as if trying to talk, but couldn't make a sound.

Herman picked up the soldier's rifle and fired three shots into the air.

He put his knapsack under Rüegg's head and turned him on his side. He opened one of the pockets on the soldier's ammo belt and pulled out the small packet of medical supplies. All the while, he talked to him: "I'll take care of you, Hans; don't worry. I'll find whoever did this to you. Just lay still now . . . don't try to talk. Save your strength . . . ." He opened the soldier's coat and the buttons on his jacket. Careful not to hurt him, he put a pressure pack between the shirt and wound and pressed down until the bleeding stopped, then fastened the bandage with first-aid tape.

Schuller couldn't believe this had happened. Tears of frustration clouded his eyes. "Who are you people? Why did you do this? Cowards!" he cried into the dark. Then guilt gnawed at him. *I knew that something was going to happen. It's all my fault! Oh, Hans, why did I leave you?*

Then guilt turned to excuses and accusations. *But I didn't know—how could I have known? How could anybody have known? I can't be blamed! Damn you, Lieutenant! I told you to put up two guards—told you, but you wouldn't listen. No one ever wants to take any responsibility. The hell with this outfit!*

He raised his fist to the dark sky. "You'll pay for this, whoever you are! How dare you take my bunker? How dare you assault my friend?"

Frei and Spiller came running up the road, sweating and breathing hard.

Herman stood to meet them. "Hans has been stabbed in the back! He's hurt bad!" he cried. "Ruedi, go back and alert the medic and the ambulance driver. Stay on their butts until they move, and only then go get Lieutenant Stucki wherever he may be." He gestured impatiently, and Frei dashed away.

"Thanks, Hanspeter, for getting here so fast. Hans may be in shock! Roll up your coat and put it under his head. It's softer than my knapsack."

The soldier took off his coat, rolled it tightly, and slid it under Hans's neck.

Schuller said, "The pressure dressing might not hold when Hans begins to shift around." He took Spiller's right hand and guided it to the dressing. "Here, press your fingers to it, just in case. Yes, right there. Not too hard, now—just enough to keep it from bleeding again. I'm going to have a look around."

Herman shone his flashlight at the wide-open door. The motive for the attack was clear. The cut chain and steel lock were lying on the ground next to the discarded bolt cutter. Cartridges had spilled from an open box, likely dropped in a hasty retreat. He picked up one of the shells and recognized it was steel-piercing machine-gun ammo from the purple firing cap. While it was of the same caliber as the standard Swiss army rifle, its steel core and stronger powder load gave it extra penetration. Without a thought, he put two handfuls in his pocket.

He entered the bunker and meticulously counted the cases of ammunition stacked against the walls, comparing them to the inventory list he and the feldweibel had tacked to the door earlier that afternoon. None of the rifle ammo was missing, and if he added the spilled case of machine-gun shells, it, too, was accounted for. But six full cases of 9-mm ammo were gone. He sat on a box and shook his head, amazed and disbelieving—why would anyone want so much ammunition? Each wooden case contained three wax-coated boxes with 1,200 shells each—wow! That was more than 21,000 rounds, enough ammo to arm an entire company. Those cases were heavy, too, each weighing a hundred pounds at least.

How could they move that many cases? No trucks or wagons had been seen or heard passing the barracks to the east, and Passo di Novena to the west was closed to traffic because of snow. That left the mountains to the south. Herman thought of the creek below the road and the trail that led to Passo di San Giácomo into Italy.

"Italy!" he screamed. His mind raced. The Passo, the border, was only a few kilometers distant. The trail was passable only on foot or with animals. Packhorses! They were using packhorses and headed for the border. He had never been surer of himself.

But his thought was sharply interrupted. Hand grenades! Herman rushed back inside the bunker where he counted the high explosives in the one open case against the back wall—twenty-one grenades plus the six used in the exercise. It was all there, and the seals of the remaining two cases were intact.

He rushed across the road and shone his flashlight below the embankment. There were fresh hoof tracks as he had expected. He dropped to the ground—the hoofs were too small to be from horses. Donkeys! They were using donkeys, and the deep tracks confirmed that they were heavily loaded. Schuller saw there were three animals. That would mean two boxes for each—a good-sized load for such small animals, especially in view of the steep grades. Enough to slow them down.

Schuller slid down the slope and followed their tracks. The trail pointed to the pass. No doubt the robbers had headed for the border. Could he cut them off and pin them down until daylight? The thought was tempting, but the distant rumble of the ambulance pulled him away. He ran back toward the bunker.

As Herman climbed up the embankment to the road, an object, glowing in the moonlight, caught his eye. He pointed the flashlight. It was an automatic gun partially hidden by shrubs. Schuller breathed deeply from excitement. He picked up the gun. It was the same 9-mm model as in the arsenal of Swiss troops, with some small differences. A phosphorous tape had been glued to the backside of the magazine to make its position recognizable in the dark—ingenious, Schuller thought—and the rear sight had been replaced with a night sight. The fifty-round clip was fully loaded. To his surprise, however, the slide-bolt was closed, and when he pulled it back, there was no ejection of a shell—the gun was not ready to be fired.

The rumble of the ambulance came closer and its headlights shone in the distance. Hans was still unconscious. Herman told Spiller what he'd found in the bunker.

"I put you in full charge of the squad, Hanspeter." He stood up and put the automatic in the soldier's hand. "I found this below the embankment; must have been dropped in the retreat. Give it to Lieutenant Stucki. Tell him that six cases of the 9-mm ammo are missing. Everything else is accounted for, including the hand grenades."

He pointed to Hans Rüegg. "Make sure they take care of Hans before anything else!"

"Where you going, Corp?" Spiller's eyes had grown large.

"I'm taking up the chase."

"You're what?" Spiller's mouth dropped open.

"You heard me—I'm going after them."

"You're crazy, Corp; you can't just leave! Wait for the lieutenant. He'll organize the pursuit."

"No and hell no! He'll have to ask the captain, he'll have to ask the colonel. By the time this army gets going, the thieves will be long gone."

Spiller shook his head and raised his eyebrows. "I say it again, Corp: you can't just go off on some wild goose chase."

"Don't waste your time trying to change my mind, Hanspeter. It won't work. My mind's made up; I'm going after them. With some luck, I might stop them before they reach the border."

Hanspeter pointed. "Over that pass? The trail's too steep, too dangerous in the dark; they'll never make it that way. Passo Novena is a better choice, and I'll bet that's where they're heading."

"There's no way to get through the snow up there. I'm telling you, they took the trail along the creek, and I'm following."

"All the way to the border?"

"And beyond, if necessary."

"The Italians will arrest you. Think of the consequences, Corp."

"I have."

"Then change your mind!" pleaded Spiller.

The corporal put his hand on the soldier's shoulder. "The bunker and this squad are my obligation. I was put in charge to protect them both, and I failed. Anyway, I'm still in charge, and that ammo is my responsibility."

"They'll arrest you, throw the book at you!"

"I'll argue that point when the time comes. Besides, Lieutenant Stucki will stand by me."

"That you can count on," said Spiller, calmer now. "Well, have it your way, Corp. I'll keep things rolling while you're gone. Good luck, then." He gave Herman's arm a squeeze, but the corporal tore away from him and slung his knapsack and rifle over his shoulder. After a last gaze at the injured soldier, he slid down the embankment.

Spiller didn't want to call attention to the corporal's departure by calling after him, so he watched silently and helplessly as he disappeared below the road. Soon there was no sound but the noisy creek.

The moon shone through a veil of mist and lit the trail through broken clouds. Rifle at his shoulder and flashlight in his hand, Herman was moving fast. The going had been easy while the trail ran along the creek but then it pulled away, got steep, and Herman started breathing hard. The sound of the creek, so loud moments ago, faded quickly. All he heard now above his labored breathing was the sound of his boots grinding on loose rocks.

He froze. There was a sudden glow. He dropped to the ground, heart pounding, as he strained to see. The glow faded and came back with changes in the moonlight, too still to be human. He pointed the flashlight. It was a signpost.

Going toward it he stepped ankle-deep into an ice-cold water-hole. "Dammit!" He hadn't once slipped into the icy creek and now he'd got his foot wet in a puddle of snowmelt from the slopes above.

Three hand-painted pointers gave directions in hiking time: All' Acqua 58 Min, Passo Novena 3 Hrs 10 Min, and Passo di San Giácomo 2 Hrs 5 Min. The latter was too close. Probably he couldn't catch the thieves before they crossed the border. Still, he pushed on.

Occasional patches of manure left no doubt of the path they took—a blind man could have sniffed it out. He wasn't sure how long he could keep up this pace—that was the problem. Scrambling around the steepening turns and towering slopes was wearing him out. His legs began feeling like sticks of lead and his knees like rusty pliers.

Thick clouds were hiding the moon. When they parted, Herman pushed himself to the point of recklessness. When the trail was dumped in darkness again, he began to trip and scrape his knees.

It had to happen . . . . Without warning, the clouds closed in, and the trail disappeared. The timing couldn't have been worse. Herman slipped, the ground gave way, and he slid down the slope unable to stop, uprooting shrubs on the way. A small tree caught him. He frantically held on to it with both hands, afraid to breathe, sick with the notion that his feet were hanging over empty space. His eyes adjusted slowly. He was lying on his stomach at the edge of a cliff, hanging onto the skimpy tree.

He wrapped his left arm around it, unhooked the rifle with his right hand, and flung it above where it hit with a nasty thump. He froze. The tree moved slightly, tearing free from the meager soil. He lay perfectly still and flat against the ground. The tree seemed to hold. He chanced slipping the straps of the knapsack over his head a fraction at a time and slung it powerfully after the rifle. It was too much. The tree pulled loose again.

Herman was at a loss. If he moved, the tree might come uprooted completely. If he didn't, he'd be glued to that ledge indefinitely. Just then, the moon broke through the clouds and showed him a small rock that was solidly embedded. Barely breathing he drew up his left leg until the rock was caught in the bend of his knee. Then he shifted his weight onto his left leg and ever so slowly began to straighten it, sliding forward. He hadn't moved much, but he wasn't sliding back. He repeated the process over and over, drawing up his legs very carefully, pushing off with just enough energy to move further from the sheer drop.

He was drained of all strength when he reached the trail, but his spirits were high. He spread out his chart on a large rock, and examined it under his flashlight, recognizing the switchback turns that were behind him. He was more than halfway to the border now, but the closeness of the contour lines meant that the most difficult part of the trail still lay ahead.

Was that sound a rock bouncing from the distant slope above? He held his breath, listening with hands cupped behind his ears. Was he imagining things, or were those hooves scraping granite? If so, they were too faint to hear now. It was dead quiet again.

He folded up the chart and sat on the rock, ate a cookie, and took a swallow from his thermos. The short rest allowed Herman to think things through. If they were on the slope above, whoever they were, he should prepare himself. Before moving on he pushed the grease from his rifle barrel. He loaded six shells into the clip and a seventh round into the chamber.

Bushes closed in on both sides of the narrow path, and the changing light played tricks on his imagination. There was the shadow of a giant donkey and beyond it a man with his gun pointed toward him. With each sighting, Herman took cover, and was forced to acknowledge that he'd been spooked.

Again he hit the ground. A faint shimmer just ahead made him drop low and hold his breath. He lay flat, eyes and ears straining to penetrate the dark. There was no sound. Reluctantly, he crawled forward. A silk scarf was caught on a branch. He carefully freed it, felt its softness, smelled its faint perfume.

The scarf! The perfume! He clenched his fists; his forehead broke out in a sweat; a voice rang in his ear.

" . . . Keeping that stuff around sounds risky . . ."

The woman's voice was as clear as if she stood beside him. Then he remembered his own words. "I'm sure they've found a secure cellar or an old bunker with strong locks."

No! The rifle slipped from his hand and hit the ground. He had to sidestep to keep his balance, then let himself go and dropped hard onto the rifle butt. But no physical pain could mask the guilt and repentance he felt. How was this beautiful woman linked to this? His lips trembled, and his eyes burned from the sweat running down his forehead. Yet . . . he refused to accept what his mind was telling him.

He examined the scarf under the flashlight beam—it was silver. It wasn't hers! Or was it? He pressed it to his nose again. This was not her perfume, he was sure of it! The thought of her involvement was absurd . . . she would never associate with such men! Or would she?

The agonizing thoughts pounding his head softened some-what—*the attackers' haste has made them careless.* He folded the scarf, put it into his pocket. He repeated his denial to himself as he pushed on. It wasn't her scarf. Nor was it her face on the serpent in his dream.

Somehow the scarf in his pocket, whether it was hers or not, had calmed his fears. It had made the fleeing thieves more real. The very thought of a woman struggling up this trail in the dead of night had changed the way he felt about his mission. There were no more phantom shapes in the brush beside the road, only shapes to hide behind, ways to take the enemy by surprise.

Bolting from bed to answer the phone, Colonnello Zanardelli's head caught the slanted ceiling before he could unhook the receiver. "Stupid telephone!" Holding his head with one hand, he knocked the handset off the wall with his other and watched it disappear between the headboard and the mattress. "Shit!" He traced the cord and pulled the receiver into view.

"Say that again," he demanded over line static.

The caller told of an attack a mere hour ago at an army depot outside All' Acqua at the Swiss border. Some boxes of ammunition were missing, the sentry had been stabbed . . . they didn't know much more yet . . . . The Swiss authorities wanted Italian help if the attackers should cross the border.

Zanardelli said he would do what he could and got off the line. There was no blood where he'd hit his head. Still, the first thing he needed to do was wash his face and wake up properly.

Ideas started coming to him in front of his washstand. Was Giulio capable of a theft like this, right from under the Swiss army's nose?

Why not? It was just like one of his actions to start like an unlikely prank and end with casualties and possible loss of life.

In his office he took a chart from his desk and traced the Bedretto Valley to All' Acqua, where he drew a circle around the tiny town. Zanardelli had been along that stretch of border during the war, fighting alongside the guerillas, and he knew the rugged area south and west of there as well as any local.

Two mountain passes linked All' Acqua with the border. One led over Passo della Novena, from where it branched off south as a little-used trail over Griespass, a route notorious for high winds and snowdrifts.

The other trail, much shorter but considerably steeper, led over Passo di San Giácomo. It crossed sheer cliffs, and was risky in the dark, but it made for a quick escape. Giulio had the requisite death wish, and the strategy would have appealed to him (as it did to the colonnello). Anyway, both trails led to the headwaters of the Toce River at Riale, a rugged village surrounded by hostile peaks.

His mandate was simple: stop the thieves before they entered the lower valley, where escape routes would be plentiful. He traced Formazza Valley to search out the best place for an effective roadblock, then picked up the phone and dialed the regional headquarters of the Carabinieri.

Curfew was long past, and the *gasthaus* tavern was deserted. The chubby woman cleaned up behind the buffet. A single swag lamp burned above the table in the far corner of the tavern, squeaking a little on the hook as it swung in the draft of the partially open window. Two officers bent over spread-out maps, drawing lines and circles under a magnifying glass.

"Close that damn window, you hear?" the woman cried for the third time. "It's cold enough as it is!" The looks on the men's faces told her, "Leave us alone," as they had all night. She continued washing the beer mugs and the wineglasses the waitress had left.

Suddenly, she'd had enough—she might as well have been talking to the open window. She squeezed between the officers and the wall and cranked the window shut.

So far, the officers had done everything in their power: transported the injured sentry to the army hospital in Lozone, where the doctor was unable to predict Hans Rüegg's chances; contacted the Swiss Consul in Milan; and evaded the company commander as much as possible in the little town.

A hard knock at the door made them look up. The chubby woman unlocked it.

The captain's orderly rushed in and saluted the lieutenant, clicking his heels. Out of breath he said, "Hauptmann Roth wants you at headquarters on the double!"

"Dammit! Both of us?" asked Lieutenant Stucki.

"Preferably both, and he wants you there now."

They left the maps on the table and hurried to headquarters.

There they were ready to face Hauptmann Roth but didn't expect to see the battalion chief behind the makeshift desk. Stucki and Ott shot to attention.

"At ease," said Hauptmann Roth, who stood beside the colonel.

The colonel took a puff on his cigar. "What do you have to say about this mess, Lieutenant?"

Lieutenant Stucki took a deep breath. "They took some boxes of ammo, that's it . . ."

The colonel shifted his weight on the wooden chair, which squeaked under him. "They rob our bunker and almost kill a man and 'that's it' is all you can say? If you'd had your ears on, Lieutenant, you'd know more than 'that's it.' Do I have to spell it out for you?"

Lieutenant Stucki bit his lip. "What's to spell out, Colonel?"

"The rumors about your corporal, that's what."

"Corporal Schuller?"

With a startling thump, the colonel brought his fist down on the plywood desk. Pencils and paper clips went airborne, and the penholder fell off the edge. "Your corporal is in on the plot!" he cried. "Well! Do you have something to say now?"

Lieutenant Stucki looked at Feldweibel Ott. Neither of them was prepared for such an absurdity. Red in the face from all the blood that had shot to his head, Stucki forced himself to keep his voice calm. "He's *not* involved. I'd put my career on the line for Corporal Schuller."

"I wouldn't be so hasty, Lieutenant. Let me tell you some of the facts!" He was visibly offended by the lieutenant's scarcely hidden rage, which bordered on impertinence. He shifted his weight on the squeaky chair trying to hold back his own wrath. "Two disturbing facts have come to light. Schuller came Sunday afternoon, quite early I'm told, in a Fiat that had Italian license plates. The driver was female." He puffed on his cigar. "Very beautiful, too, so I heard. A day later, in the middle of the night the same female inquired about Schuller's room at the *gasthaus* and then was seen walking upstairs carrying a bag. There was a witness."

The lieutenant looked to the feldweibel for signs of support, but the colonel hadn't finished. He said angrily, "I think it's very suspicious that the attack took place on Schuller's guard. Now he has vanished! How do you explain that?"

Appalled, Lieutenant Stucki held onto the chair in front of him. His eyes were blazing. "I don't know anything about this woman, but Schuller's loyalty has never been in question. When we find the woman I'm sure we'll find that everything between them is unrelated to the attack tonight."

The colonel had had enough. "And how do you explain his absence from his post?"

"He went after the thieves. He left word that he was going to try to stop them before they had a chance to cross the border."

"By himself? Ha!"

"By himself! He felt that time was of the essence. Schuller is a man of action—he has proven it many times. He's also a man of his word. You can be sure he's doing exactly what he told the men—"

"Cut it out, Lieutenant! It wouldn't be the first time that something in a skirt twisted a young man's mind," the colonel sneered. "This situation is serious! I don't need this kind of scandal in our battalion. I want solutions, not excuses. There's no room for fancy character portrayals or sympathy!" He slammed the desktop for a second time, bouncing more objects onto the floor. "I'm waiting for your reply, Lieutenant!"

The feldweibel stepped in, surprising everyone. "Character isch important, Colonel, and I schay thisch without dischrespect to you." His eyebrows fluttered, a sign of passionate conviction that everyone who knew him recognized. "The corporal'sch a scholdier of great integrity and schkill, but I don't have to tell you that, Colonel. He showed thisch again thisch morning at the shooting exercische; thosch NATO men were plenty impresched, no doubt about it. We need men of Schuller'sch merit."

Silence. When the colonel spoke, his voice was an octave lower. "It was indeed a great performance." He leaned back in his chair and blew cigar smoke for a moment. "All the more reason to find a quiet solution to this mess while our friends from NATO are still with us at headquarters in Airolo. All right, because of the corporal's good record, I'll give you thirty-six hours to clear up this mess."

When the colonel had stomped out Hauptmann Roth had to give his own warning. "Remember: thirty-six hours, or by noon the day after tomorrow." He, too, left the room, responding weakly to the men's salute.

Lieutenant Stucki sighed. He sat down on the chair in front of him and fanned the smoke from his face.

Feldweibel Ott sat down beside him. "Well, Franz, do we have a plan? What'sch next?"

The lieutenant pointed to his holster. "First we get some better weapons. We've got to assume the runagates are carrying automatics like the one we found."

There was a moment of quiet as the same thought occurred to both men coincidentally—Lieutenant Stucki was still in the possession of the automatic gun the thieves had left behind.

The Swiss Cross came to life in Herman's flashlight, embossed on a bronze plaque. Beside it, a large wooden sign with the Swiss flag painted on it, left behind from the war, read, "You are leaving Switzerland." Schuller hesitated, thinking of the consequences should the Italians catch him wearing his Swiss Army uniform, armed with a loaded rifle and his bayonet. Would they slap his hands and send him home red-faced? Throw him in prison? He chortled. *Maybe they'll put me against the wall and shoot me?* He didn't want to think.

However, turning back empty-handed was not an option. He took a deep breath and held it to slow his racing thoughts, but he already knew the answer.

He took a decisive symbolic step across the international boundary. The moon was still playing hide and seek. He shined his flashlight on the map. Intermittent dots hinted at an unmarked path along the international border leading over a mountain crest that no man of sound mind would risk in the dark. The narrow trail that Schuller was on, on the other hand, widened at the border to a small road. It descended onto a high plateau with a series of gentle turns and followed a reservoir to a dam.

The clouds vanished. Schuller moved on through a landscape so flooded with moonlight that he could see the ripples sparkling on the narrow surface of the lake. He reached the top of the dam with long, steady strides. In the distance, down in the valley, the hazy distance glowed with the few streetlights of Riale. Schuller had barely started down the road with its sudden turns when he stopped abruptly.

It was unmistakable: the sound of hooves and muffled shouts from below. It was *them*!

Herman raced blindly down the mountain, revenge the only thought in his mind. He did not see the shadow or the rifle butt that knocked him off the road. He felt only a burning pain, and the sense of falling, falling . . . .

Giulio and the others had made remarkable progress. There had been no incidents on the way to the pass, no major slips or falls. They were in the upper Formazza valley, barren of all human activity, with a clear run ahead to the farm. There, in the barn, they would rest and prepare for the last push to a rendezvous point where a truck would be waiting to take them to Domodóssola. Steps approached fast.

Emilio. "We were followed by a soldier—a Swiss." His eyes glittered even as his dark beard hid his face. Emilio was Giulio's trusted man and perfect for bringing up the rear. "The automatic would have wakened half the valley. I just busted him good—smack on the head," he went on. He showed the others how he had clobbered the soldier with his rifle butt. "He went over the edge. I doubt anyone could survive a whack like that, much less the fall."

"Here we go again!" moaned Benny. "How'd I ever get mixed up with this outfit!"

"Calm down, Benny," said Giulio. "Did he have any choice? That soldier would have been at our heels the rest of the way." He put a hand on Benny's shoulder. "Besides, Emilio has a way of blowing things out of proportion. I'm sure the soldier's doing just fine."

Benny set his jaw and quickened his pace. He knew it was too late to back out.

Giulio, too, was moving faster, thrilled that the man who had followed them was out for good. His goal, the empty barn, was but a couple kilometers down the valley.

Angelina Bianci slowed the Fiat and stopped abruptly. A policeman, standing in front of a makeshift wooden barrier, signaled with a flashlight. He pointed his rifle at her windshield.

"Stop right there, signora," he cried.

Angelina rolled down the window. "What are you doing out here in the wee hours of the morning?"

"I'm asking the questions here," replied the *carabiniero* calmly. "First, show me your papers."

"I'll do no such thing! Who do you think you are, holding up innocent people?"

The policeman repeated coolly, "I need to see your papers, signora."

"I'm Italian, and the last time I heard, this was still a free country where we are able to roam about at will without being pestered by *carabinieri!* This is preposterous . . ."

"Ho, ho, calm down, Signora," a manly voice called from the shadows. "The officer is only doing his job. Besides," he said, pointing his flashlight at a machine gun mounted beside the road, "you don't want to tangle with this, do you?" A man stepped into the headlight beams.

Angelina froze. He was tall, and his broad shoulders made him look small at the hips. He wore black pants, a black coat, and a black turtleneck sweater. But it was his voice that made her shiver.

He put his hand on the policeman's rifle barrel. "Put it down, officer; we don't want to scare the signora any more than we have to, do we?" His voice was meant to put her at ease but suspicion radiated from his eyes. "Now, signora, can we start over? I'm Zanardelli, Colonnello Zanardelli. Uh, would you cut the engine and kill those lights? No need to alert the neighborhood."

Angelina did as she was told. Another policeman brought a kerosene lantern and held it above their heads.

"My name's Bianci, Signorina Bianci." She reached into the glove compartment and retrieved her papers. "Here's my passport and my driving permit. You'll find everything in order."

The colonnello riffled through the passport and handed the papers back to her. "Now, where would you be going in such a hurry at this late hour?"

Angelina bit her lip. "If you must know, I was going fishing. There are great trout in this river."

"Signora—"

"Signorina!"

"Signorina, then—would it be possible to get some cooperation? After all, I could . . ."

"Could what?"

"Well, for openers, I could detain you for defiance, take my time checking your papers, even lock you up."

"In jail? You'd be asking for a heap of trouble, Colonnello—"

"Call me Vittorio. Vitt." He was looking hard at her now. "Have we met before?"

"I don't know any colonels," she replied coolly.

"Only generals, I presume."

"How did you guess?" she said snippily. "Ever heard of Generale Gianotti?" She immediately regretted using his name. She hated gaining the upper hand by throwing names around; it wasn't her way.

"Giuseppi Gianotti? We served in the war together. You know the general?"

"Yes, I know the general and his wife Barbara very well." Angelina heaved a long sigh. "And if you really need to know what I'm doing here—"

Zanardelli waved his hand. "No need for that, Signorina Bianci; probably visiting an ill aunt." There might have been a bit of kindness in his voice this time.

Exactly what she was going to say! She shuddered.

The colonnello turned toward the policeman. "Come on, take that stuff off the road and let this woman pass." He leaned on the window frame. "Perhaps we'll meet again someday, signorina? It would certainly be my pleasure." He tipped his hat and stepped aside.

Angelina nodded and said, "Someday, perhaps." She started the car, switched on the headlights, and accelerated past the barricades.

Though happy about the outcome, Angelina was apprehensive. She didn't like the young commander's pleasantness, and she kept one eye on the rearview mirror as she raced up the valley. No one followed.

Just beyond Canze, Angelina veered onto a dirt road and drove to an isolated barn at its very end. She parked the Fiat in the back under the roof overhang and stepped inside. Giulio and his band had not yet arrived.

It seemed colder inside the barn than it was outside. She sat on a bale of straw and rubbed her arms and legs, thinking about the officer at the barricade. There was something special about him, something at the edge of her memory. She had seen him before and not all that long ago. But Angelina had a weakness for resolute men and she always felt as if she had met them before. This time probably wasn't any different . . .

The double door flew open, and the band, donkeys and all, stormed into the barn.

Giulio walked up to Angelina. "What did you find?" he asked harshly.

"Things don't look good, Giulio," said Angelina calmly. "I passed a roadblock just this side of La Frua, and I have the distinct feeling it's not the only one."

"Police? Military?"

"Carabinieri."

"How many men? What weapons?"

"There were six of them beside the commander. There is a machine gun set up beside the road, and the policemen carried rifles."

"What else?"

Angelina met his stare straight on. "That's all I can report. Their commander seemed plenty sharp." She went to join the rest at the other end of the barn.

Emilio was still bragging about the way he'd put some soldier out of action. "One less to worry about!"

"What's this?" asked Angelina.

"Nothing I couldn't handle, take my word." Emilio laughed. "But if you want to know; I knocked a soldier down a cliff; taught him a lesson he won't forget."

"Knocked who? Where? What's going on?" she cried.

"The Swiss soldier who was on our heels! I knocked him out cold with my rifle butt. He's probably still lying below that cliff by the road."

"You did what?" cried Angelina, her eyes large.

"Don't worry; he's no more of a threat to us now than his friend at the bunker."

"At the bunker?" The words barely passed her lips.

"Giulio had to stab one of the guards. Don't worry, we're in Italy. We got away!"

Angelina felt as if she'd just awakened from a nightmare. The veil had finally been lifted from her eyes. She pressed her hands to her face, shivering from disgust. Then she exploded in Emilio's face. "You promised that no one would get hurt! You lied to me! All of you were lying!"

Giulio held her shoulders from behind. "Calm down! It's not the end of the world," he said. "Emilio had no choice. It was either him or the soldier—can you blame him? Okay, things didn't go quite as planned, but we achieved our goal."

Angelina tore loose from Giulio's grip and went to the dark end of the barn. She was even more disgusted with herself than she was with them. She had only one desire—to get away from here. But people were hurt, and she was responsible. What could she do to put things right? The more she thought about her new role in this, the more she became convinced of what she had to do. That soldier needed help! How could she get to him? She knew very well that Giulio wouldn't let her out of the barn no matter what her excuse. *But I must find a way to get to that soldier!* She was determined. *I must sneak out of here!* She stole to the barn's darkest corner, keeping the others in her view. Then, when they all were looking the other way, she slipped silently out of a side door. She took her leather jacket and a flashlight from her Fiat, and disappeared into the night in the direction of San Giácomo Pass.

Dawn brought traffic to the lower valley as the populace, mostly on bicycles and scooters, went to their jobs at the factories and granite pits. The roadblock was making some of the locals angry—perhaps not so much for the delays it caused as because police were tightlipped about the reason for it and asking too many questions.

Colonnello Zanardelli remained in his car. Except for the beauty in the Fiat, the night had been quiet. Something still bothered him about her. Not so much that she didn't belong there—though she didn't, of course. He kept wondering where he'd seen her before. She had the refined style and movements of . . . of an actress. Vitt Zanardelli had an exceptional memory for faces, but this time he had a mental block.

With approaching daylight, the roadblock was of little use, and Zanardelli was saying "Porco Dio!" right along with the peasants— he'd been so sure of catching the renegades during the night. He looked at his topographical map and studied the area around San Giácomo Pass. Had they been crazy enough to take the trail to Basódino peak? He remembered that unmarked path along the glacier. A group, though? At night? Well, it made sense strategically, offering an ideal escape into the scarcely populated Val Bavona.

"Tenente Ponte," he said, pointing to the chart and a dotted line. "Take four of your men along this path to the east until you reach the crest, then follow the trail along the Swiss border toward San Giácomo Pass. Here." He turned the chart toward the officer. "It's marked occasionally with chiseled boundary stones that indicate the border. When you get to about this point—uh, right about here— block it. If they don't show by one hour before sunset, move on to the pass, where I will wait for you. Expect snowdrifts along the way, so be careful."

"What about the two men I'm leaving behind?" asked the tenente.

"I'll send them on patrol with the truck to check out remote farms and look into abandoned buildings and empty barns."

The tenente saluted and assembled his men. He quickly checked their charts, their gear, their arms, and then he started up the slope with them.

❧❀❧

The light of early morning had reached the high cirrus at the eastern edge of the mountains. The air was brisk. Herman was shivering, but his mother was covering him with a blanket from his feet right up to his chin. She tucked the edges around him and pressed out the wrinkles. Then she held up his head and put two aspirins on the tip of his tongue, which he swallowed with hot coffee from her thermos cup. She looked at him lovingly, ran her fingers through his hair, whispered encouragement. Herman moaned. She bent over him and pressed her cheek against his. She touched his forehead with her lips and gently kissed away his pain. Tears fell from her eyes, and she brushed them away with the back of her hand.

Well-being flooded his heart. Herman had never forgotten his mother's unselfish care during times of sickness. Feeling safe and warmed by her love, he fell into a deep, tranquil sleep.

Someone wiped Herman's face with a sponge. Was he dreaming? Herman wrinkled his nose, opened his eyes . . . and looked at a beast's awesome teeth. He cringed. The beast jumped back, alarmed by the corporal's sudden move. Frightened but equally amazed, Herman stared at the biggest dog he'd ever seen. It let out a bark, then another. But it was a friendly bark. The dog, a beautiful male Saint Bernard, paced and barked, flapping his huge ears.

The corporal sat up, but a fierce pain in his head made him lie back down. What had happened? He thought back to the path across the mountain—yes, the blow to his head. Someone—one of the thieves had doubled back, he guessed. Knocked him off the mountain and left him for dead. How long had he been lying here? It was bright daylight . . . his watch showed ten after eight. He touched his forehead. A bandage was tightly wrapped around his head.

Herman couldn't think. Someone had taken care of him. The dream of his mother was so real . . . but who was the woman who had spread his tarpaulin over him from head to toe, who had put the stuffed scarf under his head?

The scarf!

He sat up in spite of the pain, untied the scarf, and shook

pine needles out. He paused and let the scarlet silk slide through his fingers, then pressed it to his nose and inhaled its sweetness. The softness of the scarf, the richness of the fragrance . . . he'd never forget.

"It's hers!" he cried.

The Saint Bernard lowered his head and barked once, frightened by his outburst.

Herman laid the scarf to the side and rolled out the tarpaulin and the blue leather jacket draped over him.

The blue jacket! Confused, he lay back down and pressed the scarf to his face—the woman with the red hair and blue eyes absorbed him completely.

His rifle, field glasses, and the knapsack were lying neatly by his side. The Saint Bernard sat now, watching and waiting for his next move. Herman opened the knapsack and took out a military-ration chocolate bar, pulled off part of the wrapper, and tossed a section of the chocolate to the dog, who caught it in flight.

Herman unscrewed the thermos. It was down by a third, just as it should have been after the scene in his dream. He filled the cup with hot coffee, swallowed two more aspirins, and leaned back to wait for the tablets to bring relief. The Saint Bernard kept his distance. After a second piece of chocolate, he rose and made his way to the stranger's side. With a yawn and a grunt, he spread out in front of Herman as though they were old pals, his head tucked snugly between his immense paws, licking his chops.

"That's a good boy," said Herman. He scratched the dog's neck and gave him one more treat. A simple tag on the leather collar said: "Barry Mendali."

Herman scanned the side of the mountain, amazed at having survived the fall without any broken bones. Where he'd come to rest he could see the road below. He was ready to quit the hunt. All he wanted now was to go home.

He rose, rolled the blue leather jacket inside the tarpaulin, and tied it to the knapsack. He wrapped his fingers around the dog collar. "Go ahead, Barry, take me home." He was badly hurt and he didn't care where Barry took him as long as it was near.

❖

Inside the barn the temperature had dropped to freezing. Tony, the oldest gunman, was flapping his arms to stay warm. "I'm freezing, and I'm getting tired of this," he cried. "What the hell are we waiting for?"

Giulio snorted, "You want to take on those Carabinieri? Be my guest! Maybe you could clear the way for us."

Tony didn't answer. He knew what was going on. He gathered straw and splinters of wood from a loose board and brought out a box of matches.

"Oh no, you don't!" cried Giulio, and kicked the pile apart. "That's all we need—smoke to attract someone passing on the road!"

When Angelina got back to the barn, she headed straight to her car. That soldier needed care, and she was going to get it for him.

Giulio had been watching and waiting. As soon as the engine turned, he was on top of her.

"Where do you think you're going?" He turned off the engine and yanked the key from the ignition.

Angelina bit her lip. "I've done my job, Giulio; I'm going back to Milan." Her lips were trembling and her knuckles were white on the steering wheel. "Now give me back my keys!"

"You're not going anywhere! We're in this together." His tone left no room for argument. "Besides, where were you?"

"Walking around in circles, trying to stay warm. But it's none of your damned business." She couldn't stand the sight of Giulio. She slid to the passenger seat and turned her back on him. Now, when the soldier most needed her help, she was going to be useless.

She heard Giulio go back to the others, heard his voice raised in anger. He was saying something about an army truck that was roaming up and down the road that had all but killed their chances of escape that way. And how the way down the valley was permanently blocked . . . so there was only one route left: back to the pass and along the rim of the glacier. First, however, Giulio had to outfox the Carabinieri who patrolled the main road. They should leave that to him—he had a daring plan.

CHAPTER 6

*A*lice Mendali was in her kitchen making *caffellatte* for her husband's mid-morning break. After putting the pots on the table and covering them with knitted cozies, she went from balcony to balcony of her three-story chalet watering her geraniums from a goose-necked copper can. Alice was slim and blond. Though there were streaks of gray in her hair, she looked younger than her age, chiefly because of an expression of childish innocence in her wide-set, hazel eyes.

She paused on the second floor to admire the farm. She filled her lungs with the fragrance of the flowers festooning her balcony, mixed now with the scent of cherry blossoms carried by a morning breeze from their nearby orchard. Out in front of her home was a pond where ducks were paddling among blooming irises and cattails bent by the breeze. Chickens fussed in the coop at the end of the barn. Around the corner facing her, a row of clean milk cans stood against the stucco wall. Below the balcony, a cord of split firewood was neatly stacked against the house. Smoke blew from the chimney and brought with it the smell of freshly baked bread.

"My bread!" Alice rushed back to the kitchen. With a long wooden spatula, she removed loaf after crisp loaf of perfectly baked bread from the cavity of her green-tiled oven. All the while, she kept an eye on the road by the dam. What was keeping Bernard?

There was a movement outside. She smiled and opened the sheer curtains . . . and her eyes grew wide. Instead of her husband, a soldier in a familiar uniform was walking across the dam. Barry, her Saint Bernard dog, trotted beside him as though they were old friends.

The soldier carried a rifle!

Alice wavered. She had great trust in her dog. She spun away from the window and rushed downstairs, one hand on the rail, the other ripping off her apron and straightening her hair.

The moment she opened the door, Barry jumped up as he always did, wagging his tail. Even more than his appearance, the soldier's voice gave pause.

"*Ich bin Herman Schuller* . . . I hope you understand German," he stammered.

"*Grüezi,*" was her surprised reply. She was almost too keyed up to talk, clinging to the doorpost to keep her balance. "Come on in," she said in perfect Swiss dialect. She straightened slightly. "I'm Alice Mendali; welcome to my home."

"I was lost," said Herman. "Your dog led me here. You speak Swiss . . . where am I?"

"You're in Italy, just across the border. But you're hurt. You need help. Step in." She had often wondered what she would do if a stranger turned up at her door. Now that one had, though a little jittery, she was still thrilled. She had a hundred questions, but they'd have to wait, he needed help. He was probably hungry and thirsty as well.

He followed her up the three granite steps to a small vestibule. Everything was bright and clean, from the white tiles on the floor to the polished parquet steps on the stairs. Even the leaves of her rubber plant were clean and shiny. Alice beckoned for him to follow her into a small chamber, saying, "Let me look at that bloody bandage first. Everything I need is right in here."

Herman leaned his rifle against the wall in the entry and put his knapsack beside it on the floor.

"Sit on this bench and hold still," Alice said. She gently unwrapped the bandage from his forehead but stopped where the blood-soaked fiber had gotten stuck to the skin. She soaked a washcloth in warm water and dabbed at the crusted blood until the bandage came loose.

"Oh, *mannaggia!* What a cut! Might need stitches," she said, concerned. "Now close your eyes." He twitched, and a moan escaped him as she cleansed the wound with cotton drenched in alcohol. "It burns, I know, but this wound needs to be disinfected." Without further comment, she repacked the bandage with salve and fresh gauze, and wiped his bruises with alcohol.

The washroom, as the farmwoman referred to it, was the place to scrub down after work and slip into comfortable clothing and warm slippers before entering the living quarters. Overalls and windbreakers hung on brass hooks along the wall, and below them were work shoes and watertight rubber boots. Across the room was a ceramic sink with a single faucet, and beside it, propped on concrete blocks, a modern washing machine. Tinder glowed in the boiler, partially visible through an open vent. The farmwoman untied his shoes. "Your foot's all wet and freezing cold!" She wiped his feet with a fresh towel and made him put on sheepskin slippers. ("They're warm and comfy.") She put his shoes in front of the boiler and hung his socks on the clothesline that stretched across the room.

Herman, still shaky but feeling better, stammered a timid, "Thank you, Frau Alice."

"Don't say another word, soldier. We'll have time to talk soon enough. For now, let's go to the kitchen for some cider; I'm sure you're thirsty." She picked up his knapsack, but Herman wouldn't let her carry it. He followed Alice around the rubber plant, which was growing from an old copper pot, up the stairs to the second floor.

She waited for him at the top. "That's the living-room straight ahead, and the kitchen to your right. There's the bathroom." She gestured to make sure she had his eye. "I'm sure you want to wash up. You'll find soap, towels, and hot water in there. Come to the kitchen when you're done."

In the bathroom Herman stared at himself in the mirror, shocked by the bruises on his face and his bloodshot eyes. He washed his hands and face with soap, then cupped his hands and splattered cold water on his cheeks and on the back of his neck. The cool water felt wonderful now that he was warm. He drank some.

When he sauntered into the kitchen Alice was tying her curtains. She wanted to see her husband before he came into the house. She already felt a little guilty, wondering how her husband would react to the soldier's presence in the kitchen, in his favorite slippers. "Here you are. Are you feeling any better?"

He said he was.

"You're pale. Here, take a seat." She gestured to the bench by the table. She opened the pantry door, took out a large bottle, put a glass in front of him and filled it. "Drink this." She watched him empty half the contents in one gulp. Alice smiled. "You are thirsty. Bernard—that's my husband—makes the best cider in this valley. He allows it to ferment halfway, then pasteurizes it to retain some of the sweetness."

Herman knew the process from his aunt's farm; there wasn't a better thirst-quencher. He emptied the glass, and the woman quickly refilled it.

An oblong table with a built-in bench on each side stood in the bay window. The table was set for three, with plates, silverware, and white napkins in silver clasps. For a centerpiece, a ceramic vase had been filled with fresh-cut, yellow roses.

Alice saw him staring at the bouquet. "My husband cuts me fresh flowers throughout the growing season," she said proudly. "He should be here any moment for his mid-morning coffee. I wonder what's holding him up." Alice glanced over at the loaves of bread lined up in the heart of her oven. "They got done just in time."

The door opened. A man of medium height stepped into the kitchen. Suspicion clouded his face as he took in the presence of the rifle in his hallway and the corporal in his kitchen. Alice lost no time.

"This is Herr Schuller, Bernard. He's a corporal in the Swiss Army. He got lost and injured and needs our help."

"What the hell . . . ?" The farmer held his tongue when his wife put her hand on his arm and shook her head. "I meant to say . . . will you have some milk and coffee with us, Corporal?" His Swiss dialect was almost as good as his wife's. Without waiting for a response, he poured coffee for everyone. He wasn't about to stop being suspicious of a soldier in the uniform of another country—with a bandage and bruises and bloodshot eyes—but his wife was right, the man needed their help.

The farmer's neck was wide, his shoulders broad, and his black hair was in stark contrast to his wife's fair skin and light hazel eyes. As he stretched out his hand to Herman, muscles rippled in his rolled-up shirtsleeve. "Welcome to our home, Herr Schuller."

Herman rose to take his hand. The grip of it was very firm.

Alice put a fourth setting on the table. She passed around a platter with dried sausage, boiled bacon, and a large hunk of cheese, and brought a freshly baked loaf of bread.

"Here, Corporal," said the farmer. He put a wedge of cheese and a piece of bacon on his plate, and cut off a slice of bread. "Try this bread. My wife is Italy's greatest baker."

"Let's not start that again, Bernard," said Alice, blushing.

Herman was hungry as a bear. They ate in silence, though questions were hanging on their lips. Finally Herman felt he had to say something. "I love your cheese; it has a distinct flavor."

"We make it ourselves right here on the farm," said Bernard proudly.

Herman nodded. "I'm sure I've had it before."

"Bernard sells it to stores and taverns all over the Bedretto Valley," said Alice, chuckling. "He always says that the Swiss are the only ones with cash these days."

"Of course," said Herman, with fresh excitement, "we practically lived on your cheese while in All' Acqua. It's a little like Parmesan, but I prefer its softer texture."

The farmer smiled appreciatively. Gone was any trace of his former suspicion.

"My husband makes the journey twice a year on foot, all by himself. It's a tiresome walk, and risky too; I wish he didn't have to do it."

They resumed eating, and the tension began to build again in the silence. Herman put down his fork. He couldn't stall any longer—he had to tell his hosts what he was doing here.

"There was an attack last night on a bunker in All' Acqua," he said plainly. "In the process, one of my soldiers was stabbed and several cases of ammunition were taken. I took it upon myself to give chase. But whoever did this thing outsmarted me, set a trap for me in the dark, and knocked me down a ravine. Your dog found me in the morning and led me to your door."

The farm couple's amazement showed in their faces.

"But someone must have helped you, corporal," said Alice. "That was such a neat bandage on your forehead.

Herman nodded. "Yes, someone did take care of me while I was unconscious. In the first light of morning I came to, shivering, and a woman held up my head and gave me aspirins from my pack and coffee from my thermos. She put my tarp over me, and I fell asleep. The whole thing was like a dream to me. I thought she was my mother."

"Your mother?" Alice put down her knife, astonished. "Do you have any idea who she really was?"

Herman sighed. "I do. Last Sunday afternoon, a beautiful woman gave me a ride to All' Acqua in her Fiat." He pulled the red scarf from his pocket. "This is her scarf. She made a pillow out of it with pine needles, and covered me up with her leather jacket. I'm afraid she's involved in this, somehow. Probably against her will!"

The farmer rubbed his chin. "Nothing like this ever happened around here. How many of them were there?"

"Six at the most, and two of them are women." Herman felt very tired suddenly. "They used donkeys to transport the ammo . . ." he barely had the energy to finish the sentence.

Alice stood. "You're not well, Corporal. Come into the den and lie down on the couch until you're stronger."

But Herman shook his head. "I'm fine, Frau Alice, truly." She sat back down. He continued, "It's important that you know who these people are. They must be capable of just about anything."

The farmer set down his cup and smiled confidently. "Don't worry about us, Corporal," he said. "I keep a shotgun in the barn, and I know how to use it. What about you, though? What are your plans?"

"Go back to All' Acqua, I guess," he said. "Face my commander. He won't be too happy about this."

Alice suddenly remembered. "There was talk about a roadblock farther down the valley," she said. "A newsflash on the radio earlier this morning—a squad of *carabinieri*."

Herman Schuller looked up. *So the Italians knew about the attack!* "That is good news," he said. "Let's hope they get these people before they do more harm. Well, I'd better be heading back. I'm out of the hunt now, for sure." He stood up, but dropped right back down, his face going pale.

"You'll do no such thing!" Alice said firmly. "You're shaky and in no shape to travel. First you'll have to rest."

"My wife's right," said Bernard. "You'll be safe with us. A few more hours shouldn't make any difference to your commander."

Alice added, "Then, when you're ready to go on, Bernard will show you back across the border."

"That's right," said the farmer. "I know an old trail that will get you there unseen." He wiped his mouth and stood up. "I'll finish some chores while you get rested up. As soon as you feel ready to make the trip, just let me know." He nodded kindly and left the room.

⊰⊱※⊰⊱

Herman took off his jacket, got out of his slippers, and spread out on the couch.

Alice insisted he drink one more glass of cider before trying to sleep. Herman raised up and emptied the glass. He felt silly lying on the couch, being cared for by a stranger.

Half asleep already, he gave voice to a question that might have sounded out of place had he asked it earlier. "What do you think your dog was doing out there below that cliff?"

Alice turned an easy chair around and sat, facing the couch. "Barry escorts our two children—we have a boy and a girl—to school every morning and picks them up again in the afternoon. He's done this for the past two years. He sticks to the road while the children are with him, but takes shortcuts when he's on his own. He's exceptionally smart. The way he took care of you is typical of him."

"You're not Italian," he blurted.

"And you'd like to know what I am doing here in Italy?" Alice played along. "I was born and raised in Gruyère. I'm sure you know where that is. My maiden name's Stüssi."

"From cheese country, how apt!" Herman reconsidered. "I don't mean to sound rude."

"It's okay, Corporal," she said. "And while we're at it, yes, my husband is Italian."

Herman shook his head. "But he speaks Swiss almost perfectly."

"He spent much of his youth in Switzerland." She smiled broadly, but her thoughts were elsewhere, perhaps in the past. "There are few husbands as good as Bernard."

"I know," he said.

Alice raised an eyebrow.

"The roses on the kitchen table. Flowers say a lot."

Alice smiled and pulled her chair closer. "My parents met my husband's parents under the Christian Cross at the Amphitheater in Rome while they were all on their honeymoons. It was at the end of the First World War. Since both men were in the dairy business, they had something to talk about that led to their friendship. Bernard and I were born the same year, same month, nearly the same day. When the Depression hit Italy in the late twenties, Bernard came to live with us in Gruyère. He became a Swiss citizen and consequently served in the Swiss military during the second war, a proud soldier, just like you. He still has a soft spot for the military . . . respects what you stand for." Alice paused. "Even though we were raised like twins, we fell in love and got married."

"Then you moved to this farm?"

"Not until after the war. Bernard's father was killed serving his country. His mother couldn't handle the farm by herself and fled to Switzerland in '42. She never talked much about her flight across San Giácomo Pass in the height of winter, but it must have been a horrible ordeal; out of five women, only two survived. She lived with us for the rest of the war." Alice waved her hand. "But that's another story."

"Is that extra setting on the table for her?" asked Herman.

Alice smiled. "No, Bernard's mother died of cancer a few years ago. The setting is for my father. He's taking his mid-morning nap. He should have been down by now."

The corporal's face had flushed. She touched his forehead with the back of her hand. "You may have a fever. Not much of one, thank God, but, just to make sure, I'll get you some more aspirins." She ignored his objection and brought back the tablets and a glass of water.

She held his head so he wouldn't have to sit up. Herman blushed; he wasn't used to pampering. "You're so kind, Frau Alice. Thank you." He could barely say the words and his eyes were drooping.

She pulled her chair up to the divan until her legs touched the frame. "You're dizzy," she said. "Close your eyes while I tell you about the farm." Isolated from the world, Alice had little opportunity to talk. A flood of words came now as she told of their winter farm farther down the valley, where they lived and milked their cows until the snow melted in the Alps. She told of how the economic downturn forced Bernard to take the risky trips across the pass to sell their cheese in Switzerland. And of how Alice worried each time. She wasn't sure that Herman was listening. His eyes were closed. His breathing was light and slow.

She went to her bedroom, brought back a blanket and spread it over the sleeping soldier. Then she pulled her chair away from the divan and sat near the window, wondering why fate had brought this young man to her door, wondering about the purpose of everything that had happened to her, to him. Through the window, she watched Barry trot over the dam on his way to school. *He's early*, she thought, but that wasn't unusual, he often played with the children during their last break.

When Bernard stepped into the living room, Alice was dozing in her chair, and Herman was in the process of covering her lap and legs with the blanket from the couch. He slipped into his coat, put on his slippers, and the men quietly left the room together.

Herman felt refreshed and his headache had all but vanished. "I'd better get going," he said.

"Why don't you stay for supper?" asked the farmer. "Another hour or so won't make any difference. Besides, there will be a news update in thirty minutes."

Herman was unsure. "You two have done so much for me already; I don't want to be a bother."

"Nonsense," said Bernard. "While we're waiting for the news, I'll show you how I make my cheese."

Herman had plenty of other things on his mind, but he knew how proud the farmer was of his cheese and felt that he could repay his kindness somewhat by taking a keen interest.

The operation was divided into three chambers and occupied one third of the barn that was built partly into the adjacent slope. After having been laced with whey from a previous batch, the milk was heated to fermentation temperature over a wood fire in a giant, 250-liter copper pot. A young, dark-eyed Italian girl, dressed in a striped seaman's shirt and sturdy denim pants stuck into tall rubber boots, sliced the curd with a long-handled knife. She pulled cheese-cloth around the curd and lifted it from the kettle with a chain-operated winch. In the adjacent chamber was a wooden cheese press where the curd was formed into wheels. The pressed cheese was submerged in a wooden brine bath for twenty-four hours before being aged in a naturally chilled storage room carved out of the hill.

Herman counted over a hundred cheese wheels on the shelves. The farmer watched him with an amused smile. "We store the cheese for a full year before taking it to market, which gives it a somewhat harder texture than the typical Swiss Gruyère."

When the men returned, Alice Mendali had made fresh coffee and filled a tray with walnut cookies from the cookie jar.

The farmer tuned the radio and listened tensely. He translated: "There's been no sign of the renegades, and the military has taken down the roadblock," he said. "The troops are searching empty barns now, but the constable thinks that the band has left, if they were here at all."

Herman shook his head. "That's wrong. They're still around; no one disappears into thin air." He was getting edgy. "It shames me not to be able to help. I should be getting back to my unit."

"I thought you'd stay for supper," said Alice, disappointed. "I'll have it ready in no time."

"I'm sorry, Frau Alice, but I really must go. Everyone will be looking for me by now, and I want to make that pass while there's still daylight." He put on his cap and buttoned his coat.

"All right, then. But here . . ." She handed him his knapsack. "I filled your thermos with hot tea, and I wrapped up a piece of cheese, some cookies, and a loaf of bread."

"Thanks for all your kindness, Frau Alice." He hooked the pack over his shoulder. "Thanks for everything. I'll never forget what you've done for me." He shook her hand. "And someday I'll be back; I promise."

He went downstairs, put on his shoes, and slung the rifle over his back.

Bernard Mendali walked with the corporal as far as the trail, then he, too, said goodbye.

Feeling stronger, Herman started up the trail, now anxious to get home. On the last ridge he stopped to look back at the peaceful farmhouse far below. Smoke still poured from the chimney, and the smell of fresh-baked bread lingered. Someone waved a white cloth from the rear balcony. Herman raised his field glasses.

It was Alice.

The temperature in the barn was still below freezing. Angelina Bianci was tired and depressed. She thought of running away and going to the police, but her instincts told her to see through what she had started. Besides, Giulio's threats against her partner had frightened Angelina even more than the threats against her. "Why have I done this?" she cried, her regrets mounting. "God, tell me why!" She had always hated guns and violence. Avenging her parents was one thing, but robbing that bunker and getting innocent people hurt was quite another.

How naive she had been! Yet Giulio's methods and aims had seemed credible as they were first explained to her: staging rallies to show the ruling party that someone was watching it; forcing unfit officials to resign; punishing those who were corrupt; acquiring weapons and ammunition for self-defense in case of a dictatorship. Robbing the bunker would be child's play, Giulio had insisted—no one would get hurt. Collecting information from the village— Angelina's job—couldn't have been easier. She'd never given it a second thought.

Giulio was pacing back and forth now, waving his arms. It was clear that his well-thought-out plan had come unraveled. He wanted everyone to think his fall-back plan would be just as good, but he wasn't convincing. They were cut off from major roads, already shivering from cold. And they were desperate—Giulio most of all, though his authority had never been in question.

The sun was well past its highest point when the band moved out of the barn onto the trail at the edge of a pasture, concealed by trees and shrubs. Their goal was a lone farmhouse but a short way north.

CHAPTER 7

*B*ernard Mendali brought the last wheelbarrow of manure to the back of the barn, washed down the floor with a rubber hose, began spreading fresh straw about the stalls. The livestock would be returning from the pastures later in the day, ready for milking. He was late at it, later than usual . . . but then, this very day had been unusual. Some suspicious movement across the pond caught his eyes. He dropped the pitchfork, reached for the shotgun, stepped from the stable to face the two strangers, dirty and unshaven, who had just crossed the dam.

The man on the left hailed him with an open hand. "We're lost and need directions."

The farmer stood his ground. "This road leads nowhere. Go back onto the main road!"

The obvious spokesman said, "We don't mean any harm, signore."

His companion added, "We're thirsty and need some water."

"Sorry, no deal—turn around!"

The first man made a suspicious move.

"Don't!" cried the farmer. After only a second's hesitation he fired a warning shot above their heads. No sooner had he pulled the trigger than his chest exploded in fire and he was thrown against the wall of the barn. The shotgun dropped to the ground.

Shocked by the blast, Alice Mendali rushed to the window in time to see her husband slide down the white stucco wall, leaving a trail of blood.

Herman leapt to his feet. *That was a shotgun! The farmer!* He raced back along the crest of the ridge and didn't stop until he could see the farmhouse. Taking cover behind some rocks he raised his field glasses.

All was peaceful. The farm was just as he'd left it. Smoke poured from the chimney, ripples glittered on the pond. *Too quiet!*

He descended further, out of view of the farmhouse. His goal was a stone fence bordering a pasture some two hundred meters from the farmhouse. Across it he'd have a clear view at one side of the house and barn and the central courtyard between them. When he reached the stone fence he came up from behind just enough to focus his glasses.

A man sat on a milk can in front of the barn, his hands on the muzzle of an automatic gun. Herman did not recognize him.

Two men were crossing the courtyard carrying someone into the house. Alice Mendali walked behind, hands clutched to her face. Beside her walked two women . . . the corporal forgot to breathe. One of them had long red hair.

Giulio tore the phone off the wall as soon as he stepped inside the farmer's house. Then he ordered the men to take the wounded man to a third-floor bedroom. Before they laid him on the bed Angelina pulled back the comforter and the blanket and covered the sheets with a curtain ripped from the bathroom shower stall.

The farmer lay still. The men had removed his heavy, dirty shoes before carrying him up the stairs, but it was too soon to cover him. "Get his filthy pants off," she commanded, "and then turn him on his right side," and when the men obeyed, she wedged a pillow behind him and pulled the blanket and comforter up to his waist. "And you," she motioned to the farmer's wife, "come help me with his shirt."

Alice was in a trance and didn't move. The men went past her into the hall.

"I need your help, dammit!" No response. She stood by the door, blood drained from her face, arms lifeless by her side. Angelina, who had been crouching over the man, flew to the woman's side and shook her, slapped her. "Come out of it! We've got to try to save his life!"

Alice revived then and, with Angelina, hastened to her husband's side.

Angelina propped him from behind. "Now take his shirt off."

The bullet had hit his fourth rib, diverted, and exited under his left arm. It left an almost fist-sized wound and left the skin in tatters like a pencil pushed through paper. The towel that Angelina had pressed against the exit wound was quickly full of blood. The woman handed her a fresh one, clean and neatly folded.

"Who are you people? Why . . . ?"

"I'm Angelina Bianci," she interrupted sharply. "There's no time to tell you how I got mixed up in this. All you need to know is . . . I'll do anything to save this man. Now get more towels. Bring any bandages, pressure pads, medicines you've got."

Sofia walked into the room, and Angelina assumed that Giulio had sent her up to keep an eye on them. "You!" she pointed at the girl's chest, "make yourself useful. Get a pot of boiling-hot water from the kitchen." When Sofia didn't move she raised her hand. "Dammit, girl, get going!" Sofia turned around and ran back down the stairs.

The farmwoman was back in moments. She brought rolls of bandages, more clean towels, and alcohol.

"Your . . . leader . . . has my father tied to a chair in the kitchen. That screaming you hear is my father telling him where to go in Swiss dialect. I'm Alice Mendali. I can tell you're not one of them. Not like him . . . will he hurt my father?"

"It's hard to say," said Angelina, wearily. Then, with a nod toward the man beneath her, "Let's concentrate on saving *him*."

Alice bent to her husband, who was unconscious still, and pale. From the sound of his breathing, his lungs weren't full of blood.

"I'll get hot water." But Sofia walked through the door that moment with a steaming kettle. Alice took it from her. "Can we clean the wound yet, or is it still . . . ?"

"Still bleeding," said Angelina. "I hope the pressure will keep him from losing too much blood. Hurry!"

Taking turns, the women replaced the towels on the wounds, careful not to tear loose any congealed blood. Sofia wrinkled her nose. She couldn't stand the smell and left the room. Then Angelina was exultant. "Signora, I think it's stopping!" She carefully uncovered the exit wound, where he'd lost the most blood. "See!"

Alice dropped to her knees, hands folded in prayer. Tears had already soaked the collar of her dress.

"We'll still have to get him to a doctor."

"But the doctor is too far . . . my God!" Alice scrambled to her feet. "The children!"

"Not so loud! Here, hold this against him. Not too hard!" When Alice took her place, Angelina rushed to the door, down the hall, back the other way to the head of the stairs. Coming back into the room she watched from the window as Benny went into the barn. *He's checking on the donkeys.* "Now tell me . . . your children?"

Alice nodded and glanced at the wall clock. "They'll leave school at three. I must get to them."

"If you go running out, they'll shoot you down! Help me get this wound cleaned up and we'll think of something. But not another word about your children around the others."

"He wouldn't hurt them . . . ? Not the children!"

"Alice, he's desperate."

"I am too!"

"Signora, for the sake of your children, get hold of yourself. I can help you get away, but we first have to clean his wounds and bandage them. Here, soak the towels in alcohol."

"Yaaah!" Herr Stüssi had started in again on Giulio, screaming in Swiss dialect, "If I had my Swiss Army rifle, you'd be in a heap of trouble! You hear? You're nothing but a cheap crook, a criminal of the highest order, a rogue, a pig, a miscreant—you hear me? You villain, you brute, you—you . . ." his insults echoing up the stairs from the second floor.

Angelina shook her head. "Some character, your father." She continued cleaning the wounds. She spread an ointment on some dressings and pressed them gently over the wounds. "Hold him up a little." Alice did as told, and Angelina wrapped his chest with sturdy bandages to hold the pressure pads in place. Then she removed the pillow and Alice eased him back on the bed until he was completely supine.

The women straightened, came around the bed, and hugged each other. Maybe, just maybe, they'd won this battle. Indeed, the room looked like a battle hospital with blood-soaked towels everywhere. In spite of all the alcohol, there was a heavy, sweet smell of blood in the air.

The wounded man's hands were ice cold, and the women covered him with additional blankets from an armoire. He opened his eyes and moved his lips but said nothing. He closed his eyes and his breathing was easier now as if asleep. Angelina heaved a sigh of relief. But for the moment, it was all she could do for him. She turned to the farmwoman.

"Did Giulio see you come up here with this alcohol?"

"I don't think so. He was in the kitchen with my father—at the window with binoculars. He didn't see me get these things. But he's got one of his men at the foot of the stairs, right by the front door. One of the men who was just up here—the older one."

"Tony. He saw you?"

"Just all the towels, I think."

"Good. Follow me. You won't have much time. That man out there, sitting on a milk can in front of the barn? He keeps dozing off . . . as long as you're quiet . . . but that's Emilio. He's crazy. He won't hesitate to shoot you if he sees you getting away. Is there another way out?"

"To the ground floor and out the back patio."

"Perfect! Let's go!"

"What are you going to do?"

"I'm going to pick a fight with Giulio in the kitchen. You just run out the back door and then across the dam!"

The women clattered down the stairs. On the landing she called down to the ground floor: "Hey, Tony! Let the signora pass. She needs to go to the basement for some brandy to clean her husband's wounds."

Tony looked up, bored. "Go ahead, send her down," he said.

Just as Alice started downstairs there were sounds of a huge struggle in the kitchen—screams.

"My father knows we don't keep the brandy there . . ." said Alice in a tense whisper.

"Go! Go!"

As Alice reached the bottom of the stairs, Tony, startled by the noise, was coming up. "What's going on?" He let the woman pass, and Angelina watched long enough to see Alice flee . . . by the front door!

"No!" she called after her. But it was too late.

Time stood still for Angelina. Tony was looking right at her. It seemed like her "No!" had echoed all over the house. She should have realized that the children were everything to Alice; she'd think nothing of giving her life for her family. With all the screaming and Tony starting up the stairs, the poor woman thought she had a chance to run for it. Maybe she could have made it, too, if Angelina hadn't yelled "No," tipping off Tony that the woman had done something foolish. Perhaps her "No!" had alerted Emilio.

But the screams in the kitchen were suddenly quite different. That was Giulio screaming in pain! Tony came rushing up the stairs now. Alice Mendali was forgotten for the moment.

Angelina stormed into the kitchen ahead of Tony.

The old man, chair and all, had leaped on Giulio to prevent him leaving the kitchen. When Angelina entered he had Giulio pinned against the hot stove, the cause of his screams of agony.

Before Angelina could intervene, Giulio had knocked Herr Stüssi to the floor, still tied to the chair, and begun to kick him. Tony burst into the room but didn't know what to do . . . he was confused . . .

There were sudden gunshots outside . . . the kitchen went quiet. Giulio rushed to the window and kicked it open. Angelina followed . . . but with all her strength she couldn't keep him from leveling his gun at the woman, on the other side of the pond now, who was running . . . .

There was a deafening crash. Before Giulio could get a shot off, the window had exploded in his face. Giulio dropped to the floor, but he hadn't been hit. He was looking up at Angelina in shock.

She knew! She had known at once! Those were the corporal's bullets!

⊰✦⊱

Corporal Schuller had indeed been watching when Alice Mendali ran from her house. And he had been watching when, moments before, the man on the milk can had been roused from his nap by screams emanating from the house. He'd watched as the man on the milk can dropped onto one knee, armed his automatic and took aim. But by then he was watching through the sight on his rifle, and he was the first to get a shot off. He'd watched his bullet slam into the gunman's chest. He'd heard the burst from the automatic weapon and watched the gunman's bullets tear into the cobblestones.

Then the gunman fell backward, his arm slung wide above his head, and the realization came to Herman Schuller, watching, that he'd just killed a man. He'd faced such a possibility before in military training, but the reality was different than he had been led to expect. He was much calmer than he thought he had any right to be, and when he saw the window open from the Mendali's second-floor kitchen and a pistol emerge, he didn't think twice before raising his rifle again and firing.

Alice Mendali was safe now, he thought. But where was she running? Ah, yes! Her children! Without hesitation, Herman leaped across the stone fence and raced down the open field. What if the band had a lookout, a rear guard at the main road? He closed in on the woman.

"Slow down, Frau Alice, slow down! It's me, Herman Schuller!" he shouted at the top of his lungs.

Alice turned and recognized the corporal. "Those horrible people," she cried, before collapsing in his arms. Tears were streaming down her cheeks. Herman guided her off the road and left her half-hidden behind a grassy knoll. With his field glasses he looked ahead and then back toward the farm, to see if they were being pursued. No one. Nothing. "It looks like we're clear for the moment," he said. "Let's go get the children."

He offered Alice a hand up, but instead of letting him help, she was pulling on the sleeve of his uniform, holding him back. "They shot him, they shot Bernard."

Herman had suspected that it was Bernard that the men had been carrying into the house, but he was shocked nonetheless. "I don't know why they shot your husband, Frau Alice, but right now we must

think of your children. Once the children are safe, I'll go back to the farm."
Now she took the hand he offered and joined him out on the dirt road.

"He has lost so much blood," she said; "he nearly bled to death,
and—" Her eyes brightened and she pointed ahead. "There they are!"
She rushed forward, crying, "My children, oh my children." She
hugged them and kissed their cheeks and foreheads. Barry added to
the excitement, jumping up on all three, barking and wagging his tail.

The girl's school dress, the same color as the ground beneath
her feet, was cinched at the waist with a leather strap. White socks
reached almost to her knees, and her shoes were brown with brass
buckles. She wore a white bonnet tied with strings below her chin.
"Why are you crying, Mamma?" she asked looking up to her mother.

"Yeah, why, Mamma?" added the boy. He wore blue shorts
and a checked shirt. He might have been small for his age, but he had
large hazel eyes.

"It's nothing," said the mother, fighting to control her emotions.
"I'm just so happy to see you." She took out her handkerchief, moistened the tip with her mouth, and wiped dirt from the boy's cheek.

The girl said, "Why are we going back now?" when Alice
turned her around.

"Yeah," said the boy, "and why is this man coming?"

In her excitement, Alice had almost forgotten Herman. "This
is Corporal Schuller," she said in Swiss dialect. "He's going to help us."

"Why do we need his help, though?" asked the girl. "Where's
Papa?"

"Yeah, where's Papa?" the boy repeated. "He's the one who
always helps us."

Alice sighed. "I'll tell you all this later, children. First, tell the
corporal your name. And you must speak Swiss so he can understand you."

But sensing something wrong, the boy hid behind his mother,
pulling on her skirt.

The girl stepped forward and stretched out her hand. "I am
Marianna, and I am older than my brother. He is just scared. He's
always scared," she said in perfect Swiss dialect.

Herman stooped a bit and shook her hand. "My sister's name
is Marianna, too; it's a beautiful name," he said, smiling.

"Is your sister as pretty as I?"

"She's very pretty, but no one's prettier than you," he said. "And how old are you?"

"I'll be nine very soon."

Encouraged, the boy left the sanctuary of his mother's skirt. "I am Marcello, and I'm seven, and I'm not scared," he said proudly. He stretched out his hand. "Is this a real gun with real bullets?" He put his fingers on the rifle butt.

"It's a Swiss Army rifle."

"Children," said Alice, "we are going to visit Signora Rossi down the hill."

"Why are we not going home, Mamma?" asked Marianna.

Marcello joined in. "Yeah, why can't we go home? I'm hungry."

Alice managed a smile and straightened Marianna's bonnet. "Signora Rossi has a large plate of cookies and hot chocolate just for you," she said. "Don't you like her cookies?"

This did the trick and the children raced ahead.

Alice turned to Herman. "You saved my life and maybe theirs, too," she said softly. "And for that, you had to shoot a man."

Herman bit his lip, and Alice sensed the struggle within his mind. She wished she hadn't mentioned the shooting.

"I'm sorry I was too late to save your husband," said Herman. "I should have stayed with you at the farm. Things might have turned out differently. Bernard has lost a lot of blood, is that what you said?"

"He was alive when I left, that's all I know. I think he *would have* bled to death were it not for that woman."

Herman looked up and she saw that he, too, was struggling with a suppressed emotion. "It was she who stopped the bleeding and saved my husband's life." Alice saw him squint and press his lips together. "She is a nice person and very beautiful. You're right, though, Herman, if she's involved with those people, it must be against her will. She's doing everything she can to stop them . . . Is she with the police?"

"I don't think so."

"Well, in spite of the horrible things that have been done to us, I have learned to like her. I have embraced her in my heart."

The children stopped inside a white picket fence in a yard that must have been the Rossi's.

Alice embraced the corporal. There was no question now of taking her back with him. Perhaps there never had been—she couldn't leave her children. This meant that her husband had to be alone with those horrible men. The thought of what he might have to endure made her head spin, but then she thought how much her children needed her and was able to control herself again.

Corporal Schuller was moving much faster now that he was alone, taking long strides back toward the farm. She kept watching until he disappeared beyond a bend in the road.

The field radio sprang to life. It was the local constable, broadcasting from his car. "The terrorists are holed up at a farm just this side of Riale," he yelled. "There are possible hostages—one injured man." He had to repeat the message a second time. Loud static made the prehistoric radio hard to hear.

"Okay—okay, I've got you this time," yelled the colonnello with equal force. Vitt Zanardelli was now kicking himself for sending the *tenente* up on that ridge. "Those bastards!" The thought of them attacking a farm family in their home . . . "Goddamned business!" he cursed. "You're wrong no matter what you do. This thing hasn't gone right from the start."

Still shaking his head he jumped into his Fiat and raced toward the farmhouse. He stopped the car beyond the dam as soon as the farm came into view and looked it over through his binoculars. Nothing moved. The house and barn seemed abandoned.

Then he spotted red stains on the white plaster wall. He adjusted his binoculars and saw the body outside the barn. Without giving it another thought, he drove the Fiat across the dam. Near the barn he stopped again with the car between him and the farmhouse. Moving low to the ground, with his Luger in his hand, he ran to the lifeless shape on the cobblestones. He lifted the man's wrist to search for a pulse; he was dead.

The man was heavily bearded, dirty, and there was a strange

contentment in his eyes that the colonnello recognized. The man's pockets had been turned inside out. There was no weapon near him, but the cobblestones were torn up by gunfire and there were empty shells. Other signs of a gun battle, besides blood on the barn wall, including a second-floor window of the farmhouse that had been shattered, the empty frame fluttered in the wind.

Was that a voice? The colonnello spun around. Yes, a faint sound from inside the house, a man's voice. "Help; up here!"

Luger in hand, the colonnello crept into the house, carefully entering each room and corridor on his way to the top floor. He expected an injured man when he broke into the room on the third floor, and he was no stranger to the smell of blood, but he was still appalled. He went to the windows with his hand over his mouth and nose, and threw them wide.

"Who are you?" asked the man on the bed.

"Colonnello Vittorio Zanardelli, *agente di polizia.* I'm here to help. Is it too cold for you with the window open?"

The farmer raised his head. "My wife—my family—are they still safe?"

The colonnello sat on the side of the bed. In spite of his compassion for the man, he was puzzled by his use of the word "still."

"Yes, farmer. Your wife and children are fine," he lied. The constable had told him nothing, but he didn't want to upset the man. The farmer was struggling to raise his head. "Lie back, sir, and hear me out." said Zanardelli. "I want you to save your strength for the trip to the hospital. I called the doc as soon as I learned there was an injured man here. He's on his way with an ambulance. You'll be going to Domodóssola, where doctors are standing by. Let me have a quick look, though, to see how they've fixed you up." Zanardelli looked under the blanket. There was more blood on the towels that littered the room than there was on his bandages. *Not a bad job.*

"I've got a few questions," the colonnello went on to say. "Simple answers will do, okay? Don't tire yourself."

He asked Bernard how many attackers there were, and if they said where they were headed.

"I was talking to two men when I was shot. There were others . . . and a woman's voice when I came to. But not my wife's."

"I was told there were hostages."

"My wife's father—I heard him yelling at them. Someone said they'd be taking him along for insurance."

"Anyone else, do you think?"

"There's a Swiss soldier."

The colonnello was dumbfounded. "A *Swiss*? You know this man? His name?"

The farmer stalled, but after the colonnello's urgent nod moved on. "Herman Schuller. Corporal Schuller. He came to our door earlier this morning. He was exhausted and injured. We took him in, bandaged him, and fed him. I showed him the way back to the border. Then these evildoers came . . . When I came to, I heard the leader steaming about the soldier . . . saying he should have got rid of him when they had the chance. He accused one of the women, claiming he knew that she took care of him. All their trouble was because of her, he said."

"And this woman . . . she's still with the gang?"

"I think so. Since they left I've been alone here. Except, just before you got here, colonel, the soldier came by to see if I was all right. He said that help would be on the way. He told me that my wife and children were at the Rossi's, down the road. Would you please check to see if they're still okay?"

"Of course!"

Colonnello Zanardelli thought of the man lying on cobblestones in the courtyard. "Who shot the man in front of the barn? Did the soldier do that?"

The farmer ignored the question and said instead, "I'm afraid the corporal is after these people alone. When he left he said he'd make them pay."

Zanardelli was shaking his head. "He's some brave soldier, this Swiss."

"He certainly is. You can leave me here, colonnello, I'm not afraid. The corporal needs your help now more than I do."

Fed and rested, the donkeys dictated a fast pace. Angelina had pleaded with Giulio to let her stay behind with the injured farmer, but it was no use. Giulio had lost all trust in her, refused and forced her to move out with the band. He'd shoot her if she gave him "any more trouble"— and had told Benny and Tony they were to do the same thing. Only Sofia wasn't a danger to her now. Sofia was listless, utterly spent, and seemed not to know what was happening. Who did, though? thought Angelina. All of them were just blindly following orders at this point; only Giulio knew where he was taking them.

Herr Stüssi could barely keep up. There were cramps in his leg and the rheumatism in his lower back was almost unbearable. Angelina had taken him by the arm and kept talking to him, to raise his spirits. "Don't worry, Herr Stüssi. I feel that rescue is near at hand," she told him at one point when there was no danger of them being overheard.

He looked at her sideways. "What are you doing among these people?"

Angelina only shook her head.

"You don't belong with them."

She sighed. "Please save your strength, Herr Stüssi."

"I'm not going anywhere until you answer me!" He sat down on a rock.

"Please come along." She pointed to Giulio, coming closer. "He'll hurt you."

"He wouldn't dare!"

She pulled him off the rock. "Don't tempt him. Try to get through this for your daughter's sake. She loves you."

The old man staggered to his feet. "All right, but I'm not going to let you off the hook. It doesn't make any sense. A nice girl like you running around with this madman! Anyway, where is he taking us?"

"I honestly don't know. But don't worry, I know we're being followed."

"The soldier? The Swiss my daughter told me about?"

Angelina nodded. Talking about the corporal sent new shivers down her back. Her thoughts had been with him ever since Giulio and his henchmen had been fired upon. Angelina, too, was waiting for the right moment to take action. She would do everything she could from now on to prevent more violence. She, Angelina Bianci, would stand up to Giulio and oppose his every move—and she was deadly serious.

Giulio knew the area well. Whenever possible the donkeys were made to pad softly on soaked grass, and he used every tree and rock for cover as he led his band along the creek. Still, he wasn't worried about the hee-haws, or the sound of grinding hooves and feet on granite rocks, or the men's carping about the rugged trail. The remoteness and rushing waters covered the noise. His big worry was time. There was less than four hours of daylight, and the route along the glacier would be almost impassable in the dark.

Another concern weighed heavily on his mind: the stranger watching their every move. Giulio had seen him run after the woman at the farm, but since then, there had been no sign of him. Had he given up the chase? Giulio knew better. *Men like him don't quit.*

There was only one sure way to get rid of him, and Giulio knew just the perfect place for a deadly trap.

Lieutenant Stucki and Feldweibel Ott had started late, held back by their commander who thought chasing after the thieves was ridiculous. As they puffed up the trail toward San Giácomo Pass the lieutenant wondered if the captain had been right. Based on their progress so far, this undertaking was beginning to look like a staged symbolic gesture.

"This trail leads nowhere," Stucki said. He had explored a path that forked from the main trail. "It's just another dead end like the others."

Ott grunted. "I wonder where the corporal isch and what he'sch up to now?"

Both men had already expressed their amazement at how Corporal Schuller had managed a climb like this in the dark.

They stopped and pulled up their binoculars.

"That muscht be the pass up there," said Ott. "What do you think, Franz?"

"It's the pass, all right," said his friend. "And look, there's some movement along the ridge. Looks like men and animals—why, I can almost make them out."

After some careful scrutiny of the pass and the rest of the difficult trail that would take them there, the men set out with renewed hope.

Herman dropped to one knee and put his elbow on the other to steady his field glasses. He adjusted the focusing knob until the image came in clear. Two men, and a woman with long black hair, walked along the distant crest. The woman held the rope of the first donkey, which was leading two others, each tied to the tail of the one up front in a picture-book caravan.

Two more figures appeared. One was a man who struggled to keep up. The other—Herman's heart began to beat wildly—was a woman, her red hair lying loosely about her shoulders. He followed her until she disappeared behind some pines.

There had to be one more man . . . yes, there he was, a cap with a green visor pulled low over his face, an automatic gun at his hip. He turned around repeatedly and scanned the trail behind him.

Herman had a long but good shot—he let the temptation pass. It was not the time to act rashly or too soon; the success of his mission could be at risk. But he had them in his sights! That was a huge advantage: he had seen them, they hadn't seen him yet.

Giulio gave the order to halt and dropped his gear. They had reached a clearing, a ridge shaped like a saddle with a precipice to either side. Stunted, alpine rhododendrons and a few scanty trees dotted the landscape, but no boulders to obstruct the view. The place was protected, but not isolated. A perfect spot to rest—or set a trap.

Spent, the band dropped where they stood when Giulio gave the order. Angelina and Herr Stüssi were still side by side, now perched on a rock, though both were tired to the point of exhaustion.

Tony came up from the rear. He told Giulio he was convinced they were no longer being followed.

Giulio took him aside. "That's what he wants us to think. He's been breathing down our necks ever since the action back in All' Acqua." He pointed to a row of boulders farther up the trail at the upper limit of the saddle. "Up there you'll have a perfect view. Get in position and set up an ambush. No one can follow us without crossing this open space."

Tony made a face. "I haven't seen a sign of him or anyone else since we left the farm. Whoever it was who shot Emilio has obviously given up." He smirked. "You worry too much."

"I call it 'thinking,'" snapped Giulio. "Now get going. This is no time to slack off!"

Cursing, Tony picked up his gun and walked to the boulders at the far end.

Giulio was pacing now. Maybe he *was* worried. He missed Emilio. Emilio never questioned an order. The more Giulio thought of Emilio, the angrier he became. "It's all your fault," he screamed at Angelina. "You helped that woman escape. I hold you liable for Emilio's death!"

Angelina shot to her feet. "Look who's talking! You have no right to accuse me or anyone else!" Her eyes blazed. "You alone are liable for Emilio's death; you and no one else!"

The rest of the band was astonished. No one had ever challenged Giulio this way.

Angelina backed off for a moment. Then her bottled-up frustration exploded right in his face. "You're a liar, a selfish snob with no respect for human life! You bring misery and disaster! There's not a shred of truth in what you say—or what you believe!"

"You bitch!" screamed Giulio. He leapt forward and slapped Angelina's face. They were coming dangerously close to the drop-off on that side of the clearing.

Boldly, with hatred and frustration augmenting her strength, Angelina punched Giulio in the face. He swayed beneath the blow and all but dropped to his knees. Out of control now, he struck back—with stiff fingers he stabbed at her chest repeatedly. She backed away without seeing the depression in the ground, disguised by a low shrub that was growing in it.

"Watch it!" cried one of the men.

But the warning came too late. Angelina tripped and fell flat on her back.

In numb horror, the others watched the slope begin to roll her toward the edge of the cliff, her face twisted in shock and pain. She managed to stay on her stomach long enough to reach for a root, a rock, a clump of grass, anything— "God help me!" she cried.

In vain. The ground gave way. She was gone with flying hair and a frightened cry. There was a distant jolt—and that was the last of Angelina.

Herman Schuller sank to his knees and reached for his chest. He felt as if he had been gored. He leaned against the rifle, stunned by a spasm that had suddenly racked his being. Something was terribly wrong. Spurred by an inner urgency, he forged ahead with new determination, convinced now more than ever that he would make good on his promise.

Tony had found the perfect spot. The boulder was just lower than shoulder height, and a small depression in the surface, softened by pine needles, was ideal to sight the barrel of his automatic gun. The "seat of the saddle" was spread out before him. The sun, low at the horizon now, was blinding—"Damn!" But Tony had made good shots under worse conditions.

The fingers of his right hand slowly curled into his palm while the left crept like a caterpillar along the gun's ventilating grooves. Leaving the gun on the rock, he pulled back and folded his arms, trying to relax. He tried to pretend this was a deer hunt, but he was apprehensive and riddled with second thoughts. He had killed Germans toward the end of the war, when they had been the aggressor, the enemy. The man he was about to kill had done nothing wrong. He should at least hate the man if he had to kill him. Tony felt no hatred. But then—the rifle the stranger carried was no toy.

Tony raised his head. He heard something, the snap of a twig, the crunch of a rock under a heavy shoe. He strained his eyes. There was his foe, within range of his rifle and coming up fast. The stranger in the foreign uniform was too young for this kind of work, Tony thought; too young to die. The soldier walked into a gully until only his green cap showed. He emerged by degrees: first his face, then his shoulders and his chest, then the hand with the rifle that had proven to be deadly accurate.

The soldier steadily came closer, completely unaware of the fate that awaited him, a perfect target. Tony pushed the safety lever, aimed at the stranger's chest, and squeezed the trigger.

Herman had never slowed his pace. Spread before him was a peaceful place, a notch in the mountaintop that had been smoothed into a saddle, with little gullies where it neared the mountain steeps. Rhododendron bushes in their red winter beauty dotted the softer slopes, but there were no large trees to hide behind, and because of the suddenness of the drop-off to either side it was impossible to walk around. Herman had no choice but to move through the open space.

He froze. *The perfect place for an ambush!* In a split second he dropped to the ground behind a hummock just as a burst of bullets ripped into the slope and showered him with rocks and dirt. Numb from shock, Herman hugged the ground, unable to move. Then his instincts came to his aid again, and he rolled farther below the crest of the hill and out of sight.

He waited and listened, nerves on edge. The hand that held his rifle trembled. He waited . . . but all was quiet. Under the cover of the rise, Herman crawled to his right, pressed close to the ground, until he came up against the cliff. Cautiously, he pushed his binoculars through the last twigs on the crest. He stayed perfectly still as he scanned the saddle and the boulders at its far end. He saw nothing— there was no sign of the gunman.

Had he left? Then something caught his eye. An object, no larger than a wristwatch, reflected in the sun. Herman pored over the spot. He saw it: the visor of a cap and the vented barrel of an automatic gun.

Herman slid backward and brought up the rifle, pushed the muzzle slowly through the shrubs. It was a clear, easy shot. The head and cap were in his sight now; the gunman was just a trigger-pull away from certain death. Yet . . . Herman hesitated. He lowered his eyes and took the tension off his trigger finger. He was recalling the submachine gun the thieves had dropped at the bunker. That gun had not been armed, the person who'd carried it had not been ready to kill. What if those shots—aimed much too low, he thought—had been fired in warning, meant to tell him to stay clear?

But the gruesome image of the knife in his friend's back returned to him, too. He put pressure on the trigger once again, the rifle recoiled and the bullet whisked from the barrel.

The two officers stopped in their tracks for the second time since hearing bursts from the automatic gun.

"An Army rifle!" shouted Lieutenant Stucki, out of breath. "That was one of ours!"

"I'll be a monkey'sch—it'sch him, it'sch the corporal," cried the feldweibel excitedly. "I know the schound of our rifle, I've heard it too many timesch. He'sch all right! What good newsch! The corporal'sch fine!"

They searched the ridge with binoculars pressed to eager eyes.

Herman had rolled below the crest before the echo of the shot returned. He waited for a hail of bullets.

All was quiet.

He came back up from a different spot, scrutinizing the boulder for any sign of the gunman, but the green cap and vented barrel were gone. He scanned the area bush by bush and rock by rock. There were no signs of anyone, even the slight breeze had died down so not a bush or branch would sway. The minutes ticked by slowly.

I can't stay here all day. He set a time limit: if nothing happened within the next three minutes, he would move out and continue the pursuit.

⋖⊱✦⊰⋗

The boulder was abandoned. Trampled grass and a dozen cigarette butts attested to the gunman's presence. Two dark spots on the rock might have been caused by his blood. The corporal found nothing more of significance except fresh tracks leading up the mountainside. He walked back to the clearing, convinced now that the band had moved to higher ground.

He dropped to the ground. Was that a voice? He listened intently, but all was quiet except for a new breeze wafting through the shrubs. I *must be hallucinating*. He rose and instantly dropped back down when he heard it again. He held his breath. Ducking low, he searched the clearing. There were no movements, no signs of life. Then he heard it again, a woman's frightened cry for help coming from below the very cliff he was standing on.

Without hesitation, Herman dropped the rifle and the knapsack to the ground. He wrapped his feet around the gnarled base of a tree stump and leaned over the edge. All he saw were weathered pine trees growing randomly from the sheer wall that dropped a hundred meters down into thickets of tall shrubs. The whimper was just below him, coming from a hidden ledge of which he could only see the edge along with the branches of a scrawny pine. He inched forward, stretching until only the tips of his shoes clung to the base of the stump. He cringed when it began to move, but it held. Pushing hard with his hands and then his knees, he scrambled up.

"Hang on," he shouted over the edge. "I'm here to help; I'll find a way down to you." He needed a rope, but where was he going to find one? His mind raced. A year ago, in another part of the Alps, he had made a rope from soldiers' leather belts when his squad had been caught at the dead end of a steep trail. That brainstorm had saved the day, but where was he going to find belts now?

While he was sitting here thinking of all the reasons he couldn't help, the thieves were getting away.

The tarpaulin! It was made of tough fiber and should support his weight. He removed the straps on the knapsack and unfolded the tarpaulin. He draped the blue leather jacket wrapped inside over a flat rock. He opened his Swiss Army knife, hesitated a split second—

it felt strange to be destroying military gear—and cut the sturdy fabric into nine equal strips. He tied the ends together with pathfinder knots, and then jerked on them repeatedly to test their strength.

Voilà, a beautiful rope! But would it support his weight?

Herman kicked the tree stump. It moved a little, but was sturdy enough, he thought. He knotted one end around the trunk and dropped the other over the cliff. Once more, he gave his makeshift rope a hard pull. Experience had taught him to remove his heavy shoes and socks thus improving his foothold on the rope. Slinging the knapsack over his shoulders, and gripping the rope with both hands, he backed out over the precipice.

CHAPTER 8

The sunshine bathed her in warmth and brightness . . . there were birds twittering in the trees, flowers and butterflies . . . the sweetness of honey in the air . . . when swift as a lizard's tongue the shadow of a creature with giant wings blocked the sun. In the sudden cold, mighty claws were gripping her neck, taking her to the highest mountain peak. There, where she was utterly without hope, a seraph glided from the sky. He hurled his spear. There was a shriek as the shaft sliced through the creature's heart. The claws let go and she was falling helplessly. The ground was coming up fast . . . but there he was: the seraph, transformed; a soldier in a strange uniform, waiting with open arms.

A voice was saying words in her language, *Dio mio . . . Dov'é sono?* It was her own voice. Angelina blinked in the sudden light. Pain scampered from emerging consciousness to her head, nibbling, biting. *Where am I?* Above her was a sheer cliff and beside her the frightening awareness of empty space. Her memory replayed the scenes leading up to her fall. She shivered.

She raised her head, but the pain pushed her back. She put her hand to the pain, and when she pulled it back, her fingers were stained with blood.

A pebble hit the ledge, then another. Angelina looked up. Something was being lowered . . . a strip of tarpaulin knotted at the end. Someone was coming for her—she was not alone.

Herman's feet slid along the makeshift rope dangling freely above the cliff now—moments later they reached the last knot at the end of the tarp. He moved one foot in a widening circle until he was brushing the foliage of a small tree. Encouraged, he lowered himself using only his hands. His head cleared the protruding boulder and he could look down upon the narrow ledge. A woman was lying right at the edge—a woman with stunning red hair.

The two officers on the trail had been watching the attempted rescue with bated breath.

Lieutenant Stucki adjusted his binoculars. "He's on the ledge!" he shouted.

"I'll be a . . . he made it. I'll be damned, our boy made it," cried Feldweibel Ott. He motioned with his head. "How far do you think we are from that cliff?" He got no answer. Instead, Stucki pointed to the pass where a man was walking briskly along the ridge. They followed him with their binoculars until he had disappeared from their line of sight.

"Dammit! We're not alone."

Angelina looked up at the corporal. *It's just a dream.* But as she looked at him her lips widened almost imperceptibly in a shy smile. The veil shading her eyes lifted, revealing a tiny sparkle. *It's him; it's no dream.* "Corporal," she murmured, "you came after me." It was too much effort. Pain tore into her smile and she fought fainting.

Herman dropped beside her onto his knees. "Just lie still." He put his fingers on her forehead and turned her head gently to examine the dark spot in her hair. Softly, he parted the stiffened hair and exposed the skull just above her neck. She had an inch-long gash that needed stitches, he thought. "Relax," he said calmly. "I'll fix you up for now, so just relax."

Angelina still wasn't sure if she was dreaming. She watched him open the knapsack and take out a bottle of aspirin and a small thermos bottle. He unscrewed the cup and filled it halfway. As carefully as one would handle fine Baccarat, he held up her head, put two tablets onto her tongue and the cup to her lips. She swallowed the pills with small sips, and he insisted that she drink it all. *It was no dream!*

Herman poured some of the tea over his handkerchief. "This might hurt a bit, so close your eyes and be still," he said. He dabbed the crusted blood from the wound and from the surrounding hair. The cut began to bleed. Seeing the trickle of her blood made him shudder. His eyes burned and his heart tapped wildly against his chest. He wanted to say something encouraging but was unable to form the words. Instead, he gently caressed her hair, letting the tips of it flow through his fingers.

The bleeding stopped. Herman unwrapped an alcohol-soaked, cotton patch and dabbed at the wound. She squeezed his arm when the pain surged through her head. He wrapped her head with the last of his muslin, like a little turban, and secured it with an elastic clasp. How odd, he thought—early this morning she'd been taking muslin from this very roll to bandage him.

The aspirin began to take effect. Angelina opened her eyes.

"Can you stand up?" She nodded. He put his arm under her shoulders and pulled her to her knees. "That's good, real good." He kept her in balance. "You're doing great, now relax for a minute or two." His words gave her strength, and with his help, Angelina rose gradually to her feet. Then she fell against him—he thought she had fainted—and slung her arms around him and held him tightly about the waist. The pallor slowly left her cheeks. Fear left her eyes.

"You came after me. Oh Corporal, you came after me. I knew it was you behind us; there could have been no one else. You threw that spear and caught me when I was falling. I knew you were there, right by my side. All along, you were in my thoughts, my prayers . . . ."

She kept on and on, and Herman did not stop her. But she wasn't making much sense. Must be a fever, he thought with growing concern.

Then she stopped, embarrassed. Tears came to her eyes. Seeing them brought anguish to Herman. But when she pressed her hands on his cheeks he suddenly felt her breasts against his chest and her abdomen firm against his, and he could smell the sweet scent of her skin. Strong feelings rose in him. He was very tense and at the same time, spinning. Then, just as suddenly, the strange affection turned to something like greatness, a triumph, like the time of his crossbow championship. If someone had said this was heaven, he'd have believed it. He had the desire to kiss her, to fall in love with her—if only he had the courage. *This is a dream. Wake up, Corporal; wake up!*

Herman pulled away and clutched at a limb of the tree. "This, uh, gnarled old dwarf, um, deflected your fall, uh—but you got a nasty cut when you hit."

Angelina shuddered. Only now did she sense how close her brush with death had been.

"You're too weak to climb on your own. The best we can do is tie you to this tarp and pull you to the top." He pointed at her legs. "Use your knees to keep free of the rock."

She looked at him blankly.

Herman smiled. "Let me show you what I mean." He reached for the rope and pulled himself up with his hands until his knees were in contact with the rock. Then he "walked" his knees along the surface. "Do you see?" he said. "It's not all that hard." No sooner had he said this than the rope suddenly went slack, forcing him to let go and drop back onto the ledge.

Angelina screamed and grabbed his arm. What had seemed a simple rescue had suddenly turned doubtful. Herman jerked on the rope. It held. He blamed the short slip on the type of knot he was using. "It's nothing, nothing at all. Just a little slack that had to come out of the rope anyhow." He yanked hard on the rope one more time. "You see? Nothing to worry about." Inside, however, Herman was terrified—what else had he overlooked?

He held out his hand. "Is her majesty ready to take the plunge?"

This brought a smile to her lips. In fact, she was almost laughing. Whatever her feelings, it was a beautiful smile.

He crouched in front of her and wrapped the scarlet scarf around her one knee and the silver scarf around the other. "This ought to protect your knees . . . keep your pants from tearing on the granite." While he tied the knots, she ran her fingers through his hair, playing with his curls. When he looked up and his blue eyes met hers, a tingle started in the back of her neck and spread over her shoulders to her chest.

Herman took off his leather belt, encircled her with it, and buckled it under her arms. Then he undid the knot at the end of his makeshift rope, and tied the two together. He jerked on the ends repeatedly to be sure of their strength. "That's it," he said.

The rope left no slack and forced Angelina to her toes as she stood with her back against the rock. He put his hands on her shoulders. "Once I'm at the cliff above you, face the rock and prepare for the pull. And try to stay away from that sharp granite!"

He grabbed the rope with both hands above her head, and climbed over her with his feet to either side. Angelina watched with her heart in her throat, expecting the rope to break at any moment and send him to his death. Finally, only his feet showed.

⋖⋗⋇⋖⋗

"Take my hand," thundered a voice in flawless German. Herman grabbed the huge, extended hand, which slung him powerfully over the top.

"Let's get the one who's still down there."

Before Herman had the chance to size him up, he and the stranger with the commanding voice were using their combined strength to pull Angelina up over the edge of the precipice. She collapsed into the corporal's arms with tears of joy pouring down her cheeks.

The helpful stranger had moved away before Herman could thank him, but then he stopped near some rocks where there was a commanding view.

Herman helped Angelina to higher ground. He found a place out of the wind where there was a mound of grassy earth to lean against. He helped her sit and crouched beside her. She shivered. He fetched the blue leather jacket where he had left it before he started down the cliff. "I believe this belongs to you," he said humbly, as he draped the jacket over her shoulders. Angelina looked up and moved her lips but made no sound.

The scarves had slipped to her ankles, and the granite had rubbed through her pants and scraped her knees.

"Let me wipe your knees and elbows." Moistening his handkerchief again with tea, he removed all the bits of rock and dirt from her elbows, careful to spare her pain. He blushed. "I would do your knees, but . . . uh, your pants . . . " but before he could go on she covered her lap with her jacket, lifted slightly from her seat and began lowering her pants to just below her knees. He hesitated. But her open smile—he thought she was amused by his blushing—made him forget his shyness. He dropped to his knees and dabbed her wounds with his moist handkerchief, afraid to look up, though. She couldn't resist and again ran her fingers through his curly hair, and as she did, that tingle in her neck was back. She inhaled deeply and closed her eyes.

When Herman had finished, he rose and, out of respect, turned his back to her. Soon he felt her hand on his arm pulling him to her side. With a sigh, she let her head fall against his chest as she snuggled into his arms. The helpful stranger had reappeared, wearing a benign smile. "Corporal Schuller, I presume." He reached down for the young man's hand. Herman got to his feet.

"And you are Signora Bianci, as I recall?"

"It's signorina," said Angelina with a touch of obstinacy.

He grinned. "I am Colonnello Vittorio Zanardelli of the Italian secret service," he told Herman. "I've already introduced myself to the lady. But to simplify things, just call me Vitt."

After shaking hands with Herman he stretched out his hand to Angelina, who nodded and shook it. She still felt she recognized him from somewhere—somewhere other than the roadblock.

The stranger's broad shoulders and superior height impressed Herman, as did his Borsalino hat and black turtleneck sweater, yet he wasn't in the least intimidated.

Zanardelli was telling Angelina, "I have searched my memory but can't place you."

"I thought you just did? Late last night you checked my papers, that's all." Yet she was almost certain now that this ruggedly handsome man was no stranger.

Zanardelli was shaking his head. "No, that's not it. I've seen you before, I'm sure of it." All of a sudden his look of puzzlement was changed by a huge grin. "I know—aren't you working for Signora Mosani? Of course you are! That's it. I saw you at her fashion show in Milan." His smile was very good-natured now. "You wore that yellow chiffon dress, and come to think of, you were definitely the prettiest of all the models."

"I'm Signora Mosani's partner," said Angelina, coolly, having regained her composure.

Like a madman, Giulio drove his gang to the breaking point, disregarding their safety.

No one spoke. Even Sofia, with all her dislike of Angelina, had been shaken by what happened to her. Herr Stüssi had shed tears, something he hadn't done since he'd buried his wife.

Tony was still bringing up the rear, but with even less self-assurance than before. He found it puzzling that there had been no sign of the stranger since he had shot at him back at the saddle. He retied his handkerchief over a cut above his right eye, the result of rock fragments from the stranger's bullet.

Benny was scouting ahead again. The woman's fall over the cliff was bothering him a lot, and he had begun to question his commitment to the cause. He wasn't as quick as some of the others, and it often took him longer to react. But what he lacked in brains he made up in mountaineering skills, so he was well-suited to the job they wanted him to do. Benny knew how to make his way over rocks and snow, and he soon outpaced the band. The going was much tougher than he had anticipated, though, and at higher altitudes the snowdrifts were very deep.

A voice thundered: "Stop right there, and don't make another move!"

Benny froze for a moment, then dove behind a boulder. Gunfire erupted, and bullets ricocheted from the rock he was crouching behind.

The shooting stopped and there was more shouting. "You'd better come out from behind that rock if you know what's good for you!"

Benny yelled back, "Who the hell are you?"

"I'm Tenente Ponte of the 12th division. Throw down your gun and show yourself."

Benny's mind raced. This had to be a squad of *carabinieri*, close enough to cut off any retreat from here.

He yelled, "Come and get me, Tenente, if you dare." Then he reconsidered. "No—okay, okay, I'm willing to talk." To show his cooperation, Benny tied his brown neckerchief to the gun barrel and held the gun high above the boulder while the tenente and his men approached.

In talking to him the tenente quickly realized that Benny wasn't quite sure what he was fighting for, and in any case, that there wasn't any fight left in him. It would have been a waste of men and resources to guard him or bring him in, but by disarming him and sending him back to his comrades, he might persuade the rest to surrender—at least the ones whose loyalties were now marginal, like his.

He had no trouble persuading Benny to go along. It was a deal.

Giulio dashed behind a tree when he heard the gunfire. Things were changing fast. Hostile fire ahead meant that his escape path was blocked. Behind him, the lone soldier with the rifle would cut off his retreat, and by now there might be reinforcements. He had no place to go. His face was as white as the snow piled beside him.

He heard heavy steps on the trail and crouched down. He cocked his handgun and took aim. It was Benny, whistling an old army tune. He was unarmed!

Benny walked right up as if he knew where to find him. "It's over, Giulio. We're trapped, and there's no place to hide. Trust me, there are too many of them for us to take on."

Giulio knew at a glance that Benny no longer cared about the cause. He wanted to go home and face the lightest possible sentence, which was why he was cooperating with the authorities.

But Giulio was not ready to give up. Maybe there were too many of them for him to fight his way out, but he might not have to fire a shot if he could make good use of his hostage.

"Those are my boys," cried Zanardelli at the far-off shots. He had an ear for gunfire and could tell a shot from friend or foe. He had gained quick respect for the young tenente, whom he had known for only a few hours. Zanardelli contemplated joining the squad of *carabinieri*

farther up the trail, but the corporal had another idea.

"I think we should wait for them right here," he said. "We're not really sure what took place up there, colonnello. Should things have gone wrong, the band most certainly would come back through here, and this saddle would make the perfect spot for a trap."

Angelina looked admiringly at the young soldier. What sweet revenge if Giulio would get what was coming to him at this very spot. But it wasn't the corporal's good sense Angelina admired most; she saw in him a savior, a giant even more formidable than the imposing colonnello. She was so tense from all the excitement she couldn't breathe. She ripped off her scarf and shook out all the hair below her bandage, letting it flow freely over her shoulders. The gesture freed her emotions, too. She was taking deep breaths, and felt as if she was being flooded with a new awareness that enabled her, in spite of all the threats to her freedom, and all her fear, to feel beautiful.

Giulio ordered the band back down the trail, back over the same treacherous terrain. The donkeys kept pace unwillingly. Benny was armed with Emilio's old gun, but Giulio had him taking the lead, where he could keep an eye on him.

Out of breath, too tired to go on, Herr Stüssi stumbled and dropped to the ground. Tony helped him to his feet.

Giulio at last relented, on the pretext that the risk to the donkeys and their precious loads was getting to be too great. "There's a small path on the other side of the saddle that cuts to the west straight down the slope." If they reached that point unseen, they might slip below the cliff hidden from the trail above and have a last chance to get away. The saddle, peaceful and deserted, spread before him.

Giulio grinned fiendishly at the thought of outsmarting his foes. There was only a hundred meters to go.

"Stay right there!" thundered a voice.

A man, tall and broad chested, with a Luger held high in front of him, had appeared like magic from behind a rise. Giulio turned. Three ear-splitting shots ripped through the air. The band froze.

"Drop your guns!" shouted the stranger. "I am Colonnello

Zanardelli. I am ordering you to give yourselves up!"

Giulio wavered. A fourth shot rang out—the corporal's rifle—then the short burst of a submachine gun came from behind. All eyes turned to the burst fired by two military officers who climbed up from behind the rise.

With everyone facing the other way, Giulio saw his chance. He grabbed the farmer by the neck and pushed his revolver against the old man's temple. "You let us pass or the old man dies! You hear me?" he screamed. "The old man dies if you so much as sneeze!"

In an unprecedented move that fully went against his nature, Benny stepped forward and ripped the revolver from Giulio's hand. With a quick jerk, he pulled the farmer to his side. "It's over, Giulio," said Benny calmly. He slung out the cylinder, emptied the cartridges to the ground, and tossed the revolver after them. He pulled the clip from the automatic he had been carrying and let it drop to the ground. He then led the farmer to the colonnello.

Tony shook his head, dismayed, but he too tossed his automatic to the ground. The donkeys bucked. Sofia, holding onto the lead-rope wrapped around her wrist, glanced at the pale Giulio. She looked for anything to tell her what to do. But Giulio, numb, unable to move or think, had no eyes for her. With a shrug, Sofia got free of the rope and joined the others behind the colonnello.

Suspiciously, Zanardelli eyed the Swiss officers' rapid climb up the rise. Satisfied that they were no threat, he stored his gun in his shoulder holster, walked over to Giulio, and handcuffed him. At that instant, Tenente Ponte and his *carabinieri* came storming down the trail. They lost no time and tied the other gunmen's hands, but, at a wink from the colonnello, spared the two women that fate. The guns and ammunition scattered about the ground were quickly gathered and secured.

The events had played out so quickly that Herman Schuller was almost at a loss. He greeted his superiors with a carefree grin. But inside him was a strange dejection, a feeling one might have after reaching a long-sought goal without a follow-up plan. Lieutenant Stucki sensed the turmoil in his young corporal and did not press him for information. There was plenty of time for that, he thought.

There were handshakes and introductions, some modest talk

and a little boasting. As the evening chill set in, the *carabinieri* gathered wood, and in no time at all, a lively fire brought some pleasantness to the scene. They made coffee and passed it around in their canteens. Everybody gathered at the fire, except Herman. He was after the spooked animals that had strayed dangerously close to the drop-off on the left. Stubborn at first, at last they followed him back to camp. He tied them to shrubs and unloaded their heavy cargo. One of the soldiers examined Angelina's head and applied a new bandage. Zanardelli was engaged in conversation with the two Swiss officers.

Angelina was sitting on a little knoll with her back against a flat rock, relieved that the ordeal had finally ended. But she felt deserted. As much as she thought of Giulio as a monster, her hatred for him wasn't nearly as strong as her anguish and frustration about herself. She found no defense or justification for her conduct no matter how deep she searched.

She watched the corporal carry on a one-sided conversation with the donkeys. What is going through his mind? *He must be disappointed in me, dismayed about my conduct.* She had betrayed him, misused his trust, made him look foolish. No wonder he avoided her and kept his back turned to her. But Angelina needed a friend. *Look at me,* Corporal; *please look at me.* He kept his back to her.

Herr Stüssi sensed Angelina's anguish and walked over.

"He's quite a man, the young corporal, isn't he?" he said, consolingly. He sat on the rock she was leaning against. "Angelina, what I'd like to say . . . there are no suitable words to thank you for your help and the concern you had for me. I won't forget you. The way you stood up to Giulio, this madman . . . you were so very brave . . . and when you fell over that cliff I almost jumped after you."

But Angelina was hardly listening. "What's in his heart, Herr Stüssi?" she asked, staring straight ahead. "Does he care for me at all?"

He patted her shoulder. "The corporal? Of course he does, my dear. Trust me, he cares a lot."

Angelina shook her head slowly. "He hasn't looked at me, not even once. All he cares about are those donkeys."

"He cares for you, Angelina. He thinks of you. Do you . . . ?"
He stalled. "You like him, don't you?" She didn't answer, and he left
the question lying there. A peaceful silence set in, the kind where
thoughts say more than words. Angelina pulled his hand to her
cheek; she felt secure in the old man's presence.

Herr Stüssi sensed her longing for companionship. "The corporal is very young. Have you thought about that?"

"I'm not sure what it is, Herr Stüssi," said Angelina, "and I
wish I knew what it all means." She kept staring. "I liked him from
the very first, from the day we met. Something about him . . . he's different. It's as if I have known him all my life—and not known him
at all. At times I think he feels the same about me, but then I'm not
sure what he thinks."

Herr Stüssi nodded. "Like that birthday present—you know
what's inside, but you're not really sure until you open it?"

Angelina smiled at his remark. She turned toward him. "You
must think I'm childish," she said. "But it feels good talking about
such things, Herr Stüssi." She sighed. "It feels good talking about
him." She covered her face with her hands. "Oh, Herr Stüssi, what
will come of all this?"

The old man gently patted her shoulders. "Don't rush anything, young lady. Give it all the time you need."

Herman's world had been turned upside down again—how many
times today? Twice in the last two hours. He was grateful that the
donkeys were giving him something to do.

Until the thieves had given up, he had been living a dream.
From the moment he started after the thieves in the dead of night he
knew that he would never again be the same Corporal Herman Schuller
who had come to All' Acqua for training exercises, and commanded a
small squad of men who had become his friends. *That* Corporal Schuller
had always tried to do a good job, to be a good soldier, to have the
respect of his men, but he wasn't a career soldier—his chosen career
was in the hotel-restaurant business. He wanted to have his own restaurant, his own small hotel, perhaps even his own resort some day.

He liked being a soldier for a while each year. He liked his command; it meant a lot to him to have the respect of men his age, and to be counted upon by older soldiers and men with much more experience and authority than himself, such as the feldweibel and Lieutenant Stucki. Both men outranked him, and in any military situation where soldiers were to behave as soldiers, his main job was to carry out their orders. He would report to them and answer their questions. However, things hadn't happened by the book in his unit where officers and soldiers came from the same county, same neighborhoods, patronizing the same taverns, attending the same churches. Though Herman didn't know these two officers in civilian life, he had grown close to them. They'd taken it upon themselves to ignore the differences in rank and behave as friends. They had asked his opinion on many occasions, and more than once they had come to join him and his men when they were having a beer or were sharing a bottle of wine. Now, for the first time since he'd worn the uniform, Corporal Herman Schuller had been involved in a real action with a real foe, and it wasn't over yet. When the feldweibel and the lieutenant had arrived he had known at a glance—so much can be learned from a glance between men in uniform—that he wasn't in trouble for taking matters into his own hands and going after the thieves without waiting for his superiors to authorize the action and give him permission.

But there was a slight problem. For the last twenty-four hours or so, he hadn't felt like Corporal Herman Schuller. He recognized a lot of things he'd felt before—especially his fears and certain aches and pains caused by the extreme demands he was making on his body—but many of the things he was doing and feeling were new. He didn't think of himself as a hero, but one glance at his superior officers (that very same first glance) had told him that they did. And for that matter, from the way he had been treated by Colonnello Zanardelli, he was aware that this high-ranking Italian officer thought of him as a hero, too.

Herman was proud of what he had done. He was grateful for the good opinion of the men here. But he also felt a little like an imposter. Because everything that had happened in his life since the woman with the red hair came into it two days ago had seemed like a dream. True, it was good old Corporal Schuller who set off after the thieves, and he could well remember that his main idea at the moment was to avenge the attack on the bunker that had made a bloody mess of his friend Hans Rüegg. However, even after he found out that Angelina was involved with the thieves somehow, and had her scarf in his pocket, he had risked his life for Alice Mendali, a woman he hardly knew. And when he risked it for Angelina just minutes or hours ago, dangling at the end of his makeshift rope, he hadn't known who was on the ledge. He had heard a human sound, there was a human being between life and death on the ledge below, and he had gone there to do what he could, almost without thinking . . . as in a dream. And somehow, as in a dream, he wasn't surprised that it was Angelina who was between life and death. The rescue had been difficult and awkward *in reality*, but Herman knew perfectly well that he had been gliding to her side like an angel, just as she kept saying in her delirium.

Then the dream had ended. She had held him . . . and wanted him. From where she was sitting across the saddle—he knew exactly where, though he hadn't once looked at her—she was thinking about him. She was wondering why he was paying attention to the donkeys instead of her. O *God!* How much he wanted to believe this to be true. But his upbringing had taught Herman Schuller his place in life, and this place left no room for someone as beautiful as Angelina. It would be fruitless thinking otherwise, no matter how much he longed for her, dreamed of her . . . yet he wanted to be close to her, talking, holding her . . . more than anything else in the whole world.

Why did the dream have to end, though? Why, when the blissful moments in her arms were as close to heaven as Herman Schuller had ever been? Weren't dreams made in heaven? And if she wanted him, really, why couldn't the dream become reality?

The answer was right in front of him: in the huge, smart, patient, glistening eye of this donkey, where, because it was starting to get dark, the colors of the sunset were reflected, and flames were dancing from the fire the men had lit to keep warm. There were to be no more chances for heroism from here on. Life would go on pretty much as before—for Herman, and for this donkey. No doubt the donkeys would continue carrying their heavy loads until the ammunition could safely be returned to where it belonged. Then, if Giulio continued to refuse to talk, they'd be let loose to follow their inborn homing instinct to find their owner's farm—whether it was in Italy or Switzerland—from where they, almost certainly, had been abducted.

Probably Herman Schuller wouldn't be crossing the San Giácomo Pass anytime soon, however, or even visiting Italy. There were further military duties to be seen to in All' Acqua and then, in fulfillment of another dream that had been with him day in day out for the last several years, he would be enrolling in a hotel school.

By the time the Swiss and Italian officers came for him, and very politely asked—insisted—that he take part in the discussions which were to decide the fate of the prisoners, Herman had decided something about his dream and was no longer completely despondent. Ever since he went up on the mountain last night after the thieves, his dream of a career had been far from his mind, but Angelina, somehow, had been with him. Even though it wasn't her scarf in his pocket at first, and he knew it wasn't, her image had been with him every step of the way. She'd been present in that dream . . . only more imaginable, more beautiful . . . and the dream was living on, down the treacherous, beautiful trail all the way to All' Acqua, to the tavern and the tiny Fiat where it had all begun . . . like the making of a sweet prophesy.

He was reliving that dream, that moment, yet one more time when Lieutenant Stucki put his hand on his shoulder and asked him to join the others to help decide what was to be done with the prisoners.

Everything was decided just as Herman was sure it would be. Almost. Though everyone else had known the outcome in advance— the officers had been deliberating lengthily about the detainees' fate—they had staged the discussions and put the corporal in charge, giving him a chance to complete his mission . . . like a reward, a boost to his image. The corporal played along like any good soldier would—though there was a small smile warping the corners of his lips—and all went well just as they thought it would . . . until . . .

The ammunition would be returned to the bunker in All'

Acqua on the backs of these donkeys; then, if their rightful owner could not be identified, the donkeys would be let loose to find their own way home.

Colonnello Vittorio Zanardelli would take charge of Giulio the mastermind and most dangerous of the band. He was implicated in many actions in Italy—not to mention the embarrassment to the Secret Service Commander at that riot—besides the recent ones involving weapons possession, kidnapping, and the assault on the farmhouse that resulted in injuries and death.

The *carabinieri*, on the other hand, would be bringing in the other members of the group. But that's where a disagreement had surfaced when Corporal Schuller insisted on taking one of the detainees to All' Acqua as a witness. Though Lieutenant Stucki thought it unnecessary, as he doubted much would come out of this incident once the ammo had been returned . . . whereas Corporal Schuller stood his ground . . . and the colonnello came unglued.

"Corporal Schuller!" cried Zanardelli. He walked over to the corporal and the two separated from the others. They stood by the cliff facing the spectacular sunset. Zanardelli's tone softened as quickly as his rage had elevated. "Uh, Herman," he said. "Okay, if I call you Herman?" He delayed for a moment then said, "Nice sunset. Amazing how the colors can change so quickly." He watched the young soldier intently, though he was looking straight ahead, and the wrinkles of concern on his forehead did not escape him. "Want to tell me what's on your mind?"

Still facing the sunset, Herman said, "I shot a man in your country. He could be dead for all I know."

Zanardelli had expected the young man's disclosure at some point, and was prepared for it, but had hardly expected that it was uppermost in his mind. He put his arm about Herman's shoulder. "I assume you're talking about the dead man at the dairy farm," he said, sounding like a concerned father. "Well, I've given it some thought. It's going to be your word against the farmer's. He insists that he shot that man in self-defense." He coughed into his hand. "Since, to my knowledge, no one can say for sure who fired that shot, I have no reason to doubt the farmer's word." He looked down on Herman. "Corporal," he said, turning him around by the shoulders, "and I mean this with the utmost sincerity—I consider the case about the dead man closed."

Herman let out a sigh of relief. Almost too quickly, he asked, "What's going to happen to Signorina Bianci?"

The colonnello shot him a crafty smile. *Now! His persistence is making sense!* "Hmmm! Um-uh." He coughed again. "I think I might . . . " he lowered his voice, "I might have a solution for all this."

Angelina had watched the proceedings with interest. Naturally, she wanted to know what would be said about her. If the corporal didn't speak up for her she would be taken into custody with the rest. She had sensed that the discussions were staged, but was impressed with the respect that was shown Herman, and when he and the colonnello spoke privately she was able to catch threads of what they were saying and realized that her fears had been unwarranted. In addition, she was seeing Herman Schuller in a new light—as a man who could hold his own against men of considerable experience and stature.

While waiting to find out what would become of her, Angelina was sick with worry, and her injured head was throbbing with pain. For a moment she had convinced herself that she would become the corporal's witness and accompany him to All' Acqua. But that notion evaporated in the face of other options. Tony had shot at the corporal, and Benny was partially responsible for the sentry's injury at the bunker. No matter how Angelina tried to manipulate her thoughts, her self-esteem began to fall apart.

If she was forced to return to Milan as the tenente's prisoner Angelina could see herself being chased through Milan's streets, heckled by onlookers who made faces and spat on her and threw rotten eggs. She could imagine being thrown into a dark, rat-infested dungeon and imprisoned until bond could be posted, if it was allowed at all.

Angelina made her way back to the fire where she dropped to the ground. She put her head down in her arms. *Oh, Corporal, I know you want me. Tell me what goes through your mind, tell me now.* Angelina shivered in spite of the closeness of the fire. When she finally raised her head and looked for the corporal, there he was, rifle between his knees and cap on straight, watching the last of the sunset.

It drove her half mad to see him sitting there like that. *Why do you have your back turned toward me, Corporal? Why are you not looking at me?* The uncertainty turned her stomach and brought a sweetish taste to her mouth. She vomited into the grass. *Oh, Corporal, look at me!* But he didn't turn around, just sat there staring at the sky. She dropped her head onto her arms, closed her eyes, and held her breath, thinking of what it must have been like for Marie Antoinette while waiting for the blade to fall.

Then she heard a voice.

"You'd better get up, girl. It'll be dark soon, and we have a long way to go."

Angelina snapped up—and looked at the corporal's grinning face. Those were the sweetest words she had ever heard. Colors were bright again, sounds were lovely; everything was beautiful. She forgot her anxiety and fear. The choking tightness had left her chest. Her eyes were clear. As soon as she got to her feet she grabbed the soldier's arm.

He offered warmth and safety.

The cabin was certainly not the Dolder Grand, but it was more than the ghostly shadow it had first appeared.

"I told you not to expect luxury accommodations," mumbled Lieutenant Stucki. "But there's a chimney, and where there's a chimney there must be a stove. I could almost bet there's plenty of firewood to assure hot coffee for a comfortable, warm night." He had spotted the cabin earlier while on the journey to the pass. He unlocked the door with a key that was hanging right by the door as if to welcome them. It was the lieutenant's idea that they stop wandering through the dark and make the cabin their quarters for the night. It was rugged, but red shutters with cutout hearts softened its appearance. Below the shutters, a sturdy birch bench invited the weary travelers, and beside it was a rough-hewn water trough kept full by the trickle from a small copper pipe.

While the others entered the cabin, Corporal Schuller led the donkeys to the back. He tied them to the wire mesh of a partially demolished chicken coop and relieved the tired animals of their heavy loads.

Lieutenant Stucki shook the petroleum lamp that hung on a

wire above a rustic table and listened for the fuel to swish around inside. The reservoir was close to empty but was quickly refilled with kerosene from a one-liter can which was beneath two stacked bunks. He lifted the hurricane glass and lit the wick. It flickered, then shot to life, throwing alternate sparkles and weird shadows on his boyish face. The small knob was deftly adjusted until the flame burned evenly.

Feldweibel Ott found a paper bag of coffee beans, and ground them himself by turning the crank on a little mill. He had also found a bag of granulated sugar and a few cans of condensed milk. After cleaning the ashes from an iron stove with a piece of cardboard, he built a fire with twigs and a crumpled newspaper. Soon a crackling fire had warmed the cabin. Lieutenant Stucki had made himself useful by filling the large enamel pot from the trickle at the little trough outside.

Angelina had taken the bristle broom from behind the stove, and whisked the dust and cobwebs out the door. In the pantry she had found crushed corn, flour, salt, and pepper, and a lone side of smoked bacon that dangled from the ceiling on a wire.

Feldweibel Ott poured perfectly brewed coffee served in tin cups he took from rusty nails above the stove. The smell lured Herman into the cabin, which was streaked with orange light from the kerosene lamp. He opened his knapsack and broke out the loaf of bread and cheese that Alice Mendali had packed for him, sharing it with the others.

The officers moved to the bunks, leaving the table and the two chairs for their "guests of honor," as Lieutenant Stucki graciously put it. Soon only the sounds of chewing and the hiss of the lamp broke the quiet.

Angelina studied the corporal. He looked tired; his eyes were dry and his lips were chapped. Still, his presence gave Angelina comfort and helped her stay at ease. She found herself increasingly drawn to him. She was tempted to take his hand and press it to her, but hesitated, held back by an imaginary gap that seemed to have grown between them. Perhaps she hesitated out of respect for his youthful innocence. Still, she sensed his longing for her and hoped he would make a first move. He didn't—just looked at her from time to time, from beneath his drooping eyelids.

Feldweibel Ott detected the uneasiness in their faces. He rose from the bunk and said, "Let me look at that bandage, schignora. Perhapsch I can improve on it schomewhat."

Visibly relieved, Herman stood up. "I'm not quite finished with the donkeys," he said, shrugging. "I'll see you later." He went around the cabin to the chicken coop. Since tending them at the pass, he had grown fond of the sturdy donkeys. He liked animals. The only creatures he had ever owned were some Silver Champagne rabbits he had raised for profit. Then there was that stray dog and those homeless cats his parents wouldn't let him keep. He untied the first animal and led it by its halter to the watering trough.

The feldweibel tightened the bandage around Angelina's forehead. "That medic hasch done a fair job, schignora," he said apologetically. "I guesch I can't improve on it with what I have with me. If it'sch any comfort to you, we'll fix you up a little better at the field hoschpital in All' Acqua."

Angelina smiled gratefully. "Thank you, soldier, but I'm fine. It doesn't hurt so much now. Not as much as it did."

Lieutenant Stucki stood up from the bunk. "You must be tired, signora. Take one of our bunks."

Angelina smiled appreciatively. "Signorina. Thanks, fellows, but the bunks are yours. I think I'll help the corporal with the donkeys." She had a deep voice, warm and sexy. She walked to the door, then turned around and saluted them. "Make yourselves at home and don't worry about us. We'll wake you when it's our turn."

The soldiers raised their tin cups, and watched the sway of her hips as the shapely woman stepped outside.

CHAPTER 9

Angelina couldn't have imagined a more enchanted setting: the pines were whispering in the breeze, an owl was hooting, snow-capped mountains towered above, the moon peeking through the soft, high clouds. Perfect for two young people about to fall in love.

She caught up with Herman at the watering trough. "You like the animals. I can tell."

"Yes," he said. "They're beautiful creatures. I wonder how they manage the heavy loads. Just try to lift one of those boxes." After the last donkey had drunk, Herman led it to the chicken coop and left it hitched beside the others.

Angelina rubbed her arms. "It's chilly. Do you think the animals are cold?"

"Maybe so. I can keep the wind away by tying them closer to the shack." He untied the donkey he'd just watered and started leading it by the halter.

"I'll help you," said Angelina. She untied the next donkey and began to follow. It rubbed its head against her shoulder. Angelina laughed. "Did you see that, Corporal? He thanked me!"

"It's a she."

"Oh." She giggled.

Herman sensed her embarrassment and avoided her eyes. He tied the last animal to an iron hook. He found hay in the shack and tossed an armful in front of each.

Angelina was impressed by his noble regard for these animals, but she was very cold. She pulled him to the bench under the cabin window and snuggled against him, with her head on his shoulder.

Where would she be now if it weren't for him? As she absorbed his warmth, she cherished the new awareness that had sprung up in her.

But with that awareness came conflict: was there gratitude mixed up in this? Was she like someone drowning, grateful for the one who threw her a rope? Angelina took another deep breath to ease the tightness in her chest.

When Herman turned his head to her there was a shy smile on his lips and warmth in his eyes. Angelina felt the warmth of his presence and her heart pounded. What made him so special? Well, his eyes were the bluest she had ever seen, and the beautiful, almost feminine curl of his lip contrasted sharply with his determined look. His sun-tanned skin was smooth and shiny in spite of his two-day-old whiskers. His hair was neatly trimmed around his ears now red from the cold. His blond curls tempted her fingers, and when she ran them through the curls they snapped back with every pass. She had the sudden urge to press her lips onto his, to let herself go and snuggle deeply into the depths of his sexy . . . yes, his beautiful sexy eyes.

She held back. After all, it was a man's duty to kiss first. Yet . . . who cared about tradition? But would he mistakenly think of her kiss as an expression of gratitude? No, she decided, it had to happen unexpectedly, and when it happened it had to be so strong that a team of oxen couldn't pull them apart.

"You're quite young, aren't you, Corporal?"

"I'm twenty-one."

"Then you're mature for your age. When's your birthday?"

"In July. I'll be twenty-two then," he said with a note of pride.

Angelina let her fingers wander through his hair. She still wasn't sure what it was about the corporal, what drew her to him with increasing force. The men in her circle in Milan had made their mark. They were the fashion kings, promoters, and photographers; they were newsmen, people in government and politics—and all of them were in stark contrast to the corporal. He had an unworldly air about him, like some dream-inspired fantasy. Along with his youthful innocence, that caused her to hold back, he had an unbridled spirit that drew her on.

Angelina began to shiver, not just from the cold. By tacit agreement, they rose and made their way to the cabin's warmth.

⊲⊱✻⊰⊳

Adjusting the lantern to a mere flicker, Angelina cried, "This is romantic!" Her eyes were sparkling and there was a blush on her cheeks. "They must be exhausted," she said of the soldiers, who were snoring loudly. Then she quickly added, "I feel so wonderful, Corporal; I could be up all night."

Herman simply nodded.

Except for the soldiers' snores, the cabin was quiet. He's not a big talker, Angelina thought.

"What's inside your heart?" she asked, her voice seeming loud to her. He liked her, she had no doubt, but so did most men: she had a pretty face and sexy figure. After all, it was her business to look beautiful and appeal to men. She touched his arm. "Come on, you have to tell me something about yourself. Where do you live?"

"In Zürich," he said, "with my parents. For now! There's going to be a job for me in Basel. I just spent a year in Scandinavia as part of my ongoing culinary training."

"You're a cook? Wow! But . . . why Basel?"

He shrugged. "I've made my apprenticeship there. Three full years."

"Do you have a girl in Basel? You must have a reason for going back."

"It's only a stopover. I'm on the waiting list for the Belvoir Park School in Zürich."

"Belvoir School?"

"It's the finest gastronomical institution in Europe."

"Hotel school, hmmm, interesting," she said, nodding her approval. "But you keep ignoring my question." She sighed. "I guess you won't tell me if there's a girl in your life. Tell me your goals, at least. I mean, what do you intend to do with your life?"

"I want to become the finest chef de cuisine."

"You want to stay a cook?"

"Yes—well, maybe not all my life. But tell me, signorina, what's wrong with being a cook?"

"Nothing!" she said quickly. She sensed sensitivity, a hurt pride. She put on her most dangerous smile. "I'd be honored to be married to a cook."

"Why the sudden change of heart?"

"Then I wouldn't have to do the cooking . . . ."

"You'd have to do the dishes."

Angelina burst out laughing. "It's a deal, Corporal—I'll do the dishes. But I'm sure you have other desires besides being a cook. If you wanted to remain a cook, you wouldn't need to attend hotel school."

He grinned. "Yes, I want to have my own restaurant someday . . . like my parents' place in Zürich. Or a hotel. That's what I really want, a large hotel, maybe a resort with flower gardens and a swimming pool, and fountains and ponds with goldfish and ducks."

She laughed again. "That sounds exciting. Perhaps you should start by taking over your parents' restaurant."

"No, I don't think so. I have applied for immigration to the United States."

Her face fell. "America?"

"Yes."

His "yes" was too quick. "When is this to take place?"

"Hard to guess," he said. "There's a small quota for Swiss immigrants, and at the moment it's been filled. It could take as long as three years to get a visa, maybe longer."

In the ensuing silence Angelina closed her eyes. Why all this anxiety? Her palms were sweating. She had been ready for certain obstacles to overcome: a girlfriend; time away for schooling; travel to gain experience. But America? It sounded so distant, so permanent.

She was forced to acknowledge her feelings for the young soldier. She took his empty tin cup from the table, walked to the stove, and refilled it with coffee. "That's a big decision. Do you really want to go to America?"

"It's been my desire for many years."

"What do you expect there that you could not find right here in Europe?" she asked in a challenging tone.

He took a sip of coffee and looked at her as if astounded she didn't know. "The opportunities in America are bound only by one's imagination." He went to the stove, opened the hole, and dropped two small logs on the embers. A spark shot up and flew onto the woodpile. He extinguished it with his shoe. When he came back to the table, Angelina reached for his hands. Her fingers were ice-cold.

He rubbed them one at a time, slowly, from the knuckles to the tip of the nails.

Before long, the silence was uncomfortable. "I'm puzzled . . ." Herman said, finally.

"Puzzled?"

"Yes . . . about your part in Giulio's organization. You didn't belong with them."

"I know," sighed Angelina. Then, in a much louder voice: "I was foolish, downright stupid!"

Herman thought for a moment. "Your anger tells me that there had to be a reason. There's always a reason when we do something stupid." He cringed a little; his words hadn't come out the way he wanted.

Angelina didn't flinch. "You couldn't say it any better, Corporal. Behind my anger there was a desire for revenge."

Herman looked up. The word did not fit the lips that spoke it.

"Yes, revenge! My parents had done no wrong. They were nice people."

"Both parents?" he said solemnly. "I had no idea." He couldn't imagine being without parents. "It was the doing of the war?"

Angelina nodded. "In a way, yes. But it happened after the Germans had left my country." She released his hands to pull out a handkerchief and dab her eyes. "They came in the middle of night— the *carabinieri*—with guns and an official warrant for my father's arrest. They took him to the station and interrogated him.

"My father had been a military man and was injured in North Africa. Unable to return to active duty, he became the chauffeur of Mussolini's household. It was this, and his link to General Bruno, the last commander of Milan's military garrison and a close relative of my mother, which infuriated the guerillas who dominated the new government. Before his assignment to Milan, General Bruno was stationed in Torino assigned to hunt down the guerillas roaming the Aosta mountains. The general was hated for carrying out that assignment. When the war ended, he was put under house arrest.

"All papa wanted when accepting the chauffeur assignment was to put bread and milk and an occasional stick of butter on our dinner table. His wages couldn't even pay the rent on our little

apartment. The day of his arrest was the last time I saw my papa."
Angelina wiped her eyes. "Mamma couldn't live with the injustice;
she fell ill almost overnight. She died in my arms two months later.
They said it was pneumonia, but I was old enough to know better. I
knew what really killed her."

Angelina clutched his hands. The look in her eyes gave added
poignancy to her story. "I was alone and abandoned in a country that
was at peace, yet so much at war. Then my father's sister, Aunt
Virginia, took me into her home in the quiet valley of Antigório. She
became my mother and my tutor, and she taught me right from
wrong. But she had no knowledge of the hatred deep inside me, didn't
know about my sleepless nights, and even her strong influence could
not stop my craving for revenge." Angelina shook her head contin-
uously. "Now look at me! I got people hurt, and for what?"

Herman bit his lip. "I'm really sorry about your parents," he
said. How could he have doubted this beautiful woman, even for one
second? Suddenly, he felt unworthy of her. Dozens of questions
flashed through his mind as he assessed the emotional events that
had pushed her into this. But all he could manage to say was, "I had
no idea. No one can blame you for what you did."

Angelina looked upon him with loving respect. "You're so
sweet, Corporal, thinking the way you do." Out of fervor, she lifted his
hands to her lips, and he could sense a small quiver. She said, "I used
to lie awake swearing to avenge my parents, but only when I met
Giulio did I see a way to fulfill that pledge. I was so sure that I was
doing right until"—her breath caught for a moment and a slight
tremor came into her voice—"until I met you at the tavern. I didn't
know it at the time, but you gave me an awareness of decency. From
then on, I was no longer sure about my involvement with Giulio." She
raised her eyes and said almost to herself, "God sent you to me. I
know he did."

The silence now was easier, less tense. Her eyes were glowing,
her hands no longer trembled. Then loss began to darken her face
and he quickly asked her, "When did you move back to Milan?"

The bright sparkle in her eyes told him she welcomed that
question. "I moved there in the fall of 1947. As much as I loved life
on the small farm with Aunt Virginia, I knew that it was not my

destiny. On impulse, I applied for a waitress job at the Grand Hotel Puccini in Milan, a job I heard about from our neighbor's daughter, who worked there as a desk clerk. I'll always remember the morning I took the train to the big city: my aunt was wishing me well, but her face was sad; the leaves on the chestnut tree had started to turn . . . ."

Milan had meant excitement. Corso Buenos Aires, the street of the Grand Hotel Puccini, was the center of high fashion, with great hotels and fine restaurants, ice-cream parlors and chocolate stores. Heavenly voices from the tiny church on Mozart Street raised her spirits. The Duomo . . . the park . . . everywhere were memories of her carefree youth. The chains of the swing her father had made for her had rusted, but the board was still hanging from the tree.

Angelina finished her dining room apprenticeship and became a star waitress with a loyal clientele. She set aside her substantial earnings for higher education. She shared a small room at the hotel with her neighbor's daughter, who thought it her duty to watch over her young friend.

Angelina smiled at the memory. "In a way, the arrangement kept me out of trouble—the owner did not allow male visitors." And justifiably so because the gangling, almost undernourished girl had somehow been transformed into the sexy phenomenon of Angelina. At twenty-one, she was a small sensation. Men of wealth and status lavished flowers and small gifts upon her which she instinctively refused.

"I never refused an honestly earned gratuity, though." Playfully, she was showing him a mercenary smile. "I dated a young waiter, but when I refused to sleep with him, he dropped me cold."

Then came Angelina's big break. "I became friends with one of my regular clients, Signora Mosani, who owned the Fashion House at the Galleria across the Puccini promenade. She was a great beauty; designed and modeled her own fashions—she even did much of the sewing. The war had taken her spouse, 'My one and only love forever,' she would say. She never dated and turned down all marriage proposals. She had so much talent and style, and when she offered me a part-time job, I accepted without a second thought. We turned out to be perfect companions: she needed a friend; I needed someone to look after me.

"I'll never forget that first day on the job going through the clothes racks, putting on dress after gorgeous dress, turning in the mirror unsure about my own reflection—a girl with so much poise and charm just couldn't be me! After weeks of tutoring, Marie Theresa allowed me my first appearance on stage. You cannot imagine, Corporal, what that meant to me. I was a little jittery, but I knew I had found my vocation."

Success did not come easy, though, she went on to say. There were struggles with fashion executives, the media, even with herself about style and her principles—Angelina refused to give in to producers' personal demands. Yet within a year, she was in great demand.

Herman's mouth had fallen open. "I once saw a fashion show at the Belvedere Hotel in Davos," he said at one point. "All I remember are the skinny models and my uncle flirting with one of them. My aunt got angry with him. Do female clients ever become jealous of you? Because you're so gorgeous, affectionately appealing?"

Angelina covered her mouth to keep from laughing.

"Sometimes they do," she said. "You see, Corporal, it's all part of the game." Her small smile lingered. "So what's wrong with that? The man flirts a little—it's their inborn right the way I see it—but all is well at the end when he buys her that gown without looking at the price tag."

Instead of objecting, as she expected, he said, "I would like to meet your partner. She sounds like an interesting person."

"She is," said Angelina. "On my day off from the restaurant, Marie Theresa would take me in her Fiat to Aosta and the mountains. We picked wildflowers in the spring and blueberries in the fall. We picnicked under the cool pines and fished for trout in the Toce River." Angelina raised her shoulders and filled her lungs. "I can still see those fresh rainbows lying so prettily in the creel."

"Who caught all those trout?"

"Me, of course."

"Who cleaned them?"

"I did!"

"Who cooked them?"

"Me, again!"

"What did your partner do?"

"She ate them, silly!" They both laughed out loud, almost waking the two soldiers, who turned and moaned.

Angelina could not remember a more carefree conversation with a man. She pressed his hands against her cheeks. His palms were warm and comfortable—like everything else about him. Her voice turned poignant. "It saddens me to think that such moments come to us only once in a great while. But," she said, changing course again, "there's always excitement if you know where to look for it!"

Her mood was buoyant. "Like that Saturday evening five years ago," she sighed. "We had a wonderfully successful week at the Fashion House. Marie Theresa had laid out a new dress for me that she had sewn herself. I can still feel the silkiness of the yarn and the freshness of the fabric against my skin. I looked stunning. A delivery boy whistled after me as we left the store.

"Once we were at the curb, Marie Theresa tied my eyes with a scarf. No sooner had she done so than I heard the rhythm of horseshoes on the cobblestones. She removed the scarf, and I saw a stylish carriage. High on top there was a coachman with a mustache, dressed in long tails, unbuttoned frock, and top hat. In his hand was a long leather whip that he swished playfully above my head. I hesitated; this could not be real. But Marie Theresa pushed me onto the seat. She sat beside me and covered our laps with a fluffy tiger fur. We drove down Corso Buenos Aires, waving at puzzled onlookers and the passing cars that were sounding their horns. After a twenty-minute drive, the coach stopped at Ruffino."

"What's Ruffino?"

"A fashionable restaurant close to the Duomo."

"What's the Duomo?"

Angelina smiled. "Our cathedral, the most beautiful church in Italy, maybe in the world. It stands majestically on its own piazza in the middle of the old town where tourists have their pictures taken with hundreds of pigeons pecking around them, sitting on their heads and shoulders, messing on them—you know." She chuckled. "I always wonder who's the real winner in this: the tourists with that unique shot, the photographers charging a hefty fee, or the dry cleaners?"

Herman laughed. "I'd like to see the Duomo."

"I'll take you there some day, Corporal Schuller."

"And to Ruffino?"

"There, too, for their specialty, ossobuco Milanese with home-made pasta." She continued. "The dining table at Ruffino was decorated with balloons and red roses, and seated around it were our favorite models and two of my closest friends, Generale Gianotti and his wife, Barbara. Corks popped, and it was Asti Spumante, exotic foods, and more Spumante.

"At some point they brought out a large cake with a single candle and an inscription: 'Happy Anniversary, Angelina.' That was how we celebrated my first year with the Fashion House."

There was more. Attached to the cake were a deed and a declaration—the legal basis of a partnership. It brought tears and kisses. "I quickly promised to quit my waitress job at the Puccini!"

"And the sleeping room with the strict rules?" Herman surprised himself again, not meaning to sound judgmental.

Angelina pulled back and her eyes grew big. The pleasantness had left her face, though her smile still lingered. Then her smile was gone, too. She picked up her tin cup and took a hasty swallow of coffee, cold by now. She wanted to ask what he meant by that, but said instead, "Yes, I moved in with Marie Theresa. And because I can't be other than I am in front of you . . . yes, something happened between us that night." She slapped her hand over her eyes, hoping for a laugh, but he said and did nothing. She peeked between her fingers. His face was looking at the ceiling—he either didn't hear or didn't care! She sighed. Her face relaxed and her hands unclenched. Then she saw his lips shape into a small smile.

"It . . . it happened only that one time. I was not comfortable and . . . I, it . . ." Her cheeks were bright red and her voice wavered. "Well, Corporal, something had to happen sooner or later. I was twenty-one then, and I . . . I had never slept with a man."

How strange, she thought. Now that it was out in the open, she didn't mind at all. These were feelings she had expressed to no one, yet she felt surprisingly relieved now that she had. She touched the corporal's arm and looked at him, not entirely without shame but with surprising steadiness. She thought of her first love affair with a man she didn't love, how she had allowed it to happen without fighting the intrusion on her innocence.

"I had an affair with a man," she said. The words just tumbled out, and she thought, "let them"—even if she was just talking to hold back the silence.

Jacques was tall and good-looking and had that French charm. He lived in a suite at the Puccini and was a regular guest in the dining room. Jacques had perfect manners and that rare gift of making compliments without fawning. Of course he tipped well. Then, one morning, the florist brought Angelina a bouquet of red roses with a note: "I'm recalled to Paris but will see you in a month. Your Jacques." Angelina could barely wait.

"He returned on a Saturday evening just as I was about to close down the fashion shop. I was overjoyed at seeing him and did not resist his embrace. He chose several revealing gowns 'for my sister who lives in Paris,' he had said, and I didn't doubt his word."

Naively, Angelina didn't think twice about it when Jacques asked her to model the dresses in the privacy of his hotel suite. It was all arranged: the soft music, the candlelight, the champagne, and the hors d'oeuvres with expensive caviar. Deprived of her natural defenses by the champagne, Angelina fell for Jacques . . . or (as she put it) "he swept me off my feet."

"From that day on, Jacques introduced me to high society; to elite receptions, afternoon teas and feasts arranged by the Chaîne des Rôtisseurs. We were present at special opera showings at La Scala and traveled to Rome's great museums. He even flew me to Zürich— my first flight—just to dine at the Dolder Grand. I met people from high government and attachés to foreign administrations, and we dined with movie stars, newspaper editors, and politicians. It was new and exciting, a Cinderella story. We were a striking couple and the center of attention wherever we went. Jacques gave me a life I had not dreamt of even in my wildest fantasies; he showed me a world I had heard about but never seen."

Angelina took a deep breath. "Marie Theresa did not trust Jacques, but I brushed her concerns aside as signs of jealousy."

Jacques arranged a small dinner party with an older diplomat from England who had a slight crush on Angelina. "If I'm late," he had said, "start without me. I'll join you later for dessert."

"I dined with the Englishman at a nearby restaurant. He was quite charming, but something didn't feel right and we cut the dinner short. A maid found him later in his suite, shot to death, and Jacques had vanished. After depressing weeks of police scrutiny, I was finally cleared."

Silence fell again. Although he made no sign, Angelina was sure that Herman was troubled by her talk. *He must think I'm a slut, a playgirl.*

In fact, Herman was amazed by her revelation, told plainly and without fanfare. None of his girlfriends had ever been so forthright. He was a little embarrassed, but he admired her openness. He reached across the table to take her hand, knitting his fingers into hers.

"I like your Topolino," he said.

Angelina felt as if she'd been cut in half by a ray of sunshine. "I bought it from Marie Theresa after she got herself a new Porsche," she exclaimed. "First thing, I had it painted red to match my hair. I was quite an attraction."

Herman grinned. "So I noticed!" He got up, picked up the coffeepot, and dropped two more small birch logs on the fire. Angelina followed him, took the coffeepot from his hand, and refilled the two tin cups on the table.

"Thanks." Herman punctured a fresh can of condensed milk with the awl of his pocketknife and added a few drops to each cup. He wrapped his hands around his and took a sip.

Angelina thought she saw him make a face. "I'll make you some fresh," she said.

"Not necessary. It's still good."

"It's barely hot."

"It's fine."

"I don't mind."

"I'm telling you, it's okay. Sit down and enjoy yours."

"It wouldn't take but a few minutes."

"I'd rather hear more about your life."

"You would?" Angelina was astonished . . . overjoyed! . . . though she didn't dare show it. She put down the cup and pushed her chair back far enough to lean against the wall and allow her legs to cross.

To earn her diploma in fashion, Angelina had taken courses at the Scuola di Moda Burgo at Piazza San Babila, and quickly risen to the top of her class. In addition she had signed up at the *Istituto di Lingue Manzoni* to study French and German languages, and to polish up her high-school Latin.

It wasn't easy. But Angelina was determined; her schooling had priority over all else.

"I graduated with honors in all fields," she said proudly, "exceeding even my own expectations."

She rested her head against the paneled wall, contentment still shining from her eyes even as rueful thoughts began to bombard her. What future awaited her in All' Acqua? In Milan? Surely there would be a trial, maybe imprisonment. She couldn't think of it. Tears smarted behind her eyelids.

Herman saw the sudden change in her. "Are you okay?"

"It feels so good being here, sitting with you," she said. "I wish we could stay right here in this simple cabin. I know I'll have to pay for what I've done. That doesn't bother me so much. I've always been able to face the consequences of my acts, even if they're humiliating. But when my acts involve others, like my partner . . . . You see, the Fashion House will be dragged into this. It will hurt Marie Theresa, her reputation, her lifelong efforts. Oh, Corporal, tell me what to do! Tell me it won't be that bad!"

Herman rose and said soberly, "I suggest we take a walk. The fresh air will do you good."

He took her blue jacket from the chair, draped it over her shoulders and held the door open.

The high clouds had all but disappeared, and the moon shone brightly. Angelina was leading the way, and Herman followed with a leaden step. It was always like this in the presence of an attractive woman. Except there had been one big difference, heretofore: his girlfriends had been his social equals, Angelina was . . . oh, so different. Yet he wanted her, wanted to kiss her, hold her, feel her lustrous skin.

What if she pushes me away or slaps me? Maybe she would just laugh and make him feel worse than he already did.

Angelina had her own thoughts: Am I worthy of him? He's so

pure, so innocent. *Kiss me Herman; hold me tight.* She slowed her steps. He caught up and walked beside her.

"Look at the moon and the stars," he said, "aren't they magnificent tonight?"

"You must come to Milan, Herman." It was the first time she had called him by his given name. She put her arms around his waist and pulled him to her, her face close to his, her breath warm and sweet against his cheeks, her eyes wide open, her lips moist and inviting.

Teasingly slow, he ran his fingers through her hair then to the back of her neck, gently caressing her skin. His hand slid to her shoulder then to her spine, applying pressure, pulling her to him. Her breasts against his hard chest felt so good—it was all so good.

She felt his leg slide between hers till there was contact—flush. Now his lips were pushing hers apart—tenderly at first, barely touching, searching, with a teasing nibble—then ardently, hurting, burning for want of love. Their tongues were probing, pulling them into each other.

"Oh, Herman." Angelina closed her eyes and let her head drop against his shoulder. She held onto him tightly, almost reverentially, overwhelmed by contentment.

Thoughts whirled about them both, mocking their romance, if that was what it was.

He was not yet twenty-two, of medium height and build, with an average education, average intelligence, and an ordinary way about him. A cook whose prospects were yet to be determined. Yet he was creative, devoted, brave, and loving. He judged people well and had his feet on the ground.

She was almost twenty-seven, a woman in her prime. She stood tall and slender and was beautiful beyond imagination. She was skilled in her work, well educated, and her future was assured—she was a match for any man. Yet she was vulnerable to abuse, often falling victim to her honesty and willingness to please.

In spite of the odds, love kept tightening the bonds between them.

"We can make it work, I know we can!" The words just slipped from her lips in one long sigh. Angelina blushed and snuggled closer. Again, it had happened. Her mind was overflowing with joy, her heart pounding with passion, her chest tightening and robbing her of breath. She loosened her hold a little to inhale his kindness, his mannish sweetness. Bewildering feelings arose in her.

Herman sensed her tension—released his grip and held her at arm's length. "Do you want to be alone for a while? A walk by yourself might do you good, give you a chance to sort things out."

She stared at him with her big blue eyes. She felt small at the end of his stretched-out hands, confused, not truly sure what he wanted of her.

Herman pressed his hands to her cold cheeks, and his stare almost burned her eyes. "I'm serious, Angelina!" he said confidently. "Go ahead, let nature relax your heart. What you really feel inside will guide you." He kissed her on the forehead and gave her a gentle push in the direction of the pass.

Angelina was hesitant, but she trusted Herman. She started out along the moonlit trail, hesitantly at first, then with longer strides. She longed for a relationship that would make her truly happy, for that someone she could laugh with, love with, pick wildflowers with. Catching trout with him, cooking them over an open fire . . . O, *Herman, my love.* His tight embrace was with her, her lips still burned with his kisses. Her thoughts wandered back to the same question: would he take her with her faults, with her impossible behavior? Could he adapt to a lifestyle that was as demanding as it was unforgiving? Would he value her work?

My work! Her life always turned around her work and a hectic schedule that left little time for flights of emotion. What if she were convicted and thrown in prison? Would Herman wait for her? What if he asked her to give up her career—but that was entirely out of question. *Oh, I'm so selfish! What about Herman's life? Could he give up that career he is dreaming about—the resort hotel with the ponds and the fountains and the fine dining room? Would Milan bring him the happiness he is searching for in America?* He was very young, true, yet he displayed such solid maturity.

Angelina stopped walking and chuckled to herself. "What in God's heaven are you so concerned about?" Her voice rang loudly up the empty trail. She continued addressing herself in her mind. "You're not in prison, not yet—besides, you barely know Herman, and you're already worried about making plans."

But Angelina was incapable of brushing her thoughts aside; her nature was to plan, to think of the impossible, to dream of the promises. Besides, that kiss had been no ordinary kiss.

The donkeys were nervous.

"It's only me, Fuzzy," mumbled Herman. He was scratching the smallest and oldest under the neck. It responded with a snort. When he scratched it behind the ears, it rubbed its head against him. He had named this donkey Fuzzy because, in spite of its age, it still had fuzzy hair on its head that grew around the root of its ears and all but covered its eyes.

"Tell me, Fuzzy," he said, "have you ever been in a situation like mine? When you were young, did you fall in love with a mare in the neighboring pasture past a giant fence that would take years of growing up to jump? Yet your desires were then, right then—not years away!" The answer was a short snort. "I thought so; I'm not alone."

His crush on Angelina was taking on a new form, one he didn't know whether to enjoy, suppress, or shake from his mind altogether. She didn't fit the pattern of the women he had known, not even the ones he had pictured in his wildest dreams. Her deep voice and large blue eyes with the long lashes, her slender hands and stylish nails, her long red hair that flowed so lushly past her exciting breasts . . . it didn't fit. Yet there was no doubt he was falling in love, and there was nothing he could do about it.

He hopped onto the wooden fence. Would there be a chance to make it work between them, as Angelina had said? As he thought of all the odds, a sour taste built up in his mouth. There was so much against them. Her education, for one—few people he knew had the chance to go to university. From his hometown high school class, only two had gone. Should he forgo his career and settle in Milan instead of emigrating to America?

His thoughts turned to a young woman he had met in Norway. Marit had been just seventeen. She lived in Oslo close to

Vigelnad Park, where he met her late one evening. Marit was very beautiful and would not have given Herman a second look except she was drunk and had fallen over a park bench. Hard liquor was strictly forbidden in Norway. Her condition was not surprising, though, as there was a copper still in every home distilling cheap wine and sugar water. Marit was a Norwegian ice-skating champion related to Sonja Henie, whom Herman had met at the Hotel Nobel, where he worked. From that brief encounter at the park, a relationship evolved. They went to the movies and the park and picnicked at the old Olympic ski-jump site. As a close bond began to form, Herman learned of a job opening at Berns' Salonger in Stockholm—the largest restaurant in Europe—a career opportunity hard to overlook.

But he was in love. He asked his mother for advice. She wrote: "Son, your career comes first! How else could you support such a relationship? If your love is deep and true, it will survive time or distance, even oceans!"

Herman had learned quickly that their love wasn't strong enough to survive even a short time and a short distance.

Angelina walked west and suddenly felt alone with the moon and the stars—and the future. It made perfect sense to her at the moment to think that the moon and the stars could answer her questions about the corporal, so she asked them. What are my chances? Is there a future for us? Will we be together soon, the way I hope and pray we will be?

Not even a bashful cough answered her, yet asking the questions had calmed her and made it easier to contemplate a future that was as exciting as it was uncertain. She wandered farther up the trail, but as she neared the mountains the tension reappeared in all its fury until she could hold back no longer. She stopped and faced the valley, and, making a megaphone of her hands, shouted at the top of her lungs. "O God, dear God, please help me! I am falling in love and I cannot help myself! I feel so wonderful, so magnificently fulfilled! What shall I do?" Her voice echoed across the valley.

Herman smiled when he heard the faint echo of her outcry. He heard her steps descending the stone path, heard the heels of her shoes grinding on the rock. Powerless to conceal his feelings, he rushed up the trail to meet her.

The moment Angelina saw Herman she ran up to him and passionately kissed his eyes, his cheeks, his lips. Her eyes were bright and her cheeks rosy. Her body shivered, aching to be touched by love. Herman was stunned by the onslaught, reacting slowly.

"I love you, Herman, yes, I love you . . . I don't know how or why . . . but I love you, I love you, I love you!" She paused to look at him with her shining eyes. "Do you love me too, Liebling?"

Liebling—darling! No girl had ever called him that. It sounded like some exquisitely beautiful Marlene Dietrich line, a word worthy of love.

"If I ever have a child," she continued, turning crimson, "I want it to be from you!" She was embarrassingly sincere, and to attest to her statement, she kissed him again long and passionately, pulling him tightly to her. "Oh, Herman, I love you. Tell me that you love me, too."

His voice was a surprising whisper, almost a croak. "I do, Angelina. I love you." He squeezed her tightly, taking her breath away. "You're desirable, Angelina, my love, oh, so desirable, but here . . . this just isn't the time or place."

She sighed softly. "I know. The time isn't right."

Arm in arm, they strolled back to the cabin, stopping to kiss again and again.

"Are you surprised, darling?" asked Angelina. "I mean, have you thought you could love me?"

"Yes."

"Is that a 'yes yes,' or just a yes?"

"It's a definite 'yes yes,' my love."

"Oh, I'm so happy! Are you happy too?"

He smiled and said, "Very happy. That's a 'very very' happy!"

"You're making fun of me, Herman," she said, sounding disappointed.

"That would be the last thing on my mind."

"I know you love me. I can feel it. You're so wonderful." She stopped and held him back to fling her arms around him and kiss him again. "Oh Herman . . ."

A cluck from the chicken coop behind the cabin disturbed the quiet. Angelina loosened her grip and pointed at the ripped wire mesh. "I could have sworn I heard that racket when we first got here!"

Herman grinned. "I wonder how these birds survive the foxes, the night owls, and the hawks, much less hungry travelers like us."

"I don't know, but where there are chickens, there must be eggs." She roamed around the cage with Herman close behind.

"Look, sweetheart, I found the nest and there *are* eggs." He quickly put five eggs in his cap while the provider clucked in protest.

"And here are wild onions—chives," said Angelina, thrilled at her find.

"What are you going to do with them?" Herman teased. "Put them in your ears?"

"Hush." She pinched his arm. "I saw crushed corn in the pantry; let's cook some good Italian polenta for your soldier friends."

Angelina started back inside, then turned around. She pulled him to her and kissed him on the lips.

"Watch it," he cautioned. "The eggs—I nearly dropped them."

She smiled. "I'll sacrifice these eggs any day for this." She kissed him again.

They made it inside with the green onions and the eggs intact. In no time, she had the fire rekindled, and breakfast was being made.

"Chop the onions for me, Herman darling," she said, "I've done enough crying for one day. And while you're at it, cut me a few slices from that side of bacon."

"Yes, my dear," he said, and laughed. He brought a chair to step up on and cut a sizable slice off the bacon with his pocketknife.

Soon the air was filled with the smell of fried bacon and onions and freshly brewed coffee.

Hands on hips, Angelina said, "I need cheese; it is not polenta without cheese! Herman, find me some cheese!"

It was a simple demand, but Herman couldn't help wondering what his attitude might be after a few years with this woman. Fortunately, he still had a wedge of the Mendali cheese in his pack. He cut it into small pieces.

"You're a genius, darling," she said, looking over his shoulder. "Thank you." She gave him a grateful hug and kiss.

"Hey, cut that out! You're not alone!" cried Feldweibel Ott, rising from the bunk.

"Did you people get any sleep?" asked Lieutenant Stucki, sitting up and wiping his eyes.

Angelina smiled. "Who needs sleep when there's love? Come on, boys, get up and join us for some good old-fashioned Italian polenta."

The officers came forward out of hunger even before they'd voiced their assent, as this polenta represented the first hot meal they had eaten in some time.

Sunrise brought life, color, and warmth to the hazy valley. The young sentry was still cold. The heck with regulations, he thought. He leaned the rifle against the concrete wall and flapped his arms. But he was tense. He looked from left to right as his comrade patrolled the road, rifle at his hip and eyes nervously on the creek and trail below. Occasionally the sentry on the road stopped, removed his helmet, and listened. But there was little to be heard above the noisy creek.

The soldiers were jittery. The events of two nights before had put the company on high alert. News of the incident had spread through the camps like a roaring fire. One account described an attack launched by the Italian military to test Swiss readiness; another had it as a prank by a rival company to embarrass their unit. The most popular rumor pointed to the notorious Italian Mafioso Giuliano, who needed the ammo for his fight against the *carabinieri*. It was rumored he was coming back to clean out the hand grenades, which would suit his personality. In Switzerland, Giuliano was a hero for his fight against authority, known mostly from a pumped-up feature story that had been a favorite in the magazine *Schweizer Illustrierte*. The fact that Salvatore Giuliano had been killed years ago at the hands of his own alliance seemed to have escaped the young, over-reacting minds.

Suddenly the sentry on the road stopped in his tracks and crouched. He tightened his grip on the rifle and pointed it toward the creek.

As he had been trained to do, the soldier at the bunker quickly climbed the hill above and hid behind a bush, ready to give cover to his friend below. He now, too, heard what sounded like hoofbeats above the creek's noise. The soldier's mind raced. Should he alert the guardhouse? *And embarrass myself like the previous patrol?* No way. Those warning shots had triggered a major alarm that later pointed to a trigger-happy sentry frightened by a herd of deer. No, they could handle this.

There was movement on the trail. "It's them," said the sentry to his friend below, a chill surging through him. With frightened amazement, he saw donkeys loaded with boxes led by men in uniform turn a bend on the trail, and there was a woman in the rear, just as the rumor had it. The sentry lifted the helmet from his forehead, wiped his eyes, disengaged the safety on his rifle, and aimed at the last man in the column. "Always shoot the last goose of a flock first," he remembered his instructor lecturing.

"It's okay, soldier—they are friends," said a calm voice behind him. A hand pushed the barrel of his rifle to the side. Pale as a ghost, the soldier jumped to his feet, his wits almost gone. He saluted with a trembling hand.

"Easy, soldier," said Lieutenant Stucki, who couldn't suppress a chuckle. "You only did what you're supposed to do. Only—next time keep an eye to your rear."

The sentries helped carry the ammo boxes back to storage.

Feldweibel Ott was in a good mood. "I'll be a monkey'sch uncle," he said after the door was closed. "No one can ever tell that an exchange took place."

Lieutenant Stucki added, "All's well that ends well." He turned to Herman Schuller and slapped the corporal's shoulder. "Well done, soldier. Well done, Herman!"

Herman nodded. He had not given it much thought until this very moment, and now that it was over, he felt somewhat let down. Oh, he was more than pleased the way things had turned out, but something precious had ended, too. He looked to Angelina, who sat on the shoulder beside the road, the rope of the lead animal wrapped around her wrist. He walked across the road.

"The animals need oats and water," said Angelina. "All they've had for the past three days has been grass and hay, and not much of that."

Herman agreed. "Signora Monika, uh, that's the farmwoman by the barracks—"

"I know Monika," Angelina said with a surprised look.

Herman smiled. "That woman seems to be getting around. Anyway, I'm sure she'll let us have a bucket or two of oats."

Lieutenant Stucki walked up to them. "Feldweibel Ott and I will find out what has taken place at camp while we were gone," he said. "We'll keep you posted. Let's meet at the tavern at, shall we say, about 0900?"

The two officers returned the guards' salutes and left for the barracks.

Signora Monika was only too happy to provide a sack of oats.

"You really like the corporal, do you?" asked Monika while Herman was in the barn.

"Oh, I do, I do." Angelina reached to her hair instinctively.

"He is a nice guy, and a blind man could see that he has a crush on you."

"I don't know how it got started, Monika, but I think I've fallen in love!" Angelina blushed. "There's something about Herman that makes me shiver every time he puts his hands on me."

Monika chuckled. "You have it bad, Angelina. Still, he's younger than you . . . ."

"I never gave it a thought. Herman's mature for his age."

Monika turned to hide a giggle. "You going permanent? I mean, what's in the future?"

Angelina shrugged. "We haven't talked about it. Maybe . . . for him . . . this is just a fling."

Monika detected sadness. "Would Herman move to Milan?"

"I doubt that. Herman wants to pursue a career of his own; besides, and you might call it a woman's intuition, I have the feeling he's spoken for. I think he has a girl in Basel."

Herman leaned against the fence at the far corner of the barn, observing the two women (who did much of the talking with their hands). Angelina had removed her scarf and wore her hair loosely over her shoulders, exactly the way he liked it. Her blue jacket, zipped halfway, showed her bosom, and her tightly fitted waist made her appear especially slim and tall. She was so beautiful, so mature, and yet so terribly innocent, too. He blinked repeatedly to sharpen his vision. And as he watched Angelina his chest tightened, his breath quickened, and his lips burned for want of her.

I should be happy, jump up and down ecstatically, and cherish her love. Yet he could not. Deep down was the sadness of knowing that this fairy tale journey would end. In a few hours, she would be back in Milan with her partner and her work, with her modeling and her high society. Herman had no doubt she would resolve her legal problems with her brains and her charm—and the help of powerful friends. And while her thoughts of him faded, he would command his squad, shoot tracer bullets, carry his heavy pack, and dream of her lovely face and tender lips. His insides churned. Would fate be kind to him? Would she ever again let him feel the loveliness of her lips, the intoxicating sweetness of her skin? Would she bring back the sparkle of her eyes—

"Corporal Schuller? Corporal?" Monika was tapping on his shoulder.

"Monika wants to say goodbye," said Angelina.

"Yes, uh, thanks for the oats, Monika," he said. "That was very nice of you. But then, of course, I knew I could count on you."

"Pleasure's mine. See you around camp. Ciao."

Angelina shook Monika's hand. "Ciao, Monika."

"Ciao!" said Herman melancholically.

Herman removed the rope from Fuzzy's halter. The donkey rubbed his head against his shoulder and waited patiently until the others were freed.

Herman slapped their rumps. "Get going, you faithful creatures. You have done your duty!" The animals cantered toward the creek.

"Are you sure they'll find their way back home?"

"They're smart animals. I have no doubt that they will. I'm sure the owner, whoever he is, will be happy to have them back."

Released of their cargo, the donkeys trotted freely down the road. After a short stretch, they stopped and turned their heads. Angelina waved them on and they took off at a slow gallop. They crossed the road headed off on the trail along the creek.

"Someday, I will own a few of these creatures," said Herman dreamily.

Angelina took out her handkerchief and wiped tears from her eyes. Soon it would be their turn to say goodbye. Arm in arm, in utter silence, they walked the short stretch to the *gasthaus*.

The chubby woman with the tight skirt was most generous. She not only allowed Angelina to use the upstairs bathroom but also gave her a fresh towel and a bar of soap. "There should be enough hot water left in the boiler, sweetie."

Herman showed Angelina the way up the stairs. He slipped into his room, then returned and walked with Angelina down the hall to the bathroom. He handed over his toiletry case. "Here," he said with a grin. "I have only this one toothbrush, but you're welcome to it."

"Thank you, darling. I'll take good care of it."

There were still embers under the hot-water heater. Herman put two small logs on, then crouched and blew on the cinders until fresh flames licked through the new wood. He closed the little grate and pushed the air flap to the halfway mark.

The water was as hot as the chubby woman had said it would be, and Angelina adjusted the faucets until she had a pleasant mix.

"I think you're all set," said Herman. "I'll see you downstairs."

Angelina took his hand to her lips. "You're so sweet, Herman," she said. "I won't be long at all. You'll see."

Angelina rolled up the towel at the edge of the tub, nestled her head onto it, and slid under the water up to her chin. It was her first bath in several days. Soaking in steam, she let her body sink deep into itself, allowing her thoughts to wander.

Suddenly, it dawned on her. Herman had known from the start what he wanted from that staged negotiation, and the dialogue between him and the colonnello was pure theatrics—she, Angelina, had been on his mind from the very first. He would have had no one else on that trail with him.

Oh Herman, you thought of me all along! A tingle shot up her spine, then another and another. It was a feeling she never before had felt so strongly, and it felt so good. *Oh Herman, oh my sweet love, will I see you again? Will our love bring us together to share our lives, to share in its pleasures?* The tingle spread to her legs, her arms, her breasts. A pleasant moan escaped her. Was this feeling what the poets call "true love?"

All' Acqua was deserted except for a squad of sentries, its young corporal at the guardhouse and the medic on duty at the field hospital. It was a few minutes after nine when Angelina, looking her best, and Herman Schuller, clean-shaven, entered the tavern. The two officers were at the window table set with cheese, butter, preserves, and croissants, and two pots of milk and coffee.

Lieutenant Stucki gestured for Angelina to sit in the chair in front of him. Angelina did as she was told, returning the lieutenant's smile.

He stood up, took a step back, straightened his shoulders, and with a voice of authority said, "Under the powers entrusted in me through the white cross . . . As an officer and a gentleman . . . being of sound mind . . . in view of *all* the evidence and lack of such, and taking full consideration of all circumstances"—the lieutenant took a fresh breath—"I hereby declare the case of the missing ammo closed."

There was a moment of pregnant silence. "The accused is free to go!"

Angelina turned to Herman. He nodded favorably, and she let out a high-pitched giggle. Jumping to her feet, she embraced the young lieutenant with all her might. "Thank you. Thank all of you!" She threw her arms around the feldweibel. "You're wonderful. You all are wonderful!" She kissed his cheeks. Then she put her arms around the corporal and kissed his lips, whispering, "Thank you, Herman darling, thank you for everything."

CHAPTER 10

$\mathcal{T}$he sun had dissolved the last shreds of mist over All' Acqua, and the air coming in at the window was warm and pleasant as the four-seat Fiat rumbled down the mountain road. Lieutenant Stucki was at the wheel, Feldweibel Ott in the passenger seat, and Angelina and Herman in the rear. The drive to Lozone would take two hours; from there the border was another twenty minutes. There was little talk.

Angelina was leaning against the corporal's shoulder, hands knitted into his, juggling indescribable happiness with deep sorrow. Was this the last chapter of their journey? Why should it end? Why couldn't they be cuddled close together another few hours? One more day—was that too much to ask? A cramping pain was steadily crowding her heart. *Oh, Herman, I can't leave you. Not now.* She closed her eyes, and with a sigh dropped her head against his chest.

Herman could only guess what was in Angelina's mind. He felt her love, but had never stopped feeling the gap in their social status. He tried to push it away and not think of it, but it was all he could think of: how different they were. He let the strands of her soft, rich hair flow between his fingers. Would he ever feel that loveliness again? He glanced at his watch—only an hour and thirty minutes to go, too little time to give love a chance. Tears began to burn in his eyes and there was a lump in his throat.

Even with her eyes closed, Angelina filled his world with her sunshine. He sensed the rise and fall of her chest—she was asleep, her first rest in two days. Herman leaned back in the seat. He looked a long time at her silk cheeks, and her eyebrows thin like pencil lines elegantly sweeping down to that narrow nose where her tiny nostrils showed her breathing.

Reverently, almost shyly, he bent down and kissed her eyelids and her nose, and the fleet response beneath her skin tickled his lips. Then, as the car moved left and right in a kind of rhythm through the endless curves, Herman, too, succumbed to sleep.

The rifle sight was right on target. The corporal squeezed the trigger . . . but the target blurred, and out of it emerged two fiery eyes, blue as the sky flying toward him at lightning speed.

Herman snapped from his sleep, his eyes wide open—he didn't know where he was. His head was at Angelina's chest; he had been unaware of their change of position.

Angelina smoothed his hair. "You had a dream, darling," she said softly, pressing his head harder to her chest.

He sat back and clutched her cheeks. "Your eyes, I will always dream about your eyes," he said. His stare and the intensity of his voice almost frightened her, and Angelina knew she had been part of his dream. She cherished that thought, but the pain still wrenched her heart.

"Oh Herman, does it have to end?"

Herman buried his hand in her hair. "I guess it will have to end somewhere."

She touched his cheek. "But why so soon? Why does it have to end at all?"

He kept at her hair. "I don't know, my sweet love. It's out of our hands now; I truly don't know why."

"Oh, Herman, I love you so! I have never felt this way before."

Herman didn't know what to say. It would end no matter what he said. The silence hung heavy between them.

At last, Angelina had the courage to say what had been preying on her mind. "If your visa comes through, Herman, are you really going to America?"

"That's the plan."

Why are you so quick about it! Anger flared in her. "America is all you think about. You don't love me, not really; all you think about is going away, running away from me, away from our love. I can't take it, Herman, you must change your mind." Her eyes were blazing, her hands trembling. Herman said nothing, and his silence shook her to the core. "Oh, Herman, I don't want to quarrel, it's just I . . . I can't think of losing you. My country is healing from its war wounds rapidly. Could you imagine living in Milan?"

"Yes, I could, and I will come to Milan and spend my future at your side." How he wanted to say those words, but he didn't, he couldn't. He just stared out of the window at the rushing landscape, thinking of her beauty and her love, of the short hours they had spent together. *Wake up, wake up!* This woman was not for him—she belonged to all the people; she belonged to high society.

"You're not answering me, darling. Could you live in my country?" Her voice was very soft.

Instead of answering, he said, "My sweet Angelina, you have your duties in Milan. You have your fashion shop, your partner, and your modeling career. These are your choices, and you could never walk away from them. The military, for one, made my choice. But I have my own choices, too, such as hotel school, family, dreams of a career . . . and America."

Angelina shook her head. "Sometimes, Herman, you are a most difficult man to understand." She knew in her heart that Herman was right, that he was saying exactly what she lacked the courage to admit. Almost timidly, she said, "Does that mean we should separate for good?"

All of a sudden it became important to him to use exactly the right words. He caressed her cheek while he thought what to say. He thought of his mother's advice, her ideas about true love, and the words came. He pushed her gently from him, groped for her hands, and held them gently. His eyes were steady on her, warm, and quite unblinking.

"You'll always be in my thoughts, Angelina; in that way we'll never be apart." He paused. "If your love for me is built merely on gratitude—or if my love for you is only for your beauty—then the roots of our love are shallow, and it will fade soon. Yet if our love is deep and true, if God wants us to be in love, if destiny has played its hand, then no power on earth can keep us apart for long—no frontier, not even oceans. If fate wants us back together, my sweet

Angelina, there will be a way for that to happen."

She did not answer. But she *did* understand, and her heart was no less troubled. Silence hung heavy in the little car.

Lieutenant Stucki stopped at a small grocery. "Let's get Hans a present," he said. Everybody thought it was a brilliant idea, and soon they had a large wicker basket filled with sausage, cheese, chocolate, oranges, and bananas. Angelina did her own browsing in the back of the store.

The hospital was on a plateau overlooking Lago Maggiore, whose surface glittered as if strewn with shiny confetti. They parked in the driveway and took the elevator to the second floor.

"Good evening, Hans; you have a visitor," said Lieutenant Stucki upon opening the door.

The soldier grinned from ear to ear and used the grab bar above him to pull himself up. His grin turned to surprise when he saw Corporal Schuller enter the room. "You made it, Corp! I'll be goddamned, you made it," cried Hans Rüegg. "I heard you were after them, and I just knew you'd get back in one piece! No hoodlums could get the best of you! D'you teach those thugs a lesson?"

Herman burst out laughing, overjoyed to see his friend in such good spirits. He sat on the side of the bed and shook the soldier's hand. "You'll hear about it soon enough, Hans. For now, I want to know how you feel. Boy, have you worried us! I never thought . . . "

"The damsel!" interrupted Hans Rüegg. "The chic dame from Bedretto with the red Topolino, who gave you a ride, though you wouldn't admit it! But Corp, what is she doing here?"

Angelina moved close to the bed and shook his hand. Her voice was deep and sweet. "I'm Angelina." She took the corporal's place at the edge of the bed and took his hand warmly in hers. "Your strong voice is telling me that you're back among the living. Now, tell me, soldier, how are you?"

"I . . . I'm okay. But . . . but what's this all about? What are you doing here?"

Angelina patted his arm. "Don't exert yourself, soldier. Corp will tell you all about me later. I'm so sorry about what happened to you."

"Sorry? Why should you be sorry for me?"

Angelina could hold back no longer. A tear slid down her cheek. "I'm partly responsible . . ."

Hans pulled back his hand. "Responsible? What is this? Tell me, Corp, what is this all about?"

Herman could only grin at his friend's reaction. "It's okay, Hans. I'll fill you in later."

Angelina said, "Relax, soldier, everything's fine now. Take my word for it."

"Yes," added Herman, "everything's okay. Angelina is a wonderful woman, and all you need to know right now is that she cares as deeply about you as we do."

Feldweibel Ott brought out the fruit basket and pushed away a newspaper to set it on the nightstand. He removed the red ribbon from the handle and peeled away the cellophane wrapper. "Here," he said, "We all pitched in, including Angelina."

Out of nowhere, Angelina brought out a brown paper carrier bag. This was opened; a bottle of wine removed and handed over with the label facing up. "And this is from me," she said with the sweetest smile.

Rüegg looked from the bottle to her face. "I . . . I'm stunned, don't know what to say," he stuttered. "And a bottle of Barbera; I'll be damned."

"It's your favorite, is it not?" asked Angelina. "I heard you brag about it at that tavern in Bedretto."

A nurse came in. "Is one of you Corporal Herman?" she asked.

Herman stood up, surprised to hear his name. "That's me, I guess," he said.

"You have a phone call. You can take it at the nurses' desk." She walked out the door. Herman pointed at himself questionably, and raised his shoulders. Who would call him here? Who even knew he was at the hospital?

He picked up the phone. The voice at the other end was female, speaking German with a heavy Italian accent. "Are you Herman?"

"Yes, but I don't—"

"You don't know me, yet you might have heard of me." She paused a moment. "Please meet me downstairs," she continued urgently. "I'll be waiting in the lounge by the registration desk, in front of the elevators." She paused. There was an uneasy silence. He knew she was still on line as he could hear her breathing. "Corporal, this is very private," she said guardedly. "I don't want you to tell anyone about meeting me. Please tell no one, and hurry." She hung up without waiting for his response.

Herman walked back to the room and excused himself, then hurried to the elevator.

The moment the elevator opened, a woman stood up from the sofa across the waiting room. She was dressed in a black pantsuit and wore exceptionally tall high heels. A light, black cashmere coat was draped over the sofa backrest. She had elegance and style, the looks of a movie star. The buttons of her jacket were open, showing a white blouse with a stitched collar and a generous amount of cleavage. A black scarf hid part of her black hair, and her gloved left hand held the other full-length black glove. Her long fingernails were filed to perfect ovals and painted deep red to match her large, moist lips. She could have come from a funeral, except she looked sensationally beautiful.

Herman judged her to be in her late thirties but knew she had to be older. Except for her black hair and dark eyes, she markedly resembled Angelina.

As soon as she spotted Herman Schuller, she rushed to him and hugged him. Overwhelmed, he let his arms dangle at his side, though tempted to grab her around her tiny waist. Her perfume was heavenly, adding to her allure; Herman had come to know it well.

She sat down on the divan and gestured for him to sit beside her. She was obviously tense, and her deep voice trembled a little, which she tried to hide. "I'm Marie Theresa Mosani, Angelina's partner."

Herman had sensed who she was the moment he laid eyes on her, but he showed surprise nonetheless, his face flushing. "I'm Herman Schuller, and I'm speechless. I'm sure you understand, signora."

"Angelina must never learn of this meeting, Herr Schuller," she said. "I want your promise!" She waited until Herman nodded. "Angelina called from All' Acqua. She told me all about you—your deeds and how she feels about you. She thinks a great deal of you, Corporal, as I'm sure you know." She reached for his hand, and when she resumed talking her voice had put on warmth. "I'm so grateful to you, Herr Schuller, for what you have done for Angelina. You are very brave. I don't know how to thank you."

Herman blushed; he'd never thought of himself as brave. "How in the world did you know where to find us?"

Marie Theresa played with the collar of her blouse, rolled the hem between her fingers, and then flattened it. "Angelina told me about your planned visit to the military hospital in Lozone—that poor soldier. I had the sudden desire to talk to you, and the moment Angelina hung up I left Milan. I got here just in time to see you step into the elevator. I'm going to meet Angelina later at the border crossing in Brissago."

Herman rubbed his neck. "But what can I do for you, signora?" he asked. "Are you sure you don't want to talk to Angelina? I'll get her for you."

She gripped his arm, held him back. "No, please. Angelina should never learn of this talk."

"But—"

Marie Theresa tightened her grip. "Please," she repeated sternly. "I worry about my partner and what might happen to her after this thing." She threw up her free hand in frustration while keeping the pressure on his arm. "Angelina is very fond of you, Corporal, and I don't want her to get hurt."

Herman was not sure what she meant, but her devotion to her partner impressed him. "I would never hurt Angelina," he said truthfully.

"I'm sure that's not your intention, Corporal," she said with a nod. "Angelina will be under much stress until this is over; she becomes easily vulnerable when stressed, and I want to make sure—" she gripped his arm even tighter, her sharp nails hurting him through the fabric—"that no one takes advantage of her. You don't know Angelina as well as I do. She is honest and trusting, in many ways as innocent as a child. We have been a team for many years. I don't want anything to come between us."

Herman squirmed. "Come between us?" he asked cunningly. Angelina had talked about Marie Theresa's tendency to be jealous. "Do you mean between us like in business, or do you mean in a more personal sense?"

His directness made Marie Theresa uneasy. But she saw there was nothing devious in him. *There's something about this young soldier that*

I *like*. Marie Theresa decided to be straightforward. "Both, Corporal, both. I don't want anything to come between us."

"You don't want anything to spoil your intimacy." He instantly regretted his bluntness. His face turned even redder than her fingernails.

Marie Theresa let go of his arm and, for a moment, was speechless. "Corporal!" she said sharply. "How do you know about this?" She said it almost viciously but quickly smoothed her tone. She bit her lip, said collectedly, "Yes, there was intimacy. But that's all in the past. Angelina is like a daughter to me now."

Herman sighed with relief. But there had to be more. "There must be more to this to justify your presence, signora."

"There is," she said sadly. "I have a heart condition I inherited from my father. My most recent exam revealed further deterioration. Angelina does not know that I might die before the end of the year." She closed her eyes and took a deep breath. "I'm determined to keep it secret from her as long as I can."

"That's not fair to Angelina," Herman babbled. "She ought to know!"

"Knowing about my condition wouldn't change a thing. I see no reason why she should worry about something only our good Lord can reverse."

Herman felt tightness in his throat. The signora's revelation left him stunned. He thought of Angelina's love and respect for Marie Theresa and how such news would affect her. The silence tore at his conscience—why had he made that earlier, idiotic remark. And then, what was the purpose of her telling him? "I am so terribly sorry," was all he could think of saying.

Marie Theresa put her hand on his arm. "Don't be," she said. "I can cope with my dilemma, but I worry about Angelina and what will happen to her once I'm gone." She swallowed as if unsure how to go on—Marie Theresa had never talked of this to anyone. She didn't know anything about this young man, except that something about him gave her confidence, an unprecedented trust. Could he provide the stability Angelina needed? "Unknown to Angelina, I have placed all my business interests in a trust for her. And since I have no worthy relatives, I have willed all my other holdings to her as well. But . . . it will be difficult for her to carry on even under the best of circumstances.

She once had an unfortunate affair, and I worry that she will fall into such a trap again. In a word, I want to know how deeply you two are involved. After all, Angelina is mature, and you seem quite young."

How dare you mix in your partner's personal life, Herman thought. "I love Angelina," he said defensively.

Marie Theresa chose not to respond. She sensed that he mistook her concern for interference. Maybe she *was* sticking her nose in.

"Angelina and I have decided to break up," said Herman suddenly. Marie Theresa looked up astonished. He continued. "The differences between us are just too great. Neither wants the other to sacrifice career or give up anything sacred. As you can see, signora, your worries are unfounded."

Marie Theresa was impressed. This young man was more grown up than she had thought. Now she was sorry she had doubted him. She thought, but did not say, that the Fashion House could easily support the two of them. But so many questions remained that would influence the future.

Marie Theresa took a deep breath. "This thing, of which I know almost nothing, will surely have grave consequences. What is going to happen to my partner?"

Herman shrugged. "I have talked to Colonnello Zanardelli—"

"Vitt Zanardelli? I know Vitt," interrupted Marie Theresa.

"I thought you did," said Herman. "I heard him talk about a fashion show he attended at the Galleria." Herman mused for a second. "The colonnello thinks there's a good chance of keeping Angelina out of prison."

"Prison? My partner is going to prison?" shrieked Marie Theresa.

"Please relax," he said in a take-charge voice, not surprised by her reaction. "No one thinks it will come to that. But there is a price to pay. Angelina might be called as a witness. It is her decision, though."

"What's there to be decided?"

"First, she'd have to admit to the crime. Then it would be up to a judge to extend clemency. Since Angelina is friends with some of the accused, testifying against them might prove difficult for her. We have not discussed this at any length, as I'm afraid Angelina would follow my suggestions blindly. Better if she decides on her own." Herman perked up. "On the other hand you, signora, would be in a better position to reach out and give her advice. And I beg you to discuss it with her seriously."

"I shall, I shall!" Marie Theresa's eyes began to sparkle. "Yes, I will talk to Angelina, and I will also talk to Vitt. You can count on me, Corporal." Her hand groped for his; found it and squeezed.

A shiver shot to Herman's neck—was he attracted to Marie Theresa? Without thinking, the words rolled off his lips. "You're very attractive, signora! Angelina was right, you're exceptionally beautiful." His unintended admission turned his face into a fireball. Embarrassed, he pulled back his hand and stood. "If there's nothing else I can do for you, signora, I would like to go back to my friends now."

Marie Theresa smiled at his youthful bashfulness. "I can see now why Angelina feels so strongly for you." She stood up and looked into his eyes. Then she pinched his cheeks with both hands and gave him a friendly kiss on the mouth. "Not a word, Corporal, you must promise!" She pulled a handkerchief from her purse and wiped the color from his lips.

Herman walked to the elevator, turned, and looked one more time at the beautiful woman. Her eyes sparkled, the beautiful smile was still on her lips, and her bosom was inviting. She waved her handkerchief until the elevator door closed behind him.

"Here you are! We began to wonder where you were!" Hans Rüegg joked as Herman came back into the room. "The lieutenant told me all there is to know, and the next time you wander about on your own, Corp,"—he pointed at Angelina— "I demand you take me along for personal protection."

Angelina laughed wholeheartedly, her old self again. Seeing her happy was all that mattered to him.

The drive along Lago Maggiore passed quickly, like an unfulfilled dream. No one spoke. The two lovers had said everything that needed to be said; more talk could only make it worse. They were in each other's arms with cramps in their stomachs and tightness in their chests. All the kisses could not make up for the love that would soon be missing from their lives. The collar of his shirt was damp from Angelina's tears, and he gently kissed her wet eyes. The border neared all too quickly.

The Fiat passed the first houses of the romantically unique border town, Brissago. Lieutenant Stucki slowed and then stopped on the promenade a block from the international boundary. He suggested they walk the rest of the way.

"This is it," said Herman, slowing his steps. He kissed the tears from her eyes, as he had done so many times before.

Angelina shivered. "Is this really the end, Herman?"

"Not the end, my dear Angelina. There will never be an end."

"It feels like the end; my tight chest and confused mind say so."

"I'll always think of you, my love."

"But we won't be together. Oh, Herman, I can't leave you now."

"We'll be together in thought." He held her at arm's length, longing to see her beautiful body. "I'll never forget you, Angelina. I can't." His voice was a mere croak.

They hugged and kissed and wiped each other's tears, making every step count. The soft touch of his voice, even more than the meaning of his words, had a calming effect.

From the corner of his eye, Herman caught a glimpse of Marie Theresa showing her passport to the Swiss Guard. "This must be your partner," he said somberly.

Angelina turned around, and her eyes sparkled. She rushed to her partner, all but dragging Herman behind her. The women hugged and kissed.

"Marie Theresa, this is Herman Schuller; he's the corporal I was telling you about."

Marie Theresa gave Herman a hug, then pinched his arm as a reminder of their secret.

A last hug, a last kiss, a few last words—"Oh, my sweet Herman, oh my darling,"—and the two women crossed the border arm in arm.

A new black Porsche convertible with white leather seats was parked at the curb beyond the border. A final smile, a final tear, a final wave, and the convertible sped away. It was quickly out of sight on the road which wound beside the glittering surface of Lago Maggiore.

PART TWO

September 1956 came in cold and dry. Geneva wore a silver coat of frost that quickly thawed under a warm sun. It was a cloudless, almost perfect Saturday afternoon. Along the lake, sunbathers stretched out on bleachers to soak up the season's final warmth. As the sun got low in the sky, the wind picked up and the cold was back. With a deafening roar, the Jet d'Eau surged for the sky, bent downwind like a coachman's whip, and plunged thunderously back into the gray lake.

Beyond the billowing mist, the magnificent skyline of Geneva was silhouetted against a cloudless sunset. A million lights sprang to life to brighten city streets and parks, residential neighborhoods, posh hotels, and famous restaurants. Jazz enlivened the nightspots where sudden explosions of laughter and Dom Pérignon could be heard as the very rich chatted and pampered themselves with caviar, langouste Thermidor, Dover sole, and thick Cuban cigars.

Marble steps beneath a dimly lit porte cochère led to the stylish Du Nord, a restaurant that was famous for its elegance. The doorman tipped his top hat, his coattails swaying as he opened the car doors of well-to-do guests who were arriving in search of another epicurean adventure. The slick maître d'hôtel took over and led his guests to the comfortable tables where they would spend the next few hours being feted and cosseted.

The chef de cuisine announced the orders—"*Deux carrés d'agneau à point avec les asperges au Mousseline—deux tournedos Rossini saignants et des pommes Dauphine*"—and the cooks went to work.

Herman Schuller liked his job. This kitchen, with its renowned chef, was the perfect place to further his career. Well known in elite society, the Du Nord's *Salon Rouge* and *Salon Bleu* were Geneva's most stylish dining spots. Many of its guests were in the city to do business at the Palais des Nations, and many were from the United States. This pleased young Schuller, as his visa to America was only a matter of time, and he was eager to meet people from his future home.

It was a typical Saturday, hectic all day with a brutal evening rush. Herman, late for a date with his girl, hurried out the Du Nord entrance, turned the corner—and bumped into a giant. Herman bounced back and hit the asphalt.

"*Pardonnez-moi, s'il vous plaît!*" said the broad-shouldered stranger in strongly American-accented French. He tipped his wide-brimmed Western hat, bent down, and helped the gawky youngster to his feet.

"Are you hurt?" asked a woman in the background. When he didn't answer, she asked, "Do you speak any English?"

Herman looked in the direction of the deep female voice—and almost swallowed his tongue. Her black evening dress hugged her slender body, and a silver fox coat was draped over her bare shoulders. She was tall to begin with, but her satin high-heels made her just about as tall as her huge escort.

Waiting for an answer, she couldn't help a chuckle. "W-e-l-l?"

In preparation for his trip to America, Herman had taken a correspondence course in English. Now that he had a chance to use what he had learned, however, he couldn't think of a thing to say. Instead, he blushed from head to toe, triggering more chuckles from the lady. He brushed the dust from his pants. "A little, uh, I speak English a little," he stammered.

"I'm Marvel, and this is my husband, John. We're from Texas," said the lady. She extended her right hand. As she leaned forward, her fur slid off her shoulder, exposing her ample bosom and pale skin.

Herman swallowed. "I'm Herman Schuller," he said, "a cook here at the Du Nord." This time, he didn't stammer. He clasped her hand firmly and managed to say, "It is a pleasure meeting you, Lady Marvel."

Lady Marvel? The woman muffled a chuckle but did nothing to correct him.

John, an officer of the United States Air Corps, was in Geneva on diplomatic assignment. He was a physical giant with a naturally dark complexion. He stood out because of his broad shoulders, hands the size of baseball gloves, and his thin-lipped, ruggedly handsome face. He was friendly by nature and loved to talk about business in a deep, croaky voice that was sometimes difficult for Herman to understand because of a strong Texas accent.

Marvel accompanied him on his extended trips abroad. She loved to roam the French boutiques and lively bazaars, shop the exclusive jewelry stores, and dine at Geneva's renowned restaurants. Besides being elegant and beautiful, Herman found her to be as friendly as her husband, and never tired of listening to her dreamy talks about her parents' cattle ranch a hundred or so miles west of San Antonio. "The most lavish spot in Texas"—it was where she had been born and raised.

For the next few weeks—on Herman's days off from work— they met for cocktails, bistro dining, and language practice. John was fond of a cozy place in Vieux Ville, the L'Escargot Sauvage—the Wild Snail—known for the spicy treat that gave it its name. It wasn't clear then whether the bistro's escargots or John's love affair with Wild Turkey bourbon, which he consumed abundantly, lured him there. John tried to hook his young friend on this high-octane stuff, but "this stubborn Swiss," as John called him, preferred his less potent cognac, Campari and soda, or café Kirsch.

Communication was difficult at first, as Herman had a very limited English vocabulary and knew only the rudiments of grammar. But he was a fast learner and under Lady Marvel's tutelage became quite fluent. Whatever their talks concerned—the business climate in America, Marvel's love for the ranch, or teaching Schuller the right Texas vernacular—their visits to the bistro were always filled with fun and laughter.

Once after a long tiring night at the Du Nord, Chef Herman was late for a rendezvous with his girl. He brushed his teeth, combed his hair, buttoned his jacket, and bolted out the service door into the chilly night.

"What's your hurry, young man?" asked a deep female voice.

Herman whirled around and bumped into a woman dressed in a full-length mink, almost toppling her. "Gee!" she said laughing. "Aren't we pressed for time!" She removed his hands from her shoulders.

Only now did Herman recognize Lady Marvel. Truthfully, with her dark coat, he hadn't seen her there, alone in the shadows, and he told her as much.

She waved away his explanation. "It's okay, Herman. But why the hurry?"

"I have a—" *date with my girl*, he wanted to say. Instead he stammered: "Um, I mean, uh, I have something going, but it's nothing big."

"Well then, hop in the taxi; I'll take you for a drink."

Herman hesitated. He had never broken a date with his girl, who waited for him at the Café de Paris, where she worked as a waitress. Besides . . . "Where is your husband?" he asked timidly.

"John was called to Zurich; just overnight," said Marvel.

Here was a unique opportunity. Lady Marvel looked exceptionally beautiful in her mink coat, and her perfume was even more intoxicating tonight. You're out of your league, he thought, but what the heck!

The taxi sped across Mont Blanc Bridge. The De la Paix, one of Geneva's great hotels, was but a few blocks away, and after a short ride, the taxi came to a screeching halt under the green, canvas-covered porte-cochère.

"We rent a suite at the hotel," explained Marvel.

The uniformed doorman, his brass buttons rivaling the doors' bright hardware, tipped his top hat. "*Bonsoir*, Monsieur, Dame," he said politely, opening the door.

Marvel nodded. "*Merci*, Jean-Jacques." She took Herman by the arm, and her mink brushed his skin, giving him goose bumps. They crossed the lobby to the lounge tucked away behind the marble columns and Oriental tapestry.

Cocktail waitresses in tight skirts and revealing blouses swirled between tables taking orders, carrying trays crammed with glasses, champagne, and bottles of expensive wines. Elegantly dressed couples, and older men in the company of younger women, filled the cozy booths along the wall. The floor was covered with a thick carpet so that one heard nothing but whispers and soft laughter, and long damask tablecloths hid flirting hands and searching toes. Soft piano music added a serene warmth.

Marvel stopped at the entrance. "Herman?" She gestured with her head, and when he didn't react, asked, "Are you going to help me with my coat?"

He quickly took it off her shoulders, surprised at the mink's unexpected weight. A whistle almost escaped him. Lady Marvel looked stunning in the long, black dress which hugged her shapely figure. A young receptionist, elegantly gowned, hung it in a closet, and then led the unusual couple to a marble table with two upholstered armchairs opposite the piano.

"Have you been here before?" asked Marvel.

"Yes, about a month ago," said Herman. "My aunt took me; that's my uncle's wife, uh, he is my mother's brother . . . His name's Bob. He's the maître d' here at the De la Paix."

Marvel patted his arm. "Take it easy, Herman. I know Bob. He's great people—and very professional. He has the gift of making people feel comfortable. So—he's your uncle?"

"What's it going to be, madame?" asked the young, scantily clad cocktail waitress.

"I'll have Wild Turkey on the rocks—I mean, over ice," said Marvel, "and monsieur—" She giggled seeing that Herman couldn't tear his eyes away from the woman's prominently displayed breasts. "Uh, monsieur will have a Campari Siphon."

Their reflection in the gilded mirror on the wall beyond the piano gave him a pang—the couple in that image had as much in common as a thoroughbred and a mule. He looked disheveled beside her, though he had pressed his pants and shirt the night before. Instinctively, he ran his hands over his pants to flatten any wrinkles. He held his ground, however, sitting an arm's-length away from her gorgeous body and the strong perfume that inebriated him.

Marvel let out a high-pitched chuckle that she tried to soften with her hand. "Are you all right, Herman?" she asked. "You seem tense."

"I'm fine."

"D'you want to try another table?"

"I'm fine."

"I'd say you're not cushy."

"It's cozy, maybe, uh, perhaps too cozy," he said, checking the mirror again.

Marvel chuckled. "I'd say you'd be happier at another table where we're not so intimate. I've noticed the way you keep looking in that mirror."

"Oh no, this is just fine," he said quickly, his face turning the shade of her dark-red fingernails.

"Okay, Herman, as you wish."

Marvel reached across the table and stopped the drumming of his fingers. He responded with a firm grip. She asked, "When's your visa due, Herman? What I mean is—when do you move to America?"

"It's probably two years away; uh, the Swiss quota is full for now." Her warm hand was helping him get the words out. He put his other hand on top of hers.

"When you get to America, you must come and visit me," she said. "John is buying the ranch from my parents and has already started the paperwork."

"I'd like that," Herman said, almost too quickly.

Marvel sighed. "It's the most tranquil spot on earth."

Immediately, Herman was excited as a kid on a hayride. "Are Texas ranches as big as they say?"

She nodded. "Yes, they are," she said with a smile. "Ours is not the largest by far, just over 10,000 acres."

"Sounds big—almost too big . . . How many hectares is that?"

"I heard John say 40 square kilometers, but I don't know how many hectares that would be. Our neighbor, the famed YO Ranch, is five times that size. While many of our pastures are bare and rocky, there are large stretches of rich coastal Bermuda and buffalo grass and plenty of prickly pears."

"Wow! I can hardly believe this," gasped Herman. He tried to drum the table again, but she held his hand tightly. There was a brief pause, and then he asked, "Uh, what's a prickly pear?"

"It's a cactus that has the most beautiful yellow blossoms in May. It also has large leaves with sharp thorns." She laughed. "If one sits on a prickly pear, it's over someone's knees with tweezers to pull a million thorns from one's—well, you know what I mean; it's not a very pleasant situation. During long droughts, my father and I used to burn off the thorns from the cactus so the animals could feed on them."

"Eat the cactus?"

"They provide moisture and many nutrients. Cows will feed on anything when they're hungry."

"Are there deer on the ranch, and jackrabbits? How about coyotes? I heard there are lots of coyotes in Texas." Herman had read a small booklet about Texas but still didn't know quite what to believe.

As Marvel satisfied his curiosity about deer and jackrabbits, Texas longhorn steers, coyotes, bobcats, rattlesnakes, and mountain lions (that she called "cougars"), his eyes grew in proportion to his interest. He did not interrupt until she talked of her schooling and the thirty-minute trip to the schoolhouse that she made bareback on her pony.

"On a pony? Wow!" He shook his head. "They would not even let us bring a bicycle to school. Thirty minutes, just to get to school?"

Marvel giggled. "It was a way of life," she said. "To shop for clothing and to get away, Mom and I would travel on buckboard to the nearest town, the only place that had a Pampell soda fountain. We would crank our own ice cream in the winter, using the ice from the frozen water trough that we mixed with salt. But Pampell's treat with Maraschino cherries, crunchy nuts, and chewy chocolate toppings crowned with gobs of fresh whipped cream was something even more exciting than my early romantic thoughts. Unfortunately, those trips took all day, so they were far apart."

Her eyes were suddenly lost in the depths of some fantasy. "When the sun sets, it looks as if the prairie's on fire. The most comfortable place is in the swing on the porch, listening to the windmill and watching the last of the sun shimmering through its blades—smelling the honeysuckle and the ivy-leafed geraniums climbing along the porch. Just thinking of it makes me want to rush back home."

❧❀❧

As Marvel dreamed about her ranch, Herman stared at her in a way he never had allowed himself to do before. Marvel sensed his attention. She lifted her hair from her pale neck and let the tresses fall freely over her bare shoulders.

Herman was overcome. His gaze lingered on her hair, her eyes, her lips—her bosom and shoulders that radiated a sexy presence. When she moistened her lips, he tightened his grip on the armrests . . .

The young server swished to their table and put two drinks and a bowl of chocolate-coated coffee beans in front of them, lifting the spell.

Marvel raised her glass. "Cheers."

"Cheers," parroted Herman.

Marvel took a sip and put her glass down. "Hunting season is in late fall. When you visit us, Herman, I want you to shoot an eight-point buck and a wild turkey gobbler."

Herman came out of his trance-like state. "Isn't it sad to shoot those animals?"

Marvel smiled. "I've never shot a deer on our ranch, and I don't intend to, but there's a need for game control. Besides, it's a large portion of our cash flow."

It didn't sound right to him, obviously. But he beat her to an explanation. "I guess . . . uh, some of the animals must be shot in order to grow healthier herds?"

Marvel nodded, a little surprised by his reasoning. "Hmmm. You've guessed right, Herman. But I've been doing all the talking," she said suddenly. "I think it's your turn."

Herman scratched his head. "I wouldn't know where to start. Well, I always wanted to have a pony. I used to ride horseback with a friend, Paul Weiher, whose father owns a large riding stable. But I really don't know what could be of interest to you, Lady Marvel."

"How about your career as chef, the cities you have visited in Scandinavia, your planned trip to America, and then, of course, your love life? Don't you dare leave that out!"

"My love life? You'll be bored."

"Let me be the judge," she said encouragingly. "Besides, it will be good practice for your English."

Herman took a handful of the coffee beans and sank deeply into the leather chair. He bit into a bean. It crunched noisily and squirted a drop of bittersweet chocolate onto his lip. He licked his lip and chewed another bean, his mouth closed now to muffle the crunch. All of a sudden the words were coming. "Following my school years," Herman began, still chewing coffee beans, "I worked a full year for a wine farmer in Grandvaux, a small hamlet in the wine regions above Lake Geneva, northeast of here . . . ."

It was a first important step in Herman's life. At sixteen, he was still a kid. There were neither commitments nor a girl to worry about. The farmer taught him winemaking from the start—the trimming and spraying, the weeding and hoeing, the art of tasting wine without getting tipsy, the fall harvest.

Scores of women migrated to the wine region from nearby French Savoie to help with the harvest. Most were in their thirties, married, and a few of them were quite attractive. A shapely redhead took an interest in Herman. After an exceptionally hot day, she persuaded him to join her at the lake. He hesitated—her finger showed the markings of a ring—but her smile was enticing. They lacked bathing suits, and she persuaded him to swim with her in the nude.

Marvel held back a chuckle as she watched Herman struggle for words.

He continued. "She walked toward me at the water's edge. I still can see the sand pushing up between her toes, rolling on top her foot then flying off at the next step, her hips rocking and twisting, her breasts swaying with her strides. And her fiery eyes—she was simply beautiful. Very tempting." Then her lips were on his, moist and eager and the sweetness of her breath overwhelmed him like no other sweetness in the world. His inborn manliness responded, and . . . "As they say, I had grown from a boy to manhood."

Marvel couldn't hold back any longer: she laughed into her hand—his cheeks had turned redder than a fresh-boiled lobster. Unperturbed, he concluded with poorly hidden pride, "I fell in love with that redhead twice my age, and, ever since, older women have had a special appeal."

His truthful innocence and careful choice of words made Marvel smile. After all, she too belonged to the category he favored.

Long before Herman's parents met, they had made their mark in the hospitality industry. His mother earned the distinction of being England's first female Maitre d'Hôtel—ever—while working at the Savoy Hotel in London. It was said that his father was the youngest, most meticulous concierge during his seven-year career at the world-class Shepherd's Hotel in Cairo, Egypt. It was his father who fostered Herman's interest in kitchen work, where he would never have to worry where his next meal came from. What influenced Herman's course eventually was the postwar economy, when finding work was tough, and apprentice jobs were few. He entered a cook apprenticeship in Basel and his career began.

The workweeks were long, and trade school fell very often on the day that he was off. In spite of the harshness of a Swiss apprenticeship, Herman found the time to bicycle into Germany and France, attend Doris Day musicals at the cinema, and bake in the sun at Eglisee, the public swimming pool. It didn't take long until his suntanned, slender yet muscular body and youthful looks were noticed. "I met my girl," he said almost timidly.

"Your first real love?" encouraged Marvel.

Herman nodded. "Margrit was young, but mature for her age, and she had a beautiful smile. But she wasn't very tall. It must have been her gorgeous lips and big, hazel eyes I fell in love with, as to me, you know, tall women are the most exciting."

"Are you ready for another drink, madame?" asked the waitress, exhibiting her bosom very close to Herman's face.

"Yes, two more," said Marvel, "and refill that bowl of coffee beans, would you, please?" She asked Herman to go on with his story.

The military was mandatory for all Swiss men. Herman had barely completed his apprenticeship when he responded to the draft. It was a new world—new discipline, new friends, an all-new outlook on life. Herman found he was well adapted to military life—excelled as a leader and as a marksman.

A unique experience led to a turn in the young soldier's life. He couldn't explain the event, couldn't grasp the phenomenon that was as fascinating as it was frightening: being at the right place at the right time, doing the right thing. An investigation failed to explain how steel-piercing ammunition had found its way into a clip of harmless blanks during field maneuvers. A hunch, perhaps the difference in weight, had alerted Herman to the deadly ammo in that light machine gun magazine, ready to be fired at a group of unsuspecting soldiers.

"Later, I brushed the experience aside as a mere fluke, a one-time occurrence. But it followed me, and I eventually accepted the strange phenomenon as part of my life. It even had a way of affecting the people around me, like the time Margrit stepped from a streetcar several stations ahead of her destination, and, quite unexpectedly, ran into me at a remote plaza—unknown to her, I had just returned to Basel after a one-year absence." Was he truly as "weird" as some of his colleagues had said?

"Here we are," said the waitress as she put the drinks on the table.

Marvel raised her glass. "To you, my fascinating friend." She wanted to hear more about Scandinavia. "You never told me what inspired you to go."

"While I was in the military, my mother found a job for me in Norway, and I left my country shortly after the service."

Oslo's Nobel, a hotel of great distinction, was the meeting place for diplomats and dignitaries. It would become his new home and place of work, sharing his room with a waiter who became his best friend. He cooked for, and occasionally met, selected world leaders, superstars, and many of the rich and famous. One of those celebrities was ice-skating champion Sonja Henie, who stayed at the Nobel during a goodwill tour.

"I met Miss Henie at a reception in her honor. I carved the Châteaubriand roast, and she asked for an extra slice. She had a wonderful smile for me, or so I thought. Later that evening, my roommate, a Dane from Åbenrå, and I celebrated with the champagne the party had left behind. It was my first taste of the bubbly."

"You'd never had champagne before?"

"No, and I didn't care for it, not one bit. It said *Brut* on the bottle, I remember that well, and—ugh," he said, making a face, "it was awful, what a disappointment."

"How about now? Do you still not have a taste for it?" asked Marvel with an amused smile.

"I've learned to like it but still don't care for the real dry stuff. It has to have some sweetness to it, like Asti Spumante or Pro Secco—

well, maybe not quite that sweet. Nonetheless, the Italians have a better feel for what people really like."

"I couldn't agree more," said Marvel with a passionate nod. "I go to receptions, and guess what? They pour the driest Brut champagne and everyone makes faces as though drinking sour lemonade while bragging about its extraordinary qualities."

"Gee, am I glad."

"Glad?"

"That we have the same taste."

Marvel chuckled. "Well, all right, Herman."

Swimming among the islands in the cold fiord, strolling under the Nordic sun that barely sank below the horizon, climbing the Olympic ski-jump ramp, or peeling shrimp from paper cones as one peels roasted chestnuts back home was to experience Norway at its best. Vigelnad Park had expanded his cultural awareness with its statuary dramatizing the joys and perils of humankind. In the hour before sunset, when a golden light suffused everything, the statues stood out prominently against the deep blue sky.

An important job opportunity led Herman to Stockholm, and Sweden had been heaven for a lonely Swiss. Scores of Finns had migrated to Stockholm looking for work, taking the tedious jobs. The Finnish women were bright and beautiful, and their way of looking at the human body was different from what Herman had been taught. He liked their openness and passion, and never felt a shred of shame with them.

"It was an interesting way to live, if I may say so," said Herman with a grin. "But sooner or later, every man in such circumstances had to accept the reality of a 50-kronen trip to the doctor's office."

"Did you take that trip, Herman?" teased Marvel. But after glancing at him: "Bad question, Herman. Please go on."

He worked as *hors d'oeuvrier* at Bern's Salonger, said to be the largest restaurant in Europe. "I learned much from the Chinese cooks who had their kitchen adjacent to ours. My friends called it 'spying on the Commies.' I was impressed by the way they made their noodles, swinging and stretching the dough above their head then twisting it time and again until it was reduced to the size of vermicelli—the shortest of the cooks using a ladder to gain the necessary height. It was probably the free world's first functional relationship with that people: they cooked for us, we cooked for them—we had a great accord."

When the planned year in Scandinavia had ended, Herman returned to Basel. He reunited with Margrit who, in spite of his exciting life in Sweden, had been constantly on his mind. "We'd lost none of our feeling for each other and spent a beautiful summer together." Herman paused then murmured almost to himself, "I never made love to Margrit, though. Must be the reason for my strong memory of her."

"Good evening." The voice was familiar. Herman swung around. It was Uncle Bob—in tails, with his black hair neatly trimmed and cologne wafting from his cheeks. He was smiling, but clearly surprised.

"We're having an intimate discussion, Monsieur Maître d'hôtel," said Marvel gaily. "But if you must know, your nephew's quite a coquette."

"No need to explain, Madame Orgain," said Uncle Bob. "I'm sure you know what you're doing." He quickly left the table. Soon, the waitress brought a bottle of Moët & Chandon—brut—with the compliments of the maître d'hôtel.

They exchanged glances then burst into laughter. Would they actually have to drink it? Disaster!

When Herman continued his life story, Marvel saw how proud he was to have become Corporal Schuller—a leader, someone the others depended on. But the glow didn't last. A shadow clouded his eyes. Gently prodding, she forced him to acknowledge what troubled him.

The story finally tumbled out: of a fashion model more beautiful, more lovable than any woman he had ever met; of the simple eye contact in a small tavern that had progressed to love outside a cabin in the crisp mountain air, in the wee hours in the moonlight. And as Herman retold the story act by loving act, Marvel was spellbound. Then came a farewell that broke his heart. Marvel watched him slump, saw him shudder. He leaned back and closed his eyes, a lone tear clinging to his cheek.

Marvel's hand groped for his, found it, and squeezed. With passion of her own she acknowledged his struggle, his lingering love, his longing for the woman he could not forget. She made no attempt to lift the silence that had come down hard.

Then the waitress brought him his bowl of chocolate coffee beans and he revived.

His voice was croaky. "At the end," he said ruefully, "I also lost Margrit. I had never told her of that hopeless affair, but neither could I hide my divided heart. I've never been more lonely."

Still Marvel did and said nothing. She had known Herman only as a cheerful lad who could do no wrong. If his love for the fashion model was as real as he wanted her to believe, she would be forced to reckon with a different personality. In a strange way, she felt envious.

"Hell, you just can't forget that woman in Milan," she said finally, surprising herself.

"I know. I've tried. But I can't. Sometimes I think I'm nurturing it."

The friendly bartender reminded his guests of Geneva's strict curfew laws. It was time to leave this cozy environment. As they walked from the hotel lobby, Marvel took Herman's arm. He responded with warmth. Marvel understood his struggle—she had been there herself—and decided she would pay the fashion model in Milan a visit next time John was called to Italy. Then it hit her.

The way Herman had described the fashion model, why . . . he could have been describing me.

The doorman had left for the night and they were alone. She clasped his cheeks with both hands. Their eyes met, and she felt his ardor. Then she kissed him, hesitantly, waiting for the response she expected . . . but it was too slow in coming. She mussed his hair.

"Let me get you a taxi, Herman. It's too late to walk."

"Thank you Marvel, you're so kind, but I really want to walk. All these emotions have been too much . . . I need to be alone."

He lumbered across the river, along empty streets and lonesome alleys to his flat, a knot in his stomach and a lump in his throat. How well he remembered that lump in his throat! Now, dragging along aimlessly, he was forced to confront the renewed desire that filled his mind, and all of a sudden he knew, he knew that there was more to the story with the fashion model—and a different ending.

CHAPTER 12

*I*n September 1956, the postwar economic roller coaster was beginning to show stability in Northern Italy. No longer a mere wishful whisper, a once great industrial giant had awakened after a long uncertain sleep, and the Po Valley was again taking the lead in commerce, tourism, and the world of fashion. Milan was booming. Riding on the coattail of success, Moda di Masoni, the Fashion House at the Puccini Galleria, on Corso Buenos Aires, contributed on its own a new, exciting look.

Bordering rich, woolen carpets, shiny marble had replaced the old tile floors. Modern, chrome-plated clothes racks enticed shoppers with the latest fashions, and new privacy booths with beveled mirrors reflected the giant crystal chandeliers. Clients could ride the glass elevator to the new modeling stage on the second level or amble up the fan-shaped marble staircase in the comfort of air-conditioning (a novelty at the time). Well-trained fashion models of rare beauty added unrivaled buoyancy to the establishment.

But not all was well at the Fashion House.

Two kilometers north of Corso Buenos Aires, at the edge of metropolitan Milan, Cimitero Monumentale lay under a thin blanket of the fall's first morning frost.

"—And lead us not into temptation. But deliver us from evil. For Thine is the kingdom and the power and the glory forever. Amen."

The woman spoke these words on bended knee, in a barely audible voice, then stood to gaze at the inscription on the cold granite stone. Almost timidly, she ran her fingers along the shallow grooves. There was no flourish in the script, no pride. "From One Friend to Another" was written in Gothic letters above the deceased's name, date of birth, and the day that she had died. The simplicity of the statement was a true memorial to the way the deceased had lived her life.

The sun's first rays shot over the ivy-covered masonry wall, casting ghostly shadows from rows of cenotaphs and Gothic stones. The air was still and crisp. A flock of doves swooped through the brightening sky. The woman, wearing a black pantsuit that was tight about her waist, her hair bound by a purple scarf, watched the way the birds unfurled a dark blue banner across the sky, then with coordinated turns changed its color to silver, then back to dark blue again. Something about the way the doves changed course and color in perfect cadence was giving her the assurance that life was keeping to its inevitable course.

Angelina Bianci—her silhouette distinct now in the early light—dwelled upon her memories without finding any philosophical comfort in them. Her heart was with the deceased, Marie Theresa, her friend and partner, who had been gone for three long months. Gone was her kind voice, gone her winning smile, only the memory of her gentle ways remained. Angelina buried her face in her hands and wept.

"Go ahead, take a deep breath—then shout it out!"

Though her head had snapped back as if responding to a familiar voice, there was no voice. She thought often of the person who had taught her that line—the corporal, Herman Schuller—when she was lonely or at the end of her strength.

Angelina filled her lungs, then shouted, "O God, why have you taken her away? She was so young!" She unfolded her hands and stretched them to the sky. "I can't go on! O God, I can't go on. The burden is too great."

Yet this wasn't the first time she'd felt this way or said these words—and she kept on, in spite of feeling the burden of Marie Theresa's sudden absence that lay heavily on her shoulders. Now that the fashion house was hers alone to lead and organize, the work piled up no matter how many hours she worked each day. And as business days turned into nights, she was getting her only rest, ever more often, on a couch fully clothed. She sought salvation in prayer, but no matter how hard she prayed, she got no relief—no counsel from above. In spite of all the pain of her regular Sunday morning visits to the cemetery, she looked forward to them with passion, as, so it seemed to her, even from the grave Marie Theresa was giving her faith and strength.

The day of Marie Theresa's death seemed to have been decreed by the heavens, as towering clouds had risen over Milan and thunder had rolled through streets. While sheets of rain flooded the sidewalks and subways, Angelina, following an inner prompting, had rushed to 10-Aldrovandi, Marie Theresa's apartment. There she found her partner lying on the floor beside her bed. Angelina got her to the hospital, but the heart surgeon was emphatic: her friend wasn't going to make it.

From her deathbed, with the strength left in her, Marie Theresa revealed to Angelina that she would be the sole inheritor of her assets. Then she raised her concern about Angelina's ability to run the Fashion House, about her failed relationships with men.

"Dear Angelina," she had said. "Think of that corporal you used to talk about so often—Herman Schuller? What a nice young man. He would be someone you could trust, who would always be there for you." These were very nearly Marie Theresa's last words. She died in Angelina's arms later that afternoon.

Suddenly, Angelina had acquired wealth she hadn't dreamed of: the Fashion House at the Galleria, the 10-Aldrovandi apartment complex that was now her home, the Porsche, and a treasure in gold and precious stones she had yet to find the courage to put on. It was all hers—yet she found no joy in it.

To overcome her grief, Angelina threw herself into the business from dawn to dusk, and after everyone had left the shop, she bent over the drawing table night after lonely night. Her efforts paid off. Fresh designs brought great reviews from a growing clientele as sales and profits soared. Yet . . . what had started as a way to conquer sorrow became a habit—a ruthless pattern that took its toll. Her strength faded.

When, finally, she was convinced she could no longer go on alone, she hired an assistant, a young woman with red hair and blue eyes. As if to leave no doubt that she wanted a younger version of herself as her protégée, the young woman had been working as a waitress in the Puccini dining room when Angelina noticed her. Sabrina was married to a carpenter, and they had one child, a daughter, who had just taken her first steps. Angelina employed both, husband and wife—she had her team.

With her energy and endurance, Angelina rebuilt the Fashion House, financed by liquidating her personal assets. She mortgaged 10-Aldrovandi, took a loan on the Porsche, and sold her Fiat. Then, with a heavy heart, she sold Marie Theresa's jewelry. As she was organizing her affairs, she was enthused to discover a new side of herself—a shrewd trader, a businesswoman who was winning the support and respect of bankers and colleagues.

But Angelina was lonely. And as loneliness gripped her heart, her work became a substitute for intimacy. Before long it was the only love she knew.

Angelina watched the doves till they were out of sight, then turned her attention to the weeds that were pushing up between the begonias which adorned her friend's grave. As the sun rose higher above the masonry wall, the shadows grew shorter, and the cenotaphs became more affable. Still, the image of Herman Schuller was strongest in her mind, as it had been for the past few weeks.

"Oh, corporal, where are you?" she whispered. "Do you ever think of me?"

$\mathcal{T}$he bell tower of Geneva's Protestant Church began to strike the hour. A flock of white pigeons, perched on the adjacent rooftop, scattered with a confusion of wings and flying feathers, then went back to their roost. It was three o'clock.

The salesman leaned against the dealership sign advertising their latest model. Hefty, with short black hair, he wore designer pants held up by black suspenders and a starched white shirt with a blue-striped tie. The toothpick in his mouth had been ruthlessly gnawed.

He stood next to a pedestal that displayed the *Vespa Grand Sport*. A sign next to the scooter promised "supreme performance."

The salesman hiked his foot up on the pedestal, rubbed his nose and chin, and cleared his throat like someone about to deliver an important speech. "It'll go a hundred, and we can finance most of it," he said cautiously.

His expression changed like a fisherman's, thought Herman— one minute cautiously baiting his hook, the next minute gleefully reeling in. The Italian-made two-wheeler, the VGS, was a lot more than bait, though, where Herman was concerned. In fact, he'd never seen such a sexy piece of machinery and thought of it as a work of art.

Of course, the seasoned salesman sensed his interest. "Go ahead—sit on it. Get a feel of the tandem seat," he said.

Herman climbed onto the seat. The salesman put the key in the ignition and gave it a quarter turn, and the steering column unlocked. Herman's fingers molded into the handgrips as if they had been made specifically for him.

The salesman said, "Okay, now push it off the stand. Yeah, that's it. Now rock it. Oh, much harder than that. Don't be timid now; give the suspension a chance to prove itself. That's it—thaa-at's it. You see? What did I say? Those larger wheels do make a difference!"

Herman bounced up and down. I *have to get this scooter!* Yet he was undecided. Would his finances allow it? He had saved enough to make a substantial down payment and wanted to pay off the rest within a year.

The salesman also sensed his client's indecision. "Why fight it?" he stated routinely, though his eyes were keen in tracking Herman's response. He grinned crookedly. "The girls will fall all over you; I ought to know—they always do with me." The expected reaction wasn't there. "Here, let me take you for a ride."

Before Herman knew what was happening, he had his arms around the sizable man whose body odor was only partly hidden by strong cologne, and they were racing down the road as if their tails were on fire. The salesman turned his head and pointed to the speedometer. "Didn't I tell you? What did I tell you! A hundred, just as I said, and with all this weight on it!"

Herman mumbled something about the downgrade, but leaning into curves and racing up and down the hills he quickly forgot any reservations he might have had. I *have to get this scooter!*

Still he wavered. He had hoped to find an apartment and share it with his girl, Suzanne, the waitress at the Café de Paris. But even if they split the rent, as they had agreed, the higher rent would put a strain on him. At the moment, the small studio room he rented from a couple felt adequate. It was close to work and had all the comfort he needed. His landlords—watchmakers working at home late into the night—did not allow female visitors, though, but had been lenient when Herman occasionally broke the rule. Why change? Or more to the point, perhaps—did he really need this scooter?

It was an easy twenty-minute walk from his flat to his place of work, but Herman often chose a longer route through a shopping mall where there was a car dealership. Three U.S.-made Studebakers were on display—the most stunning creations of modern man that Herman had ever seen. He stopped there for a moment each day to admire the cars, dreaming of hitting the wide-open Texas roads behind the wheel of that red convertible with white leather seats.

Suzanne shared in his dream and was already begging him to take her with him to America.

"You'll need a visa."

"How will I get it? I've always dreamt of going to America. It sounds so exciting. Will you take me with you, Herman, really?" In discussing their plans, the love between them deepened.

Back at the dealership, his thoughts swimming, Herman climbed from the seat of the scooter.

"Well?" asked the salesman, as he jumped from the seat with the ease of a featherweight boxer who had just won his fight. "Can we wrap it up?"

The bell tower announced the half hour. Herman looked at his watch. "Shit, I'm late. I'll be back. Count on it!" He jumped on his touring bike and pedaled away.

The sun was bright on the choppy surface of Lake Geneva. Suzanne submerged her toe in the water, and with a "wow" quickly retreated to her bleacher. Though only September, the water was already cold. She stretched out and pulled a towel over her slender body. Suzanne chose her friends among fun-loving people, so she and Herman were well matched. They had met at a local nightclub on New Year's Eve. That brief encounter had ignited a spark, but it was March before they had decided they were made for each other.

Suzanne put her hand over her eyes and ground her flawless little teeth. Where is he? Herman was an hour late. This wasn't like him, and last night he hadn't shown at all! Had something gone wrong between them? *Why are you late! Especially today?* Her sister, sunbathing right beside her, was in Geneva on a two-week visit. Ursula had always been a rival in the matter of attracting men and Suzanne had been eager to be seen with Herman.

She looked at her watch again. *Where the hell are you!* But then she saw him on his bike peddling furiously. When he reached her section of beach he leapt off the bike and bounded up wearing a big grin.

She scrambled off the bleacher and greeted him with a hug.

"Hey, Sis, meet my friend Herman," she cried. When her sister had turned around, Suzanne kissed Herman on both cheeks, then full on the lips. Ursula introduced herself with a tentative smile.

They might be sisters, Herman thought, but they were as different as black and white. Suzanne was tan and slender—Ursula was pale, full-figured, and very bosomy. Suzanne had sparkling blue eyes and an abundance of soft hair—Ursula's hair was short and stringy. Still, with no sparkle in her eyes and no luster in her hair, Ursula seemed to be getting more attention from the boys on the beach.

Suzanne was exactly the friend Herman needed. They talked for hours, often late into the night, and no matter how silly their discussions—about friends, what they had for lunch, America, menstrual cycles—they enjoyed spending time together. Herman took Suzanne to fine bistros and the movies, and she responded to his attentions with increasing fondness. In time, they understood their feelings as love, and their relations became intimate.

Suzanne pulled Herman onto the bleacher. She rolled her towel tightly and put it under his head. She cuddled close to him, knitted her fingers into his, and positioned her head on his chest so her hair just touched his chin. His warm, steady breath in her hair was reassuring; she welcomed his closeness and the feeling of belonging to him. She had never felt so intimate with a man, and would have been completely happy with Herman—if he weren't so popular with other girls.

Herman dozed off on his wooden bench and Suzanne woke him with a cold shower from her swim cap. "Hey, stop that!" He jumped up and chased her, and when he caught her, dragged her playfully into the chilly lake.

But their afternoon break was running out of time—they had to report back to work by five. Suzanne would be off an hour later, and Herman promised, as he always did, to pick her up at the Café de Paris. He would never show.

The evening at the Du Nord had been unusually slow and the chef brigade was leaving early. With extra time left before going to Suzanne, Herman decided to stop by the car dealership . . . continue the exciting dream of a red Studebaker convertible on wide-open Texas roads . . . . He turned the corner and . . . the car in the middle, the red convertible, was gone. In its place was a slick Fiat Topolino with its top rolled down—insignificant, almost lost next to the American models.

But memories came back faster than Herman was able to absorb. He dropped to his knees and pressed his palms flat against the showcase glass . . . *Angelina!* The memory of her had grown dim, almost gone . . . now it was back with all its love and beauty, stirred by the magical appearance of the car that so resembled hers. As though she was right in front of him, his head filled with the images of her mystical smile and her bright blue eyes, with the sweet smell of her soft skin, and the touch of her luxurious red hair. He sensed her breath warmly against his ear, her lips nibbling at his earlobe, her fingers deep in his own curly hair . . . it was as if they had never parted. A stabbing pain pushed against his side, his chest tightened— and the lump in his throat was back.

Herman had vanished. Suzanne, already worried by his absence, immediately sensed a change in him when he showed up three days later at her place of work. A nebulous veil was hiding the bright sparkle in his eyes, his gaze was unsteady, wandering, and she didn't believe his feeble excuse of having been ill. She questioned him, begged him—Herman remained tight-lipped. And as the week passed by she came to realize that something had gone wrong. Another woman? Suzanne couldn't take it, and they began drifting apart.

Chapter 14

In October, Herman could resist no longer and bought the sporty Vespa. He and Suzanne had been separated for two weeks, but all seemed well when they got back together again.

"How neat! I like it!" was Suzanne's response when he drove up. "Where to, Herman? What do you have in mind?"

"The next stop is Aix-les-Bains, for lunch."

Suzanne's eyes went wide. "Aix-les-Bains? You mean, like Aix-les-Bains, France?"

"Yes, of course."

"Isn't that a little far?"

"Not really. Have you got your passport?"

Herman put on his brimless leather cap and goggles, stepped on the starter, and the scooter took off with a roar. It was a cloudless day; the air was still and warm—perfect for an adventure, according to Herman. Suzanne agreed and was holding onto his waist with both arms, her face flattened against his back, her eyes narrow slits against the wind.

Herman knew his way around the endless city blocks. The border, only a few minutes out of the city, was soon behind them. They rode deep into the Savoie, leaning into the gentle curves, absorbing the beauty of the hilly grazing lands beneath the towering French Alps.

The scooter swayed as it snaked along the shores of the Lac d'Annecy. Sailboats bounced on shallow waves like rubber ducks in a youngster's bath, their white sails glistening in the morning sun. Young people in skimpy bathing suits played soccer on the sandy beach, laughing and falling over each other, rolling in the sand. Herman honked, and they interrupted their play long enough to wave.

This was his second trip to Aix-les-Bains; ten days ago he'd made the trip to test the scooter's performance. There was plenty of new territory to explore, beautiful lakes and mountains, why take the same route again? It couldn't be for the cute garden restaurant in Aix-les-Bains where he had stopped for lunch . . . where he had been teasing with Monique, the waitress . . . ? He didn't know for sure, or perhaps he didn't want to know, because the answer might have had something to do with Aosta, the Italian Alpine village across Petit-St-Bernard Pass where he had stopped for fuel . . . where he had fought the temptation of turning south toward Milan instead of north . . . .

Racing away from the lake along the Leschaux Valley they passed little streams slipping out of the hills; fed by recent storms, the Laudon River was swollen. Suddenly, Aix-les-Bains spread out beyond the Sierron River Bridge, seeming close enough to touch. Herman slowed and cut the engine under a chestnut tree.

Suzanne relaxed her grip on Herman's waist and straightened in the seat. She pointed to the peninsula dotted with white stucco houses and exclaimed over its beauty. Blue-and-white-striped cabanas with loungers and umbrellas in front of them lined the sandy beach.

"How wonderful!" she cried. "Look, people are still swimming. How thrilling! Can we join them?"

"Did you bring your bathing suit? I didn't!"

"Uh, I guess we're not going swimming. Too bad—would have been fun."

Herman drove through the city center to the Du Monde, known for fair prices and great food, where he had met Monique. "Here we are," he said. He stopped at the garden terrace gate. Suzanne climbed from the seat, a little stiff from the long ride and glad to be on solid ground. Herman shouted over his shoulder, "Reserve a table, while I park the Vespa," then drove across the street to the parking lot.

Lime green napkins with silver holders were arranged on the glass-top tables like the spokes of a wheel, the core being a bud vase with a single yellow rose. Young patrons dined and chatted; almost all the tables were occupied. Sweet honeysuckle twisted through the wrought-iron rail, its scent blending with the yellow roses'. Suzanne chose a table set for two, close to the gate.

An immense stained-glass panel separated the indoor dining room from the garden terrace. The artist had used cut glass inlays and smart strokes of his brush to create a horseshoe-shaped lagoon with a sky full of color. Seagulls and waves supplied movement, and in the foreground there was an abandoned rowboat, its bow partially buried in the sand, a broken oar projecting from the gunwale.

"Interesting place, isn't it?" asked Herman, coming through the gate.

"I love it!" Suzanne beamed. "But then, my dear Herman, you always know the best places to eat." She pointed to the stained-glass panel. "Isn't it marvelous? That must be the dining room."

"It is. And yes, the panel is a masterpiece," he said. "But . . . you must be hungry, sweetheart. They have a great cold-cut platter with true Bünderfleisch, prosciutto, and fresh Gorgonzola cheese. Also, you must try their crunchy pickles . . . ."

The sun shone brightly, and it was getting warm, but a soft breeze across the terrace kept things cool. While Suzanne visited the rest room, Herman tried to spot Monique. He watched the patrons, most in their teens, chatting and giggling. *Where was she?*

"Have you ever heard of stand-up toilets?" Suzanne was in high gear when she returned to the table. "They look like urinals, and I was certain that a man would walk in on me! To add insult to injury, there were no doors for privacy!"

Herman smiled. "Welcome to France, sweetheart, you'll get used to it."

"No thanks." She screwed up her nose. "I'd rather hide behind a bush or a tree."

"And get bitten by ticks and ants? I had enough of that in the military."

They burst into laughter.

A waitress dashed by their table. "I'll be right with you," she said. She was back in a moment and recognized Herman. "Hello, *mon ami. Mon dieu*; where have you been? It's about time you came back to see me."

Herman jumped to his feet. "Hi, Monique. Please meet Suzanne."

Monique viewed Suzanne with mock-suspicion, then shook her hand. "Welcome to Aix-les-Bains, sweetie." Monique gave Herman a sideways glance. "Hum, a girl this time around," she mumbled under her breath, while pulling a notebook from her apron pocket and a pencil from above her ear. "Today's special is pork chops with green beans and *boulangère* potatoes, and the soup du jour is Potage Du Barry."

"What's 'Du Barry'?" asked Suzanne.

Monique shrugged. "Beats me," she said. "I only know that it's made with cauliflower."

Herman's knowing smile was almost too knowing. "You're right, Monique; Du Barry is associated with cauliflower, always is." He looked quickly from one woman to the other to gauge the response to his expertise, then hastened to add: "Madame Du Barry was the mistress of King Louis XV until his death. She fled to England at the outbreak of the French Revolution but later came back to retrieve some jewelry she'd stashed away. She was betrayed, caught by the militia, and promptly guillotined."

Monique chuckled. "I guess the soup won her the king's heart but failed to save her head."

"I think I won't have soup today," said Suzanne, making a face.

Herman ordered a platter of cheese, dried meat, smoked ham, French bread, and a carafe of Beaujolais.

Monique took a short break and sat with them to chat. "Tell me, *mon ami*," she said, "where are you going from here?"

Herman pointed east. "To Aosta, Italy, then over the Grand-St-Bernard pass back to Switzerland."

"Why the same route again?" asked Monique.

Herman was at a loss—he didn't know himself. Monique seemed put off by his silence, but cheered up promptly when he said, "Because of you, Monique, what else?"

She turned to Suzanne. "You must keep an eye on your *ami*; he's quite a flirt. Besides, I bet he has a girl in every town. I like him, though, he's cute."

Suzanne shot Herman a stern look. He threw up his hand in self-defense. "How can you say that in front of my girl, Monique? Besides," he smirked sheepishly, "I'll bet I haven't been in half the cities of France yet."

"You're right, Monique, I'll have to keep an eye on him." Suzanne was keeping back a laugh "There's no way we girls can trust a boyfriend these days . . ."

"Or a husband," cut in Monique. They carried on for some time, interrupted only by the occasional, impatient wave of a customer.

Herman raced through the French countryside—Chambery-Montmelian-Albertville-Moûtier—to Petit-St-Bernard Pass. A fast bike, a full tank, hard asphalt, a girl on the seat behind him, a bright sun in a cloudless sky—how could life be any better for a man his age? But unexplained disquiet filled his thoughts. As they neared the Italian border, apprehension gave way to carelessness. He shifted late and misjudged some curves. *I had better stop before I run us off the road.*

Shortly after Bourg-St-Maurice, Herman drove into the parking lot of a modern hotel with an adjacent restaurant. A bronze crossed fork and knife pointed to a short staircase that led to the dining room.

"Something wrong, Herman? You look a little pale," said Suzanne.

He shook his head and seated her at a table by the large picture window. Below them was the long stretch of road to Petit-St-Bernard Pass. After a sigh of relief, Suzanne told him: "Whatever made you stop, I'm glad you did—my rear end was giving me fits."

Herman ordered coffee.

The waitress, dressed in a tight skirt and freshly starched white blouse, brought two cups. Each had a ceramic coffee filter on them.

Suzanne indicated the drip filter. "I like having fresh-brewed coffee, but tell me, my sweet love, how do you drink this one without messing up the white table cloth?" Coffee dripped from the filter, and there was no place to set it down.

"Here, let me show you how it's done," he said. He lifted the filter above his nose and began to drink from the cup. Coffee dripped on his nose and chin.

Suzanne burst into laughter. "Big help. Here, let me try." She put the filter onto her cupped left hand. "Ouch! Hot!" She quickly put it back onto the cup and licked her palm. Then they figured it out. The drip filter had a lid that doubled as saucer—genius! The waitress had watched them curiously but had not come to the rescue.

"She must think we're crazy," said Suzanne in Swiss.

Herman paid the bill and they laughed all the way to the scooter. Suzanne's carefree attitude had made him forget what had bothered him. Almost.

The highway to Petit-St-Bernard Pass was paved, and thirty minutes later, they were at the summit. The French border guard gazed up from his blue-white-and-red-striped cubicle, yawned, and gestured a "go on." Herman nodded and drove across the white line. He stopped at the Italian flag.

The young officer greeted them with a cheerful "*Buona sera*," his right hand at his cap in salute.

Herman came back with "*Bonjour*."

The officer replied in French, though with a heavy Italian accent. "May I see your papers?" he said. Herman handed him both passports. The officer flipped through the pages, one eye on the woman on the tandem seat. "Traveling through?"

"Yes," Herman said. "Over Col du Grand-St-Bernard to Martigny, then back to Geneva."

"Hmm."

Suzanne's curious nature took over. She asked, "How do you decide when to search a person? I mean, you can't search everybody."

The young officer smiled. "Oh, we know. Anybody hiding something becomes just a little nervous."

"Aren't people, by sheer nature, anxious in the presence of a uniform? I ought to know—I'm always jittery," confessed Suzanne.

"True. You were a little nervous, but have I searched you?"

"No, you didn't. I guess that comes with experience." She fell silent for a moment, then asked, "Isn't Petit-St-Bernard the pass where

Hannibal crossed the Alps with his elephants, on his way to Rome?"

The young officer smiled. "You're well up on your history, mademoiselle. With thirty-seven elephants and 40,000 troops, Hannibal, age twenty-six, left Spain in 218 B.C., climbed through the Pyrenees, forded the Rhone River and then crossed this pass on his way to meet the Roman legions. Publius Cornelius Scipio, the Roman general, tried unsuccessfully . . ." and on it went until Suzanne gently intervened.

"This is very, very interesting, officer," she said. "Thanks for the chat."

If he was offended by her cutting in, he didn't show it. "Have a nice trip," he said cheerfully, returned the passports, saluted, and waved after the accelerating Vespa.

The descent to the Dora Baltea River was rapid, then the grade wasn't so steep and the curves, to Suzanne's delight, became less threatening. The Aosta Valley wore its fall coat of turning leaves. At the end of the valley they stopped at the city that bore its name, nestled along the highway near the start of the Valpelline Valley.

After a trip to the service station, they had settled on a nearby café for a *boccalino* of red table wine when the strange feeling crept up on him again. His chest tightened and that familiar symptom of heightened awareness—the lump in his throat—was back. He pulled out the roadmap and matched it up with the crossroads that ran north into Switzerland and southeast toward Torino and Milan. Without realizing what he was doing, he added up the distance to Milan—*197 kilometers, three hours of driving at the most.*

Suzanne watched him with concern; was he going all the way to Milan? *No way, my bottom couldn't last that long!* But something else bothered her: his eyes. The look in his eyes was cloudy, distant. How could the mileage markers on a map have such an effect? Before she could intrude upon his thoughts, however, he finished his wine and stood up.

"Time to get on our way," he said abruptly. He put down six francs to cover the tab and an extra franc for tip. Suzanne sighed with relief: they were heading north.

Buthier River snaked along the highway on their right, gradually turning northeast to form the heart of Valpelline Valley.

"Isn't it beautiful?" Herman shouted over his shoulder.

"What did you say?"

He pointed to tiny hamlets stuck like beehives on the steep slopes. He drove to the narrow, sandy shoulder and stopped at the safety cable strung between chiseled granite blocks.

He indicated the entire scene with a sweeping gesture. "This is Val Valpelline, the last major valley between Aosta and Switzerland." He removed his headgear and hung it on the steering column. Suzanne, always ready to get off the seat, slid to the ground and walked to the cable.

"It's beautiful," she said. "Wow, look at the color of those maples."

"Those are chestnuts."

"Chestnuts? You can't tell from this distance."

"I drove down to the valley ten days ago. They're chestnuts, trust me," he said.

Suzanne gave him a sideways glance. Was there a hint of resentment in his voice? She watched him secure the scooter and sit back on the tandem seat, sideways, but his movements were sluggish, as if his mind were somewhere else.

"What is it?" Suzanne asked with concern.

Herman didn't answer, just stared at the valley and the adjacent slopes. He bit his lip. "The valley," he said lastly. "The valley; it was in my dream. At the time I didn't know it, but now I'm sure. It's the valley in my dream!"

"What about the valley?" asked Suzanne.

He shook his head. "I don't know," he said vaguely "There was darkness in the valley, and then light came from those mountains. I was confused—the dark, the light!"

Suzanne looked at him, bewildered, almost frightened. Then, in a few seconds, the agitation subsided and his customary warmth was back. He pulled the roadmap from his pocket and spread it over his knees.

Suzanne walked to his side and pointed to the map. "There's a lake at the end of the valley," she said.

Herman nodded. "A reservoir . . . dammed."

"Did you drive all the way up there?"

"No, I didn't. It's quite far, and if the map's contours can be trusted, too steep for my scooter." Abruptly, Herman swung his legs around the seat, put on his leather hood, and kick-started the engine. Suzanne quickly got on behind him and wrapped her arms around his waist. He looked over his shoulder. "We should make the hospice and Switzerland in about thirty minutes." He shifted into low gear and the scooter whined through switchback curves and steep inclines. After a short tunnel, they passed the border and were now back in Switzerland.

The plaster walls of the old monastery across Summit Lake shadowed Mont Vélan, white from a recent snowstorm. Herman stopped briefly.

"I wonder what made the monks settle in such rugged country two centuries ago," said Suzanne.

"Yeah," agreed Herman. "Cut off from civilization, no doctors, no hospitals, surrounded by cold granite rocks and eternal snow. Not much food either, besides milk from cows and goats and an occasional beehive for honey. I wonder if the monks still make beer from honey?" They would find the answer in the monastery, which they entered moments later.

Posters of tales of heroism and self-sacrifice plastered the monastery's walls along the corridor leading to the chapel. They took the time to read the stories of stranded travelers and monks with dogs the size of calves braving snow and ice to save the lost and freezing.

"Saint Bernard dogs are intelligent and brave and have great endurance. They are the prize tools of rescue teams, and their success in saving human lives has been well documented," said one plaque. Suzanne read aloud from another: "Barry One, the most famous of the Saint Bernard dogs, saved forty lives all by himself. In honor of his deeds, only the best male dog of a litter may bear his name."

The chapel, illuminated by only a few candles, was at the end of the hallway, dark and eerie, almost ghostly. A low hum, like mumbled prayers, came from its dim cavity, though no one could be seen. The darkness and stale smell gave them the creeps, and they left quickly.

The hotel across the street was closed for the season.

"Look at these gorgeous dogs, and the fine furs and soft colors," shouted Suzanne excitedly. They had obtained permission to visit the kennels at House Saint-Louis. Indeed, the dogs were stunning. A male, large even for a Saint Bernard, wagged his bushy tail. Herman leaned against the railing—the male looked just like Barry from the Mendali dairy farm. A bitch with offspring was in the kennel next to him.

Suzanne pointed to the male. "He must be the father, look how proud he is." As if to confirm her judgment, the male rose and walked to the sturdy fence. The little ones rushed to him and stuck tiny tongues through the wire mesh. Concerned, the bitch grunted and got to her feet. The pups rushed back to her, all ten of them, fighting to get their teeth on her enormous teats. Suzanne laughed at the comical scene. But where was Herman?

She found him sitting on the outside stairs leading to an upper floor, face buried in his hands. Had the dogs anything to do with what was troubling him? She walked up to Herman and put her hand on his arm, determined to find out. "Something's bothering you, Herman," she said. "You've kept it a secret long enough. I want to know what it is!" She planted herself in front of him, hands on her hips.

Herman did not yield.

"You're spoiling everything," Suzanne cried. "If you can't tell me what it is, at least say *something!*"

But Herman's thoughts were far away, in Milan, at a galleria. A cramp was in his stomach, and the lump in his throat was stifling him. What had started as a day for mending was being ruined by suspicion and resentment. Herman knew that only straight answers would resolve the issue—and of course, there were none.

The gods responded with a downpour that drenched the travelers on their way home.

The roar of the Jet d'Eau was deafening, so the young couple moved farther from its base. Suzanne had suggested the spot to settle their differences. The lively waterspout, she thought, might help him to be more spontaneous and—well, tell her the truth. She had her back turned to Herman, arms crossed, chin up, eyes cold and suspicious. He moved closer to her and put his arms around her, but she pulled away.

"Don't!" she cried. "I don't know what it is, but something has come between us." She looked straight ahead, away from him.

"What do you mean, Suzanne? There's nothing between us; it's all in your mind."

Suzanne shook her head. "I don't believe you; you're not here, not with me, not really. We don't talk like we used to. We even quarrel, something we've never done before." Frustration shook her body. "There's someone else," she cried. "Maybe it's my own sister."

Herman shook his head. "What makes you say that?"

"You wouldn't be the first man dropping me for her."

"Of course not, Suzanne. I have no interest in your sister. What gives you that idea?"

"I saw you look at her big bosom with, with—with lust in your eyes," she cried.

Herman inhaled deeply. "I don't care for your sister. I think she's a bore, a tart."

"You see," cried Suzanne. "You don't care for my family; if you really loved me, you'd care for them!"

Herman lifted his shoulders, didn't answer. Suzanne was right, of course; she had a rival. But how could he explain? Suzanne was strong in character. She had a deep sense of loyalty and expected the same in return.

She cried above the noisy fountain, "There's another woman in your life, Herman. I know there is. I feel it."

"No, there isn't," he said.

"Something's wrong. I know there's another woman—we haven't made love in a week. It's just not like you." She looked over her shoulder, eyes blazing between tears.

"Please, Suzanne, have patience with me. It'll pass. I'll find myself—you'll see."

"You're a poor liar," she screamed, her body shaking uncontrollably. "I know there's someone else!"

"No!"

"Admit it—there's another woman!"

"Okay, okay, but it's over; we broke up a year ago, long before you and I met."

"I knew it!"

"It's over."

"You still care for her." Her voice was now a high-pitched shriek.

"She isn't here, she's in Italy; I'll never see her again." At that moment, Herman realized the extent of his love for Angelina. Tears smarted behind his eyelids. "Yes, I love her, I love her, I love her! She's the only woman I have ever loved!" he wanted to shout, but he said nothing.

Suzanne shook her head wildly. "You see, you still love her. I can see it in your eyes!" she cried.

The ensuing silence swallowed every noise, even the mighty waterspout.

Herman bowed his head. "I'm sorry, Suzanne, so very sorry," he said. "But you and I have made wonderful plans. You're the only person in my life, and I don't want to lose you. We'll work things out—you'll see." His shoulders slumped more, and his head dropped lower—he was the picture of wretchedness. His voice was barely audible over the fountain's roar. "Can you forgive me?"

She shook her head, got up, and walked away.

Herman was crushed. Suzanne was his only friend and the only woman close to him. He begged, pleaded, promised—but she turned him down this time, and the next time, and the next. Herman was left to himself with a love without love, with a dream that would remain a dream.

He thought of leaving Geneva for another job, but that would mean running away from himself, betraying his principles, and losing his last shred of self-respect. His life had become a roller coaster while his future was a cartoon. Fate seemed to require him to stand helplessly by while his innate sweetness was made bitter by experience, while his innocence decayed before his very eyes.

Le Velour Rouge on Rue du Rhône had been unusually quiet that night. Most of the clients had left, and the waitresses blew out the candles, gathered glasses, cleaned out ashtrays, and replaced the burgundy tablecloths with fresh linen that was beige. In the background, the band packed up their instruments. The bartender behind his bar across the dance floor pointed to the pendulum clock above the antique mirror.

"Last call before curfew," he said to his two remaining guests, one a young man, the other a woman of questionable character. The first two buttons of her stained blouse were undone and the hem of her skirt was above her knees.

"I'll have one more," said the young man.

"I think you've had enough," said a female voice in a tone neither soft nor overly authoritative. The woman who spoke came forward, looking tired. The skirt of her lavender evening dress was being thrown from side to side by the exaggerated swaying of her hips as she came up behind the young man's stool. She picked up the glass of cheap Madeira and gave it back to the bartender.

"What's going on here, madame? Isn't my money good enough for you?"

"Now, now, Herman, don't you get smart with me," said the woman in the lavender dress. "When I say you've had enough, you've had enough—that's all there is to it." Everybody knew her as Rosie, the owner. She ran a clean business and did not tolerate foul language, arguments, drunkenness, or fights, and her guests respected that. She knew Herman from his trips to her club with a young woman. Something must have soured between them, but Rosie made it a policy to keep her nose out of her clients' business. She only knew that Herman worked at the Du Nord across the street. She liked him and was tempted, against her principles, to learn more about him.

The dubious woman on the stool beside Herman jerked back her head. "C'mon, honey," she said. "Let's get the fuck out of here. Your business is not appreciated." As she slid from her seat, two more buttons of her blouse sprang open, entirely exposing her sagging bosom. She put her arm around Herman's neck and blew a strand of greasy hair from her face.

"Shut up and get the hell out of here!" cried Rosie. "I don't need your kind of trash in my place!" The employees looked up in shock. The woman with the low-cut blouse didn't dare to argue with Rosie and staggered out the door mumbling.

Rosie turned to the bartender. "Charles, take him home. And don't ever get him drunk again!"

Was this his life? Was Herman this person who was pub-crawling night after night, getting drunk in bad company? It was Herman all right, and in a very short time he'd fallen quite deeply into the devil's pit. Alone one night, overcome by despair, he cried out: "O my God, what's happening?"

"Why not try to be yourself?"

Herman shot up. The voice had been so loud, so real. But it was *his* voice, and he was talking to himself. Then it was the corporal talking to him from on top of the desk across the room that Herman called his home. His feet were on the chair, elbows on his knees, hands folded under his chin.

"I see you're surprised to hear my voice. You shouldn't be."

"I need help," Herman said, wincing. "I'm lost and don't know who to turn to. What can I do?"

"First, stop feeling sorry for yourself!"

"But I have no friends—no one cares for me."

"Hush!" said the voice from the desk. "Haven't you learned anything from our previous talks? Have you forgotten the man you were? Think about it and stop whining and feeling sorry for yourself. Get hold of yourself, straighten out, grow up, and put the past behind you. And one more thing—don't start a new relationship until you sort things out; you've done enough harm."

The vision disappeared.

"Monsieur Schuller?" The knock on the door was timid. "Monsieur Schuller, are you all right?" The landlady knocked again, harder. "Anything I can do for you, monsieur?"

Herman rushed to the door. "I—I'm fine, madame," he said through the solid slab of wood. "I'm okay. I—I must have dozed off and had a dream."

Herman was awake now. But his revelation had left him in shock. The admission that his life was adrift had given him a deep desire to put things right. And so he put his life back together piece by piece. He reread the inspirational novel *Mr. Howard und die Kinder* (in English, *Pied Piper*) by his favorite author, Nevil Shute. He retired early and rose before the sun was up. He took up English where he had left off and filled his files with new recipes and menus.

He began feeling better, but there were lonely nights and weak moments. At a time of solitude, he wrote to Margrit, the girl in Basel.

Dear Margrit,

I cherish the moments you spent at my side; I dream of your embrace and kiss—

Dear Margrit,

My nights are filled with the dreams of you; my heart is pounding for your love—

Dear Margrit,

Do you remember our song? "Oh Margarita, I love you so dearly; from far away I come to you. Your shining blue eyes—"

But they all ended on the floor, crumpled, stepped on, kicked aside. He couldn't do it. His mind was empty yet filled with desire— desire for a fashion model at a galleria in a city he had never visited.

$\mathcal{T}$he Porsche convertible was parked at the Puccini Galleria curb, its top stored neatly inside the well behind the white leather seats. The galleria was dark, and the only light came from the hotel entrance and from behind the fashion store's glass doors. Sabrina gave the car door a gentle push, and the lock caught with a crisp click.

"Have a wonderful vacation, partner," she said, leaning on the door, "and don't worry about us. Things will be just fine. Be sure and write me that postcard."

Angelina put her hand on Sabrina's arm. "So sweet of you to get up so early just to say goodbye," she said. "Now that I'm actually on my way, I'm glad you encouraged me to take this trip."

"You earned it, partner, every bit of it. Just enjoy yourself and stay out of trouble." She bent down and kissed Angelina on the cheek. "Get going now, before you change your mind."

Angelina pushed the start button, the engine sprang to life, and she sped off down the Corso Buenos Aires. Sabrina watched until the Porsche turned the corner, a last reflection on its bright red chassis from the corner streetlight.

Angelina was in an unparalleled good mood. *I finally did it!* Only now was she coming to grips with the reality of her trip, a vacation planned for weeks and postponed repeatedly. *Restore your strength and self-confidence,* she had told herself time and again. *Forget the struggle that threatened your sanity, put the ugliness of the trial behind you once and for all.*

Giulio's trial! It was time to wrest it from her mind, bury all the images that brought those events into focus.

It was a peculiarity of Angelina's mind, however, that what she so much wanted to forget was usually the first thing that came into her mind, and Giulio's trial wasn't any different . . . .

At Marie Theresa's urging, Angelina had been the state's star witness. She had worked long hours with Vittorio Zanardelli preparing for the trial. And as the days of sorting through evidence had turned into nights, she began to feel close to him and recognized his longing for her. She could not deny his charm or tall, muscular, good looks—he was desirable to any woman in need of love. In struggling against his lust, which became obvious as the trial dragged on, she was able to keep from taking a hard look at feelings of her own.

Back at his office after a long day sifting through evidence, Vitt had pulled out a bottle of wine he had hidden in his desk. He pulled the cork and slowly, teasingly, filled two glasses just below the rim. As Angelina reached for hers, he held onto her hand and looked deeply into her receptive eyes. His lips moved closer to hers.

"Vitt, you're married—I couldn't," she had said, resisting his hug. But it was too late. Her glass shattered on the parquet floor as his kiss stifled her words and his embrace took away her breath.

"He's married, he's too smooth, and I don't trust him," Marie Theresa had said repeatedly. But Angelina was helpless. Vitt's vow—*Trust me, my sweet rose, we'll make our plans when this thing is over*—had all but blinded her, and they made love often right up to the end of the trial.

The sentences were harsh. Giulio, as the mastermind, received ten years in the penitentiary. The remaining members of the band, due in part to Angelina's favorable testimony, got shorter prison terms—infuriating Giulio. For Angelina's considerable help in reconstructing events and allocating responsibility for the band's misdeeds, the judge dropped all charges against her.

It was over.

Giulio was led in handcuffs from the courtroom by two guards. As they passed in front of Angelina, he broke loose, jumped the rail, and leaped at her. "I'll kill you!" he shouted. A policeman wrestled him to the floor. As Giulio was taken away, his screams—"Someday I'll take care of you, you traitor!"—echoed through the courtroom until the doors were shut behind him.

Back at the office, Vitt had charmed Angelina into making love to celebrate their victory. Unfortunately the colonnello's wife had business with him that day also, and walked in on the lovers *in flagrante delicto*. She had come in quietly and watched with disgust for a few moments before making her presence known, which she did by picking up a chair and bringing it crashing down on her husband's skull. The blow wasn't life-threatening, but an ugly scene ensued during which Vittorio Zanardelli, having been scrutinized and pressured by his wife, admitted that he had been intimate with both women, often on the same day.

Hurt, betrayed, but mostly appalled at herself, Angelina fled the colonnello's office, dressing as she ran. She vowed never to speak to him again.

The red Porsche moved swiftly through the suburbs. At the northwest edge of Milan, Angelina turned off the highway and followed the road to Cimitero Maggiore. She was delighted to find the gates unlocked.

During the night, frost had fallen over the monuments like a crystalline blanket that glittered in the early morning light. Leaving the warmth of her car, she followed the cobblestone path to two graves with simple granite crosses. She dropped to her knees and said a silent prayer. A little guilt rose in her; she hadn't visited her parents' graves in weeks.

Angelina thought of that warm July day ten years ago when Aunt Virginia had brought her to the cemetery to say a last farewell to her mamma and her papa. It had been a clear, dry Milan day in one of the pleasantest summers on record. The sky had been bright, the air pure. It had been a time to celebrate and a time to grieve, a time for nature to heal and a time to forgive—a time for Italians to put evil behind them. But there lay her papa, a strong, gentle man who had never hurt a soul. He had worked hard providing for his family and had so little to show for it.

Now, ten years later, Angelina had come to grips with the realities of life, of wars where the innocent suffer most, where some die for others, sometimes just for the chance to raise their voices against injustice. Angelina thought of her papa as a pioneer. The brutal death of her father and others like him had forced a confrontation between the government and the people it served, clearing the way to true Italian justice.

Angelina scraped the dry soil with her fingers. She rose and walked to the water faucet at the wall, unhooked the copper watering can from its bracket, filled it three fourths full, and took it back to the grave. She removed the spray-spout and poured the water between the blooms, careful not to splatter the tender petals. With the remaining water, she rinsed the frost off the gravestone.

Slowly, she went down the path she had walked with Aunt Virginia on that beautiful summer day to the train that had taken her to her new home at Valsesia Valley. As if it were yesterday she remembered how she'd gone down this path with her father's priceless gift beside her: a bicycle made from surplus parts and lovelier than any she had ever seen.

Angelina raced through Aosta and up the winding road across Petit-St-Bernard Pass, through endless hairpin turns on the way to Aix-les-Bains. Angelina dreamed of sunbathing on the sandy beach, soaking in the hot spas, and dining at fine restaurants. Maybe she would even dance at the local nightspot with the Parisian band. Was she in need of romance? The thought made her blush.

A year ago, while on a short vacation with Marie Theresa, Angelina had met Maurice—tall, handsome, with plenty of French charm. He was the general manager of the Le Manoir Hotel, where she'd made her reservation, and his signature was on the room confirmation card. "I'm anxiously awaiting your arrival," he had scribbled at the bottom. Maurice was one of few men who had attracted Angelina, and she looked forward to seeing him again.

Since her affair with Vitt Zanardelli, Angelina had shied

away from having relations with any man and fought her desires for intimacy. But the long days and lonely nights were a constant reminder that she was a woman with all the cravings and lust instilled by nature. As she shed admirer after admirer, brushed off one marriage proposal after another, she often thought of Marie Theresa's advice: "That young corporal is the type you can trust, someone who will always will be there for you."

Thinking of Herman Schuller made her breasts ache with desire for his strong arms around her and made her lips burn for want of intimacy. When she dreamt of him, her dreams were shaped around these desires and, dreaming, she denied herself nothing in their fulfillment. Angelina was torn between a strong sense of loyalty to Herman Schuller and an equally strong need for physical intimacy.

Perhaps Maurice would be the one to fill that need. She honored the love she had felt for Herman just as she honored the love she had felt for her parents, but both of these great loves belonged to the past. Still, her need for intimacy was very much a part of her day-to-day life. It would be insistent tonight, more insistent tomorrow. She'd come to the point of acknowledging to herself that she needed *someone*, and of the men in her life since Herman, Maurice had been the only one able to sustain her interest. What if she didn't say yes to him, and this were not only her best chance of happiness but her last?

CHAPTER 16

*E*very year, fall brought peace and quiet to the Palais des Nations. International negotiations dwindled, many dignitaries left Geneva. Even the popular Du Nord restaurant felt the pinch.

Herman had given his customary two-week notice to his employer, and this was his last day at the restaurant. It was unusually slow, and the *chef de cuisine* allowed him to check out early. Herman gathered his knives and rolled them lovingly into their leather pouch, then said goodbye to his friends on the *brigade de cuisine*—all people he had enjoyed working with. Walking out of the restaurant for the last time, his final pay envelope in his jacket, he was racked with chest pain. Taking a long last look at his place of work did nothing to ease the pain of leaving.

As Herman dawdled along the sidewalk, he had the sudden desire to see the Fiat Topolino at the dealership. The pain in his chest forgotten, he ran down the middle of the empty street and hard around the corner to the show-window . . . there was the Fiat, looking puny between its two American cousins, but full of associations that made him weak with desire.

"I can't forget you, oh, my sweet Angelina! I can't forget you!" he cried. "I love you, I need you, I can't live without you. I want to be in your arms. I want to spend my life with you." He pressed his face against the cold plate glass, smudging it with his tears. He heard a noise from across the street but he didn't care. Something bittersweet gathered in his mouth and he spat it on the sidewalk. He put his hand over his mouth, but it was too late—his dinner and farewell champagne shot from his mouth. The pain in his chest eased—then it was back with renewed fury. He slumped against the showcase glass.

When the spasms ended he felt embarrassed and looked around. He was alone. He pulled out his handkerchief and wiped the smudges from the glass.

In a week, he would report to his military reserve unit in Winterthur. Following his service, he would enter the Belvoir Park Hotel School in Zürich. He had not seen his parents in six months and had planned to spend a few days with them. He owed it to them, especially to his father, who had made going to school financially feasible.

But here was the Fiat.

He tried to concentrate. What if he drove to Milan, to the Galleria, to the fashion store? Maybe he'd get a glimpse of Angelina, even find the courage to talk to her. Or would he? Herman had no illusions. He was no longer the courageous corporal Angelina had admired. The All' Acqua incident, and his part in it, was a once-in-a-lifetime series of events. In his wildest dreams he couldn't imagine being tested ever again by circumstances remotely like those. True, he had outdone himself while Angelina had been vulnerable and confused, but he was no longer the man she had looked up to.

Yet . . . he still wanted to see her, needed to . . . what if she rejected him, laughed at him, threw him out onto the street? Angelina wouldn't do that, he was sure, as sure as he was about being unable to confront her. The more he thought about her, the more he wanted to be with her.

Then he devised a plan that seemed sensible at the time. He'd drive back to Aix-les-Bains and have lunch with Monique . . . continue via the Petit-St-Bernard Pass to the crossroads at Aosta . . . . And by the time he got there he'd know what to do, which way to turn: left back to Switzerland or right to Milan.

"That's it," he cried aloud in the empty street. "I'll do just that!"

SATURDAY, OCTOBER 20.

Herman was up early. He took a final look at the city he had come to love, and it seemed harder this time to say farewell. But he did not brood for long. He looked forward to his trip through France and Italy—a journey filled with expectation and uncertainty.

The scooter hummed dependably. Almost without realizing it, he crossed the French border, and three hours later he was on the last stretch to Aix-les-Bains, five kilometers down the road. He didn't know what was pulling him toward that city with such force, nor did he really care—he had eyes only for his first goal, beyond the next hill. At first glance, he was just another tourist on an excursion, but up close, his tension was apparent: set jaw, pale cheeks, glassy eyes. Herman's mind was a mosaic of colorful but disconnected thoughts, and the trip with its promised pleasures had become an obsession.

He stopped abruptly. Below him spread a familiar sight— Aix-les-Bains at the lake, the sandy beaches, cubicles with colorful umbrellas, people sunbathing along the shores, and sailboats skimming the gentle waves. But Herman did not see the beauty or feel the warmth; all he felt was frustration and indecision. He cut the engine and rolled the scooter under the shadow of a large camellia tree.

What's wrong with me? I'm supposed to be enjoying myself, he thought. He removed his leather cap and brushed back his hair. As he sat askew on the seat, he calmed somewhat. He had plenty of time to get to Milan before dark, if that was what he wanted. But that would cut short his time at the Du Monde and his planned visit with Monique. Should he spend the night? In the struggle for preeminence, no one thought took hold.

He untied the saddlebag strapped to the rear of the tandem seat, removed the engine cowling, checked cables and bolts and fluttered the carburetor—but he knew nothing was wrong with the engine. He replaced the cowling and the saddlebag, sat back on the tandem seat, and let his eyes wander about the lake as if looking for an answer from below its waves. Perhaps spending the night in Aix-les-Bains wasn't such a bad idea. If he couldn't achieve a more relaxed state of mind he would be in no condition to meet Angelina in Milan. Besides, he'd always wanted to visit that nightspot across the lake that Monique had mentioned. She might even join him. Would she? Though she was married, Herman had a feeling that she liked him.

That's it! I'll spend the night. He jump-started the engine and sped into town in search of a hotel room he could afford.

◄►◄✴►◄►

Angelina was still asleep, worn-out from the long drive through the mountains. The rising sun reached her pillow through the brocaded curtains. She squinted, opened her eyes, closed them, turned the other way. She wasn't ready to wake up—wanted to know the end of the dream. But she couldn't reconnect, the dream was gone. She sat up on one elbow.

I can't lie in bed all day. She sighed. *The heck with it—you can do as you please.* She lay back down. Wasn't the point of taking a vacation to do whatever she wanted?—spread out, sleep longer, and dream some more. The dream, that beautiful dream—*oh, Corporal!*

She suddenly realized that this was the first time she had not been working, striving, pushing her way up the ladder of success. From the moment she had left the serenity of her aunt's home, her ambition had been to be, quite simply, the best. Best waitress, top of her class at the university, clawing her way up the seemingly impossible path to triumph—to the highly recognized fashion model she was today. Then, with Marie Theresa's unexpected death, the whole process was starting all over again, slaving, thriving, building momentum to assure her business a place at the top. But now all this was behind her, if only temporarily, forgotten among the fluffy pillows and soft sheets and the warming blanket.

Angelina shot up—she must have dozed off again. She pushed the comforter to the foot of the bed, stretched, twisted, and pressed her fingers onto her tummy. *Better do my sit-ups.* She counted, "One, two, three—" and stopped at twenty-four. The exercise made her heart pound and her breath come fast. She gazed at the chandelier and watched a half-dozen flies swirl and dive in the sun's narrow spear of light. Angelina remembered as a kid watching them zigzag around the light bulb in her dormer room. There was magic lying in bed and staring at the ceiling and prophesying about a wondrous future.

Her suite—number 71—was the same she and Marie Theresa had stayed in for two nights a year ago. The same antique furniture, the curtains she remembered with layered, hand-stitched fabric, and the fresh-cut, red roses on the table spreading the same sweet fragrance. Her gaze fell on a card she'd overlooked inside the bouquet that had arrived the night before. She slid from bed and opened the tiny envelope. It was from Maurice.

> I'm anxiously awaiting your arrival. Give me a call at the office, please! Your humble servant,
>
> Maurice.

Reading the card gave Angelina a hot flash. She unlocked the glass door to the balcony, pushed it open, and let the cool air hit her face.

Angelina had not seen Maurice in the afternoon when she checked into her room, and he wasn't there when she returned from an early dinner. Anxiously, she picked up the phone, but placed it back in its cradle after only two rings. She wasn't ready to meet Maurice, not yet. *All in good time.* She'd have breakfast first. Then perhaps she'd be ready to face him.

She took her time. She ran the water in the bathtub, rolled a hand towel onto the rim, pushed her head into it, closed her eyes, and soaked in the hot water. She lathered her feet and her legs and thighs. Her breasts were more sensitive than normal as she spread the foam around her nipples. She shivered. *Must be because of the long sleep.* She pushed her feet against the bathtub, bit her lip, dropped the sponge, and gripped the rim with both hands. The sensation passed slowly.

She toweled in front of the full-length mirror, watched her breasts move with the rhythm of the towel, her nipples pink and stiff. Seeing her naked body renewed her awareness, and an itch brought about a touch of narcissism. Her body ached. Angelina was in need of intimate love, a man's rough touch. She closed her eyes, clenched her fists, and pressed her nails into her palms.

She rifled the armoire, not sure what to wear, then chose a light blue, sleeveless blouse that generously showed her cleavage and a dark-blue skirt that was too tight and much too short. She turned in front of the mirror. *Rather blatant!* She left her suite and walked down the stairs.

The young porter spotted the woman from suite 71 coming down the steps, her legs long and slender, her hips swaying, her breasts moving in harmony with her steps. A whistle escaped him involuntarily.

Angelina smiled. The young lad had helped her with her luggage the night before. "*Bonjour,* Henry."

"*Bonjour,* madame, it's so nice to see you again. You look so— so beautiful today."

"*Merci,* Henri—*merci beaucoup.*"

"Are you going to have breakfast?" But he didn't wait for an answer; he walked ahead and opened the glass doors to the breakfast room. She chose a table by the window, and Henry helped her with the chair.

"Thank you, Henry." She gave him a tip.

"*Merci,* madame, that wasn't necessary," he said, but quickly tucked it in his shirt.

A young waitress came to the table. Angelina ordered the *petit déjeuner* of *café au lait, croissant,* butter, and black cherry jam. She was a little nervous. Maurice knew that she was here. Thinking of his tall, good looks filled her with fresh desire. She had felt comfortable at his side, and he was the only man she could even think of having an affair with—though she still blushed at the thought. She slid the silver clasp from the rolled pink napkin and spread out the silverware on the white damask.

"May I, madame?" asked a tall man dressed in a stylish black suit. He put down a basket with two croissants, a silver bowl with iced-down butter, and a pony jar of black cherry jam. He poured her coffee and milk from both pots simultaneously.

Angelina looked up. "Maurice, what a pleasure to see you. I missed you last night," she said with almost too much vigor. She stretched out her hand. "I was just thinking of you. Please join me for coffee."

Maurice stood behind the chair across from her and put his hands on the backrest. "How nice of you to think of me! I looked for you last night, but you had left for dinner by the time I came back from an errand. I was tempted to call your room, but"—he turned red—"You hadn't left word. I didn't want to disturb you if you needed to rest after your trip." Leaning across the table, he took her hand to his lips and kissed her fingers.

The pressure of his moist lips made her neck tingle, and she had to hold back a moan. "I was tired and fell asleep almost immediately," she sighed. "Mountain driving is so demanding. Still, I wish you had made that call."

He turned the chair sideways and sat. "Madame, you should let me do the driving. Let me do everything for you. Save your energy, so you can have fun in the evening."

"Of course, Maurice," laughed Angelina. "I'm here to relax, not to exert myself."

"*Bien sur*, madame, but remember, Aix-les-Bains is for lovers; its sole aim is to please the soul and brace the heart. It is where one forgets one's pain to find life's beauty, where one finds new love, where one—"

"Okay, okay, Maurice, I've got the picture," said Angelina between giggles.

He took her hand and kissed it again, almost forgetting himself, his voice a low murmur now. "Angelina, my dear, my love, I must see you in the privacy of your room. I couldn't sleep last night knowing that you were so close. I couldn't wait to see you." Flustered by his unpremeditated outburst, he turned a shade redder than Angelina's hair.

She smiled. "It's okay, Maurice. Don't be embarrassed. I, too, could barely wait to see you. Tell you what—I'll finish breakfast and be back in my suite in thirty minutes."

He jumped to his feet. "I'll be there! You can count on me!" He backed up a step or two without taking his eyes off her, then flew from the room.

Angelina couldn't help smiling and shaking her head. She finished her breakfast. The tingle in her neck was back and was now affecting her shoulders and chest, but she was having second thoughts. She put down her cup, an uneasy feeling in her heart. Was she going to go through with this? She liked Maurice. He had charm, he made her laugh, and he was honest, maybe too honest. Could she love him, though? Or could she learn to?

But there was no simple answer, and right now, Angelina didn't care to find one. Yet . . . hadn't she come to Aix-les-Bains for an answer to just this question? Wasn't the reunion with Maurice what she had dreamt about for weeks? Her feelings had carried her this far and it was too late to back down—her desires were now, not tomorrow or next week. Was she losing control? *What's wrong with that—why can't I lose control just once?* It was now or never. She took another sip of coffee and hastened to the elevator.

The key to her room didn't fit. She tried again, but the lock wouldn't turn. Her hands shook like leaves in a storm. *Get hold of yourself.* Then the key turned and the lock clicked open. She entered—*light, I need lots of light*—she threw back the heavy curtains and opened both balcony doors. The blazing sun hit her face. *I'm hot!* She shut the curtains, ran to the bathroom, and splashed cold water on her cheeks and neck.

Angelina could not remember feeling like this before. She dropped onto the wingback chair and closed her eyes. *You must calm down. Get hold of your emotions or you'll spoil everything!* But her body ached from desire. She heard steps running up the stairs and coming closer. She rushed to the door, intoxicated with anticipation. The knock on the door was timid. She opened.

"Angelina, my love," Maurice murmured as he stormed into her suite. He slung his arms around her waist and pressed his lips onto hers. His desire was real, his kiss was deep and solid, his breath was heavy on her face, smelling good, feeling good—everything was so good. His stomach rubbed against her stomach, his thigh was hard and muscular between her legs, oh heavens, how long had it been! Suddenly his hand was coming up inside her skirt, higher, closer—

Something did not feel right. A second before, Angelina had been prepared to do anything Maurice asked of her with passion and desire. Now she wasn't sure. His breath lost its sweetness, his lips no longer had that tender touch, his hand didn't belong *there.* The magic, the dream, the desire faded as if scratched through with the stroke of a fountain pen. This was not *her*—not what she wanted. She pulled away, hesitantly at first, then vigorously, still not sure why. Then it hit her—the dream—how could she do this!

"Not so fast, Maurice," she said, in control again. She kept him at bay with both hands. He gave her an astonished look. She said, "I—I don't know. Let's talk this over before we do something we'll both regret."

He did not want to let go, and she dragged him to the love seat where she pushed him into the cushions.

His eyes turned the size of egg yolks. "But Angelina, my love—"

"Shhh." Angelina put her finger to his lips and sat as far from him as she could. Even though it endured mere seconds, the silence was awkward.

"Please listen, Maurice," she began. She swallowed and searched for the right words. "I gave you a sign this morning of what I wanted—what I thought I wanted. Then, just now, something else came over me, something I can't control. Maurice, I—I can't go through with this."

"But you—"

"I gave you hope. I'm sorry, awfully sorry. In a moment of passion, I gave you my pledge, but I should have thought it out better. Forgive me, please. But I won't change my mind—to do this would be wrong."

"I thought you liked me," he whined.

"I do, Maurice. I like you. You're a decent man, but my feelings for you are more like friendship. There's a difference between *like* and *love*."

"I don't believe this. I thought—"

"So did I. I'm truly sorry." She stood and went to the door, still slightly ajar. He followed, hangdog, and squeezed by her with eyes lowered to the floor, white teeth showing between slightly parted lips. Angelina felt a rush of passion for his letdown and buried her fingers in his hair. Then she kissed his cheek. He mistook the gesture. His eyes lit up again, a smile was changing his mouth . . . He grabbed her waist. But Angelina quickly pushed him into the corridor and locked the door.

She stood for a moment with her back against the door, trembling. Then she flung herself onto her bed, letting the tears come. Fighting for control, she choked back her sobs and stopped trembling.

There was a knock at the door. I *must have dozed again.* She opened it hesitantly, but it was only the chambermaid. "Give me five minutes, please," said Angelina.

"Thank you, madame, I'll be back," said the woman.

Angelina looked at her watch. It was half past eleven; she had slept for a solid hour and felt good. She brushed her hair in front of the mirror. Her blouse was wrinkled, and she changed it to one with long sleeves and a high neck. I *should get out of this sexy skirt,* she thought, but didn't. She walked down through the hotel lobby and to the parking lot unnoticed. Just as she unlocked her Porsche, a tap on the shoulder spun her around.

"*Pardonnez-moi,* madame, *s'il vous plaît,*" said a stranger in a light-gray raincoat, checkered scarf, and black felt hat.

"I beg your pardon?" snapped Angelina, puzzled by the coat he was wearing on such a lovely day.

"I didn't mean to frighten you, madame, but this is your Porsche, isn't it?"

"Yes, but what's this all about?"

"Then you are Signora Bianci?"

Angelina nodded apprehensively. "It's 'signorina.'"

The stranger cleared his throat with a short cough. "I'm with the police department of Grenoble, mademoiselle. We need to talk." He showed his papers. "But this is not the place. It must be private. Can we go to your hotel?"

Angelina shook her head. "I first want to know, monsieur, what this is all about."

The detective became impatient. "As I said, I'll explain in private, in your hotel room or wherever you would like for us to meet."

Angelina gave in. "I'm on my way to a restaurant to dine. The Du Monde has great food and is only a few blocks up the road. You can ask me your questions while I'm waiting for my lunch."

"Will we have privacy?"

"On a beautiful day like this? Of course, monsieur. Everyone will be sitting on the outside terrace. I'll take a table inside. Will that be satisfactory?"

"*Magnifique!* I'll meet you at the restaurant."

Angelina drove to the Du Monde and parked across the street. She killed the engine and sat back, her gaze wandering about the sky. It hadn't sunk in yet completely, but the detective's secretiveness was starting to bother her. She shrugged and walked across to the restaurant.

"*Bonjour,* madame," said the young waitress. "So nice to see you again. Isn't it a lovely day?"

"A very nice day, Marcie," said Angelina, recognizing the waitress from last night. "If at all possible, I'd like to sit inside."

"But the garden terrace is so beautiful on a day like this . . . wouldn't you be more comfortable out here?" But her manner changed after a glance at her customer. "You may sit wherever you'd like, madame."

Angelina chose a table at the back. Marcie turned on the lights in that section and began to remove the excess silverware.

"Leave an extra setting; someone will be joining me."

Marcie quickly reset the table. "What would you like to drink, madame?"

"Two deciliters of Beaujolais, *s'il vous plaît*."

"*Parfait*, madame." The waitress left.

Angelina's neck stiffened. Why were the French police looking for her? She should have followed the detective's advice and met him at the hotel. Now she would have to wait for him. *Where the heck is he?* Policemen didn't get lost. She looked at her watch. He should have been here by now.

Marcie brought a small decanter of lightly colored red wine and poured half a glass. "Anything else before you decide, madame?" She handed Angelina a menu.

"Uh, just bring me your daily special. It's always good. My friend can order when he gets here."

Angelina put her elbows on the table and dropped her head into her hands. *What's holding him?* She glanced at her watch, at the door, back at her watch. To pass the time, she studied the stained-glass panel that divided the terrace from the dining room.

Herman cut the engine. He propped the scooter on its stand and swung from the saddle. He had driven around town looking for a hotel. But the rooms at the Agora on Rue de Chambéry, and the Hôtel des Bains and the Manoir on rue Georges cost more than he was willing to spend, and he thought of the others, including the Beaulieu on Charles de Gaulle and the old Métropole on rue du Casino, as unacceptable dumps. He decided to have an early lunch at the Du Monde.

He removed the saddlebag from the tandem seat and slung it over his shoulder. Two zippered pockets allowed for ample storage, more than he needed, and two smaller, waterproof pockets held his insurance papers, passport, and extra currency. The bag could be carried like a handbag or over the shoulders like a rucksack. He had everything packed for his weeklong trip: toiletry case, pajamas, warm underwear, an extra shirt, shorts, socks, a large bar of soap, a fluffy hand towel, and two soft washcloths. He had dropped off his other belongings at the train station the night before to be shipped to his parents.

He secured the scooter and was halfway across the street to the restaurant when he noticed the Porsche in the rear parking lot. The top was down, and it had an all-white interior. There was something familiar . . . But this one was a bright red; Marie Theresa's Porsche had been black.

The Garden Terrace was crowded and every table taken, including the one by the wrought iron gate. Just then a single man rose from the table close to the stained-glass panels. Herman quickly claimed the table for himself and pushed the dirty dishes to the side.

"I can't believe you're alone. No girl this time?" cried a teasing female voice behind him.

Herman spun around. "Monique! How nice to see you."

Monique dropped onto the empty chair across from him. "You won't mind my company, will you? We're old friends, right?" They both laughed. She took his hand and hung onto it while she rose and came to his side. She put her arms around him and leaned on his shoulder. Her voice was a whisper in his ear. "Nice to have you back, *mon ami.*"

Surprised at her unexpected closeness, Herman put an arm around her waist and pulled her close, so that he could feel her soft hip against him. "I've been missing you, Monique, more than any time before."

"Well, you had company, *mon ami*, remember?" she said. "But strange that you should bring it up—I thought the same just now." She pulled away.

Wow! "It's true. I could really use a friend right now," he said, trying to suppress his shock.

"Well, you know how lonely I get with a husband who's traveling all the time."

"Say the word, Monique." His words were clear and strong,

though it made his face red to say them. "I am more than willing to make good on my thoughts."

"Hush, you didn't come here because of me," she said with a shrug.

"Shall we put that to a vote?"

Monique piled the dirty dishes onto her left hand and wrist, pulled a rag from her apron, and wiped the table. "You don't give up easily, *hein?*" she said. "But where is your girl?"

"That's just it, Monique. I'm on my own now. And this might be my last trip through here, at least for some time."

"How disappointing," Monique said. "You're leaving Geneva?"

"I've got my yearly military service to take care of, then hotel school in Zürich. I'll miss you."

While arranging the dishes on a tray stand, she spoke to him over her shoulder. "I'll miss you, too." She quickly picked up the full tray and took it to the back.

Herman swallowed. Monique had never been so straightforward about her feelings. Would she go out with him after work? They could go to the nightspot across the lake, have some wine, even dance. *What an opportunity!*

Monique returned to the table. "What is it going to be, *mon ami?*"

"Whenever you get off work—"

"What . . . ?"

"Oh, I'm sorry, Monique. Uh, I thought you said—uh." He couldn't help stuttering. "I'm starved," he said quickly. "Had no breakfast, you know. Hmm, what's your special today?"

Monique shook her head at his indecision. "It's *vol-au-vent à la marinière avec les petit pois et des pommes croquette—il est très bon.*" Then, with a smile, she asked what difference it would make; wouldn't he order the dried beef and prosciutto anyhow? "I'll get your beer."

Monique's cheerful smile and laughter made Herman forget about the Porsche. But when he looked across the street, there it was again. Exactly the color of Angelina's Fiat . . . The license plate was hidden behind another car. Sure, the odds were a million to one against, but what if it were Marie Theresa's new Porsche, and what if Angelina were with her, right here in Aix-les-Bains? He shivered. "Impossible!"

"*Comment?*" Monique was back, "Are you in a dream world, *mon ami?*

"Monique . . . sorry. I thought, uh—I thought I saw a friend's car."

Monique served his beer and took his order. To her surprise, he wanted the *vol-au-vent* special.

Angelina stared at the stained-glass panel. The young lad's voice and laughter on the outside terrace were familiar. The hand movements of the man silhouetted against the glass panel synchronized with a voice that was vaguely familiar. He was flirting with the waitress.

Though convinced that the odds were a million to one against it—the man who had come to mind wasn't the type to flirt with a French waitress—she had to be sure. She stood, went to the door—and ran smack into the detective with a force that all but toppled him.

He held onto the door handle with one hand and Angelina's arm with the other. "I'm so sorry, mademoiselle."

"It's my fault. But where were you?"

"Phone calls," he said. "And I had to stop at the precinct to tell them where I'd be."

"I had the waitress leave the setting," said Angelina with decreasing tension. "If you're hungry, you can eat lunch with me."

He thanked her for her kindness and placed his raincoat, checkered scarf, and hat over the chair to her left. He sat across from her. He pulled a cigar from a silver case, bit off the end, and spit it to the floor. He stroked a match and lit the flat end, then puffed rapidly to get it going.

Angelina had thought the meeting urgent and resented all the time he was taking. Now he was leaning back in his chair and blowing smoke at the ceiling. His rather large lips were cracked and curled outward, exposing teeth that had yellowed from years of nicotine. His right eyebrow jutted out around an old scar, doubtlessly the result of a fight. A miserable specimen perhaps, but after all, there was warmth about him, and he carried himself with the confidence and charm so typical of the French.

At last he spoke. "You're staying at the Hotel Le Manoir?" he asked, more like an affirmation than a question.

Angelina nodded.

The detective took a quick puff from his cigar. "I was contacted by a friend of ours, Vittorio Zanardelli . . . ."

Blood rushed to her head. "Get to the point, monsieur; I want to know what this is all about!"

"Please, madame, give me a chance'" said the detective, surprised by her reaction. "As I said, the colonnello has contacted me. He has disturbing information . . . ."

Angelina interrupted again. "I don't even know your name," she snarled.

"Of course. I'm sorry," he said reluctantly. "I'm Jacques Simon, Capitaine Simon. Vitt asked me to find you. He knew you were on vacation in Aix-les-Bains and not much else. Anyway, I began looking for you as a personal favor to him. It took some doing, mademoiselle, but I found your Porsche; I must have checked every hotel parking lot. Vitt said—" He stopped abruptly. Six men walked in and seated themselves at an adjacent table, laughing loudly and arguing bitterly.

The capitaine was looking wildly around. The men who had just arrived were evidently making him very nervous. "We can't talk here, but it is important that we talk soon and in total privacy. It would be best if we met at your hotel."

Angelina raised a shoulder. "We can still have lunch," she said.

He shook his head. "No, they need me at the precinct—more calls." He threw up his hands. "Everybody's looking for me! At your hotel then?"

Angelina thought it over. "Well, we certainly wouldn't be disturbed in my suite. It is number 71 on the second floor." She paused. "Ask for Henry at the reception desk." She looked at her watch. "I'll be along shortly. Shall we say, uh, in half an hour?"

"I'll be waiting, mademoiselle, and don't be late. It's important."

No sooner had the Frenchman left her than a waitress advised the men at the next table that their table on the terrace was ready and they left *en masse*. Angelina was mad at herself again. *I don't even know this detective, and I invite him to my private room.* She fiddled with her napkin, creased it with her fingers, and ironed it with the back of her hand. Why would a detective drive seventy kilometers to Aix-les-Bains just to deliver a message? Why not pick up the phone and call? She shook her head. Why was the colonnello, with whom she had severed all ties, trying to reach her?

Marcie brought the *vol-au-vent*, and for the time being, Angelina forgot about the detective and the mystery man on the other side of the stained-glass panel.

CHAPTER 17

*M*onique brought Herman's *vol-au-vent*.

He directed her attention across the street. "Do you know who drives that Porsche?" he asked.

"The red convertible?"

"That's the one."

"It belongs to a charming woman. She dined with us last night. She has lots of class and could be an actress or some rich man's mistress. I haven't seen her today, though."

There was unusual urgency in Herman's eyes. "Do you know her name?"

Monique raised an eyebrow. "I heard it last night but don't remember. She's a good tipper, so I was told."

"Was her name Masoni?"

Monique shook her head. "No, I don't think so; doesn't sound like it."

"Marie Theresa?"

Monique shrugged again. "I'm not sure, but—no, it was definitely different, a longer name. I'm sure it wasn't Marie Theresa." Monique was mystified about her young friend's sudden interest in the beautiful stranger. "I think she was Marcie's guest last night; I'll ask her." She looked at Herman suspiciously. "But tell me, *mon ami*, why the sudden interest in that woman? You wouldn't know her— she's out of your league!"

Instead of an answer, Herman bombarded her with questions. "Is she by herself? What's the color of her hair? Her age—tell me her age! Does she have an Italian accent?"

"Not so fast!" Monique threw up her hands defensively. "Let

me see if I can make sense from your nonsense. The woman was alone, as far as I could tell. She had her hair wrapped under a scarf, so my guess of its color is as good as yours. Her age? Hmm," she sighed, "women of her class never seem to age. My guess is: maybe as much as thirty, but almost certainly not over that. She's definitely French—no accent." Monique laughed self-consciously. "Come on *mon ami*, drop it—you wouldn't have a chance!"

A patron at the adjacent table waved peremptorily, and Monique turned away.

Herman overlooked Monique's last remark. He was breathing hard. When he met Marie Theresa at the hospital in Losone, a black scarf had covered her hair only partially, but Angelina had a habit of covering hers entirely. Angelina was fluent in French. Could it be she? He took a bite from the *vol-au-vent*, but his appetite was gone. He poked the pastry shell with his fork, playing with it until the filling leaked onto the plate. With sudden determination, he pulled his billfold from the saddlebag and left enough francs on the table to settle his bill with tip. He dashed across the street.

Monique saw him run from the table. She stared after him, as bewildered as she was disheartened. What had gotten into him?

Herman just stood there staring at the Porsche—the license plates were Italian. He shook his head, then looked aimlessly at the horizon. *This is insane. It's just not possible!* It wasn't the first time Herman had had such feelings. He had chased after Porsche convertibles before, had gotten cold waiting for owners at curbside, and had followed female strangers—only to be disappointed or humiliated. Was this another mirage?

Perhaps not. The Porsche was real and so were the Italian license plates. He bit his lip and closed his eyes. *No way!* Time to put all these sightings behind. He took a deep breath, kick-started the scooter, and accelerated around the curve.

Angelina walked onto the terrace. A scooter shot by. She was in total disbelief. Was this? It couldn't be! The driver's head was covered with a slick leather cap, its straps loose against his cheeks. But the profile—his muscular build. Was it possible—could it be Herman Schuller? Was the silhouette in the stained-glass panel—Angelina paled. *Come on—there's no chance of that.*

She crossed the street to her Porsche, slid into the seat, and sat motionless for a minute as she brooded about the man on the scooter. She thought of her dream. Was this a coincidence? Perplexed, she started the car and drove down Main Street toward her hotel.

Her mind was elsewhere. At the first stoplight, she almost rammed a truck. She looked at her hands—they trembled. She clutched the steering wheel until her knuckles whitened. She squinted; her vision blurred. She approached the intersection at Rue de George, the street to her hotel.

I'd never forgive myself! Angelina hit the brakes. Deafening horns and curses erupted as she made a U-turn. She raced back to the Du Monde. The heck with the no-parking signs! Out of breath, she ran up to Monique and grabbed her arm. "Who was the young lad who left on the scooter just now? I need to know—it's important."

Monique was spellbound. Why would this elegant woman inquire about her young friend? But curiosity quickly got the best of her. "Let's step inside, madame. More quiet there, and I'm ready for a smoke anyhow." She shouted over her shoulder, "Marcie, I'm going for a smoke. Watch my station? Thanks!"

Angelina followed her to a table. Monique lit a cigarette and offered one to her.

Angelina shook her head. "Thank you, I don't smoke," she said. "You are Monique, aren't you?"

"Yes," said Monique, "but how can I help you? You must know I'm extremely curious."

"My name is Angelina Bianci. What do you know about the young man who sat in your section a while ago? You seem to know him; I heard you laughing and talking together."

Monique nodded and took a long puff.

Angelina became impatient. "Do you know his name?" Her hands trembled.

"Well, I don't know him well," Monique began. "He stops here now and then to dine. Last time, about ten days ago, he was here with a young woman, pretty, too. We talk, have a few jokes. He was by himself this time."

"His name, please."

Monique took two long puffs then blew the smoke from the corner of her lip. "He's a Swiss guy. Don't know his patronymic, always has been *'mon ami'* to me, but I think his first name is Herman."

Angelina was speechless. Finally, very softly, she said his name: "Herman Schuller."

Monique's eyes opened wide. "That's it! I'm not good with German names," she said, still surprised. "This is wild! You're asking the same questions of him as he asked of you. Then I saw him looking at your Porsche. Frankly, I thought he'd lost his mind."

"Please, Monique, is there anything else you can tell me? Where is he staying?"

"I don't know. It hasn't been his habit to stay over when he comes here. He said he lives in Geneva, and will be going to hotel school soon—I think he said in Zürich." She paused. "I'm a little puzzled, though, Signora," she continued. "When he asked about your Porsche, he wanted to know if your name was Marie Theresa. Is that your real name, perhaps?"

Angelina smiled at Monique and got up to leave. "You don't know how much this means to me, Monique. Thank you so very much." She hugged the waitress and pressed a generous tip into her hand. Just before running out the door, she called over her shoulder, "If you see Monsieur Schuller, tell him that I'm staying at the Le Manoir on Rue de George. Tell him that I am waiting!"

Herman felt like a coward for leaving Monique that way, but the thought of Angelina had removed all traces of desire for the waitress.

Shoppers and browsers crowded the lively bazaar. Herman mingled with them. He liked crowds. They gave a feeling of belonging, being one with the people even if they were total strangers, a different nationality.

He walked by a shoe booth that was shaded by a field-green canvas. Wooden shelves stacked four high were filled with walking shoes and slippers. Herman had never seen so many shoes. Then came a booth with racks of black leather jackets and sleeveless vests—ungodly expensive, Herman thought—and beside it, a glass display case crammed with shiny silver chains, hearts and crosses, and denominational amulets. One booth had nothing but belts, hats, and gloves. Another market stall was piled high with garish garments—*disgusting; what woman would wear those?*—and the next one displayed colorful shirts on steel cables stretched between the corner posts. Herman stopped and let his hands glide through the soft fabrics. *Twelve francs for a sleeveless shirt*—no way!

He joined a group of men around an open booth and waited patiently for his turn at front row. Mannequin legs in silk stockings protruded like corn stalks from a large square table. The owner, a slender woman, beautifully tall with a permanent smile on large, sexy lips, slid silk after silk onto her shaved legs. Men picked up pretty boxes with red ribbons, and the model stopped long enough to collect for them.

Herman strolled to a booth simply because the salesgirl was very pretty.

"Do you accept Swiss currency?" he asked. *How silly; they always do.*

"Oui, monsieur."

Herman pointed to a pile of sweaters. "May I?"

She said, "With pleasure, monsieur. What color do you prefer?"

He pointed to a stack. "The blue. No, not that one, the darker, the third in that stack."

She pulled the sweater from the pile and handed it to him. He took off his jacket and slipped the sweater over his head. He smoothed down the long sleeves. It felt soft and comfortable, a perfect fit. She held up a round mirror, and he turned in front of it longer than he usually would.

"Brings out the blue in your eyes."

Herman looked at her a little surprised, "Thank you, mademoiselle. Hmmm, it feels good, really good." He slipped the sweater over his head again and gave it back to her. "I'll take it." The girl let out a yelp as though it was her first sale. She shook a brown paper bag open and shoved the sweater into it. Herman handed her twenty Swiss franks, and she gave him back the change in French currency. He held briefly onto her hand. "Your eyes are hazel," he said. "Has anybody ever told you about the sparkle in them?"

Blood shot to her cheeks, and she quickly pulled back her hand. "Put on your sweater, monsieur. It will give you the warmth you're seeking."

"*Touché, touché!*"

Herman was back in the crowd. He shadowed a shapely woman he thought to be about eighteen. She had a slim figure enhanced by a tight skirt and fitted, white and blue-striped shirt. She clearly wasn't used to wearing high heels and stumbled across the plaza's cobblestones. She entered a Citröen car dealership, where a man of considerable age greeted her. He opened the driver door to a black Citröen and helped her into the seat, then hopped in from the other side. The girl started the engine and shifted into gear, but the engine stalled. It was her first driving lesson, or so it seemed. She tried again, and the engine stalled once more.

Herman shook his head. *How clumsy!* Couldn't be all that difficult to learn to drive, he thought—not for a man, anyhow. Still, besides Lieutenant Stucki, none of his friends owned a car and only a few knew how to drive. He shrugged and returned to the bazaar.

A pair of white tennis shoes caught his attention at a small boutique across the plaza. He'd never seen a pair like them: a leather snap-on patch kept the strings out of sight, which gave the shoes a lovely streamlined look. He tried them on, but they were too narrow.

"They're for women," said the seasoned female clerk with a chuckle.

Herman said, "They're beautifully made, very fashionable—"

"And comfortable, too," said the clerk, cutting in. "I own a pair; they're made in Italy."

"Do you have the same for men?"

"Sorry, for women only," she said.

Herman made a face. "That's not fair."

The woman pointed at racks behind her filled with bras and corsets and piles of panties. "You blundered into a lingerie booth, you know," she said, laughing. "The tennis shoes are just to attract customers."

"Men, too?" he said jokingly.

"Sure. They buy them for their sweethearts. How about it, *monsieur*? Can I wrap them up for your girl? Think of the reward."

Herman rubbed his chin. Sure would make a nice Christmas

present for his sister, Marianna; he always wanted to give her something special, and these were just her size. His face lit up. "Good idea. Pack them up. They'll make a perfect present for my sister."

"Your sister? How nice of you; I'll put them in the box."

"Forget the box. Just slip them into this bag." He handed her the bag with the sweater. Again, he paid with Swiss francs and received change back in French currency.

"Thank you," she said with a grateful smile. "Here's your bag."

Herman was delighted. But it also meant no overnight stay in Aix-les-Bains, as his purchases came to nearly as much as a hotel would cost, almost exceeding his daily budget. He stopped at a pharmacy and bought a small bottle of rubbing alcohol, aspirins, some cotton, and a roll of gauze bandages to replace those which had been used up after a fall on his scooter—at a wet railroad crossing when it had slid out from under him.

The purchases fitted into the saddlebag with room to spare. He shook the scooter, listened to the splash in the tank, and determined that it was half full. *Plenty of fuel to get me to Aosta.* But the Porsche was still with him, very strongly—he drove back to the Du Monde parking lot. The convertible was gone.

Herman slumped over the steering column. Sorrow crept into him. *I should have waited.* The deep-throated church bell tolled the early afternoon hour. It was a beautiful sound, except to Herman, who noticed nothing around him. What if Angelina were right here under his very nose? He paled—what if she were with another man? He had always taken for granted that Angelina would be by herself.

The picture of Angelina in the arms of another man couldn't be evicted from his imagination. Skip Milan, he thought. Go home, go to Hotel College, go to America, and forget forever that there was a woman in your life as beautiful as Angelina.

He drove around the block and decided to top off the scooter anyhow, at an Enco station a block away. Before hitting the highway, he drove by the Du Monde one more time, then put the scooter into high gear.

Monique walked onto the terrace as the scooter turned the corner noisily. "There's *mon ami!*" She ripped the napkin from a man's lap and waved it above her head, but the scooter kept on, accelerating rapidly.

❧❖❧

In her excitement Angelina had forgotten about the Frenchman.

"He's waiting in your suite," said Henry apologetically. "You know who. I refused to give him the key at first, but he showed me his papers. A police captain! I had no choice. He's been waiting for some time."

Angelina nodded. "It's okay, Henry. We have legal business to attend to, so please make sure we're not disturbed."

Henry nodded. "*Bien sur*, madame."

Angelina gave him a five-franc tip. "Thank you, Henry; you're sweet."

She pushed the elevator button but then decided to take the staircase. The corridor was deserted. Strange—the door to her room was ajar. She pushed on it, but something blocked its way. "Monsieur Simon, are you in there?" There was no answer. She put her shoulder to the door and managed to force the crack wide enough to squeeze through.

She entered and stumbled backwards against the door pushing it shut.

"*Dio mio!*" she screamed.

At her feet Simon was propped against the wall. His head tilted against the door. Blood dripped from two wounds at his back. With the closing of the door, he had slumped forward, blocking the entrance. Angelina stepped over him to the center of the room. She held her hands over her mouth, unable to think or scream. Then driven by instinct, she reached for the man's wrist—there was no pulse. She floundered backward, eyes fixed on the blood trickling from his wounds.

Her heel caught on the throw rug. She tripped and fell against the bed frame. She didn't feel the pain, just slid to the floor, shoulders against the mattress. She pulled her knees to her chest, wrapped her arms tightly around her legs; pressed her eyes shut. For a moment, Angelina was too terrified even to tremble. Then her teeth began to chatter and she began to shudder all over.

Was it five minutes or twenty? Angelina didn't know how long she had been sitting propped against the mattress. The bleeding had stopped, but it had left a puddle of blood from Simon's waist to the door. She crawled to the nightstand and reached for the telephone. There was no dial plate, but the phone rang as soon as she took it off the cradle. It rang a second time, a third—*why don't they answer!* She let it ring again, and again. *Answer—someone, please, please answer.* But . . . what was she going to say? She couldn't talk, couldn't even whine. She dropped the receiver back into its cradle.

Angelina climbed onto the bed and slumped, gasping for air. She had to do something, get hold of somebody. She had to notify the police. *Slow down,* she said to herself. *Hold your breath; hold it for as long as you can!* She took a deep breath and held it until her face turned red. She exhaled, took a second breath, and let it bleed out slowly. The trembling finally stopped.

A burst of wind ballooned the curtains. Only now did Angelina see that the balcony doors were open. The lock had been forced; the bolts pushed out and bent. Slowly, she regained her senses. She was back at the telephone. But she hesitated. Something was terribly wrong—no one had heard the shots!

Angelina paled. The killer must have used a silencer—only the Mafia and the underground used them to do their dirty work. Angelina rammed one hand to her stomach, the other over her mouth as vomit shot onto the goose-feather comforter. This was no coincidence—the attack was meant for her!

She scrambled to the telephone. It rang and rang—five, ten, twenty times. *Where is everybody? Why don't they answer!* The relentless beeps pounded at her eardrums and tore at her mind. Angelina closed her eyes. The detective knew about the killer; he'd tried to warn her, tried to save her. Now he was dead, dead, dead—

She dropped the phone and started for the door, but the body blocked her way. She stared at the dead man. He would be alive, she thought, if only he had made a call to the local precinct instead of coming here all the way from Grenoble. Why travel so far just to deliver a simple message? Why all the secrecy?

It hit her like a ton of bricks: bribes! The detective was afraid of bribes—in his own department! Weird as Angelina's thoughts were, they made perfect sense. Whoever was after her would stop at nothing. What about the Manoir staff? And Maurice, could she trust him?

Suddenly Angelina trusted no one. She picked up the receiver from the floor reflexively, put it back in its cradle, and then collapsed onto the floor. She pressed her hands against her ears to shut out the world. Her head ached, her temples pounded, her mind raced. *What can I do, O God, what can I do?* Gradually, one thought began to dominate her mind—get out of here, get out of Aix-les-Bains, get out of France, get back to Italy where friends can help.

As if possessed, Angelina crammed her nightgown, her toiletry case, her shoes and stockings, her blouses and her skirts, gowns, pants, bras, lipsticks, hairspray, lingerie, and sweaters into her heavy suitcase. It flew over the balcony rail, quickly followed by a second. Angelina sighed; her Porsche was close to her lakeside balcony, parked within sight purposely. She climbed over the wrought-iron rail and slid down the bars. She was two meters above ground still and there was nothing else to hang onto. She let go, hit the ground hard, and twisted her left foot.

She limped to her car. Getting out had taken less than a minute, and no one had seen her. Angelina started the Porsche and thundered down First Avenue and onto the highway in the direction of friends and sanctuary: Milan.

Herman was back to his happy mood thanks to the magnificent autumn sky and the smooth-running scooter beneath him. With his happy mood came hunger. He thought of the meal he had left behind and decided to stop at the hotel on the foot of Petit-St-Bernard Pass.

The same waitress was on duty. Herman sat down at the table by the picture window overlooking the road from Aix-les-Bains to the pass. He ordered a light beer and a platter of prosciutto, Brie, and two French rolls. The two-hour drive had given Herman ample time to forget the Porsche, yet he caught himself looking at every passing car. Traffic was exceptionally light for a Saturday afternoon, likely due to a soccer game on the radio. On the other hand, the absence of cars left the road wide open to Aosta, which he hoped to reach later in the afternoon.

What would he do at the crossroads? Would he find the courage to turn right toward Milan? There was still time to get there before dark. Indecision gripped him. He unwrapped the knife from the napkin and twiddled it. If the knife stopped with the blade to the left, he would go left. But if it pointed to the right, he'd go to Milan. The knife stopped to the left. *Two out of three.* He spun again. The knife pointed down once and up twice. *Stupid game.*

But it wasn't the game. He knew damned well that he would spin that knife until it pointed exactly where he wanted it to point. He had made up his mind: he was going to Milan.

The waitress brought his food. He drank his beer and began eating, yet his eyes were back at the window. A car turned at the outer limit of his view and picked up speed on the straight-ahead as though chased by the devil. The car was too far away to determine make or color. Herman leaned against the glass and watched it come closer. His heart raced, his eyes grew big—it was the red Porsche, and the top was down! In a split second, Herman was on his feet. He left enough cash to settle his tab and flew down the few steps to his scooter.

Like a fiend, Herman took off after the red Porsche, leaning into the curves until his shoes scraped the road. But the scooter was no match for the Porsche. Disheartened, he saw it pull away. His only chance to catch it now was through a delay at the border crossing.

Angelina clutched the steering wheel in both hands. She squinted, and her lips were pressed together. The border was in plain view— soon she'd be in Italy, and in a few hours more, home among dear friends. The French guard signaled her to slow down, then gestured that she should continue. Angelina breathed a sigh of relief; news about the dead detective had not yet reached the border.

She sped up. The Italian sentry held up his arm. Panicky she hit the brakes; the tires screeched, and the Porsche slid to a stop at the sentry's stretched-out hand.

The young officer stepped to her side. "In a hurry, aren't we? Let me see your passport."

She unlocked the glove compartment and handed him her papers.

"What was the reason for your trip to France?"

"Vacation," she said with hidden anxiety.

"You didn't stay very long. What cities have you visited?"

"Aix-les-Bains."

He pointed to the large suitcase on the passenger seat. "Please unlock your luggage."

"My luggage? You're not serious—I'm Italian."

"Just open it."

Angelina was shocked; never before had an Italian border guard questioned her. She opened the suitcase on her front seat, then the second suitcase locked inside the front trunk. Was her anxiety making her a suspect? Now he insisted on her purse. Angelina was infuriated—how dare he look inside her purse! But she bit her lip.

At last, the guard stepped aside. "Okay, signora—you may continue," he said with a grotesque smile. He tipped his hat. "Have a nice day."

Angelina was too agitated to go on. She leaned against the seat and closed her eyes—for a minute.

Herman was just passing the French sentry on his scooter. There was the Porsche! But before he made it to the Italian side, the Porsche pulled away. Herman honked. There was no response, and the car was out of reach again. Herman stopped by the Italian border guard and showed his passport without being asked.

He asked in French, "Who was that woman?"

The guard answered with a strong Italian accent. "I heard you honk and thought you must know her. She's from Milan, and obviously in a hurry. Look how she's burning rubber."

"Are you allowed to give me her name?"

The sentry raised an eyebrow. "Any reason why you need to know, Monsieur Schuller?"

"I thought I recognized a friend. I've been chasing her almost since Aix-les-Bains."

The guard hesitated. "There seems to be a great interest in that signora—three men asked about her minutes earlier; weird-looking men. Her name's Angelina Bianci."

Angelina veered around curve after curve at reckless speeds, almost cutting in half the normal driving time to Aosta.

A *telephone, I need a telephone!* She stopped at the first BP service station to have the Porsche serviced. She begged the attendant to let her use his office telephone. He hesitated but nodded after she gave him a generous tip.

Angelina was out of breath. "Is this Colonnello Zanardelli's office? I need to talk to the colonnello!" There was a long pause.

A distrustful voice asked, "Is this Signora Bianci?"

"It is; I have to talk to him. Now!"

"He left a number where he can be reached." The woman's voice cooled, reacting to Angelina's curtness. She spelled out the number and repeated it. Angelina scribbled it onto her left palm and hung up without saying another word. She sank into the desk chair, undecided about making the second call.

Hesitantly, she dialed the number—Vitt Zanardelli was the last man she wanted to ask for help.

"Hello! Hello? Is anyone on the line?" Zanardelli heard deep breathing. "Angelina? Is that you?"

"Yes."

"It *is* you; so nice to hear your voice. I have—"

"I heard you were looking for me."

"Well, yes. I'm sure Capitaine Simon brought you up to date. He's an old friend from the war, reliable, a good man." He paused. "You don't sound right, Angelina; you're out of breath. Something wrong?"

"He was shot."

"Who? Who shot who?"

"Simon. He was shot dead."

"He was—he's—what?"

"Right in my room. They shot him in my room. I found him there, dead. I panicked and ran."

"You did what?" Zanardelli didn't think he'd heard right. "Slow down, Angelina," he said calmly, "and repeat what you just said."

"Simon's dead! Someone's after me! I'm scared . . . ."

Silence hit with the force of an ax.

"Things are starting to make sense," Vitt said bitterly. "I don't know how to break this to you, Angelina, but . . . Giulio escaped from prison by faking an illness." He heard her sudden intake of breath. "In prison, Giulio pledged to get you, even bragged about finding you and killing you. His imprisonment has destroyed his identity, and his followers have lost confidence in him. This is worse than death to someone like Giulio, and he puts the blame on you. He has nothing left except revenge—and he is as dangerous as ever."

Silence fell again.

"Are you okay?" Zanardelli asked.

"How did you find me?"

"Through your friend Sabrina. Oh, she wouldn't say at first, and even then only mentioned Aix-les-Bains. She called you repeatedly without success."

Angelina closed her eyes and bit her lip. "What do you want me to do?"

His voice took on a begging tone. "I miss you, Angelina. We should get together. I have the means to protect you—"

Angelina broke in sharply. "That is out of question, colonnello! Forget it, I'll find another way!"

"Okay, okay," he said quickly. "I'll help you, no strings attached." He coughed. "I relate to your feelings completely—I owe you this one." After an uneasy silence, he asked. "Where are you now?"

"Back in Italy, close to the Swiss border."

"Hmm—Giulio has new accomplices. One is in jail for his attempt to bribe an officer. It might be best if you stay clear of Milan for a few days. Continue on your vacation—Switzerland, Austria— just stay away from here. Give me a call now and then."

"What about Monsieur Simon?" Angelina asked fretfully.

"I'll contact the state department in France and explain the circumstances of your flight. Meanwhile, I'll sort things out in Milan and make sure that no charges are filed against you." He paused and cleared his throat noisily.

"What is it?" asked Angelina.

"I'll organize protection for your business; a visible uniform should do."

"I'd appreciate that, colonnello."

"I'm still Vitt!"

❖

Herman stopped at the crossroads. *What now?* Logic told him to turn right toward Milan, yet he hesitated. What if—the Porsche tore onto the road and sped north toward Grand-St-Bernard Pass. Herman just sat there, paralyzed by what he had just seen. Then he honked and shouted, and the engine howled at high pitch as he continued his pursuit.

He was gaining on the car, lagging only a short stretch behind. Then the grade steepened and the scooter slowed. Herman brought his fist down on the steering column and rocked back and forth on the tandem seat as though it could help. It was no use—the Porsche was quickly out of reach.

Yet Herman did not despair. Leaning dangerously into the curves, he squeezed the last bit of power from the engine. He had no time to wonder about Angelina's mad dash or why she was going north instead of south to Milan, no time for anything but the next curve in the road.

The road straightened as it crossed a viaduct spanning a wide gorge. Herman rose from his seat, slowed the scooter, and removed his driving goggles. In the far distance, just before a bend in the road, a car was askew against the safety cable on the right. Herman's heart almost stopped—it was the Porsche. A Jeep, its top removed and its metal struts glowing in the sun, blocked the Porsche up front. Herman was now close enough to see two men leaning against the Porsche and a third man in the Jeep pointing a hunting rifle at it.

In the next instant the Jeep had pulled alongside the Porsche. The two men brutally jerked Angelina from her seat and dumped her into the Jeep as though she were a bag of trash; then they jumped on board as the Jeep made a screeching U-turn. Though too far still to hear her cries, Herman saw her futile struggle before the Jeep raced from view beyond the bend.

Herman brought the scooter to a gradual stop. Then he was seized by fury and opened the throttle. He raced ahead, up the steep slope and around the bend—the Jeep had been swallowed by the hills. There was nothing to disturb the sudden quiet. Herman cut the engine and rolled to the shoulder, where he slumped over the steering column, a pain in his heart, his hands trembling uncontrollably. He was outrun, outclassed, outperformed—out everything. Even if he caught up with the Jeep, he'd be no match for those thugs with their hunting rifle.

He drove back to the Porsche. The car was idling. He opened the door and sat in the driver's seat. He found the red start button at the dash, the ignition key hanging beside it, and killed the engine. The sudden quiet overwhelmed him. He trembled and his eyes blurred. He tried to focus, but his mind was like a run-down clock. With screeching tires, a car veered around the curve followed by a second close behind that nearly grazed the Porsche. Herman broke out of his mental block. He jumped from the seat and shouted, frantically waving his arms. But the cars raced past him down the road and disappeared at the end of the straightaway.

I have to get help, find a policeman. But Aosta was twenty minutes down the road. It would take an hour to find a policeman or someone in the village with whom he could communicate and get back up here. All traces of the Jeep would be gone by then.

Instinctively, Herman rifled the car's interior, not really knowing what he was looking for. There was a suitcase on the passenger seat, and below it, on the floorboard, a red travel bag. He felt along the dashboard. A flap on the very right caught his attention. It was locked. A small silvery key attached to the ignition key fit the lock, and the flap sprung open. The glove compartment was lined with black felt and was narrow and deep. Herman removed what looked like an engine logbook, insurance papers, a detailed map of Aosta Valley, a black address booklet with brass corners and a tiny slide lock, and Angelina's passport.

Herman opened it and laid the other contents on the dash. He stared at the black-and-white photograph inside. Unsmiling, Angelina looked rather solemn, but her hair flowed over her shoulders just as he remembered it. Looking at her picture created an unbearable tension and he clenched his fists. He was going after them! He would rip Angelina from their clutches! He cried, "Whoever you are, wherever you go, you'll pay for this!" The mountain valley returned his voice and made him feel quite helpless and alone.

In his anxiety, Herman dropped the passport. It fell beside the blue travel bag. He bent over but was sidetracked by a zipper in the glove compartment. He pulled on the tab—a pistol dropped into his hand: a short-barreled Beretta. He popped out the magazine; it was loaded with ten rounds. He felt a surge of life, of blood, through all four limbs. A devilish smile danced on his lips.

Inside the travel bag was a small purse filled with Italian lire and French currency—robbery, therefore, was not a motive. The suitcase on the passenger seat was stuffed with clothing carelessly tossed inside. Hesitantly, he sorted through the contents. *Angelina will need some of these things when I find her.*

He laid a pair of dark blue slacks and a woolen turtleneck on the dash, then added panties and stockings to the pile. Slightly uneasy, he put her money and her passport with the other items in his saddlebag.

He spread out the Aosta map. Would the thugs risk driving through the villages between here and the Swiss border with an unwilling passenger on board? Probably not. A few side roads turned off to either side, and one, through the Valpelline Valley, stuck out from the highway like a pointing finger.

The valley! Herman blanched. His dream! His intuition! He bit his lip—this couldn't be a coincidence—everything was fitting almost too perfectly!

As if fate meant to help him, Herman saw a dust cloud rise from the mountain slope across the valley. He shaded his eyes and followed its billowing crawl up the slope. This had to be a struggling vehicle—like a Jeep.

Herman jumped up ready to take off after the dust cloud.

Slow down and make plans.

First, he couldn't leave the Porsche beside the highway. He looked around. Behind him was the viaduct with a service road leading below. It was the perfect hiding place, and Herman decided to try it. *Well, here's my first driving lesson.* He dropped into the driver seat.

The engine sprang to life at the first try. He pushed down the brake handle between the seats, put his right foot on the brake pedal and the other on the clutch. Out of gear now, he eased his foot from the brake. The car rolled backward in neutral, fishtailing with Herman's overcorrection. He hit the brake pedal, and the Porsche slid to a stop. With feet solidly on the clutch and the brake, and following the markings on the shift knob, he shifted into first gear. He released the pressure from the pedals—the car jumped forward and the engine died. *Oops!*

Herman tried again—the engine stalled. *Not as easy as you thought, huh?* It became an emotional test, a play between clutch and brakes and just the right amount of gas, a shoving, a stalling, and an enthusiasm that refused to yield. Little by little, he steered the Porsche down the steep gravel road and parked it against a massive pillar under the highway overhang, safe from the elements and out of sight from curious eyes.

Herman drummed his chest and laughed. "I made it! Holy shit, I made it!" he shouted overjoyed.

The convertible top refused to close, so he left it alone. No reason to lock the doors, he thought, removing the keys. He hid them on top of the left rear tire.

As a last thought, Herman took a small toiletry case out of her bag. He removed a brush and comb, a small mirror, toothbrush and paste, and a half-squeezed tube of Nivea cream and slipped everything into a nylon stocking. Sheepishly, he added a heart-shaped bottle of perfume and a deep-red lipstick, then put the toiletry case back into the suitcase. He climbed back to the road with the stocking under his arm.

Herman checked his watch. Fifteen minutes had passed since he'd found the Porsche idling by the side of the road. By now, the dust cloud had disappeared, yet Herman knew exactly what he had to do: he was going to give chase. The scooter sprang to life. After a last glance at the map, Herman took off around the curve and down a gravel road into a deep ravine, then back up the hill, making a dust cloud of his own.

CHAPTER 18

$\mathcal{I}$n a cloud of dust, the Jeep rumbled down the steep road all the way to the valley floor.

"Who are you people? Why are you doing this? Where are you taking me?"

Angelina's voice, strong and demanding at first, was now weak and begging. But there was no response from the men.

The back seat had been replaced with plywood, and Angelina's hands were tied behind her and fixed to the exposed undercarriage. Shifting her weight to soften the painful jolts only hurt her arms and tired her. There were brief reprieves when the Jeep slowed, but as the trip wore on, her pain was continuous, and there was nothing she could do to lessen it.

The man beside her sat on a folded blanket, one hand on the rifle between his knees, the other on the roll bar. His name was Roberto, but his buddies sometimes called him "the Goat" for his thick, untrimmed beard, she thought, which had traces of his last meal. In her entire life Angelina had never been this close to someone with such a repugnant appearance: small eyes (more a pig's than a goat's), bushy brows, a bright red nose, thin cracked lips. His body stank, and the tobacco in his mouth put out an even stronger smell. The other men joked and hooted, but he sat silent, staring ahead, not a twitch of life on his sunburned face except for the quid of tobacco moving about his cheeks.

At last he turned toward Angelina. She sensed his attention and began to feel sick. She was ready to learn her fate and bracing herself for the worst, but instead of talking, he put both hands on her breasts. Angelina jerked away and tried to sink her teeth into his arm. Her resistance made him vicious. His right hand moved up her thigh below the skirt, and the other pinned her chest against the seat frame, cutting off her air. Summoning strength she didn't know she had, Angelina head-butted him hard. His head was thrown back and blood was dripping from his nose. Stunned by her unexpected strength, and agitated further by the giggles of his two buddies, he growled, "Shit! Damn you! Shit!" He pulled off his red neckerchief and pressed it to his nose, and for the moment it appeared as if he had had enough. But the truce did not last.

"I'll teach you a lesson, you bitch!" he screamed. The first blow ripped the skin above her eye, and the barrage that followed left no part of her head unmarked. Angelina cried out in pain and turned every which way to protect her face. Blood dribbled over her right eye.

"Leave her alone," cried the driver—Pietro, Angelina had heard him called—over his shoulder. "I don't want marks on her; the boss might not approve."

After one more blow the beating stopped. Angelina pressed her head into her arm to cover her eyes. But she was more afraid of his gaze, with its possessiveness and lust, than of his fists.

Pietro slowed the Jeep with an agonizing change of gear, pulled to the side, and stopped. He shifted his legs that barely fit below the dash and turned around. His gaze was on Angelina and the bruises on her face. He paused and scratched his thick, gray sideburns. Was that compassion in his dark brown eyes, a hint of kindness? He had nothing to say, but he was the only one of the three who gave her the slightest hope.

"What are you stopping for? Forget the whore," hissed the man in the passenger seat. He was short and stocky and his big belly bulked beyond his rawhide belt. He picked up a rag from the floorboard and polished his head. Only a few stringy strands of hair were left— a fringe in the shape of a horseshoe. The others called him "Nico" (bringing to mind Soviet premier Nikita Khrushchev, whom he resembled) or "Baldy." His red butcher cheeks above an enormous double chin glistened like polished apples, and his naturally pink, oversized lips wore a permanent smile that never seemed to match his mood. At first glance, he gave Angelina the impression of goodness and fatherly trustworthiness—in keeping with "Baldy"—but one look in his eyes was sufficient to reveal depths of evil. He puffed on a cigar that he lit repeatedly with a lighter that put out a giant flame.

Still grumbling, Pietro put the Jeep in gear. The rough ride continued until they turned into Valpelline Valley. The road became smoother as it followed a creek in the shadows of giant chestnut trees and rumbled over log bridges. The first houses of a small village came into view. With brutal force that almost broke her neck, the Goat-man pushed Angelina down onto the wooden seat. The straps cut painfully into her wrists. When he covered her with the smelly blanket he had been sitting on, her mouth and nose filled almost instantly with vomit.

The bearded man stared at his vomit-laced shoes. "Shit, bitch! Cut that out!" He punched her in the ribs. "And keep it quiet or I'll knock you out for good!"

Angelina wasn't trying to make noise, merely struggling to clear her throat so she could breathe. The spasms continued, though nothing came up.

They were climbing again, the Jeep's wheels were throwing rocks and dirt. Finally Roberto pulled the blanket off and let her breathe. Her right eye was glued shut from dried blood. She rubbed it against her right arm, and the crust came away, leaving red stains on her blouse.

A massive hydroelectric dam blocked the end of the valley. They stopped at a small dwelling beside the road. Roberto leaned the rifle against the seat, jumped out easily, and entered the stone house through a side door. He was back shortly with two bottles of wine in one hand and a rucksack in the other. He climbed back on board and packed the bottles into the rucksack that he pushed below the bench.

The final stretch to the top was almost too steep even for the Jeep and led through a short tunnel to the lake above the dam. The driver untied Angelina's hands, mumbled an apology, and helped her down. She met his eyes, determined to get her answer. He quickly turned away from her.

Angelina shivered. She slid down the embankment and sat on a rocky knoll close to the water's edge. She leaned over and watched her reflection on the glassy surface. The bruises were visible, though not as bad as she had feared. The cut above her eye, however, would take time to heal. She cupped her hands and splashed water onto her face, and the water turned pink.

Angelina bit her lip. Why would Giulio jeopardize his freedom just to satisfy his hatred? Even commit murder? She remembered the way he had leapt at her after the trial. Sickened by the horror of her fate, her body convulsed again. Acid gushed from her mouth and burned her throat. She wrapped her arms around her knees and buried her head in her lap.

"Get up here, bitch, we haven't got all day!" screamed a voice from above. It was the bearded man impatiently pointing with his rifle. But before she left, Angelina scooped two handfuls of water from the lake and rinsed out her mouth and nose.

It was incredible that so much evil could exist in such a beautiful place. Nestled between high mountains, the lake mirrored snow-covered peaks and sheer granite cliffs. Golden and copper fall foliage lined the lake along with rhododendrons that were already wearing their winter red. But the men trudging beside her barely glanced at the beauty. As did Angelina, now that she was on the move again without knowing where they were taking her or what lay in store. Once again fear held her in its icy grip.

Angelina's thoughts turned to Herman. She felt his closeness, felt him tracking them and waiting for the perfect moment to make his move. He had to be out there, somewhere; God had put him there, just as He had brought him to her on that mountain pass so long ago. *Oh Corporal, I know you're out there!*

I must leave a trail of something, a sign he can recognize when he looks for me. Her long-sleeved blouse had been torn from the beating; on the trail she was able to tear small strips from it and keep them in her hand. Only the Goat-man was behind her. Twice, three times she stumbled and each time he came alongside, brutally yanked her to her feet and dragged her along. Each time, also, she left a shred of cloth behind on the trail. She was convinced that, as in an adventure book she had read as a child, the corporal was certain to pick up her trail.

As much as she wanted to believe in his presence, she was assailed by doubts. Was she just imagining the corporal's closeness? Was it only wishful thinking? With her arms clutched against her chest like someone trying to keep warm, she kept tearing small bits of cloth.

The scooter hit an embankment and spun out from under him. Herman tucked his head as he flew over the steering column. He hit hard, shoulder first, rolled over once, and ended sitting up straight. Was he in one piece? He gripped his legs, ribs, and neck. Nothing broken, though he hurt from head to toe. The scooter whined above him. He crawled up the short slope and turned off the ignition before righting the machine. He knocked the white sand, slick as snow, from his pants and jacket and wiped the dust from his mouth and nose.

"Damned sand!" But in a moment he was back on the road raising the dust again, and grateful for the sand, as he had been all along, for showing the tracks of the Jeep.

He took a wrong turn where the Jeep's tire prints mixed with others and he came to a dead end in Doùes, a tiny village that hugged the crest of a forlorn mountain ridge. Still, he sensed he'd arrived at the village for a reason. He needed to stop his headlong pursuit, stop trying to force the course of events. Increased alertness to every aspect of the situation would help him to keep the images from crowding in—of how she had been treated, of how *they* might be treating her (whoever they were). *Take things in order!*

He went back with renewed hope and quickly located the Jeep's characteristic tracks, which he followed until they entered with Valpelline Road. Here the sand gave way to packed gravel and there were no more tracks. Unperturbed, he continued up the valley along the creek, through thickening chestnut forests and over bridges made of rough-hewn logs. He all but collided with a wagon pulled by a team of oxen, and his speed terrified a caravan of three packmules led by an old man who brandished a rawhide whip and hurled a curse at him. He passed three women on bicycles. They waved colorful scarves as he rode past, but he never looked back.

The sun was nearing the horizon when he entered Valpelline, the valley's largest settlement, according to his map. Sturdy houses crowded the narrow, paved street. He stopped at the first general store and parked behind a Citröen van. At the far side a tarpaulin-covered truck was backed against the building. A man wearing a dark-brown leather apron with thick shoulder pads used iron clamps to unload a block of ice that he slid on makeshift wooden skids through a side door. Herman bounded up the granite steps in front of the place. His entry activated a small brass bell above the door.

"*Buona sera,*" called a female voice from the back.

Herman responded in French.

"Oh, *bonsoir,* monsieur," said the woman with a heavy Italian accent. She stepped from behind the counter.

Herman said, "I need a few items; may I look around?"

"*Va bene!*" She returned to her task behind the counter and began chatting with the iceman.

It was a typical small-town country store selling everything from groceries to brooms, clothing, shoes, chinaware, pitchforks, wheelbarrows, grass seeds . . . The store was not only the valley's grocer and general supplier but also the communication center of the countryside, as was evident by the stream of foot traffic that gave little rest to the tiny bell above the door.

Herman took a loaf of bread, a bottle of sparkling water with a snap-on ceramic lid, and got down a small sausage using a broom-stick with a hook on the end. He waited for his turn in line and put the items on the counter. He pointed to the glass dome.

"Give me 250 grams of that Parmesan, *s'il vous plaît,*" he said.

The signora took a two-handled rocking knife from the counter and cut off a piece that she put on the larger pan of a Roberval's Scale. She put two dissimilar weights on the other side, and the needle centered. "Right on," she smiled proudly as she wrapped the cheese in parchment paper. She stuffed everything into a brown paper bag, pulled a pencil from behind her ear, and added up the items on the bag. Herman gave her all the French currency he had left from the bazaar, and she returned the difference in lire. The last customer had left the store, and, except for the iceman, who still roamed around the back, the storekeeper and Herman were suddenly alone.

He asked, "Did you see a Jeep drive by your store some thirty minutes ago?"

The signora pondered for a moment then told him in halting

French that there had been one motor vehicle besides the ice truck; it might have been a Jeep, she wasn't sure. "Twenty, thirty minutes ago . . . maybe more."

"How far is it to the lake?"

"Maybe fifteen kilometers, maybe a little more. The road is very steep; driving is no good. You will stay the night in our valley?"

"I may have to. Is there any shelter at the lake?"

"There is no place to spend the night there. The two buildings are for maintenance—locked up, you know."

He was about to go. "There's a big house beyond the end of the lake, though. It was a youth hostel and then the *patrioti* stayed there occasionally during the war. The road ends at the lake so you have to go on foot."

"I locked the back door, Signora Ponte. *Arrivederci!*" said the iceman from behind the counter. Coming out, he turned to Herman. "That hostel by the lake isn't a bad place to spend the night. The ground floor has been redone—nothing fancy, though." He laughed softly. "I should know. I slept there many times during the war. I've heard from some hunters hereabouts that it's still livable." His French was fluent with scarcely a trace of accent, but by the time Herman could think of other things to ask the man, he was out the door and getting into his truck.

The more he thought about it . . . "It's the perfect place!" Herman cried aloud.

"What was that, signore?" asked the store-woman.

"I need to talk to a gendarme," said Herman with urgency. "Where's the nearest *gendarmerie?*"

She made a sweeping gesture of dismissal. "There is no *agente di polizia* here," she said. "Only in Aosta."

"May I use your telephone?" When the woman hesitated, he said, "I'll pay for the call." The signora pointed to the back wall. Herman picked up the receiver—but what was he going to say? He had no proof of abduction or anything else. He only had Angelina's belongings, her money, and her passport—why, that could make him the suspect. Besides, how long would police question him before they believed his story? No! *And no again!* He had sensed from the start that he was on his own.

He turned to the signora. "I need to protect my scooter when I get to the lake."

"You have a scooter? You could park it under one of the buildings' overhang . . . But better, let Signor Bennado keep it for you. He lives in a small house in La Léchère, by the dam. He is my uncle, a good man. You can trust him."

Herman asked how to find his place.

"At the dam turn right just before tunnel. His is the first house on the right, hidden from the road. He lives by himself. An honest man, very nice."

"*Mille grazie*, signora."

"*Prego*, signore. Tell him you know me, Signora Ponte. *Arrivederci*."

"*Arrivederci*, Signora Ponte."

"*Buona fortuna!*" she called after him as Herman walked from the store under the clink of the tiny bell.

The paper bag did not fit into the saddlebag, and he put it on the floorboard between his feet. The hunt continued below the village church nestled on a scenic hill, then left along the valley. The pavement ended, yet the rough road failed to dampen Herman's spirit. He had the beginning of a plan now based on a solid hunch, thanks to the iceman back at the store. It was easy now to link things together: a deserted dwelling used by hunters occasionally and a hunter's rifle—this was surely no coincidence.

The three-story hostel hugged the crest of a steep slope dotted by shrubs and a group of tall pines. The metal roof, symmetrically streaked by rust, shone in the evening sun. A stone chimney covered with a pitched metal cap projected above the ridge like a sentry standing guard. Over the years, large patches of plaster had weathered away exposing rocks of a rusty red and pale gold, even a greenish blue. Angelina trembled at the sight of a place so desolate and out of the way. Suddenly her legs would no longer support her weight. She went down hard and could not go on. Roberto the Goat-man stepped over her and poked her hip with his rifle butt. Her only response was a faint moan. *Just go on hurting me.*

"I told you to leave her alone!" cried Pietro. Exhausted, he too dropped to the ground. "We all can use a rest." He pointed to the hostel. "There's no rush to get up there." The Goat-man shouldered the rifle and with a mumbled, "damned weaklings," pushed on by himself.

Angelina watched him climb the slope, silent and smooth as a big cat stalking its prey. She feared the others, but she was terrified by the bearded man. Nico followed but soon dropped behind. Pietro stayed put, but his gaze followed the men climbing the slope. Angelina took her chance . . . She tied her small, lace handkerchief to the far side of the bush beside her . . . her last sign, and not too soon. Pietro was at her side and helped her to her feet, and she started up the hill with him.

The scooter purring, Herman drove past lonely dwellings and small herds of cows and sheep on sloping pastures. Between the hills and meadows small stands of deciduous trees were turning red and gold. Herman slowed through the small village of Oyace built on both sides of the climbing road. It seemed as though the entire population was crowding the narrow cobblestone street and the piazza in front of a tiny church. The women were dressed in their best black gowns and knitted shawls, and the men were clothed in black suits and ties and matching hats made from the finest felt. Herman parked the scooter and approached a group of men in the middle of the street. None of them knew French or German, but his Italian was good enough to understand that, yes, a Jeep had raced through town twenty minutes ago. However, they insisted there was no woman aboard—three men. Herman didn't try to explain, and he wasn't daunted. Of course they wouldn't have driven through town with Angelina in plain view.

He continued through Bionaz, the last village before La Léchère and the dam. At the sudden sight of a small chapel, almost hidden among pine trees, he stopped the scooter for a moment and muttered a prayer.

I know, Lord, I only pray when in dire need—I always figure that you're too busy with everybody wanting things from you. But today is different, Lord, and I am not asking for myself but for a friend in need of your helping hand. You're the only one who can take me to her, help me find her, and who can tell me what to do when I get there. I'll do my part, you can put your trust in that, Lord, but I'll need you along—I can't do it on my own. Thanks for listening. Amen.

Herman wasn't Catholic, nor was he devout, but a feeling of calm came over him in that quiet moment, and he felt more sure of himself when, moments later, he was rumbling up the steepening, rocky road.

The hostel was built on top of a flattened hill, buttressed by a four-foot rock wall. On the east, away from the lake, the ground floor was carved out of the hill, adding a fourth story on this side. Steps built into a breach in the wall led to the entrance. The door, one step above ground level, was made from solid tongue-and-groove wooden planks strengthened with thick bolts. Three massive hand-forged steel hinges supported the door on the right, and at the opposite side were iron handles, hand scrolled, with a huge, turn-of-the-century lock. The door was framed by granite blocks, and there was a chiseled inscription on the header: a Gothic "R" followed by the number "1904" and the letter "F". To each side of the door were two windows with unpainted shutters of more recent construction. At the building's right corner was a concrete watering trough kept full by the dribbling of a rusting water pipe. There was a long view from here across the narrow lake to the dam at its far end. The view was beautiful—and made a surprise approach, by daylight, very difficult.

The men dunked their heads into the cool water in the trough. They ignored the slimy algae and drank from the disgusting pipe. One by one, they stepped around the corner to relieve themselves. Angelina soaked her handkerchief in the cool water and sat on the trunk of a sawed-off tree near the trough. She dabbed her face and neck with the cool cloth and returned it to the water. She was thirsty but could not bring herself to drink from the pipe.

Angelina started to walk behind the building, but the Goat-man caught her arm and jerked her back. From a concealed crack in the wall he retrieved a monstrous key that he pushed into the massive lock. He had to apply considerable force to turn it, and when it finally gave way, it clanged like a hammer striking an anvil. Goat-man put his shoulder to the door and it swung open, its rusty hinges squeaking.

The open room on the lower floor, with a closed-off staircase leading to the upper floors, appeared to have been a mess hall at one time. Now a makeshift partition cut the room in half. A few steps away from the door sat an iron stove of the potbelly variety . . . the plate on top was cracked, and the exhaust pipe had separated, rendering the stove useless. Behind it, in the center of the room, a massive wooden column supported the ceiling made from rough-hewn beams.

The window on the left was covered with red-checked curtains, now in tatters. Beneath it was a table with two benches. In the rear corner were upper and lower bunks with torn mattresses, and beside them were the broken remains of chairs and tables indicating a time when part of the furniture had become victim to the potbelly stove, apparently during a drawn-out winter storm. Someone had decorated the back wall in an attempt to give the place an atmosphere—or they couldn't find a spot to store the stuff: an ancient pair of skis with poles; a rusty glacier-pick; a climber's rucksack with the climbing rope attached to it. The place smelled musty.

Goat-man opened the window, unhooked the shutters and pushed them open, and let in some fresh air. Pietro lit the kerosene lantern dangling from the ceiling above the table. It began swinging slightly in the sudden draft.

"Here," the Goat-man grunted to Angelina, pointing at a door. "Do your shit in there!" He forced the door open, pushed her toward it, and she almost fainted from the stench. It was an open latrine and must have been used recently. She held her nose to control her nausea and was able to reach the outside door before the yellow bile and stomach acid came gushing from her mouth. She ignored the algae, dunked her face, and rinsed her mouth at the slimy pipe.

First she pressed her hands over her ears to muffle the men's joking comments from inside—then she could no longer keep back her rage.

"Shameless brutes! Worms of men! How tough you are with a helpless woman! Pigs!" And as she cried out, fright turned to sudden strength and hatred.

The key was still stuck inside the lock. In a moment's inspiration, Angelina ran to the door, pulled it shut, and tried to turn the key. She didn't have the strength, and before she could give it a second try the door flung open, slinging her inside. Nico had pulled the door handle with a force she wouldn't have thought he possessed. He slapped her to the floor and dragged her to the column behind the stove.

"You really thought you'd get away?" he crowed. "This will teach you, bitch!" He bound her hands, tight as before, passing the rope around the timber.

The men were in a festive mood as they gathered at the table: drinking, laughing, and making jokes.

But their humiliating jokes, the foiled escape, or even the rope that cut painfully into her wrists were not what brought Angelina to the point of complete despair. It was when the grinning, goatish man opened his hand and bits of cloth fluttered past her head.

Shaped like a giant V, the setting sun made the dam appear golden. Still, Herman felt there was something cold and ghastly in the way it watched over the valley. As if to authenticate this feeling, the scooter went out from under him again, this time just before he left the road for La Léchère right in front of the tunnel the storekeeper had told him about. On the sudden steep grade the scooter had flipped backward. Herman was able to jump free, and because he had been going quite slow at the moment, the scooter only suffered a couple of scrapes. He was close enough to Signor Bennado's house to walk the bike—engine running and in gear—the rest of the way.

The old man couldn't grasp a word the young man at his door was saying, but nodded when Herman mentioned Signora Ponte's name. Herman pointed to himself, to the scooter, and then to the barn. The old man gave him a toothless smile and helped him push the scooter to the barn.

Herman untied the saddlebag and hooked it over his shoulders. He carried the bag of provisions under his arm. He left the scooter deep in the shadows by an old wagon. He gave the key to Signor Bennado as they were leaving the barn, and the old man closed the double doors.

Moments later Herman was inside the tunnel, pressed against its walls. When he emerged he could see the jeep straight ahead, under a building overhang Signora Ponte had mentioned back at the store. Herman listened intently, struggled to see everything he could in the lengthening shadows of the late afternoon sun. Nothing disturbed the peace except for a waterfall hitting the lake at the far side of the dam. He checked the Beretta and stuck it back in his belt, hidden below his jacket.

Like an innocent tourist, Herman walked into the open, paper bag in hand, looking at the map as he moved casually toward the building overhang. "Anybody here?" he called in French and then in German. A soft echo came back from the sheer granite wall beside the dam. The Jeep reeked from a filthy blanket under the back seat, and there were cigarette butts, candy wrappers, and empty beer bottles strewn about on the floor.

Herman stepped onto the crude back seat, one hand on the Jeep's roll bar, the other over his eyes. He scanned the lake and the trail that ran left along the shore. A second trail zigzagged up a slope to his left, and Herman wondered which route he should follow. Something caught his eyes. He jumped from the Jeep and started for the trail by the lake. Before he reached it he found a fresh cigar butt and someone had spit tobacco juice on the short rock wall at the end of the road. *This has got to be the right trail!*

The trail was rocky and there were no footprints. Was Angelina with them? The village people said that there was no woman on the Jeep. Were they mistaken? If Angelina wasn't on board, where had the thugs left her? Doubt sprang up again—was he on track, or was he merely chasing a mirage? No—the abduction was as indisputable as the Jeep. He looked into the distance to the end of the lake, to a hostel shrouded in mystery.

Without haste, Herman walked quickly along the lake. The rays of the sun low on the horizon now had turned the snow-clad mountaintops to gold. It was a beautiful path, with rhododendrons in their early fall attire and fragrant plants with turning leaves as bright as any flower. He saw other signs of the men who had recently passed this way—another cigar butt; a chocolate wrapper—but no sign of her. Even so, he no longer doubted that she was with them. He knew she needed him—he just knew.

POP! Angelina startled, hurting her wrists—it was the popping of a wine cork. The bearded man filled three glasses and was cutting pieces off a salami he had taken from the rucksack. After cutting large wedges of bread with a hunting knife, he speared the pieces of sausage and passed them around. As they stuffed themselves like pigs and gulped their wine, they started looking at her differently. She didn't have to guess what their muffled talk was about; she saw the lust in their red eyes—and trembled.

Angelina had never thought of dying, in spite of all the friends and loved ones she'd lost. Was this the way it would end for her? By the hand of some vile criminal? She thought of the peace that death would bring, an end of suffering, an end of injustice. Acceptance of her fate brought calm; her trembling stopped. Yet her muscles were tense, there was strength in them. She was not going to give up without a fight; kicking, biting, she'd fight for her dignity by any means, even if she lost out in the end.

Angelina closed her eyes and a vision of Marie Theresa appeared, and spoke to her in a voice that was strong and clear: "Don't you dare give up, Angelina. You're still young and have the best of your life ahead of you! Let them do what they will. Staying alive is all that matters. Stay alive, alive, alive—!" Then Angelina had a vision of the corporal, his face stern and determined as she remembered him from that mountain pass. Without saying a word he was flooding her with hope and comfort.

Where are you, corporal? Where are you?

Herman had had the hostel in view for some time where it stood at the end of the valley, on a steep hill. There was no way to circle it and hide himself from view. He was forced to stick to the rough path. Then the lake ended. The trail, marked with small piles of rocks, swung sharply to the left. Herman crested a small rise—and saw two buildings at his feet that had been hidden. Herman dropped to the ground.

The structure on the right was a barn, long and narrow, and like the two-story house on its left flank was built from rocks and mortar and roofed with galvanized metal that had large patches of rust that implied its age. His interest was in the tiny windows of the two-story structure. There were no shutters and the glass reflected the setting sun. But all was quiet, and the houses seemed abandoned. Beyond the two buildings there was a steep hill to the hostel, whose metal roof was pink with the last of the reflected sun.

Cautiously, Herman made his way between the structures to the foot of the hill. There was movement at the crest. He dove behind a large bush, listening for voices and rushing steps. There was no sound at all, not even the call of a bird, and the air was completely still except for the movement of his own breath.

It was time to take a break and think this out.

He sat on a flat rock, his back against the brush. Something caught his eye. Nothing in the entire universe could have stirred him more at that moment than what he found: a small silk handkerchief. His heart pounded as he carried the soft token to his face, pressed it to his cheek, to his nose . . . was it his imagination? No, faint though it might have been, he was sure he had caught the scent of her perfume.

Angelina went completely rigid when the hands began to stroke her legs. She held her knees together with all her strength, too frightened to open her eyes. She cursed her provocative skirt. If only she had changed into slacks before fleeing the hotel! The hand had already slid above her knees, squeezed, probed, and wedged itself between her legs. Angelina grew cold and lifeless. She bit her lip to keep from crying out.

Marie Theresa wanted her to give in to the men and live, but Angelina would rather die. Forgive me, Marie Theresa, but I can't let them do this to me, I can't let them do it—I can't—I can't—

The tobacco smell came close to her face. She turned her head away from the smell, eyes pressed tightly closed, lips pressed hard together, shivering out of control.

The hand pulled back, suddenly—forced back, Angelina fantasized, by the stronger hand of God. She sensed the man get to his feet and walk away. She was too afraid to open her eyes. But she couldn't relax. She overheard the man say something to the others like, "I'll be at my house waiting for the boss—see you in the morning," walk to the door, and turn the key. Cool air entered the room and whisked by Angelina's face. She squinted. The bearded man, rifle in hand and rucksack slung about his shoulders, was leaving. He paused at the door and then walked down the step, leaving the door ajar.

Using every bush and tree for cover, Herman had climbed the hill until he was below a four-foot wall. He had hid the saddlebags and paper bag under a bush by the wall, checked the Beretta and pushed it back into his belt. Crouching low, he crept along the rock wall and up some steps to a little courtyard where at the right corner there was a water trough. To the left of the door there was an open window and he could hear the gruff voices of several men. The thought of Angelina among them made his skin crawl. Surprisingly, the hoodlums had not posted a lookout and were obviously unconcerned about being followed.

Beyond the trough were the remains of a sawed-off tree trunk and next to it a large bush Herman thought could offer protection should he . . . the thought had barely entered his mind . . . the lock clicked, and the door opened with a loud squeak. Herman dashed behind the trunk and shrub and stayed flat on the ground, his gun at the ready. Through the foliage he saw a man of middle size appear in the doorway. Though standing in the shadow of the doorframe, a mere silhouette against the weak light from inside, Herman saw that he was fully bearded and held a rifle across his shoulder. Something about the way he stood in the doorway scanning his surroundings— almost sniffing them—made Herman shiver.

The man stepped down and went to the water trough. He leaned the rifle against the rim, untied his red neckerchief, and dunked it in the water. He wiped his face and neck, wetted the cloth again, and tied it wet around his neck. Very slowly then he reached for the rifle and brought it to his hip. Again he scanned his surroundings, slowly moving his head from left to right, and snuffling like a tiger smelling its prey. Herman didn't breathe.

After what seemed an eternity, the man threw the rifle across his shoulder and went rapidly down the slope.

Herman gulped air at last and listened to the man's steps fading below the hill. With the departing danger, reality arrived, and Herman trembled uncontrollably.

He had no choice but to wait for total darkness. Heart pounding, he watched the last sunset, hoping to read a message of hope and promise there. Instead he felt plagued by uncertainty and growing fear. At last the sun dropped below the horizon, and darkness fell upon the hostel.

The hinge squeaked again . . . . This time Herman dropped below the wall. Concealed by the advancing darkness he raised his head slowly until his eyes were level with the ground above. A second man, tall and stringy, stepped outside. He pushed the door open all the way, rolled his shoulders, and walked to the trough. The light from a kerosene lamp, swaying slightly above a table by the window, illuminated the room's interior.

The tall man splashed his face, drank some water from the pipe, and spit out the rest. Unbuttoning his pants he walked away from the trough and around the corner of the house. Herman heard him urinate. Though fearful of discovery, the drive to get a first glance of the room's interior was stronger. He slid silently along the foot of the wall until he was straight across from the entrance. He raised his head. A few steps beyond the door was an iron stove and behind it, in the center of the room, was a hand-hewn column. There were bunk beds against the wall, and a pile of broken chairs and tables without legs. But there was no sign of Angelina. Dismayed, he crawled away from the door's glare.

The sound of the man's steps were coming from the trough, and when he came into the light again he went straight inside and closed the door behind him. Herman knew the door was bolted when the lock clicked like a firing pin.

It was completely dark now and there was much less danger of discovery. There were no sounds other than a dripping trough and an occasional gust of wind through the trees. Convinced now that the man with the rifle had left for the night, Herman made his way to the window by inches with so much stealth that no movement was apparent where the light was spilling. Just before he had raised his head enough to see inside, the window closed. He froze. After long moments during which the laughter and talking was unchanged inside, he inched higher until his eyes were level with the windowsill. Where a tattered curtain covered part of the window he had an unrestricted view inside.

Two men sat at a table by the window. One of them was the man with the bushy sideburns he had seen outside—the other was fat and bald. The bald man was dealing playing cards, but it was obvious that the game didn't have his full attention, as his eyes kept moving to a specific point at the back of the room. He scooped up the cards, looked them over, shook his head and put them back down. He picked up a revolver from the table and began playing with it, slinging it around his trigger finger. Herman could make out another pistol—a semi-automatic—and a box of shells. Next the bald man cocked the hammer, swung the cylinder out, emptied the chambers, and let the shells drop onto the table . . . but the shells rolled off. He reached for them, tried to catch them, and in the process bumped his head against the kerosene lamp that hung above the table.

With the men thus distracted, Herman moved so close that his cheeks were all but pressed against the glass. The lamp swung wildly, bringing light to the back of the room as it swung that way. Then the bald man bent below the table so that Herman could see into the room behind him.

Herman blanched. Angelina!

Angelina threw back her head. The sudden commotion at the table tore at her nerves, agitated by the tapping ammo shells as they hit the wooden floor. Nico chased after them, cursing, and throwing his arms about like an overexcited monkey.

Angelina froze and almost cried out—a shadow was at the window! She strained her eyes, but the shadow was gone as if touched by a wand. Was she seeing things? *It was there; I know it was there!*

Herman had retreated to the tree trunk and the bush—the only place he thought was offering safety at the higher level where he wanted to be—to calm his nerves and formulate a plan. The pistol, clamped in his hands, was shaking.

Angelina!

There was no way he could calm the turmoil in his emotions— he had found her! The knowledge took hold: *Angelina is alive! She's alive!* With this knowledge, his shivering stopped, but everything that was about to be required of him was brought home. *Whether or not she lives through this depends on me!*

The men would be going nowhere in the dark, and Herman did not expect the man with the rifle to take on the mountain before daylight. But he still had to act at the first opportunity, as he felt sure that this man was the most dangerous of the three. The military had taught Herman the value of discipline, the significance of planning logically, and the art of building on momentum to destroy the confidence of even the toughest foe. Herman took a deep breath and started drawing a mental blueprint of what was about to happen . . . he found flaws in the plan and was revising it . . . for the third time. He vividly imagined his every move inside the room.

Time was passing slowly. At one moment the fear of failure was crushing him, at the next his trust in himself was strengthening his courage.

The click of the lock spun him around. The door opened. Herman dropped to the ground to watch, pistol at the ready. The man in the door was short and squat, and the cabin's meager light was reflected on his shiny dome. He looked around, yawned, and stretched his arms above and behind his head. He left the door open and came down the step. He walked to the trough, wetted his face, bald spot, and neck, and wiped them dry with a wadded handkerchief.

Herman pushed lower into the dirt—the bald man was coming straight toward him, a mere shadow against the faint glow of the open door. Herman bit down on the hand with the pistol to keep it from shaking. The man stopped, unbuttoned, and urinated against the trunk.

The warm smell made Herman hold his breath. Only his mind stirred, threatening to destroy his last shred of self-confidence.

He lay paralyzed, too scared even to shiver. *Forgive me, Angelina—I can't do it . . . .*

Then the bald man buttoned up and walked back toward the door.

With the immediate danger gone, Herman's mind cleared, turned back to the plan he'd formulated. Herman was ready to storm the hostel and free Angelina. It was now or never!

The man climbed the step. He turned and took one more breath of fresh air before he stepped inside. He pushed the door slowly behind him.

Now! Herman leaped from the shadows and with all the momentum he could muster, crashed into the door as it was closing. The impact catapulted the bald man across the room against the iron stove. The man at the table jumped up and reached to the table for the guns, but was flattened when the intruder's gun went off right into his shoulder throwing him back into the bench. With a swipe of his left hand Herman sent the two pistols and all the ammo clattering across the floor. For a split second he pressed the pistol into the man's face then whirled around looking for the second man . . . he was lying lifeless beside the stove, blood dribbling from his bald spot.

Angelina didn't believe her eyes. She hadn't had time to think as this giant burst through the door and took control. Now the giant was freeing her and had a face: it was her corporal, Herman Schuller. Her prayers had been answered.

CHAPTER 19

Angelina's nightmare had finally ended. Freed from her bonds, she had been anxious to flee the cabin, get away from the men . . . away from the stench. But she had also felt a strange compassion for the injured man, the only one of the three who had displayed any measure of kindness toward her. She bit her lip, put her bitterness aside, and helped Herman clean his wound and then pack it with the few medical supplies Herman had in his saddlebag. Surprisingly, the bleeding had been minimal. But his face muscles were tense and his lips tight—the pain caused by the slug deep inside his shoulder must have been horrendous. Though no longer a threat to them, Herman had taken no chance and tied the tall man with a piece of old rope he took from a rucksack on the wall to the bench where he sat.

Under the threat of the gun, the bald man's hands were promptly tied to the timber column—as tight as Angelina's had been.

A first shimmer of the sun turned the cirrus above the mountains to a deep crimson. Herman had chosen a shallow indentation on a small rise above the hostel to spend the last few hours of darkness. He had to reason with Angelina—who was determined to go on— that walking in the dark across an unfamiliar mountain terrain would be plain suicidal.

The night was cold but quiet, even the slight breeze had calmed down eventually. Angelina had changed into her slacks and the turtleneck sweater Herman had brought from the Porsche, and he had draped his wool-lined jacket over her. He had cleansed the cut above her eye and rubbed it with a mild salve he had in his pack.

They had ample time to pour out their hearts. Angelina talked with a suppressed voice of her trip to Aix-les-Bains designed to bring about tranquility and rest, how it had turned into a nightmare . . . the dead detective, her subsequent flight from the hotel, her abduction, the frightening drive up the mountain . . . her terrifying ordeal among the men. Then, with tears rolling down her cheeks, she told of Marie Theresa's death. Herman wiped her tears. He made her drink the last of his bottled water, distracting her from the sad thoughts that had begun to dominate her mind.

While Angelina talked, Herman disassembled the semiautomatic gun taken from the hostel, removed the firing pin and tossed it way. He kept the revolver. It was an old Nagant, a Swiss-Army standard from WWI. It still had the original safety line looped through the eyelet at the handle. All six bores in the cylinders were loaded. Herman was well acquainted with the gun's reliability, having used one just like it for target practice. He looped the safety line around the nearest branch, opened the ammo box and put a handful of the shells in his pocket before disposing of the rest in a hole in the ground.

Herman told about his pursuit on the scooter, how he saw her being pulled from her car and thrown in the Jeep, how it had affected him, paralyzed his mind and body. He told her what he did with the Porsche, how he had tracked her to the hostel, how he had hidden outside. He was glad he hadn't known all that had happened to her or he might have followed his heart inside the hostel before he had a plan, before he knew exactly what he was going to do. "But nothing has ever warmed my heart more than the tiny handkerchief tied to a bush at the bottom of the hill," he concluded. He pulled it from his pocket and pressed it into her hand.

Angelina put the silk against her cheek, cuddled closer in his arms. She looked up at his face. Herman's eyes were closed, but she knew he was observing the surroundings, watching over her. She caressed his hand.

"The sun will be up soon," she whispered.

"I know." He looked down to her. "We must get away from here as soon as it is bright enough to see. Last night, just before darkness, I saw a bearded man with a rifle leave the hostel—I'm sure he'll be back up here checking on his buddies."

Just the mention of that man put a shiver to Angelina. She took a deep breath. "On the way up, the Jeep had stopped at a rock dwelling below the dam—I assumed it was the bearded man's homestead. Then, just before he had left the cabin, I overheard him talking to the others, saying he'd spend the night at his house, then show their boss the way up here in the morning . . . Giulio, I'm almost sure."

Herman looked up sharply. "Giulio!" He paused briefly, then added assuredly, "That will buy us some extra time. Yet whatever we do, Angelina, we must stay clear of the trail along the lake—we wouldn't have a chance in a confrontation with the bearded man. I have given it some thought during the night. Besides the valley road," he pointed to the southeast, "those mountains seem to be the only reasonable way out of here." He stood up and helped Angelina to her feet. He hooked his pack over his shoulders and the Nagant's safety line around his neck. "First we'll make sure the two men are still inside." He began walking down the slope. He stopped halfway. "Sure would give us a bigger head start if we could make them believe we were heading in the opposite direction . . . ."

Angelina nodded confidently. "You can leave that up to me."

Herman opened the shutters he had closed before they settled on the rise. He unbolted the door and entered cautiously. The dawn pushing through the window made it barely bright enough to see, but he could tell almost at a glance that the men hadn't moved. Their bonds were still tight. Within earshot, Angelina said as though she were repeating their escape plan—speaking Italian—to the northwest across the Swiss border. When they left, the door was securely bolted and the shutters shut. If no one else should find them first—the *carabinieri* most certainly would.

They reached the crest of a ridge. The panoramic view was unrestricted from the stream's beginning at a glacier on the left horizon, to where it fed the lake, and all the way to the dam on their very right.

Angelina had been laboring up the difficult slope, and Herman decided to take a break. Angelina sat down on a moss-covered rock. Herman dropped his pack, unhooked the Nagant he had been carrying across his chest, and then, shading his eyes, observed the lake and the trail below.

He turned to Angelina. "Nothing's moving—not yet."

She reached for his hand and pulled him closer to her.

"I prayed to God to bring you my way," she said quietly. "Oh, Herman, you could have been killed." A shudder ran down her neck. "I had fantasized—so many times—about seeing you again. I wondered how it would feel, what I should wear, how much makeup I should put on for you, even the kind of perfume. I wanted to look my very best for you." She pouted. "Now look at me! I'm all bruised up, with no makeup, not even a touch of rouge, and my hair's a terrible mess!"

Herman smiled at her self-deprecation. "You look plenty good to me," he said half jokingly. "I thought of you, too, Angelina, and it must have been those thoughts that brought me to Aix-les-Bains. I can't help thinking about the way fate brought us together."

"It was God's plan," Angelina said plainly as if it were the only explanation. Her feeling for Herman was increasing, but she was not sure how deeply he felt about her. After he had untied her back at the hostel, they had embraced and kissed. But it was the only kiss, the only real embrace, though he had held her tightly during the night, keeping her warm. She sensed aloofness, a barrier she could not understand. Was he, God forbid, in love with another woman?

Angelina had to know right now. She could tell he was ready to move on, but she stepped up to him and threw her arms around his neck. "Oh, Herman, I missed you so," she whispered. He slowly put his arms around her. She turned in his embrace so her back was to him, avoiding his eyes. She felt his gentle breath on her hair and his arms tightening around her. Angelina closed her eyes, absorbed his warmth, let the wondrous feelings rise again—"Oh, Herman, darling."

Darling! How he had missed hearing that word! He couldn't resist, he couldn't hold back any longer. He turned her around, pulled her to him, pressed his lips to hers and sucked in her sweetness, making up for all the kisses that had been missing from his life.

Angelina responded, snuggled into him, pulled him to her with all her strength. As she yielded to his manly tenderness, she felt as if all the promises of her dreams were coming true. They held each other for a long time, kissing and falling in love again.

But it was not the time. Herman slowly released his grip and pulled away.

Angelina, somewhat reassured by his vigorous kiss, and still dizzy from it, wanted to hear more of what he was planning. But Herman was already spreading out the Aosta map, turning it until it lined up with the landscape before them. The rise they were standing on was the perfect spot from where to plot their future course.

He pointed to the map and then to the southeast. "The contours show a possible passage between those mountain peaks. From there, it should be easy to get to the next valley."

Angelina did her own pointing—behind her. "The Swiss border really would be closer, wouldn't it? Only a short distance."

"Perhaps closer, yes, but almost impassable. On the map, large stretches between here and there are all white—indicating permanent snowfields or glaciers. There isn't a single trail. No, Angelina, I suggest we stick to our plan and take the southeastern route. I know it's long and difficult." He pointed to her feet. "Let me see your shoes."

Angelina held up her left foot. "I guess I'm not equipped for this sort of thing." She shrugged. "I could break off the heels."

Herman couldn't keep from laughing. "Sit back down," he said with a chuckle. There was a small, mysterious smile on his lips as he opened his pack and pulled out the new tennis shoes. "You'll be more comfortable in these," he said humbly. "The shoes are a Christmas present for my sister. She won't mind it, though. I hope they'll fit."

Angelina was speechless. Herman hadn't changed—the way he had taken care of her Porsche, the foresight he'd shown to bring her clothes, the chase up the valley, and now this. She knew at a glance the shoes would fit and was shaking her head in disbelief.

While Angelina put on the tennis shoes, Herman continued studying the map.

"Look, darling," Angelina cried excitedly. "The shoes are a perfect fit. Now I can follow you to the end of the world." She turned like a ballerina, delighting him with her enthusiasm. She sat back down and beckoned. "Just for a minute, darling. There's so much we must talk about, so much we must think of, so much we—"

"We'll be snuggled together soon enough," he said soundly. He pinched her butt teasingly and Angelina jumped to her feet like a jack-in-the-box. So began an uncertain trek through the mountain wilderness.

With the ridge between them and the lake trail, Herman descended along the gorge and walked down to the stream. It was the lake's main water source.

Herman poked a stick into the water. "It's deeper than I had hoped," he said. "There's got to be a ford farther downstream where the crevasse widens."

They found such a place closer to the lake—almost too close. The stream was three meters wide and, in most places, not much more than ankle deep. Because of a bend in its course, the opposite border was littered with washed-up rocks of all shapes and sizes. Herman knew what to do.

"Here, sweetheart, take the paper bag while I wade across," he said. He took off his shoes, stuffed his socks inside, and threw them across. He rolled his pants up over the knees and waded across the uneven granite bottom, balancing with his arms. He had expected the water to be cold—but this ice bath almost took away his breath. Once on the other side, he dropped his rucksack, with the Beretta inside, and took the Nagant from around his neck.

He dislodged a large rock from the border and rolled it into the water. He returned for a second rock and placed it two steps farther into the stream, then repeated the cycle until he was across. Angelina watched him, admiring his activity and youthful energy. *He must be freezing!*

Herman stretched out his hand. "Come, sweetheart, London Bridge is ready for Her Excellency," he said, shivering between words. He took her hand and waded beside her while she stepped from rock to rock, balancing with the paper bag high above her head. "You're doing great," he said, stuttering now.

Angelina pulled him down with her onto the bank. "Your feet—they're all blue. Where's that towel?" Herman pointed to the outside pocket on his pack. She found the terrycloth and slapped his feet with it to get the blood going, stopping repeatedly to massage the skin, which was soon quite pink.

Herman was restless. "We need to get out of here fast." He pointed to a small path. "Look at the way that path is trampled. Animals must be crossing here." His eyes lit up. "Here's our chance! This path has to go somewhere. Chances are it will take us to the pass." He unfolded the map.

Angelina pointed to two distinct peaks. "Château des Dames? Looks awfully steep, especially on the other side."

"It seems like a reasonable place to cross," he said confidently. "We'll worry about the bluff when we get there." But Herman did worry—the contours indicated a very steep slope with sporadic sheer cliffs all over.

"Looks like snow up there," said Angelina unconvinced, the worried look still on her face.

"Maybe so," said Herman, "but it couldn't be very deep and may be melting before we get there."

Before they left the stream, Herman filled his bottle with clear glacier water. They followed the trail along boulders that grew in size and bushes that had become dwarves in the high altitude. The trail ended unexpectedly at a sheer granite wall rising as high as the eye could see.

Angelina made no effort to conceal her anxiety. "Are we boxed in?"

Herman did not respond right away. "Hmmm, we'll find out soon enough," he mumbled. He had indeed lost the path on the hardening ground. He backtracked and moments later found the spot where the trail turned sharply uphill.

"That's it!" he cried triumphantly. He helped Angelina over the first hump.

"Animals have a remarkable sense for finding their way, don't they, Herman?" Breathing hard, she used her hands to pull herself along. The bushes had tufts of brown fur dangling from the branches.

"Must be wild goats," said Herman.

The steeper the trail became, the more their progress slowed. "You've hurt your foot," he said after observing her moving ahead of him. "What's wrong with it?"

"Oh, it's not that serious."

"It hurts—I can tell from the way you bite your lip each time you put your foot down."

"It's nothing. I just twisted it a little when I jumped from the balcony while fleeing the hotel."

Herman shook his head—what else, still, was he going to find out about her?

The trail was turning northeast.

"Sure looks like snow up there," said Angelina, short of breath.

Herman shrugged casually. "It will be okay as long as we stick to the animal trail," he said. He didn't like it, though—he hadn't expected snow this far down.

Morning warmth had turned the shallow snowfield in the shadow of a massive cliff into a slippery mess. The tennis shoes weren't up to this. Herman urged her to take the lead, "just in case." The trail wasn't such a good idea after all, he thought. Turning back, however, was not an option either, so they pushed on through the snow.

As he had been afraid she might, Angelina slipped and slid into him with force, almost throwing him off balance. He kept her in his arms.

She screwed up her face in disgust. "Stupid snow!"

Herman laughed. "Maybe stupid to you, but it's beautiful to me."

"Beautiful?"

"Well, first you fall into my arms, and second, it's fun to ski on."

"Here we are, fleeing for our lives, and all you can think of is hugging and skiing!"

"Why not? I like them both. I used to ski a lot as a kid."

"And hugging, too—I just knew it. Well, I never skied, and after this I'm not so sure I'll ever want to."

Herman was still hugging her against him. She'd turned her head up to him and was returning his grin. "You'll get to like the snow. Just wait, sweetheart, until I teach you how to slalom down the slopes."

"You make it sound so easy." The fear had completely left her eyes. "Uh—you will really teach me how to ski, someday? Is that a promise, darling?"

"Cross my heart. I'll teach you, someday."

The brief rest did Angelina some good; the climb seemed easier. The air, however, was becoming colder as they ascended, and there were thick clouds of vapor now when they exhaled. As the slope turned more southerly the snow ended, and the ground leveled to grassy meadows strewn with small boulders and dwarf blueberry bushes.

Angelina cried excitedly, "Look at those rabbits." She pointed at the half-dozen long-eared creatures grazing, hopping, and playfully chasing each other about on the rocks.

He said, "They're hares."

"Hares?" she parroted. "They look like rabbits to me. They're rabbits, I know."

"Okay, then they're rabbits."

"Thank you, darling. Can we take a short break?"

"Yes, of course, you must be tired."

"Just a little, maybe. But I want to watch those rabbits," she said almost childishly. Herman was determined to look at her ankle. He helped her onto a rock, undid her left shoe, and slipped it from her foot. She moaned and bit her lip when he rolled down the sock, moist now from the snow.

"I'm sorry," he said. "I know it hurts." He began to massage her ankle, gently, with his fingertips. "Let me know when it hurts too much." She nodded. The ankle had swollen somewhat. When he slipped the sock and shoe back on, he tied the strings loosely.

"Here we are, as good as new," he said with a smile. "Just don't push it. We've got all day."

She gave him a kiss. "Thank you, Herman, it feels better already."

He was concerned, though. To get across that mountain would be difficult even under the best of circumstances. He had no doubt that her ankle would swell again, more than it had already, perhaps. He could imagine a situation where she couldn't get her shoe back on. And if he had to carry her when they came to the pass, through snow and ice . . . well, the best way to suppress pain was to ignore it, and he would ignore the painful images in his head as well.

He pointed at a peak to the north of them. "That must be the Matterhorn."

Angelina took the map from his pocket and opened it. "It says Monte Cervino."

Herman laughed. "All the same—Cervino is the Italian name for Matterhorn. Looks different from this side, though, as the slant that makes its profile famous is in the opposite direction." Herman frowned and took a deep breath. Only now did it dawn on him that they were among some of the most rugged alps of them all—the Matterhorn and the Dufour Spitze a short way east were Switzerland's highest peaks.

"Must be nice being a rabbit," she said unconcerned, taking the map away and folding it.

They started off.

Herman smiled devilishly. "Give me one good thing about it."

"Well, they have no worries. They—"

"—make love all day long?"

"That wasn't on my mind, darling," she said, mildly protesting. "I meant to say, they have a happy life, going about it without worry."

He nodded. "I guess you're right, except—"

"Except?"

"Well, there are the foxes, the hawks, not to mention an occasional hunter looking for a quick meal, and—"

Angelina cut in sharply. "Do you always have to spoil my wonderful thoughts, darling? You know exactly what I mean." She threw her arms around his neck, almost toppling him. "Must be nice being a rabbit," she whispered in his ear, then held him back and kissed him on the lips, cutting off any chance for a response.

The rabbits scattered every time they made a sudden movement, except for one who seemed more curious than the rest. One of its ears stood straight up, the other was flopped over one eye.

Angelina laughed. "He must be half blinded, by love I presume. I guess there are always exceptions in life, even with rabbits, don't you think, darling?"

"I prefer being human."

"Here we go again!"

The man with the rifle was constantly on Herman's mind. He scanned the valley, particularly along the lake, but nothing moved, and he concluded that his worries were unfounded.

The terrain grew steeper as they struggled through a second snowfield. Angelina gasped for air, but the pass was now within reach, and minutes later they stood on its crest. The animal trail continued on the other side, down the steep slope.

Angelina dropped to the ground where she stood and Herman fell beside her. As they sat on the crest, blown clean of snow by the winds, holding hands and looking over the land below, they felt proud.

Angelina grabbed Herman's arm and pointed down the slope. "Herman, look, there's a reflection down there! As from a small mirror!"

Herman couldn't see it.

"Well, it was there a moment ago."

They froze.

A sharp impact below their feet hurled dirt and rocks at their legs, followed by a muffled pop from below.

Herman clutched Angelina about her waist and rolled backward off their stone perch the way scuba divers roll off boats. And not too soon—a second bullet whisked by exactly where they had sat.

Angelina paled. He grabbed her face with both hands. "Are you hurt?" he cried, his eyes wide. She couldn't talk, just shook her head.

"Stay down!" he urged. He peered from behind the rock and saw a flash of reflected light from field glasses or a scope—the same Angelina must have seen—far below on the lower snowfield. Then a man, rifle slung over his shoulder, came out of nowhere and stormed up the slope. Herman watched him until he was well into the snowfield.

He turned to Angelina. "We're being followed," he said. Almost panicky, he whirled in a circle, looking for a place to go, but the only way out was down along the animal trail on the other side.

He had hoped that the drop-off would be less treacherous than shown on the map, but it was every bit as steep and dangerous as he had feared. On its southern face, however, the mountain was clear of snow. The goat trail emerged again and again, dodging boulders and sheer granite walls as it wound back and forth to a tiny lake below.

Herman shivered, and his heart raced. *I will have to think fast!* The man with the rifle was at the most thirty minutes from the top. Even if they managed to keep their distance, they would be exposed to his shots. No! Herman decided. Running was not the answer; he had to find a way to stop the man.

He gripped Angelina by her shoulders and pointed to the path down the cliff. "It's our only way out, Angelina," he said, trying to stay calm, "and the goat trail is the best way down."

Trembling, she gripped his arms. "It's too steep, Herman. I'll never make it!"

He smoothed her hair. "Yes, you can, sweetheart, just follow the trail; where goats can move about, so can you." His tone more than his words had a calming influence on her. He unclenched her hands, removed the Beretta from the saddle pack, and put it in her hand. "I know this is yours, I took it from your Porsche, but do you know how to use it?"

"Yes. Colonnello Zanardelli gave it to me for protection during the trial. He taught me." She popped out the clip, viewed the ammo and snapped it back into place. She engaged the safety with her thumb and put the gun into the paper bag.

Herman just shook his head. He took her in his arms and pressed her head to his chest, and she heard his pounding heart.

Then, his voice low and tender, he said, "Angelina, my dear love, go down the cliff now and wait for me by the lake."

"What about you? I'm not leaving you. I'm staying right here with you!"

"No, you can't—"

"I'm not leaving!"

"You'd be in my way." He ran his fingers through her hair. "Whatever happens, look out for yourself. Don't look back—go on with life."

She heard his concern and knew that she had no choice. She faced the cliff for the descent, took two steps, turned around, and rushed back to him, throwing her arms around him and pressing her lips to his. "I'll see you below the cliff by the lake, darling, for sure."

Herman watched her skid and slide down the goat trail, the paper bag in one hand, holding onto rocks and bushes with the other. He went back to the crest. The man was now at the grassy strip where they'd seen the flop-eared rabbit.

The man had a beard. He was moving fast—fifteen minutes

from the top. It made Herman sick to watch him. He stormed the slope on all fours like a cat, determined and fearless! Herman's mind raced. Was he capable of stopping this man? Stealth and surprise were all he had going for him. The space between them was completely open, and the only places for cover were further down the slope, favoring his foe. He bit his lip—there had to be a way to change the odds.

"If at a disadvantage, attack!" Lieutenant Stucki used to say. Herman chose a nearby bluff that was sufficiently camouflaged with low shrubs and started toward it, moving low to the ground. The sun's glare would be behind him, and the distance was perfect for the Nagant. There was only one drawback to his plan: using Angelina as bait. Herman hoped the bearded man would be sufficiently distracted by the descending Angelina, giving him a chance . . .

Roberto had slipped in the snowfield and used his rifle to get to his feet.

"*Cazzo!*" He swore repeatedly as he brushed the wet snow from his jacket, hair, and beard. His fury, however, wasn't so much from slipping in the wet snow or bumping his head on a protruding rock as for his two missed shots. Roberto knew the distance to the rim had been at the limit of his scope-less rifle, but he had killed deer and elk at that range before. He must have been aiming low unconsciously— was he afraid of hitting the woman?

That woman! The thought of her was what kept him going. First her beautiful breasts, then the softness between her legs. From the time he'd first laid hands on her in the Jeep he'd known she was his alone, he had to have her, and no one was going to get in his way! Especially not that fool Pietro, who was only interested in doing what Giulio said and collecting his reward.

At his house, he had spent most of the night plotting to kill his two comrades at the hostel and to claim the woman for himself. Giulio didn't know of the place where they were hiding her, and they had agreed to meet in the morning at the rock house below the dam—by that time, however, Roberto intended to be long gone. He had it all thought out. He'd lure his two buddies away from the hostel, shoot them, and roll their bodies into a deep ravine. It could take weeks before they'd be found, more weeks until any suspicion would fall upon him, and months could pass before anyone could track him down. Roberto knew every desolate mountain cabin, stone house, and natural cavern, knew every mountain pass in and out of Italy. He feared no one . . . it was worth the risk.

The missed shots were but a temporary setback, as Roberto was skilled in scouting and hunting and knew every mountain trail. But he wanted to catch up with them before they reached the bottom of the cliff beyond that ridge. He wasn't too concerned about their handguns—they were no match for his high-powered rifle. Still, he'd been pushing himself, going as fast as he could go—the reason he lost his footing. The climb was much harder than he remembered it, and he was feeling his age for once. He scanned the ridge with his binoculars again, but the man and woman were gone, descending, surely, on their way down the goat trail.

He knew that trail. He'd guided climbers up and over the Château des Dames—before his license had been revoked. How he missed his old profession! Ever since the incident with the young student he'd had fantasies of rape. She had been his first . . . Before her there had been a wife. Adventurous and strong and sexy, he'd singled out that student from the first. While the others rested at a cabin, he'd persuaded her to accompany him to a nearby peak. It still thrilled him to remember her screams, echoing through the mountains. For this he spent only one year in prison. There had been a question of provocation by the student. Still, the judge had taken away his permit as a guide, and it was the only work he knew. Connections made in prison had led to Giulio. What was being asked of him hadn't seemed like much, and it was more than he'd ever been paid.

By the time he returned to the cabin he was prepared to kill Pietro and Nico and carry the woman over his back if he had to, bound and gagged. With the woman gone, however, killing them would just complicate things. He left the idiots behind. He didn't believe their story about Switzerland; whoever freed the woman was too smart for that. He spotted their tracks almost immediately. Puzzled at first by their northerly direction, Roberto had quickly guessed their route of flight. He took a shortcut along an established trail. Sure enough, he found the ford where they had crossed the stream, and the tracking became a routine.

Roberto looked up. The ridge was within reach. He stopped briefly to catch his breath and scratched his beard. He unhooked the rifle, checked the chamber. He scanned the crest from end to end, swaying back and forth like a tense tiger in a circus cage. He moved closer, then dashed for the crest, rifle at his hip and finger on the trigger.

He stopped abruptly—there was the woman. He clenched his teeth, and his eyes became slits. "*Porco Dio!*" She was almost at the bottom of the cliff. The sight of her made his head swim.

He leaned against the boulder to his right, pressed the rifle butt against his shoulder, aimed at her feet. But his aim wandered. *Don't hurt her—only her feet.* She was in his sights. He squeezed the trigger until his finger touched his palm. *That's it, steady now* . . . the boulder exploded in his face, and then again, and yet again. Rock fragments had lodged in his open eye. He cried out in pain and clutched his face. The rifle slipped from his hands and fell over the cliff.

Roberto just stood there with his back against the rock, hands pressed to his face trying to overcome the pain, his right eye on fire. Rapid steps approached. He could hardly make him out, even with his good eye. But he was young, much younger than he had expected. *Too young to do a man's job.* But the lad's gaze was determined as he came toward him, revolver at the level.

Without saying a word, Herman unhooked the binoculars from the bearded man then pointed with the revolver to the bottom of the cliff.

Roberto knew this wasn't the time to mount a challenge. With his palm pressed over his injured eye, he began the difficult climb down the cliff.

At the sound of the three shots, Angelina swung around. Her heart pounded, she feared the worst. Something came flying through the air, bounced from rock to rock, and landed at her feet. It was a rifle, its stock cracked open from the fall. Angelina held her breath as she watched the feared man climb down the cliff. She pulled the Beretta from the paper bag, released the safety catch and aimed at the man, still far away. Her hand was trembling. She waited with the gun at her side.

Herman had searched the landscape with the binoculars. Assured that there was no one else, he began to descend. He couldn't keep back a chuckle as he neared the bottom. Angelina, in total control obviously, had her gun on the bearded man and was shouting her head off in Italian. He couldn't understand a word, but the man was evidently obeying her command to get on his belly and put his hands behind his head. When Herman approached she was posing over the body the way a big-game hunter poses with a trophy. Herman burst out laughing.

Angelina heard his laughter and spoke in German. "When it comes down to it, this piece of garbage is nothing but a vile coward. And look what I found on him." She held up a long hunting knife.

"He's all yours, *genehmige Frau*. Do with him as you please," laughed Herman. He was at the bottom now and picked up the rifle.

While Angelina thought about what to do with her captive, Herman stripped the rifle's firing mechanism and slung it, together with the ammo, into the lake.

Angelina had reached her decision. She ordered Roberto to take off his shoes and socks and then she hurled them into the lake. She threw the hunting knife after the shoes. Now she sent him back up the cliff with a stern warning: "If I ever see you again, or if you ever come near me, I'll kill you! You hear? Go on," she added harshly, "what are you waiting for?"

Roberto knew he had no choice—the game was over. He made a wide circle around the young man and hobbled up the slope.

"I suggest you get lost," Angelina called after him, "because there won't be a rock large enough to hide behind or a hole deep enough to crawl into when the *carabinieri* start looking for you."

Herman clapped his hands, though he hadn't understood a word. "Well done, *mi' amore*." Angelina shot him a fighting look. But she wasn't the rock of Gibraltar he almost thought she was—she collapsed in his arms, quivering from head to toe.

The surface of the tiny lake was clear as glass. Angelina leaned against Herman's shoulder, her hands in his lap and her feet submerged in the ice-cold water. The chill around her ankle, considerably swollen now and tender to the touch, felt like a gift from heaven. "It's going to be fine, darling; you'll see," she assured him.

Herman brought out the cheese and bread. "Time to eat," he said. He opened his Swiss army pocketknife and cut off a slice of bread and a wedge of cheese. "Would Madam prefer the Beluga with the buck-wheat blinis, or will it be the saumon fumé on Melba toast?"

"Actually," she laughed, "I had my palate set for Lobster Thermidor. But cheese and bread will do."

They ate and drank water from the bottle Herman had refilled at the stream. He cut her another wedge of cheese.

"Thank you, darling, but I'm not sure if I'll get it down," said Angelina. "My stomach is still in a knot. Do you think those hoodlums will be back?"

"You mean, the other two?" Herman shrugged. "I have my doubts, but we'll find out soon enough—when we reach Valtournenche Valley."

"How much longer until we get there?"

Herman pulled the map from his breast pocket and traced a course with his finger. "Looks like we are past the halfway mark, and the most difficult part is definitely behind us—I'd say not much more than three hours."

Angelina cuddled closer to him. "It's so quiet here, Herman. It's simply wonderful." She pointed to the little stream. "Where's it coming from?"

Herman followed the stream with his eyes. "Must be from the glacier above us," he said.

"I don't see a glacier. Where is it?"

"Right up there, inside that indentation between the two peaks. Here, follow my arm."

Angelina shook her head. "The gray mass that sticks out like the tip of a tongue?"

"That's it. That's the glacier."

"I always thought of glaciers being white, you know—fluffy, like sheep fur."

Herman chuckled. "Well yes, but they carry dirt and rocks along. What you see is the moraine."

"How disappointing." Thinking of the glacier made Angelina shiver, and the cold water on her feet suddenly affected her.

Herman stood and pulled her up. The swelling on her foot had gone down, and the remaining redness was due to the cold water. He wiped her feet and helped her put on socks and shoes, barely tying the laces on her left shoe.

After a first few painful steps, Angelina's walk improved.

The stark granite fields, their constant companions since they started, gave way to meager grasslands, barren of animal life, though they did not lack for beauty.

Angelina pointed to a waterfall that was roaring down a cliff and spewing clouds of vapor that had given birth to a stunning rainbow. "What a spectacle, Herman," she beamed. "I'd never expected this up here; it's so beautiful."

Herman nodded at something ahead. "That's even more beautiful, my sweet love," he said. Angelina looked but didn't see anything unusual. He pointed. "That pile of rocks up ahead is a trail marker, and there's another just like it on the horizon."

The trail, its changes of direction marked by rock piles, made the going easier. It descended gently through a weathered forest of gnarled old pines to a large, oval clearing. The sight was breathtaking: lush grass and long-stemmed flowers waved in the wind like whitecaps on an earthbound sea. Beyond the clearing the Valtournenche Valley spread out with its inviting hospitality and the promise of a telephone.

Angelina's limp had worsened. "Can we rest for just a moment, darling?" she begged. "It's just too lovely to pass up."

"You're right. Time to take a break," said Herman. He sat beside her, stretched his legs, and lay back in the soft grass.

Angelina picked a blue flower and tickled his nose with its petals. "*Viola alpina*," she said. "It's one of the few flowers still blooming this late in the year."

Herman wrinkled his nose. "I know them as alpine pansies. Is that the Latin name?"

"Yes."

"How come you know so much about flowers?"

"From my father. He knew every mountain flower by its biological name." Angelina picked a long-stemmed flower that

Herman knew as *Sonnenröschen*, and held it under his nose.

"*Helianthemum nummularium*," she said. "It's another late-bloom-ing flower, but they are usually done by September. I'm surprised they're still in bloom up here. Look at the bright yellow petals and orange stems; don't they have a wonderful fragrance?"

"Yes," said Herman agreeably. The scent was as sweet and delicate as Angelina. Nothing about this extraordinary woman sur-prised him any longer, and when he kissed her lips, he wondered whether he was worthy of her.

"Oh, Herman . . . I feel so—wonderful," Angelina said passion-ately. She rolled onto her side and stared at the valley. Something looked familiar. She shielded her eyes. There was the river, and farther down the bridge, and on the hill the tiny chapel. "Yes," she cried, "it's the stone chapel above Losanche. And just north of it there is the crossroads and—" Angelina could clearly see it in her mind "—the tabernacle with the statue of Maria under the large linden tree." A sudden sparkle came to her eyes. "I know this place, Herman! Oh, darling I know this place," she repeated excitedly. "My father and I hiked through here toward the end of the war."

Her face contorted. Moisture glistened in her eyes. Herman supported her head with his hand and gently eased her onto her back. He pulled out his handkerchief and dabbed at her tears. She looked so beautiful with her shining eyes and naturally tanned skin. He leaned over her, and with the back of his fingers, brushed across her cheeks. There was no rush; the valley was now within easy reach.

Angelina was almost intimidated by his tenderness. His gentle ways reminded her of her father.

"My father was a good man," she said.

Herman nodded vaguely.

"In early December 1941," she began, "he was wounded during the siege of Tobruk in North Africa. They sent him home to heal, and when he was well enough to walk he took me on a three-day journey through these mountains. I was fourteen. A military convoy brought us as far as Chatillon at the foot of the valley, and a wagon pulled by mules took us to Losanche, where we started our hike. We spent the night in a tiny chalet . . . the chalet!" Angelina shouted, interrupting herself. She jumped to her feet.

"Herman, there's a small cabin two or three hours from the valley, just below that mountain pass." She pointed across the valley. "It belongs to a friend of my aunt." Angelina didn't wait for his comment, reached for his hand, and pulled him off the ground.

Herman shook his head. "What about the chalet?" he asked, in awe at her sudden surge of energy.

"It's the perfect place to spend the night! Oh, darling, we must go there!"

Determined, she dragged Herman down the slope, along a scenic trail, and across a wooden bridge covered with rough-hewn planks and curved rails, anxious to reach the chalet before dark. She knelt at the tabernacle by the crossroads and pulled Herman to his knees as well. She folded his hands into hers. "Thank you, Lord. Thank you for having changed darkness into light, grief into happiness. You have filled our hearts with joy as you lead us along a path of love. Amen."

Angelina was back on her feet, pulling Herman behind her like a puppy.

He held her back. "I don't know exactly what's on your mind, but I thought we had agreed to get help in Losanche, at least look for a telephone. That was our plan, wasn't it?"

Her eyes wandered, though she looked straight at him. "I think it's unwise, Herman," she said, searching for words. "Isn't this the first place those men would look for us?"

He scratched his head. "Maybe so," he said, "but, what about your foot?"

"It's fine—look!" Angelina jumped up. "You see? It doesn't hurt."

"It's up to you, but I still think we should seek help in Losanche."

But Angelina had made up her mind. The chalet, for whatever reason, was all that mattered. She didn't rest until two hours later. They climbed to the top of a modest hill. From its grassy crest they looked out over a gentle, open slope. Down at the bottom, on the near side of a little stream, and surrounded with grass that was unusually tall for this altitude, there stood a small dwelling with plaster walls and bright red shutters, and a corrugated metal roof. The late sun caught the chalet at an angle, giving it a rich, yellow glow that slowly turned to orange.

Angelina sat down, then rolled to her stomach, elbows on the grassy crest, head cushioned in her hands. The fresh air and the excitement of the view below her painted her cheeks a fiery red and made her eyes shine. "Isn't this like something out of a fairytale? Join me, Herman, please," she said lovingly. He lay down beside her.

He lifted his head with a sudden move. "What?" she whispered.

He put a finger to his mouth and pointed to the slope on their left. A pack of chamois, Angelina counted five, emerged from above a thicket and sauntered toward them. A mere stone's throw away, the animals stopped and nibbled on a bush. One of them was on constant alert, head up straight and ears pointed.

Angelina wrapped her fingers around Herman's. A loose strand of hair dropped over her cheek, and he tucked it gently behind her ear. Something about the elegant movements of these gracious animals, she thought, their peaceful air . . . her heart and Herman's were growing warm together.

He whispered. "My father proposed to my mother in a setting like this. Whenever they talk of their early dating, two chamois take center stage. It's all part of a love affair that is still going on today." He felt her hand tightening around his.

Angelina sat up straight. "I will—yes, Herman darling, I will, I will!"

Herman felt baffled; what had come over her? Then he caught on—Angelina had taken his comments to be a proposal of marriage. The chamois, disturbed by the commotion, dashed away.

"Now, see what you've done," he said jokingly.

Her response was a long, loving kiss on the lips.

WELCOME TO MY WORLD was carved on a wooden plaque above the door. Angelina lifted a loose stone on the path and found the key. She unlocked the door and, with some hesitation, pushed it open. They paused before stepping inside, as if entering a shrine.

The place was furnished simply. There was an oval rug made from hand-knotted stockings, looped together as Herman's mother used to do with her discarded hose—nothing was more comfortable underfoot. Centered on the rug was a rustic table, and at angles to it were two wooden chairs with bright cushions of floral tapestry, and near them, ottomans upholstered in the same fabric. There was a magazine rack, and in it an old copy of *Vogue Gioiello*. Right behind it was the sole window with white lace curtains tied back with blue-striped ribbons. A gust of wind pushed the door shut, which would have thrown the room in darkness were it not for narrow spears of light shining through heart-shaped cutouts in the shutters.

Angelina reopened the door a crack and went to open the window and fling wide the shutters. The sun, low on the horizon now, flooded the cabin. Cabinets with painted flowers flanked an iron stove; on it stood a large enamel pot with dual spouts and a wooden handle on a wire loop. From the ceiling dangled copper pots tarnished from lack of use. Beside the stove was an oblong, galvanized trough, slightly wider and higher at the back, that reminded Herman of his childhood bathtub. It was elevated from the floor with four flat granite rocks. Behind the trough was a pink curtain that separated a small section from the rest of the cabin. Angelina pulled the curtain to the side.

"Look, Herman," she cried excitedly, "there's a bed with a real mattress, made up with sheets and a blanket." There was also a pillowy goose-feather comforter, just like the one on Herman's bed at home. Angelina pushed it to the back and sat on the edge, bouncing up and down.

Herman grinned and pointed to the narrow bed. "I wonder who's going to sleep on the ottomans tonight?"

"It's not going to be mee-ee!" sang Angelina.

She took down a black-and-white photograph pinned to the wall. "This is Roselina, my cousin," she said, pointing to a young woman tending a small flock of goats. "Really just a friend, but we always thought of ourselves as cousins." Angelina took down a second picture. "This is the two of us in her mother's yard. We were—"

"—still kids, quite skinny, too," said Herman, laughing.

She elbowed him. "Hush! Inseparable, I was going to say. We spent that whole summer together."

Angelina rummaged in the kitchen cabinets, where she found crushed corn, sugar, coffee, powdered milk, dried onion flakes, salt, pepper, flour, and a liter tin can with dark olive oil that was surprisingly well preserved. Beside the cabinet hung a string of Chianti bottles in their woven baskets.

"I'm going to cook polenta for dinner."

"All in good time, sweetheart." Herman opened the door. Like a giant balloon about to burst, the sun hung low above the horizon. She took his arm and they stepped outside.

"How beautiful!" she exclaimed.

Herman held her from behind, his cheek gently against her hair, and his breath warm upon her ear. As the fiery orb slipped below the horizon, the scanty cirrus that filled the sky turned from bright yellow, to deep orange, to dark red.

Angelina rubbed her head against his chin. "Oh, Herman . . . I wish we could stay up here forever, all by ourselves."

Breathing in her hair, he said, "That would be nice. I'd like that." But he was thinking: O God, where is this going? Where will it end?

A brisk wind came up. Angelina shivered, and they retreated to the cabin, which was still warm from the sunny day. Herman unhooked the lantern and lit the wick. He adjusted the knob until it burned evenly and hung the lantern back above the table. He opened the metal damper and started a fire with crumpled paper and a few split logs from the woodpile. As soon as the spark took, he added two small logs and blew on the tinder until the flames licked evenly between them. He then filled the blue enamel pot with water from the hand-cranked pump outside the cabin and put it on the open flame.

Angelina unhooked a Chianti bottle from the string and foraged in the cabinets. "I can't find the corkscrew. Help me, Herman," she said almost demandingly.

Herman took the bottle from her hand, flipped open the corkscrew on his pocketknife, and pulled the cork. He tapped her shoulder and asked with a triumphant smile, "Would the lady of the house do me the honor and sniff the cork?"

Angelina grinned, kissed the cork, and filled two tumblers.

She raised hers. "Here is to you, darling," she said. "And may fortune smile upon you for as long as you have love for me." The glasses touched and filled the cabin with their melodious ring. The flickering lantern also helped create a mood that softened the reality of their predicament. Giulio's threats were never far from their minds.

Herman licked his lips—Angelina's polenta was delicious. He opened a second bottle of Chianti and let the sparkling liquid flow. He raised his glass. "Here's to the finest cook of all the land."

"Don't flatter me, Herman." She pushed his glass down. "I want you to be truthful with me and accept me for what I am." She turned aside. "Not until I hear your promise shall I toast you."

He raised his glass again. "Here's to the most beautiful woman in the entire universe. Now, will you let me do the dishes?"

She burst out laughing. No wonder I care so much for this guy.

Steam rose from the blue kettle on the stove. Herman grabbed it with a towel and poured three-fourths of it into the trough. With a pot, he brought cold water from the pump. Angelina removed her shoe and stocking and probed the temperature with her toe. "Hotter, please." Herman poured the rest of the hot water from the kettle.

"That's it, sweetheart," he said. "That's all the hot water for now." It was a meager bath at best—only ankle deep.

Herman opened the saddlebag and pulled out the nylon stocking he'd stuffed inside with the brush and mirror, the toothbrush and toothpaste, the heart-shaped perfume bottle, the lipstick. "I thought you might like to have these," he said humbly. "Now is your chance to make yourself beautiful for me."

Angelina looked from one item to the other in complete astonishment. She wrapped her arms around him. "Oh, Herman, I don't know what to say."

But Herman hadn't finished. He pulled his pajamas from the bag and draped them over her arm. "They might be a little large around the waist but they'll keep you warm during the night." Before Angelina had a chance to respond, he walked to the door. He looked over his shoulder. "I'm going to have a look around while you take your bath."

Angelina stared at the door long after it was closed. When she turned around, she saw something on the table. It was her small purse. She opened it apprehensively. Inside was her passport and her money folded exactly as she had left it. Mechanically, Angelina took off her clothes and sat in the tub.

Was this really happening? She began to lather. First, her arms, then her neck and breasts. Her breasts responded to the soft cloth. They were so sensitive! Angelina moaned and leaned against the slanted back. She closed her eyes. "Oh, Herman," she said lovingly, "I never knew how much I missed you." She looked back at the door. What was he doing? What was going through his mind? She was certain he was thinking of her. She unscrewed the heart-shaped bottle, closed her eyes, and inhaled its sweetness. Oh, what sweet feelings. *Herman, Herman* . . .

As she lay in the tub, her thoughts drifted to a valley, to a small tavern with a jukebox, to the shy smile of a blushing soldier. How strangely, how wonderfully fortune had smiled upon her!

Her gaze fell upon the curtain. Curtains concealed secrets and pleasures to be unveiled. Her breasts began to tingle. Was she thinking of—? Everything in her—her thoughts, her desires, the itch in her breasts—said yes. Would Herman? The itch spread to her thighs, her arms, her neck, her lips.

Dim halos from streetlights below the valley shone in the

misty night. Herman leaned against the doorframe and listened to the gurgle of the creek behind the cabin. Clouds had gathered overhead, and the smell of rain was in the air. A sudden lightning bolt illuminated the surroundings of the cabin, then a second—brighter, closer—shot down from the clouds. Instinctively, Herman counted the seconds until the thunder hit, and found the storm to be within three kilometers. Storms had fascinated Herman ever since he was a kid. He could sit in his tree house half the night looking at the lightning and listening to the thunder—the wilder, the better.

Tonight was different, though. The fiery civilian and the sober corporal were fighting it out. Both were hopelessly in love, but that was where the similarities ended.

Said the first Herman, "I'll marry her, move to Italy, have many children, and live happily ever after."

"Here we go again," warned the latter. "How do you plan to fit into her lifestyle, her circle of friends? How would you deal with high society? How do you expect to make a living in a strange city whose language you do not speak? Think about it—you have precious little to offer."

"You're just negative; our love will solve any situation we might find ourselves in," insisted the fiery civilian.

Corporal Schuller had had just about enough. "Nonsense! Love will fade in time, and reality will assert itself. Do you want to take the chance of destroying the very thing you love and care for so dearly?"

The argument was over.

The heavy raindrops sounded like cats chasing across the metal roof. Herman opened the door slowly. The room was deserted and the curtains pulled tight. As they had agreed, Angelina had left the meager bath water for his use. He undressed, sat in the tub, lathered, brushed his teeth, and rinsed them with a swallow from the water bottle. Just as he toweled, the curtain moved ever so slightly to the side. First, two hands appeared, pulling the curtain just wide enough to expose Angelina to the waist. Her breasts were pushing hard against the buttons of his pajama top. Her lips were parted in a dreamy smile, her eyes sparkled. She had never looked so desirable.

Her voice was neither timid nor excited. "You have my permission to share my bed," she said. She closed the curtains. Herman toweled, put on his briefs, and turned the wick down to a flicker.

Angelina was lying on her back, eyes closed, the comforter snuggled to her chin. Herman looked at her serene face. The bruises were barely noticeable in the dim light. He bent over her and ran his fingers through her hair, over her forehead, along her cheeks. A whiff of perfume enriched the air . . . he couldn't hold back . . . he kissed her eyelids, then the tip of her nose. He put his lips to hers, feather-like, and she responded with a tender moan. He lifted the comforter just enough to slip beneath, his feet sliding down between her legs.

Her hand went to grope for his, found it, and pressed it against her stomach. Slowly, deliberately, she wrapped her legs around him and rolled on top, her nipples sharp against his chest. Angelina was naked.

Her breathing quickened. She straddled him, her eyes filled with expectation, her cheeks a deepening red. Impatiently, she kicked the comforter from the bed, tore his briefs off, clutched his hair. She bent down and kissed his eyes and cheeks and lips, tenderly at first, then with quickening desire. She kissed him long and hard, feeling his arousal. Hips twisting with anticipation, she lowered herself onto him, probing, pausing at the slightest discomfort—it was sheer heaven. She wanted to shout but bit her lip—nothing was going to disturb this precious moment. And as he joined in the rhythm of love, Angelina and Herman got lost in each other. Finally, Angelina shivered; the climax spread, pulsating again—O God—and again. "Oh-oh-oh, oh, my darling," escaped her in a whisper. Then she felt his warmth entering her womb. *Oh, my God. Oh Herman, Herman, Herman.*

They rested linked in divine eternity—neither wanting it to end, neither wanting to let go.

The petroleum lamp flickered. The rain intensified, the drumming on the metal roof was louder and faster. Angelina rested in his arms, deep in thought. Her lips moved, but she didn't make a sound.

Herman sensed her apprehension. He ran his fingers through her hair. "Are you thinking of Marie Theresa?"

Angelina raised her head. "Marie Theresa?" she asked surprised. "What makes you think of Marie Theresa, darling?"

"She was your best friend. You shared your happiness with her . . . ."

She kissed the palm of his hand. "Oh, Herman, you're so sensitive. I *was* thinking of Marie Theresa. I still love her and miss her."

With a nod, he said, "I've never met a nicer person."

Angelina sat up. "You met—how could that be? You *saw* her once, I guess."

"No, I talked to her."

Angelina's mouth popped open. "How could you have—she never told me!"

"It was a secret."

"When did you—" she closed her eyes. "The hospital in Losone! There was a call for you."

Herman was embarrassed. Timidly he said, "She was concerned about you and about who I was."

Angelina stared at the ceiling. "Marie Theresa checked up on me. She didn't trust me." There was a heavy silence. Then her eyes were sparkling again. "Just as my mother would have checked on me," she said with pride. "Oh, Herman, my sweet darling, she truly was my mother." Angelina lifted his fingers to her lips and kissed them. "You must tell me all about it."

Herman sighed with relief. "She wanted to know how closely we were involved. She told me about her heart, and that she was going to die." He kissed her hair. "Marie Theresa's only concern was your happiness."

The rain let up for a minute, then suddenly it was pounding the metal roof with renewed strength. Herman lay back on the pillow, exhausted. He closed his eyes. His breathing slowed, and he was asleep. Angelina cuddled his head in her arm and looked at his youthful face for a long, long time.

It had been almost a year since Angelina had been intimate with a man. She searched her feelings, trying to understand why being with Herman was so different. For the first time, Angelina felt completely fulfilled and satisfied. She had insisted on male protection in the past, but this alone, she reasoned, could not have made such a difference. There had to be other reasons, like—like love. She inhaled deeply and held her breath. Then she bent over Herman and whispered, "It wasn't true love before! Oh, my sweet darling, I care for you so deeply."

⟨⟩❈⟨⟩

The sun's first rays stole from behind the distant Château des Dames. Herman lifted Angelina's arm from his chest, untangled his legs from hers, and lifted the comforter just high enough to slide from beneath. He brought his face close to hers and admired its smoothness and soft lines. He breathed in the sweetness of her skin. Then he dressed quietly and left the cabin.

The rain had stopped, but his shoes and pant bottoms were soon wet. The squall had covered the peaks with a second winter coat. Herman was not concerned, as the clouds had vanished and the sun was rising in a clear sky. He strolled through the meadow, his eyes on the ground to avoid stepping in puddles. He picked flowers, and as the bouquet grew, he buried his nose in it and inhaled its fragrance.

Last night couldn't have happened—but it had. He, Herman Schuller—profession, cook; rank, corporal—had made love to the most beautiful woman in the world. As he put together the pieces that had led to bliss, he almost patted himself on the back. Everything began to make sense now: Angelina's sheepish smiles; her obsession about making the chalet before dark; her mysterious, gleaming eyes, all but begging. Blinded by love and duty, he hadn't caught the signs—or hadn't believed in them, even when asked to share her bed. Even now it was almost more than he could grasp.

Herman went back to the cabin, arranged the flowers in an empty pot, and filled it with water from the pump. He rekindled the fire and put on a fresh pot of water for the bath. Breakfast would be elegant: coffee with powdered milk, leftover polenta fried in olive oil, bread, Parmesan, and the last piece of dried sausage. The fire crackled, the sun shone brightly into the cabin, and his mood was the best it had ever been—breakfast was ready to be served. The curtain moved and Angelina came from behind it in his pajamas.

She yawned and stretched. "What a beautifully arranged table," she said, "and those lovely flowers." She bent down and smelled the bouquet. She walked up to Herman and took his hands. "My darling, my love," she said lovingly. "You gave me a gift last night that I shall cherish for the rest of my life." She pressed his hands to her breasts. "I was never happier. Oh, Herman, you must come to

Milan; you must see how I live, meet my friends." She paused and said with a sigh, "Then, if you don't like what you see or feel, darling—God forbid!" She did not finish what she had started to say.

Herman wrapped his arms around her. She closed her eyes and opened her lips, receiving him. Their tongues pushed into each other's mouths, seeking, striving, summoning their deepest feelings.

During breakfast, Angelina revealed the happenings in Aix-les-Bains, filling in the details. Talking about the dead detective brought tears to her eyes. Herman was spellbound, right up to the conversation with Colonnello Zanardelli. "Giulio's gone absolutely crazy," she concluded.

Herman shook his head. "I can't believe it. He must be insane; it's the only explanation. But he'll be making mistakes as he has before, and those mistakes will bring him down."

"I'm scared nonetheless, Herman," said Angelina with a faint sob. "Where can we go?"

"You said that your aunt lives somewhere close to here?"

"She lives in Varallo, in the Valsesia Valley. But it's too far to walk from here. My father and I spent the night with Roselina's mother, in a small village. Uh, the name escapes me right now." She opened the map, traced her finger along a valley. "Here it is, Herman, Alagna-Valsesia."

Herman raised an eyebrow. Was it possible to walk this far through an unknown wilderness? How about Angelina's swollen ankle? Was she up to such a test?

Angelina sensed his apprehension. She said, "There's a trail over the pass all the way to Alagna from where we can hitch a ride. And look," she said, holding up her foot, "my ankle's much better now."

Herman bit his lip, then said, "It's twenty-five kilometers at least, and it will be late by the time we get there, if we make it that far at all before dark. Besides, would we be welcome?"

"It's been a long time," said Angelina, "but I'm sure that Signora Giorgianni would be pleased to open her door to us."

"It will be hard on your ankle."

"I'll be fine, darling. Please, let's push on."

They finished breakfast. Meanwhile, the pot of water boiled

and Herman poured most of it into the trough. While Herman made two more trips to the pump, Angelina cleaned the dishes with the rest of the hot water.

"Voilà, madame, the bath is ready," he said, bowing like a butler. He started for the door, but she held him back by the arm.

"Herman, don't leave." She pointed to the table. "I want you to stay with me." Herman sat on the bench, gazing at her unsteadily.

With a model's skill, Angelina unbuttoned her pajama top beginning with the button closest to her neck. Her fingers moved to the second button and let it spring open with a simple twist. Herman held his breath. He stared at her emerging cleavage, waited for the third button to snap open, then the fourth and last. With a small shrug, Angelina let the fabric slide from her arms. She pulled on the strings that held up the pants and they dropped to the floor. She stepped out of them, totally naked now, and slowly turned around like an emerging sculpture on a pedestal. Her breasts were full, very full in proportion to her flat stomach and tiny waist, and her long, slender legs made her look exceptionally tall and elegant. To be sure, Herman was delighted by the sight of her naked beauty, but he wasn't sure if he should keep looking or respectfully turn aside. Angelina stepped into the trough, sponged her arms and thighs and legs, her breasts swaying gently in a counter-rhythm.

"Please, darling, scrub my back." Her eyes glistened with desire.

He moved toward her, as she had hoped he would, and put a hand to her cheek. He took off his shoes and socks, rolled up his pants, stepped into the tub behind her, and picked up the sponge. With his other hand, he smoothed her hair, letting the tresses flow through his fingers. He lathered the sponge, slid it over her back and her neck and her shoulders, around her waist to her belly, up to her breasts, lifted them, circled her nipples, and Angelina shivered and moaned with every stroke, letting herself go. Herman dropped the sponge, placed his fingers below her chin to tilt back her face, bent over, and kissed her mouth. His other hand moved to her breasts, and he pulled her to him in tight embrace.

"Oh, Herman, love me, please." And he did—making up for so many lost moments and frustrations, so many unfulfilled needs.

The journey continued through the mountain wonderland made lovelier by their feelings for each other. A change had taken place in Angelina—not all at once, but slowly. Her eyes had become less steadfast, wandering, at times turning away from him. She blushed easily and her smiles were shy, and when she talked, which was little, her words were soft, carefully selected, almost short of an apology. At times it looked as though she wanted to say something, then didn't. Herman was at a loss. Was she having second thoughts? Was she having regrets about the night at the cabin?

The trail to the pass was marked well, "A Sunday stroll," Herman joked. He kept track on the map: there was Mount Roisetta Peak, and just beyond, Valle d'Ayas spread out peacefully before them.

Herman pointed to a small village. "This must be Saint Jacques, where there's sure to be a telephone."

"I want to go on, darling."

"It's eleven already, dear Angelina. We'll never make Alagna before dark."

Her eyes begged. "I'd like to go on. Herman—please?"

"I suggest strongly that we stop in Saint Jacques and find that telephone. You're in no condition to make it to the next valley."

"I want to go on." She sounded as if she were almost looking forward to the punishment.

"First let's take a look at your ankle."

She sat on a rock and removed her tennis shoe and sock. "It feels fine, darling. It's barely swollen, see?"

Herman touched her ankle. "It isn't any worse than last night, but I don't like the redness." He rolled up her sock and tied the shoe loosely. "If you insist, we'll go on."

Herman took the lead across a stone bridge, then up a narrow trail back into the mountains.

The trail steepened as it snaked between Cima Bettaforca and its sister mountain, Bettolina, both covered with fresh snow. Angelina was struggling, and her pleas for a short rest became more frequent. At last they saw, far in the distance, what Herman thought was the last ridge to cross. Deciduous trees in the colors of fall surrounded a large pasture carpeted with dark blue flowers. Angelina stopped and leaned on a tree, holding her ankle.

"I should have insisted on getting help in Saint Jacques," Herman scolded under his breath. He took off his coat and spread it over a knoll where there were many flowers and thick grass. "Sit here, sweetheart. It's time to take a rest." Again, he had the feeling she wanted to tell him something.

She lay on his coat while the blue flowers all around her moved like a flag in the wind. "Look at the beautiful *Gentiana*," she said. "I've never seen such blue ones. Aren't they just stunning, darling?"

Herman opened the bottle he had refilled at the cabin with boiled water. He lifted her head, and held the bottle to her mouth. She took two small swallows and lay back down again.

Herman removed her sock and shoe. The ankle had turned blue, and the swelling had doubled. He gently massaged it with the tips of his fingers. All the while, he watched her face. "There's something on your mind, Angelina. You've been trying to tell me something all day, and I think it's high time you spit it out!"

She took his hand to her mouth and kissed his fingers. "You are so good to me, Herman, and I—oh, Herman, I don't deserve your love."

He started to chuckle but was stopped short by the seriousness of her voice.

Angelina grabbed his arm. "It's about the colonnello, Vitt Zanardelli." She looked aside. The rosy color had left her cheeks.

Herman sat up, suddenly aware of what she was going to say. "You—you don't have to tell me anything, Angelina. You don't owe me." He wanted to know—oh, how he wanted to know!—but it was best not to know everything.

Angelina shook her head. "No, Herman, I must tell you! I owe it to you for better or for worse; you must know everything about me." She hesitated, then raised her head and faced him. "During Giulio's trial, Vitt and I had a relationship." She tried to look through his outer shell to read his thoughts, but Herman's expression was unchanged. "We became involved." Louder, this time. She watched him. His expression remained as though he hadn't heard. Angelina's heart sank to her ankle. "We slept together—oh, Herman, say something," she begged.

The light in his eyes gave way to a shadow, a delayed darkness like a cloud dragging across the sky. He leaned into the grass and closed his eyes.

Oh, my God. Angelina shivered and her face turned ashen. Then came a flood of guilt: "It was wrong, Herman! Wrong!" He didn't move; just lay there, eyes closed, lips pressed together. "I didn't love Vitt. I had no real feelings for him . . . please say something."

He sat up and wrapped his arms around his knees, staring vacantly at the horizon. Then he got to his feet, anger and jealousy writhing inside him. *Damn!* If it had been a stranger, someone he had never met—he could handle that. But the colonnello? Vitt Zanardelli had known how Herman felt about Angelina. Herman took a few steps away from her and faced the valley. There he stood like a marble statue, hands clenched. He squeezed his eyes shut as if blinded by the image in his head. *It'll never be the same!*

Angelina knew what he was feeling. Tears pushed through her lids and rolled down her cheeks onto the turtleneck. All day long she'd had the urge to tell him. Now she was sorry for having destroyed something beautiful between them. Yet it had to come out sooner or later; she could not have lived with herself otherwise.

Finally he took a deep breath and unclenched his hands. He rolled his shoulders as if trying to throw off a gigantic burden. Herman sat back down. What right had he to judge Angelina? He fought for understanding. When he saw her tears, the last resentment melted from him—how could he, even for one moment, feel anything but love for Angelina? "It's okay," he said calmly, but with a distinct quaver. "There's nothing to be ashamed of. You followed your heart, and I respect that."

"You don't understand, Herman. I feel like a slut, I—"

He put his fingers to her lips. "Slow down, Angelina," he said reassuringly. "No one can judge you—life's not always what we want it to be."

"I should have stood up to him, I should have—"

"It's done and past. I'm hurt knowing it, but I understand—sometimes we do things when we're vulnerable."

"No, Herman, it was consensual," she whined. "I could have stopped it."

He pulled her head to his chest. "Forget it!" He pulled on her hair, almost painfully, but she sensed growing calm flowing from his fingers. She longed for the warmth of him and cuddled closer. Herman sensed her needs.

He said, "While in Geneva, I met a lady from Texas. Her name was Marvel. She was kind and beautiful, just like you. Her husband, John, taught me a lot about American customs. If I learned anything from him, it must be his favorite quote: "There's no such thing as a free lunch," and each time he said that, he made a special point of it. Ever since, I expect to pay for everything, including favors—especially favors. If you felt you had to pay for anything, Angelina, you have done so; you're free of debt."

Angelina had yet to get used to Herman's philosophizing, and it took a moment to sink in. Then she sighed. She no longer regretted telling him—she had no more secrets.

He picked a flower and pushed it behind her left ear. It was his way of saying he trusted her and believed in her. The flower added a note of purple blue to her shiny hair, and as she hugged him, a big sigh of relief escaped her—her newfound mood hampered only by the thought of Giulio and his deadly threats.

The journey continued through the mountains. Herman counted and timed his steps, a habit he had acquired in the military. He said, "We're doing about three kilometers an hour." He watched her limp. "We might want to slow down a bit to preserve our strength. We're two-thirds of the way there."

"Thanks for your concern, Herman," she said. "But I'm fine. Trust me—fine."

But the tone of her voice was not convincing, and the strain of the trail soon took its toll. Angelina slowed and began moaning with every step. Her limp became worse, and in the end, she could only walk by hanging onto Herman's shoulder. Even the walking stick he had cut from a tree gave no relief. To make things worse, they missed a road marked distinctly on the map. An old man who lived in a small rock house at Grande Alt, a small hamlet that the mapmakers had overlooked, gave them directions along with a glass of cider that they gratefully gulped down.

Two hours were left until dark. The last ridge was behind

them now, and it was downhill the rest of the way. The road, wide enough to walk abreast on, snaked through a thin forest toward Alagna. The sun had vanished behind the shadows of taller pines, and the northerly wind that had whipped up in the afternoon gained strength and chilled Angelina. Agitated by the steep grade, her ankle worsened and her steps became unsure; she was afraid to put down her swollen foot. Sure, enough: she lost her footing, slid to the ground—an accident waiting to happen. She pulled Herman onto her.

"Wow!" He rose to his knees, unhooked the saddlebag from his shoulders, and pushed it under her leg.

Unbearable pain came to Angelina almost immediately. Her cheerfulness evaporated, and her courage faded. She cried, "I can't go on. Oh, Herman, it hurts so much. I can't take another step."

He didn't say a word, just untied her shoe, and slipped it from her foot. Her ankle was a purple mess. The skin was bloody and hot to the touch. He thought it was infected and needed prompt attention, but did not alarm her.

Angelina moaned. "Is it bad? How bad is it?" She was afraid to look at her foot.

Herman shook his head slowly. "It's not good, for sure." He thought. "But it's nothing a hot vinegar soak can't heal." He bit his lip. Guilt set in. If only he had insisted on finding that telephone! He had known of the difficult walk, of the danger of infection. Yet, while he denounced himself, he had only praise for Angelina's courage and persistence.

He smoothed her hair. "You've been courageous, my dear love," he said lovingly. "Don't worry—I'll figure out something." He pulled the water bottle and aspirins from the bag. "Here, take two of these and finish the water." While Angelina took the aspirins, Herman bandaged her foot loosely with the rest of the gauze and rolled the sock above her ankle. He removed the shoelace and tried to slip the shoe back on. But the pain was too severe, and even the slightest pressure made her scream.

"It won't work, Herman."

"Then I have to carry you."

"I can't let you. I'm too heavy."

He laughed. "I used to carry my little sister around when we were kids."

"I'm not your little sister and I'm not a kid."

He didn't listen. He stored her shoe in the saddlebag and knelt in front of her. "Climb onto my shoulders," he said. His tone left not much of an alternative, and Angelina did as she was told. He added, "All the way, sweetheart; put your calves over my shoulders." She did. "Yeah, that's the way. Now, strap the saddlebag on your back." He held it up for her and waited until he heard the snaps of the two straps. "Hold onto my forehead now, but don't cover my eyes; I want to see where I'm taking you."

Angelina folded her hands across his forehead—*don't treat me like a kid!*

"Here we go," he said, "hold on tight!" He locked his arms around her legs, leaned forward, straightened his knees, and then took two quick sidesteps to gain his balance.

He rolled his shoulder. "Hey," he joked, "you don't feel much different than my sister did, though I enjoy it more with you aboard."

"How can you joke at a time like this, Herman? I'm too heavy. I can't let you do this."

He chuckled. "You're as heavy as a feather, sweetheart. Are you comfortable?"

"Oh, Herman, darling, I don't know what to say. Yes, I am snug, but I feel terrible."

He laughed louder. "Don't feel bad. I'd do anything for a good-looking chick like you."

She pinched his ear. " 'Chick'?"

"Did I say 'chick'? I guess I did."

She pinched him again. He coughed. "Uh, would you stop pinching my ear?"

She laughed and pinched him one more time just to make sure.

Herman took the walking stick in his right hand and started down the darkening road. He breathed in or out every third step as he counted: "In two three, out two three, in two three—"

Angelina couldn't help teasing him about his babbling. "Sounds as though you're doing calisthenics."

"That's exactly what I'm doing. Want me to stop?"

"Oh, no, it's music to my ears. I like to hear the sound of your voice no matter what you're saying, my wonderful darling. But I like it best when you say, 'I love you!'"

"I love you!"

"Oh, what heavenly words. Say it again."

"I love you!"

"Say it again and again!"

So the trek continued with the sounds of cheerful teasing as they slowly gained on the distant valley. But as the weight on his shoulders hurt and then threatened to crush him, Herman fell silent, and the rest periods became more frequent. To occupy himself, Herman imagined carrying his heavy pack and rifle and diverted his thoughts as he had on long forced marches. He chuckled. Things could be worse. He could be rushing his boozy buddy back to the barracks to make curfew. Then he pictured Simon, the African, carrying the cross for Jesus—*his thoughts about his load must have been similar to mine.*

The forest ended. In an unforgettable spectacle, the sun consecrated Corno Bianco Peak before leaving them in total darkness. But far below, like a beacon from heaven, Alagna's lights shone through the hazy twilight, and even the thought of Giulio could not diminish the delightful sight.

Angelina spotted the house.

Signora Giorgianni closed the gate and waited until the steps of Catherine, the neighbor with whom she'd just had tea, faded in the dark. Kerosene lamp in hand, she walked toward her home. Then she heard the steps again. "I bet Catherine forgot her purse—she always forgets her purse!" mumbled the signora. She walked back to the gate and held up her lamp.

Out of the dark came a sweet voice. "Is that you, Signora Giorgianni?"

Though she hadn't seen Angelina in some time, she instantly recognized her by her deep, almost virile voice. "Angelina?" she asked and raised the lamp. "It is you! Angelina, what a wonderful surprise to see you." Once past the first stage of astonishment, Signora

Giorgianni opened the gate, hung the lantern on the fence post, and took Angelina into her embrace. "I haven't seen you in so long, but—but who's your companion?" She let go, unhooked the lamp, and held it in front of her.

"A friend," said Angelina. "His name is Herman Schuller, and," Angelina switched from Italian to French, "he is more than just a friend. Can we come in?"

"Of course," responded the signora in French with the typical Italian accent. She shook Herman's hand. "Any friend of Angelina is welcome in my house. Come on in; I'll cook supper." She paused. "What's wrong with your foot, Angelina?"

"I twisted it in Aix-les-Bains, and the long walk didn't help it much."

"Hmm. You can tell me about it over supper. Let's go inside where it is warm." The signora led them along a narrow rock path to the house. Angelina held onto the walking stick with one hand and Herman's shoulder with the other, hopping on one leg. She stopped at a birdbath.

"The cherub—you still have the cute cherub. I remember watching the birds wash their wings early in the morning and splash against the window."

"They still do."

Herman sniffed the air. "Smells like sage," he said.

The signora said, "You've got a good nose, Herman."

"He ought to; he's a chef."

"A chef, hmm," said the signora. "I grow sage and rosemary; nothing adds more to a mood than the scent of fresh rosemary and sage."

Herman nodded, surprised at her mastery of French. He instantly liked the woman's openness and unreserved attitude toward him, a stranger.

Signora Giorgianni waited under the porch light. "Now, let me look at you, Angelina. My, my, how do you manage to keep that tiny figure?" The door was deftly opened and they stepped into a small, stone-flagged foyer, with a door on the left that led into the family room, and a wooden staircase further back rising to the upper floor. The kitchen was to the right. The signora flipped a switch and walked into the brightened, lightly varnished, pine-paneled room. Herman helped Angelina to the oaken breakfast table in the bay window.

The signora asked if they wanted wine or coffee. "You must be thirsty."

Angelina made room for Herman on the long bench. She made a smacking noise and licked her lips. "Mmm, do you still make that delicious cider?"

"Of course I do, my dear. I should have known; you always liked my cider." The signora brought a liter bottle out of the pantry and filled two glasses.

Angelina took a long sip. "It's still the same! No one makes cider as sweet as you, signora."

"I remember you liked my caffe-macciato, too; I'll fix some for supper. Let me look at that foot now."

In no time Angelina was soaking her foot in a large kettle of hot vinegar water. They drank caffe-macciato and spread fresh butter and rhubarb preserves on home-baked bread.

"My, my, when did you two eat last?" asked the signora.

Angelina looked at Herman. "Before seven this morning?"

"No wonder you're starving. Now, tell me what you're doing here in the dark of night." She crossed her arms, ready to listen. Soon she was objecting that she wasn't being told everything. However, the answer to one important question was written on their faces: they were in love.

Angelina started to clear the dishes.

Signora Giorgianni stayed her hand. "Don't you dare, girl," she said. "First, we put a poultice on your ankle, then you two relax in the den while I straighten up in here." She went to a closet and brought out her medical box. She spread some of the contents of a milky jar over a cotton patch and pressed it onto the swelling. Then she wrapped the foot loosely with soft gauze. "Stand on it and see how it feels."

Herman helped Angelina up.

"I can't believe it! That soaking has done wonders. My ankle feels so much better. Look, I can stand on it."

Signora Giorgianni beamed. "By tomorrow, you'll be as good as new," she said. "Now, get out of my kitchen." She pushed the two playfully across the foyer to the family room.

Herman adjusted the pillow on the divan and urged Angelina to lie down. He propped her left ankle on a second pillow and pulled a chair close. "Are you comfortable, punkin'?"

"Yes, I'm very comfy. Thank you, my sweet, darling Herman."

"Anything I can get for you?"

"After all that fuss over me? No! But what did you have in mind?"

Herman rubbed his chin. "A glass of Asti Spumante, man's best friend, a grand piano, the dentist . . . ?"

She laughed. "Stop! I need only you. Here, hold my hand."

"How about"—Herman looked his most sheepish—"I tell you a bedtime story. I know Hänsel and Gretel, then there is *Schneewittchen* and—"

Angelina laughed again. "No, tell me what you've done since All' Acqua." Her voice softened. "Tell me what you did after Brissago, after the border, after we kissed for the last time."

"I wouldn't know where to begin. You wouldn't be interested in my failed relationships."

"Oh, but I am," said Angelina. "You never told me about your girlfriend. I suspected you had a sweetheart back then." But her cheerful teasing wasn't all that lighthearted. Was there someone in his life now? She would be watching him closely. "Go ahead, darling. So there was a girlfriend!"

"There was."

He did say *was*. "Does she have a name?"

"Margrit. But we broke up."

She sighed silently. "You separated? But for what reason?"

"When I came back from the military, things between us didn't work out any longer."

"I'm sorry. I mean, I feel guilty. Things between us might have contributed."

He put his hand on her arm. "No, it was nobody's fault. Our differences would have come between us sooner or later. Meeting you only hastened the process."

So, it was about me, she thought with some satisfaction. Herman had closed his eyes and was biting his lip. If silence could move trees, his would move a forest. She sensed he still had feelings for this girl. *It would be wrong to pressure him.*

"Then you mentioned, uh, was it Marvel?"

There was a sudden spark in his eyes. "Yes, the couple from Texas. I met them in Geneva. They were really good to me, especially Lady Marvel. I wonder if all Americans are that nice." There was marked excitement in his voice.

Angelina cringed inwardly at the word "America." "You liked that Marvel, did you?"

"I suppose I did." But his feelings were all too obvious. "Her parents own a large ranch in Texas where she grew up. She told me about the windmills turning in the breeze, cattle grazing in endless pastures, whitetail deer walking up to her porch. And when she told me how the sunset spreads across the prairie, how the soft light flickers through the windmill blades, why it felt like she had invited me into her dreams."

"Was this relationship more than you're telling me."

"Are you kidding? I was totally out of her league! Besides, I respected her husband."

"Do you still think of her?"

Herman sighed. "Yes, sometimes. I liked her. She favored you, a lot. When she walked on her high heels, her fur tossed casually about her shoulder, her hips swaying like a pendulum, I thought it was you. And when she talked, her voice had a deep and sexy ring, just like yours."

Angelina tittered. "Gee whiz, Herman, is that all you ever think about? How I sway my hips? Besides, I don't have a deep and sexy voice."

"Yes, you do, sweetheart—it has a deep, rich sound just like Marvel's."

Angelina was smiling but concerned. Would she be a memory for Herman someday, like this Marvel? Just another memory? She pulled his fingers to her lips and moistened them with a kiss.

"Herman?" She waited. "Is there someone else in your life now?"

He shook his head, "No, there's no one." Then, so solemnly that he could have been speaking of the dead: "I must have fallen in love with you the moment I laid eyes on you at that tavern in Bedretto."

What a nice thing to say! "I never suspected it back then. You were rather reserved and withdrawn. I never guessed you could have been interested in anything more than a fling."

"A fling?" Herman looked up with a small smile. "No, sweetheart. You were more than 'just a fling.' You were a soldier's dream. You were like the pin-ups on our lockers."

Angelina giggled. *What an imagination!* Then her mood changed to concern. *America.* It was time to face the matter head on. "Herman, do you still have that ambition of going to America?"

"Yes," came back all too quickly. "Sometimes that's all I'm thinking about."

How dare he be so quick about it! "But why so far away, Herman? Come to my country, live with me. Wait until you see my business and the future I can offer you in Milan. We'll make a terrific team!" Her eyelids drooped with these dreams of the future and her arm slipped to the side of the divan.

Signora Giorgianni walked in with a blanket over her arm. Herman spread it over Angelina and gently tucked it around her. The signora smiled at his tenderness. After putting a finger to her lips, she took him by the arm and pulled him to the kitchen.

"I'm dying to find out what really happened," she said, as soon as they were alone. They were sitting across from each other at the kitchen table. "What would you like to drink, Herman?" she asked, and quickly suggested, "how about a glass of my home-pressed wine?" She got an uncorked bottle and filled two tumblers.

"Cheers!"

"Cheers!"

"Now tell me, how did Angelina acquire that cut and those bruises? Really! You must know, I've been fond of her ever since she lost her parents and moved to this valley to live with her aunt. I know when she's holding back on me . . . So what about those bruises, Herman, and what about that foot?"

Herman hesitated, concerned about revealing more than Angelina intended. "She was kidnapped by three men," he said finally, and described the events that had led them to the signora's door.

"She's in real danger and trusts no one, not even the police. The man who's after her is capable of just about anything. He has killed already and won't hesitate to do it again. So she's afraid to go back home."

The signora had both hands on her cheeks. "I can't believe your story. It's too fantastic." She went to the stove and came back. "What are your plans? You must have a plan, Herman."

He shook his head. "There's no plan other than going to her aunt in Varallo."

"Virginia, my dear friend—she'll be overwhelmed. But you've got to contact the police . . . ."

Again, Herman shook his head. "No. Angelina believes with absolute certainty that the police are being bribed. Really, she trusts no one. The happenings in Aix-les-Bains must have been horrendous. They've robbed her of all self-confidence."

"But you must do something, Herman; you *must* contact the authorities!"

"Angelina spoke with a colonel of the secret police. It was his suggestion to stay clear of Milan, at least for the time being."

Signora Giorgianni shook her head in disbelief. "Why would anyone want to harm such a beautiful human being? And what an incredible good fortune that you were there to help her, as though someone had planned the whole thing."

"Someone did—Angelina is convinced of that."

She stood up. "Come, Herman, let's go to the basement and get some more of this wine."

They had to go outside to get to the basement. A single low-watt light bulb hung from the vaulted ceiling, swaying a little in the sudden draft. There were bins with potatoes from the summer, and bins with apples and pears for the long winter. Garlic was woven into long ropes; red peppers had been strung together. A dozen sausages and two sides of smoked bacon dangled from the ceiling on long wires, and beside them hung fresh provolone cheese in large, netted rounds. The wine rack tilted slightly to keep the bottlenecks pointing down. The cellar was clean and tidy and didn't have the usual musty smell.

The signora removed a bottle from the rack, wiped it, and handed it to Herman. Taking their time, they walked back to the kitchen.

"Here, make yourself useful," said the signora, handing him a corkscrew. Herman pulled the cork and filled the tumblers. The surroundings took on a new warmth as the young man and the woman of his mother's age settled down to sip wine and make small talk. As the wine took effect, they chatted even more cozily.

"Do you love Angelina—really love her?"

Herman pondered. *Of course I love Angelina, more than anything in the world.* But it was a complicated, an almost impossible love. He took a long sip of wine.

"I care for Angelina," he began, then reconsidered. "Yes, I love her. What man wouldn't fall in love with a woman of such beauty?"

"So you're attracted to her beauty? With no lasting intentions, I suppose?"

Herman sighed. "Quite the contrary, signora. I'd like nothing better than to spend the rest of my life with Angelina. But things are not all that simple."

"Make some sense!"

"Angelina is no ordinary woman . . . and I don't just mean because of her beauty."

"Say it, Herman," she said impatiently. "Here," she handed him the bottle, "fill the glasses." Herman did as he was told. He emptied his glass, and she quickly refilled it to the rim. "Something's bothering you, Herman. Perhaps you don't even know what it is. Men never know what bothers them."

Herman opened his eyes wide, wrinkling his forehead, and somehow looked defeated. "Can you imagine, Signora, a fashion model and a cook? Can you think of anything more absurd?"

She sensed self-pity. "Not really," she said. "But then, I've seen worse. Such a match might not be impossible."

"But the odds are against it."

She wasn't sure where he was going. "You're hard to understand, Herman. People are people, and her friends aren't much different than yours."

"Are you kidding? Her friends are theatrical producers and fashion kings, even people from the government—high society. My friends are the pastry chef from down the road and the cooks I work with—ordinary people. What in the hell am I doing in this relationship?"

"Slow down, Herman," she said sternly. "High society! You don't even know what that is. Here, have some more wine." But deep down, Signora Giorgianni knew exactly how Herman felt. Being the underdog was like planting a crop for someone else.

Then she had an idea. "Herman," she began, "have you ever thought about where Angelina came from? That her upbringing might have been similar to yours, possibly worse? What she has done with her life was of her own doing. She worked hard for what she has and deserves everything that's coming to her. But maybe she's closer to you than you think, and you're exactly what she needs."

The wine was starting to affect Herman. "Maybe, uh, maybe you're right, Ma," he said. "I just don't know how I would fit into her circus—circle."

She took his hand. "Are you afraid of the difference in age? You're young yet, Herman, and Angelina is pretty grown up."

"What the hell has age got to do with it?" He heard himself and pulled back. "But I'm scared about our differences. She went to university and all that stuff; I barely mastered trade school. You don't have to be a scholar to figure things don't add up. A chicken and a fox have more in common."

The signora smiled at his outpouring. And even though she sensed a hefty dose of self-pity in his voice, she could relate fully to his passion. She filled their glasses again and said an upbeat "Cheers!"

"Cheers!"

She put her hand on his arm. "Have you discussed any of this with Angelina?" Herman shook his head. "I thought so," she said. "Let me give you some advice. Sort things out now and put them into perspective before you get so involved that you forget what's what. Once love has reached the point of no return, your mind becomes numb to reasoning. You can't make good decisions then, and jealousy, the most destructive force in us, will do its dirty work."

Jealousy! Herman closed his eyes—*Angela and the colonnello*—it was still in him.

The signora saw him shiver. "Are you okay, Herman?" she asked. "You're suddenly white as a ghost."

"Must be the wine."

An uneasy silence fell. Was that a tear below his eyelid? Yes, he wiped it.

The signora stood. "Now, now, what's that all about?" She walked over to his side and sat down beside him. She put her arm around his shoulder and pulled his head to her bosom. Was that a sob? Moisture seeped into the fabric of her blouse. "Come, come," she said softly, "it can't be all that bad." She patted his back and hugged him close. "I know how it feels to have the odds against you. But there's a reason for everything. Sometimes we don't see it at first, and sometimes we never get to know it, but it's there, working for us, giving us time to work things out. Take that time, Herman. Take all the time you need." She smoothed his hair, her passion for the young lad growing. "Love is a wondrous thing, and you should be proud of Angelina's love."

He shook his head slowly. "But I'm not worthy of her. There will always be someone better."

"That's hogwash, Herman, and you know it," she said harshly. "You're courageous and smart; besides, you're plenty handsome. What more would a woman want? Put that inferiority stuff out of your head."

Herman pulled away; his eyes were uncertain.

She smiled. "Don't be embarrassed; you're doing fine." She raised her glass. "To you and Angelina."

"To Angelina, evasive as the moon on a cloudy night, bright as the sun yet unreachable as the distant stars!"

The signora was delighted. "I know how you feel, Herman. Love is a powerful thing but can vanish quickly when circumstances change. I've been there." She took another swallow of wine and squeezed his hand. "You must decide *now* what is best for you and Angelina—what is possible and what is not. When a relationship lacks the substance to make it work, it's sometimes best to sever it before anyone gets badly hurt. Sometimes love alone is not enough."

After more wine Signora Giorgianni recalled an affair in her mid teens, an affair that brought about a pregnancy and the consequent flight of her lover, an older man.

"I never saw or heard from him again," she said sadly. "I guess he wasn't worth it. My parents sent me to an institute in Chamonix to have my little girl. Later, I married a nice man strictly for the convenience and because Roselina, my baby, needed a father. He was a good man; still, I wasn't capable of loving him."

Chamonix, France—no wonder she speaks French so fluently, Herman thought. "I saw a picture of Roselina at the cabin; she's very attractive."

The signora's eyes sparkled. "She's still my baby, though she's married and has children of her own."

"Are you living by yourself?"

She nodded. "My husband served in the military during the war and joined the partisan movement toward the end. He was killed in a skirmish with German troops not far from our homestead. After his death, I realized that I really had loved him—but by then it was too late to tell him, and I have been living with this thing ever since."

"I'm sorry."

"Don't be sorry, Herman. He left me this house and farm free of debt. In some ways, life has been good to me. Let's get some more wine." They returned to the basement and brought back a bottle of Asti Spumante. Herman was going to fill the same tumblers, but she stayed his hand.

"Use these." She handed him flutes from the shelf behind her. "Let's not spoil the flavor of the Asti; I serve this one only on special occasions. Here's to you and Angelina."

"And to your beautiful Roselina," he said as the glasses clinked.

"She's a great girl. She occasionally spends the night at the cabin above Losanche, cleans it, and keeps it stocked, just in case some lost wanderer needs it."

"Like us." Thinking of the cabin brought fresh blood to Herman's cheeks. "It was beautifully cared for. So romantic."

As the night grew long, the bond between the young man and the woman twice his age grew deeper.

It was early morning when Signora Giorgianni gave a final word of advice. "Angelina deserves the best," she said, "and there's no doubt she'd be happy with you, Herman. On the other hand, you should make allowances for her complex personality."

She stood up, or tried to. "Must be the Asti," she said as she fell back onto the bench. "Makes my legs heavy as lead." She succeeded in her second attempt, took two steps, swayed, reached for the table, missed, and fell flat on her rear end.

Herman, already on his feet in an attempt to grab her, shot from the bench, stumbled over her feet, and landed hard across her lap. "Holy shit—are you hurt?"

The signora smiled timidly, then chuckled, then laughed heartily. Herman joined in her laughter, then made his feet and pulled her up. With his support she made it to the stove and heated some milk. "An old remedy," she called it. They sipped warm milk and began to feel better.

The signora showed him to the chamber beyond the sitting room. "It's where Roselina sleeps when she visits." After she left him Herman went to Angelina, adjusted the blanket over her, and looked at her peaceful face for a long time. He left his pajamas on the chair beside the couch, undressed, and slipped into bed. He was still dizzy from the wine, and drained from the eventful day. Soon, cold feet rubbed against his legs—it was Angelina sliding under the covers.

The sun emerged from behind the whitened mountain peaks. The air was pure and crisp, and there was not a cloud in the sky. Signora Giorgianni had already arranged for a neighbor to drive the couple to Varallo in his VW minibus. Angelina called her aunt from the post office—one of few telephones in Alagna—to announce their arrival. Her second call, lasting thirty minutes, was to her partner in Milan. Then she called Colonnello Zanardelli to tell him about the abduction, the bearded man, and the heroic deeds of Herman Schuller.

After an emotional farewell to Signora Giorgianni, they rumbled down the dusty road in the van on their fifty-kilometer journey to Varallo.

They stopped at a white picket fence surrounding a large garden; in the middle stood a modest farmhouse constructed from rock with a built-up roof cut from large timber and covered with slate shingles. Red geraniums cascaded from the second-floor balcony and from the single dormer window jutting from the steep roof. The air smelled of tart pine from smoke billowing out of the large, stone chimney. Beyond the fence were freshly weeded vegetable beds. Wooden pegs at each end still had the seed packages stuck on them. However, the bare tomato bushes and sparse leaves hinted at the end of the growing season. Even the red-tip butter lettuce was almost gone. What the garden lacked in vegetables, however, it more than made up with begonias, roses, and margaritas that were still in bloom. The air was still except for the clucking from the chicken coop next to the homestead.

Angelina pulled Herman along the stone path to the front door.

A woman in her fifties responded to her knock. "Angelina! Here you are! I could hardly wait." The women embraced amidst tears of joy.

"This is Aunt Virginia," said Angelina, standing aside and pushing Herman forward. "And this, my dear aunt, is Herman Schuller, the man I told you about, the man I love."

Herman stretched out his hand, his cheeks growing warmly pink from the introduction. The family ties were obvious: the high cheekbones, long neck, prominent breasts and slim waist, the bowed lips, and the unmistakable sparkle in their eyes. The only differences were in Aunt Virginia's dark eyes and her black hair that was turning silver one strand at a time.

"It's been so long, Angelina; I've missed you," said Virginia.

Angelina was excited as a child on her first trip to the carnival. "You don't know how much this means to me!"

Virginia stared at Angelina's foot. "Your phone call had me worried," she said. "You still limp."

"It's much better since Signora Giorgianni took good care of me; she's such a nice person."

Virginia nodded. "She's always been a dear friend. Let me finish what I've started, Angelina, while you show the young man around. I sense you can barely wait."

"I still can't hide from your motherly instincts, can I, my sweet aunt?" laughed Angelina. "Come, Herman—I'll show you around." Angelina pulled him after her.

"Here's the kitchen where I—"

"—learned to do polenta?"

Angelina pinched his arm. "Don't make fun of me, darling! Polenta is not the only thing I can cook!"

Stained wooden cabinets flanked the wood-burning stove, and shiny copper pots dangled from sturdy brass hooks above it. Centered in the window bay was an oval dining table with two curved benches, and on it a bouquet of fresh yellow roses were lovingly arranged in a ceramic vase. The tour continued to the sitting room, then up one flight of stairs to the study.

Angelina pointed to a walnut upright piano in the corner against the wall. "The closest music teacher was in Aosta, and it was just too costly to take piano lessons," she sighed. "One of the missed opportunities in my life." A large hutch, expertly crafted from rosewood, stood grandly beside the piano, and on it were rows of photographs. Angelina lifted one of the pictures.

"This was me at sixteen." She put it too close to Herman's nose. "Wasn't I pretty?"

Herman adjusted the distance. The picture was of a skinny girl. Only the hair, flowing over her shoulders in long waves, and her big, fiery eyes showed any resemblance. "You were skinny then. When did you acquire your curves?"

Angelina picked another picture that showed her in a waitress uniform at the Puccini dining room—a mature woman. "This was me at eighteen."

"Wow! What a change two years made! No wonder men were falling all over you."

"They still do," she said with a smirk and a proud toss of her head. Next were two pictures of her grandfather and grandmother. The edges were curled, and the images had yellowed through the years. Like her aunt, Angelina's likeness to her grandfather was astonishing—the same chin, the same wavy hair pulled back behind the ears, the same big, kind, penetrating eyes. "This was Grandpa. He was a proud man. And this was Grandma—wasn't she attractive?"

Herman looked at the well-endowed woman wearing a large feathered hat. "Wow! There's no doubt where you got your greatest assets."

"Yes," was Angelina's spontaneous response, "she was a very smart woman."

Herman laughed. There was no winning with this female.

Angelina's expression darkened as she reached for the picture of a couple on their wedding day. "These were my parents," she said softly. "The best parents anyone could have." She pressed the picture to her chest and closed her eyes.

Herman quietly left the study.

Aunt Virginia had prepared saffron rice for a mid-morning meal.

"Can I chop those onions for you?" offered Herman. "I'm a cook, and a pretty good one at that."

"You're bragging, Herman."

"I know. But I really am pretty good."

"Okay, then. Here's the carving board and knife; half an onion's all I need right now. And while you're at it, crush a large clove of that garlic. Careful, though, that knife is plenty sharp!"

Herman dismissed her concern with a snort. He peeled and chopped half of the onion, put the other half on a plate and into the small cooler cabinet. He peeled a large garlic clove, squashed it with the flat side of the knife, and chopped and rubbed it with salt to a puree.

Virginia nodded approvingly. "You do know your stuff." She turned away, then, and looked through the window to the mountains. "How long have you known Angelina, Herman?"

"We met last year, on May the fifteenth. I was in the military then."

Virginia faced him. "You seem to remember that date well."

"I'll never forget that Sunday afternoon."

There was a brief silence.

Virginia looked at him warmly. "I . . . I can't find words to say what's in my heart. I want to thank you for helping Angelina—that's all. I'm forever indebted to you."

"Not necessary, signora. I'd do it again in a heartbeat."

She shook her head slightly. "No need to downplay what you did. You risked your life for her. She gave me some of the details on the phone." Virginia played with the buttons on her dress but kept her eyes on him. "Angelina is all I have left in this world, my only blood relative." Virginia stepped forward and embraced Herman, and he turned redder than an overripe tomato. She loosened her grip.

"Angelina told me how she feels about you, Herman, and I want you to know that, whatever comes out of this, you have my blessing and undivided support. I wish you two the very best."

Herman reddened even more. Though thrilled by her words, he was unable to respond. He walked to the sink and began rinsing off the cutting board and knife.

"You don't have to do that," said Virginia.

"Clean up? I'm used to it. My mother wouldn't let me get away with not helping clean up."

"Our men leave the cleaning to us women. But thanks."

When he was done, Herman sat and watched her finish the cooking. She moved about with grace and self-assurance, like Angelina. He was watching so intently he didn't see Angelina walk into the kitchen.

She went straight to Herman. "Why did you leave me?"

"I figured you wanted to be alone with your memories."

"Don't ever feel that way, Herman. You should know that I want to share everything with you, the happy moments and the sad."

Herman slid from the bench and took her in his arms.

Virginia watched over her shoulder, touched by his display of tenderness. "You two go ahead," she said encouragingly. "It'll be a few minutes till the rice is ready."

Angelina perked up. "Follow me, darling."

She pulled Herman up two flights to the attic chamber.

"Here is where I slept during those two wonderful years with my aunt. It's where I put the past behind me and searched for my future, wondering what was out there, what shining knight I would meet."

Rays of morning sun shimmered through the partly open dormer window and gave the room a pleasant brightness. The walls were of tongue-and-groove knotty pine, slanted at shoulder height to the gable's roughhewn center beam. White sheer curtains with ironed pleats pressed up to the window and softened the view up the valley to the distant mountains. Herman imagined Angelina at the small desk by the window gazing across the valley and pondering life's great secrets. He inhaled the fresh air. How wonderfully refreshing, how relaxing it must have been for her to awaken here each morning to the rising sun! He bent down and smelled the three margaritas in the crystal bud vase on the desk.

Angelina watched him. "My dear aunt," she said, "always puts fresh flowers in my room when I come to visit." She pulled Herman toward her and held him about the waist. "Oh, Herman, I wish you could feel the way I do. I used to lie awake, thinking of the man I would love. And now you are here, darling, right here in this very room." She kissed him on the lips. "I love you so much. Don't ever leave me."

Don't leave me! The words were almost too much to bear thinking about. He pulled away.

The hardwood floor was partly covered with a sheepskin rug. Angelina sat on the edge of the sleeper sofa pushed against the wall. A comforter, rolled inside a zippered cover, served as backrest, and two large pillows, sewn in tapestry, served as armrests. She gestured for Herman to sit down. He began to but was distracted by black-and-white photographs mounted to either side of the door.

"My first modeling auditions," she explained. She stepped behind him and leaned against his shoulder. "They're terrible poses, aren't they, darling? Here, look how I hold my left arm so stiffly, and here—the head's all wrong and my fingers are spread like pitchforks. But my dear aunt won't let me take them down. 'They show how far you've come!' she says. Maybe so, but I still think they're awful."

Herman laughed. "Maybe to you, but they look plenty good to me. You should listen to your aunt."

"You're just trying to be nice, darling." She opened the door. "I'm going downstairs. Virginia might need my help in the kitchen. Coming?"

"I'd like to look at your pictures some more, if you don't mind," Herman said.

She gave him a quick kiss. "Don't be too long now." She closed the door behind her.

The sudden quiet made Herman feel lonely. He studied the fashion pictures, examining each as if it were a priceless work of art. He had never seen anyone more gracious or more beautiful—the way she held her head proudly, yet modestly, and positioned her hips sexily, yet diffidently—she was so far superior to models in magazines or fashion shows back home.

Then it dawned on him. There was no open cleavage, no excessively exposed skin in any of her poses, yet Angelina was charming and notably exciting nonetheless.

I should be thrilled . . . Sadly, he was not, and these pictures were the very reason. The woman in them was a stranger. Angelina was not for one man to love; she belonged to all men, to the people. The longer he held onto that hopeless image, the more frightened of losing her he became.

"Angelina, my love, why can't I simply love you?"

"The rice is ready," called Aunt Virginia from the kitchen. Herman shook free of his thoughts, wiped his eyes, and walked down the two flights.

Angelina slid down the bench to make room for him. While they dug into the bowl of rice, Virginia learned of the details that had led them to her. She didn't interrupt, just listened, occasionally shaking her head in disbelief.

"The *risotto* was wonderful," Angelina said when they were done eating. "You're still the best cook."

"Hush, Angelina, you know better than to flatter me. Besides, I had help."

"I peeled the onion," said Herman.

Angelina brought up the conversation with her partner earlier that morning. "Things don't look good at home," she said. "There have been strange phone calls. Sabrina's scared. An unknown car circled her home last night. I suggested she move her family to my apartment at 10-Aldrovandi, where I have security."

"Are the police doing anything about it?" Virginia asked.

Angelina shrugged. "A detective makes his rounds through the showroom, and a uniformed policeman is posted at the front door during our hours of business." Angelina tried to downplay her anxiety but was unable to hide the fear in her eyes. Giulio's threats were on her mind constantly.

Herman reached for her hand. "Have you heard from the colonnello?"

Angelina took a deep breath. "I talked to him this morning. He advised against going home yet. Giulio has been spotted in Milan, but none of those sightings are confirmed." She put her other hand on top of his. "I can't stay away much longer, Herman. Sabrina is overwhelmed by all the uncertainties; she needs me."

Virginia said, "Take the colonnello's advice. It would be hard to keep a low profile with that car of yours. Anyway, what are you going to do about the car?"

"Sabrina's husband has left Milan with a friend by motorbike to retrieve the Porsche where Herman left it and drive it here. They might even get here by noon."

"Wow!" said Herman. "That's less than an hour from now. Have you told them about the key?"

"Yes, but they took along an extra set, just in case."

Virginia shook her head. "Where will you go? I'd be delighted to have you stay with me; your room's always ready," she said with growing excitement.

Angelina perked up. "Why not? What do you think, Herman? We could stay right here in my dormer room."

He nodded distractedly. "Has Giulio any idea about Virginia?"

Angelina bit her lip. She had told Giulio about her aunt, and what he didn't know he could figure out. "I see what Herman's hinting at. It would be a mistake to stay here, Virginia. I'm sorry, but it's best that we go on."

Virginia's smile vanished. "But where? Where will you go?"

Angelina looked at Herman. Then the thought came to them simultaneously—the Mendali dairy farm.

"Alice invited us back," said Angelina. "Would she mind if we dropped in on short notice?"

"Only one way to find out," said Herman.

Angelina dialed information. Virginia gave her a pencil, and Angelina scribbled the number. She dialed, but the Mendali's line was busy. She waited a few minutes and dialed again, but the line remained busy.

Virginia waved her away when Angelina began to clear the dishes. "Leave them, Angelina. I'll have the rest of the day to clean up," she said. Angelina insisted that they at least soak the dishes, and they carried them to the sink. Virginia took her by her arm. "You're tense, girl. Come help me gather the eggs. The walk will do you good. Besides, we have not had a woman to woman talk in years."

From the window, Herman watched the women walk along the rock path through the garden. Virginia, a wicker basket in her hand, had her arm wrapped around her niece. Angelina still had a little limp.

"Herman seems very nice," Virginia began. "There's something special about him."

Angelina looked up to her aunt. "Thank you, Virginia."

Virginia slowed her steps. "Does his age bother you at all? You're mature and he's quite young."

Angelina smiled. "I've never thought of it that way, but don't let his young looks fool you. Herman's plenty smart and mature. I love his down-to-earth manners and his carefree ways. He's definitely different from any man I've known."

"Then your love's not mere compassion—you know, gratitude? His deeds were heroic, I must say."

"Oh no, Virginia." Angelina searched for words to express her feelings. "He's brave and thoughtful; he makes me laugh, and he makes me feel womanly without expecting anything in return. Besides, he's a fine lover." The words just slipped out.

Virginia remained unmoved. "I had a brief chat with Herman in the kitchen while we waited for you. He is sensitive and seems totally devoted to you—you're not just stringing him along?"

"Oh no, my sweet aunt," returned Angelina quickly. "I love him deeply and would marry him tomorrow if he asked me. But Herman has other plans, such as hotel school and going to America." She paused, then quietly said, "I wish he'd change them." She shook her head slowly. "I can no longer imagine being apart from him."

Virginia broke off a rose of the deepest crimson and held it under Angelina's nose. She watched her niece inhale the sweet fragrance, sensed her ardent desire for the young man's love. Virginia's motherly instinct had never been wrong. *Whatever your future, child, I want the best for you.*

At the chicken coop, Virginia unlocked the wire-mesh gate. "Here, Angelina. You hold the basket while I gather the eggs."

Angelina slid the basket handle over her right arm. "This is fun, Virginia, just like the good old days."

"Like the good old days," repeated Virginia. She found eight eggs and put them into the basket. "It looks as though one of the hens is on strike again."

On the way back to the house they halted. Was that piano music coming from the study? Angelina pushed the basket onto Virginia's arm and ran to the house.

Herman was surprised to find the piano in tune. *"Guten Abend, gut' Nacht, mit Rosen bedacht"* was an old song he had learned from his grandfather, an accomplished musician. Whenever Grandpa came to visit, he would bring along his violin and Herman would join him at the piano.

Angelina burst into the room, out of breath. "I had no idea you could play the piano, Herman. You never told me!"

Herman was flattered. "My mother insisted on piano lessons. My teacher said I was her brightest student . . . and her laziest. Lack of practice caught up with me eventually. That's why I'm a cook today."

Aunt Virginia entered the room with the egg basket on her arm. She anticipated Herman's question. "A piano-tuner from Aosta makes the rounds twice a year. He was here just last month—that's why it's in tune."

Herman nodded.

"Please play some more," begged Angelina. She didn't take her eyes off him as he continued with "Santa Lucia." Angelina hummed along and then sang: *"Sul mare luccica L'astro d'argento . . .* it's my favorite song, darling. How did you know?"

"Show me an Italian who doesn't like *'Santa Lucia,'"* he teased. "Actually, it was your selection at the jukebox the day we met."

"At the tavern—you remembered. You remembered my song!"

He said, "Do you play the piano?"

"Of course she does," Virginia broke in. "I taught her a couple of songs when she stayed with me."

"Aunt Virginia! You embarrass me. I could never play like Herman."

"Hush. You do very nicely; go ahead," she urged. Angelina sat down and played a pleasing melody.

"My dear aunt composed it for me," she said when she'd finished playing.

"And Angelina wrote the lyrics," said Virginia. "The piano tuner then put it on paper for us so we wouldn't forget it."

Angelina lifted the lid of the bench and pulled out a single page of sheet music. She put it on the music flap and smoothed out the wrinkles. She played the tune again and sang the words, and her deep voice came through clear and sweet. *"My name is Angelina—my mamma named me so. I'm smart, healthy, and pretty—like Mamma was before me. Mamma is now in heaven and watches over me. I'll be good and loving, so Mamma is proud of me. I'll be good and loving, so Mamma is proud of me."*

The road across La Colma Pass was steep and winding. The Porsche negotiated its many hairpin turns with the grace of a slalom skier. Angelina was at her best. At the sight of her shifting and steering, feet dancing on the pedals, eyes judging the ever-present curves— Herman thought of a symphony conductor. Herman, one hand on her shoulder and the other braced against the door, had never ridden in such a car, and the speed and comfort thrilled him.

After an exciting race through thick growths of chestnut trees, a challenge to both Porsche and driver, they fueled up at Omegna and ate at a small bistro. Herman insisted on stopping at a grocery store, where he bought a handful of chocolate bars. They continued through pine forests up Val Antigorio along the Toce River, leaving behind villages stuck to mountain slopes like swallows' nests. The forests gave way to steep grasslands adorned with fall's last flowers and grazing cows and sheep. Then the valley narrowed, and the road passed through steep granite quarries on both sides of the river. Giant yellow cranes lowered granite blocks to waiting trucks. After a spectacular waterfall, the stone houses of Ponté, a tiny village with narrow cobblestone streets, came into view. Angelina slowed the Porsche.

"Stop the car!" Herman shouted.

Angelina hit the brakes, and the Porsche slid to a stop.

"That looked like Barry back there! I could swear I saw Barry at that large house with the playground up front." Angelina put the car in reverse. Herman pointed. "There he is! That's the Mendali Saint Bernard! I'd recognize him anywhere." Herman leaped from the Porsche before it had come to a complete stop.

"Here, Barry," he called. Barry raised an ear but didn't come. "Do you remember me?" Herman threw him a piece of chocolate. The Saint Bernard caught it in mid-air, then charged like a bull. He leaped up on Herman, knocked him over, and licked his face. Amused, Angelina watched Herman lying on his back and caressing the dog's massive head, trying to keep the slippery tongue away. "Okay, Barry, enough, you hear?" The Saint Bernard stood back and let Herman to his feet.

Angelina handed Herman her handkerchief. "What a way to show affection! I ought to be jealous."

He wiped his face and brushed off the dust. "I have an idea," he said. "Let's wait for the children and walk with them to the farm. We can go after the Porsche later this evening."

Angelina hesitated.

"I'm sorry," said Herman quickly with regret. "How stupid of me—I forgot about your foot. We'd better skip the walk."

Angelina smiled. "I think it is a great idea, Herman," she said. "I haven't met the children, and this will be a good way for me to get to know them." She didn't wait for his response, backed up, and parked under the eave of a barn beside the school.

Children's singing came from the schoolhouse window. Angelina hummed along. The singing stopped and the children swarmed from the schoolhouse door.

Herman gestured toward a boy and a girl walking down the steps. "There they are," he said. Barry was beside himself. He leaped forward, rubbed his head against the children, and wagged his tail.

"Remember me? I'm Herman Schuller."

They just looked at him, bewildered and suspicious. Then the boy's eyes lit up. "Where's your uniform and your rifle?"

Suddenly, all shyness was gone and the children rushed into Herman's arms. He cuddled them and tousled their hair. "Here." He pulled two chocolate bars from his pocket. "But you must promise not to get dirty," he said. The children nodded enthusiastically and gave him a kiss on the cheek.

Herman nudged the children toward Angelina. "I want you to meet someone very special. This is Signorina Angelina; Angelina, please meet Signorina Marianna and her little brother, Signor Marcello."

"I'm not little anymore," objected Marcello.

Angelina pulled him to her. "Of course you're not; you'll soon be a real man like your papa."

"I like *you!*" said the boy.

"Is it all right if we walk with you and Barry?" asked Angelina, amazed by the children's mastery of German. The children nodded, and they all set out for the farm.

"Tell me about Herr Stüssi, your grandpa," said Angelina. "Is he in good health?"

Marianna replied with another question: "Are you the woman who helped my grandpa?"

"Well, yes, I guess that would be me."

"He talks about you all the time."

"Your grandpa talks about me?" Angelina couldn't help blushing. "Your grandpa is a wonderful man; I like him very much." She couldn't imagine anyone at the farm speaking well of her.

"I smudged my shirt," said Marcello.

Angelina took her handkerchief and moistened a tip of it with her saliva. She pulled the boy to her and rubbed the spot. "Here," she said, "as clean as new."

"I like you," said the boy. He took Angelina's hand. "You could be our mother."

The children ate their chocolate and chatted. They stopped now and then to throw rocks into deep ravines, and the lively group eventually reached the place where Angelina had found the corporal lying on the ground, feverish, and cold.

She gripped Herman's arm. "I couldn't stand the sight of you lying there, not sure if you were alive. I bandaged you, and all the while I prayed and shed tears." Angelina wiped her eyes. "You looked so young, so innocent, so peaceful."

Herman smiled. "I dreamt you were my mother tending to me."

Angelina put her hand over her mouth. "You thought I was your mother? Really?"

"Yes, and it felt heavenly." He paused. "Did you . . ."

"Did I what?"

"Did you kiss me?"

She squeezed his arm. "Maybe, maybe not."

"You did. I thought I was dreaming, but no—you kissed me."

"Maybe I did. Maybe I kissed your forehead." She ran her fingers through his curls. "Yes, darling, I kissed you. I couldn't help myself."

They reached the top of the cliff.

Angelina shook her head. "It was indeed a miracle that you survived that fall, Herman. God was with you that night. He had sent his best angel to watch over you."

"He sent you, my sweet love."

Alice Mendali had been in an uproar ever since talking to Angelina on the telephone. She cleaned house and baked bread—she knew how Corporal Schuller liked her bread. She shampooed her hair and put on a new dress and freshly starched apron. Soon the children would be home, and she began to keep an eye on the road. She must have glanced for the hundredth time at the mirror and was doing so again, straightening her hair and applying lipstick that she hadn't worn in months.

There was movement at the dam. *Here are the children. And walking with them . . .* She flew down the stairs, tore off her apron, and checked her hair. Barry greeted her with a loud bark, then the children, then—there was her corporal at arm's length. She embraced him with all her strength, not wanting to let go.

He loosened her grip. "So nice to see you again, Signora Alice. Do you remember Angelina?"

"Of course I do. Angelina, how could I get so carried away?" She hugged her. "My father talks of you every day. Please come in. You must be hungry and thirsty."

The house was exactly as Herman remembered it, and the washroom, where Alice had bandaged him, was just as clean and neat. The rubber plant had grown new leaves and was as shiny as ever.

Alice Mendali rushed ahead to the kitchen. "Please sit down," she said. "I'll be back in a moment." She dashed upstairs. "Pa, Pa, Angelina and the corporal are here!" she shouted.

Herr Stüssi rushed to the door and crowded after his daughter into the kitchen. The scene was comical with everybody talking and wiping tears. Herr Stüssi shook Herman's hand and patted his shoulder, and the two carried on in Swiss-German. He might have been talking to Herman, but his gaze was on Angelina. Finally, the old man couldn't stand it any longer and he pulled her onto the balcony.

"Are you going to marry the corporal?" he asked with kind, expectant eyes.

"Yes, if he wants me," replied Angelina without hesitation, not overly surprised by his bluntness.

"He'll be crazy if he doesn't. Now, let me tell you about Swiss Germans. They're a tough bunch of characters—I know, I'm one of them."

Angelina burst out laughing.

"Come and get it," called Alice Mendali. "Children, hop in first," she said, and the children moved along the bench. The early evening meal consisted of *caffellatte*, home-baked bread, fresh butter, and, of course, Mendali cheese.

"I know the dairy farmer who makes this cheese," teased Angelina, and everybody laughed. "Where is your husband?"

"Bernard is at a town meeting and won't be back till supper." She leaned towards Angelina and whispered. "I'm giving you Marianna's room. It has a good mattress and box spring, and I'll put the girl in Marcello's lower bunk. That's all the room we have. Will Herman mind sleeping on the couch?"

Angelina couldn't help a chuckle. "Herman probably wouldn't mind the couch," she said, "but I would." Then she added spiritedly, "Herman and I are, well—we've been sleeping together."

Alice put a finger to her lip. "Shhh," she whispered. "You slept together?"

"Well, yes," said Angelina in a low voice, amused by the farm-woman's astonished look. With a sigh, she added, "I'd marry Herman today if he wanted me to."

"You mean—"

"Yes, of course, we'll share the same bed."

"What are you two whispering about?" inquired Herr Stüssi.

Alice waved her hand downward. "Woman-talk, Dad. Just keep to yourself."

Angelina whispered, "I don't mind telling him of our relationship. I'm proud of it."

"Don't you dare! Not at this table," said Alice in a tense whisper, indicating the children.

"Tell me, Mamma?" asked Marianna.

"Tell you what, sweetheart?"

"What you are whispering about."

"I'll tell you when you're grown up. Now drink your milk."

Herman suggested they get the car before dark. He threw Barry a piece of chocolate. "Do you want to come with us, Barry?" he asked. The Saint Bernard looked at his mistress.

Alice gestured with her hand. "Go on, Barry, you can keep an eye on them."

Angelina laughed. "It'll be a tight fit."

"Oops!" Herman shrugged as he realized his hasty invitation. "Uh, no problem. We'll put Barry on top. If my rucksack had room in your tiny Fiat, the Saint Bernard will surely fit in your Porsche."

They walked down the winding road, Barry a few steps ahead as though he knew where they were going.

Angelina thought of the Mendali couple. "I wish this would never end, Herman. The Mendalis must be happy up here all to themselves. Where else could one find such happiness?"

"It would be nice; a life dedicated to lovemaking."

"You're making fun of me again, darling."

"Do you really think it would work out, sweetheart?"

"You're not taking me seriously."

Herman slowed his steps. "I am serious, Angelina. You know how I feel about you, but I—"

"But?" Angelina stopped walking and held him back. "But what?"

"My sweet love." He swallowed. "Have you ever thought of how different we are?"

"So what? What does that have to do with love?"

"Everything! It has everything to do with love!"

She shook her head. "At times, Herman, you're a difficult man to understand."

He grabbed her shoulders, and his stare almost frightened her. "Angelina, my sweet love, I want you to listen. It is important that you understand what is in me, how I feel about us, about my love for you." She started to say something but he put a finger to her lips. "Shhh." He pulled her head to his chest. "You have done so much with your life. You have reached success, secured a future. I have nothing to bring to a relationship, no guarantee of a future. Not yet, anyhow: only promises I might never be able to keep."

Angelina was confused. "We have each other, darling—isn't that important?"

"It's most important, but it's not enough." He exhaled heavily. "When a man has nothing to offer but his love—I just can't see how it could work out."

Angelina turned away. Then she looked back at him. "We'll make it work, Herman! The fashion shop could easily sustain a large family. The important thing is our love. I love you, Herman."

"You'd expect me to cling to your apron strings?"

"I love you!"

"I'm only a cook . . ."

"I love you!"

"You'd get tired of me soon enough . . ."

"I love you!"

He kissed her quickly and ran his fingers through her hair. "It won't work. Not the way it is now." He wrapped his arms around her, and felt her shiver. "Angelina, my wonderful love, let me succeed first on my own. Let me achieve a career level you can be proud of, one that will make us equal."

"Equal?" Angelina didn't think she heard right; she repeated, "Equal?"

"Yes. I want to be someone like you, to be able to hold up my head next to you—to be equal."

Angelina was dazed. She dropped her head on his shoulder and tried to absorb what he was saying. *Maybe we are different.* But so were she and Marie Theresa when they first met. There was the same gap then, the same difference in ambition, the same feeling of inferiority. But they worked it out just as she and Herman would work it out. And, as Angelina prophesied, she felt ever stronger about their love. She pledged to fight for it.

It was a tight fit. Barry wanted no part of any ride, but with

Herman's persuasion and a piece of chocolate, he jumped up onto the rear-engine cowling behind the seats and lay down with a grunt. Angelina accelerated. As soon as the car began to roll, Barry took to his feet. But the metal was too slick for his claws as he tried hopelessly to keep his balance. "H-o-o . . . not so fast," shouted Herman; "We're going to lose Barry." Angelina applied the brakes, and all of Barry's 150 pounds came crashing onto their laps. The poor animal never knew what the laughter was all about. They caressed him, fed him chocolate, and kissed his nose. Finally, they sat Barry on the passenger seat and Herman replaced him behind on the cowling. This time, the Porsche accelerated slowly as a happy "wrrrrrough—wrrrrrough" echoed through the valley—and it was not from the dog.

Supper was ready. Bernard Mendali returned from his town meeting and was as happy as Alice to see his guests. He underwent the usual scrutiny about his gunshot wound—all healed by now—even discussing the anatomical origin of the skin that had been used to close it up. "I couldn't sit down for a while," he said with a grin. Everyone laughed and the mood was set.

Alice put a giant bowl of steaming spaghetti on the table, cooked perfectly *al dente* and enhanced with mouthwatering tomato-basil sauce and ground Mendali cheese. She also had a bread pudding with raisins and brandy sauce topped with mounds of whipped cream. Bernard opened the first of two bottles of Barbera wine.

Alice watched Herman struggle with the long pasta. "Here, Herman, let me show you how we Italians eat our spaghetti," she said. "And don't be embarrassed—I too had to learn the trick." She took a mound of spaghetti onto the tines of her fork and spun it inside a spoon so that the pasta clung tightly to the fork. She pushed it into her mouth without slurping.

"Bravo!" Angelina said, clapping. "One less thing I'll have to teach him." It was the kickoff for an evening of story-telling, wine-sipping, laughter, more laughter, more stories, and more trips to the basement for Barbera wine. By nine, the bowl of spaghetti and the bread pudding with the brandy sauce and whipped cream had all been consumed. And as the evening turned to night, Angelina had forgotten about Giulio and his threats. Almost.

Herman turned off the light and slipped under the covers. He waited. The door opened, and Angelina stood naked with the bathroom light behind her. Barely breathing, he turned back the cover to receive her and moved his head on the pillow to make room for her head beside his. He smelled the sweetness of her skin, marveled at its smoothness. She snuggled deeply into his embrace, longing for his love and warmth.

The next days were heavenly. The first morning, after dropping the children off at school, they took a long walk to the San Giácomo Pass. Barry wouldn't leave their side. At the saddle, Angelina spread out a blanket and set a picnic with baked chicken, home-baked bread, a generous wedge of cheese, grapes, and a bottle of Barbera wine that Alice Mendali had packed for them.

"Here, Barry." Angelina tossed him a juicy chicken leg that he caught mid-flight. Herman pulled the wine cork, and they toasted each other, clinking glasses.

Angelina pointed to the edge of the cliff in front of them. "What if the rope hadn't held your weight, Herman?" she asked apprehensively.

He shrugged. "We'd still be on that ledge making love."

"Can't you ever be serious about anything? You risked your life on that flimsy rope!"

He laughed. "I'd do it again, but only for you, sweetheart."

Angelina shook her head. "That's what makes it so heroic. You didn't even know who was lying on that ledge."

"It had to be a beautiful woman."

"You didn't know that; she could have been fat and ugly."

"Not a chance—I have prophetic powers about this sort of thing."

Angelina frowned. "You're bragging again. But tell me, would you have come down that rope for any woman?"

Herman laughed. "Maybe. But what are you getting at?"

"I want to know! Would you have risked your life for any woman with a pretty face?"

He lifted his shoulders. "Whatever you're thinking, sweetheart, it is not even an issue; I knew you were down there."

"Sometimes you're—difficult!" She looked at him sheepishly. "Tell me, darling, what crossed your mind when you first saw me on that ledge?"

Herman pressed his hands about her cheeks. "I felt like your red hair had set me on fire—as if all my dreams were coming true at once. I almost let go of the rope."

Angelina perked up. "What a nice thing to say, darling," she said. "But I'm glad you didn't."

"Didn't what?"

She smiled triumphantly. "Let go of the rope." She leaned over him and kissed him.

They strolled to the cliff, arms around each other's shoulders. Herman put his foot against the tree trunk where he'd tied his rope that day, and almost broke it in half. It had rotted.

He whistled. "Luck was on our side that day, definitely."

Angelina sat down at the edge of the cliff and pulled him to her side. Barry lay down behind them with a grunt.

"I wouldn't be here today if it weren't for you, and for this alone I could love you." But this was not even close to the reason, she thought; she would love Herman under any circumstances. He had all the qualities she liked: strength, courage, wit, a down-to-earth attitude, a way of taking life as it came with just enough panache to make it exciting. "It's so peaceful up here."

Barry grew impatient and roamed about the saddle, sniffing all the bushes and outcropping rocks.

Angelina motioned toward a boulder a few steps from where they sat. "That is the rock where all you soldiers and policemen decided my fate." She took his hand to her lips and kissed his fingers. "You knew all along what you wanted from the colonnello, isn't that right, Herman? I was on your mind from the very first."

Herman smiled mischievously. "Maybe you were; maybe you weren't."

"Here we go again. Come, darling, you can tell me now. You always wanted me along; I was the one thing on your mind."

"Maybe you were—"

"It doesn't matter what you say, I know you wanted me along."

"I could have chosen that other woman; what was her name? Sofia?"

"You wouldn't dare even think that!" cried Angelina, making a face. She pinched his buttock painfully, then jumped to her feet and ran away. Herman chased her. She dove onto the blanket, giggling, hands stretched out to keep him at bay. But he wrapped his arms around her waist, and they rolled head over shoulder off the blanket and onto the grass, laughing and teasing and breathing hard. She ended up on top of him. Her eyes sparkled, and she snapped at him with her moist lips. He jerked, and they rolled again until she was below him. Angelina closed her eyes and let her heart melt. *Oh, what tender love! O God, let it go on forever and ever!*

*M*ilan was ending its busy day with heavy traffic. A downpour had left the streets wet and flashing with reflected light that was being poured onto them by passing cars and by the streetlights above on their ornate metal poles.

Angelina didn't yield to other traffic, didn't heed signal lights as she raced through the outskirts of Milan, veering around corners, tires screeching. Herman, part of his gaze on the road, the other on Angelina's face, was very concerned about her reckless driving—an anxiety on her face he had seen growing since they had left the farm earlier in the afternoon. Dread showed in her eyes; her hands, sturdy when the trip began, now trembled and her lips were tight.

The day had started with a phone call to the Fashion House from the dairy farm. As Angelina talked to Sabrina, Herman watched her expression switching from bewilderment to sparkles of hope to frustration and suspicion.

"I gather the news isn't all that good," Herman said after Angelina hung up the phone.

"I don't know—Sabrina didn't make much sense." Angelina twiddled with the buttons of her sleeve. "Last time we talked she was up in arms. Now she's saying that things are quite normal. She hasn't moved into my apartment as I had insisted and is thinking now that those phone calls she thought were strange may simply have been a stroke of her imagination brought about by Zanardelli's warning about Giulio." Angelina shook her head. "Darned, I don't know anymore what to believe. Except . . . uniformed policemen are still patrolling the main entrance, and a detective is making his presence known occasionally."

"Works for me," exclaimed Herman. "So, why the long face?" He tried to appear somber but couldn't help a chuckle.

"That's just it, Herman. Things are *too* calm . . . doesn't make any sense. If everything were well, why . . . why are the police still there?" She exhaled frustratingly. "I can almost feel Giulio watching my every move, his confederates scrutinizing the roads to Milan looking for me, waiting for the perfect moment . . ."

"Slow down, sweetheart," Herman interrupted sharply, "and take that nonsense from your mind." Waving his hand casually, he added. "Think about it for just a moment. Giulio is a loner. He has no confederates, no army of associates. His own party won't have anything to do with him, the colonnello has said so, and of the few hired guns, one is in jail for his attempt to bribe a policeman, and you can almost bet on this, three are running from the law. Giulio is clever, no doubt, that's how he traced you to Aix-les-Bains. But his luck is bound to be running out as it has before, and his bitterness toward you is only making him more vulnerable. He'll be caught before you know it!"

Herman's logic had an immediate effect on her. Her face still showing her anguish, Angelina stopped fiddling with her sleeve and calmed down, slowly. After a moment of thought she suggested, and Herman agreed, that staying away from Milan served no further purpose. There was no guessing of what Giulio was up to now—he may even have fled the country. It was decided they would leave in the early afternoon and arrive in Milan after closing hours, unannounced. They said goodbye to the dairy farmers, and Angelina even managed to smile. But as the drive was nearing Milan, her anxiety grew with renewed fury—Herman could read it in her face—Angelina was determined that things weren't right.

The race continued down Corso Buenos Aires. After a screeching U-turn, she brought the Porsche to a stop at the No Parking sign in front of the Puccini Galleria. All the shops were dark, and the Galleria had an eerie, abandoned look. Angelina pulled Herman after her past overflowing trash containers put out for pick-up and display windows with their ghostly mannequins.

The double-glass back entry door to the Fashion House was facing the Hotel Puccini across the Galleria promenade. A faint light shone from inside. Hands trembling, Angelina had trouble getting the key in the lock. When she did, using both hands, the key wouldn't turn. She pulled out the key to make sure it was the right one and tried again. Her face was twisted from frustration.

"Slow down," said Herman, alarmed. "Take a deep breath and hold it." Angelina gave him an embarrassed smile and did as she was told. This time the lock clicked open.

"That's strange," said Angelina. "There's a garment rack in front of the door and I can't push it open—Sabrina knows better than to obstruct the entrance."

"Let me do it." With his shoulder against the door, Herman pushed the rack aside. He had a sudden hunch that something wasn't right. But it was too late.

A dozen steps ahead two men were registering shock at the sight of him. Herman recognized Giulio in spite of his skimpy beard and uncombed, shoulder-length hair. Next to him was a giant of a man with bulky muscles. He had the hands and shoes of a Goliath, a squashed boxer's nose, and foul teeth showing between his large, cracked lips. But Herman's eyes were on Giulio and a revolver with a long silencer that protruded from his belt.

Time slowed while Herman's thoughts raced. They must have been leaving as we came in and they never heard the door because of the clothing rack . . . There are two of them! . . . Giulio! . . . The gun, I've got to get hold of that gun . . .

Giulio's movements were tauntingly slow and clumsy as he pulled the revolver from his belt.

Herman made his move in the same instant, leaping through the air like a tiger with his claws out. *The gun! Get hold of the gun.* He didn't see Giulio's wretched face or the giant's sluggish reaction. All he saw was the gun with the steel-blue barrel. The hammer went back, the cylinder turned, and the sight began to level at his chest . . . *God help!* . . . he screamed . . . there was a loud report just as his fingers contacted cold steel. The flash was in his face, and he heard the whistle of the slug. His momentum had knocked Giulio onto a brass table that collapsed under their weight. The gun was wrenched from his fist. Giulio's head was tilted back, his throat exposed . . . With a quick blow Herman drove the edge of his hand into Giulio's throat . . . his eyes went wide, he wasn't breathing. Then his eyes rolled back.

Meanwhile, like a wildcat, Angelina had jumped on the giant's back and clawed at his eyes with her sharp nails. Cursing and roaring, he'd shaken her off, sending her flying against a standing mannequin. Angelina slid to the floor, stunned.

The giant swung around. He lifted Herman by the collar like a toy and with a quick move locked his arm around his neck. Herman, wiggling like a worm, kicked and pounded his fists into the brute's abdomen, but he couldn't twist loose, and his blows had no effect. The giant increased the pressure and the arm lock was about to break Herman's neck . . . he felt himself blacking out.

With his last shred of consciousness, Herman caught a glimpse of a shiny object. Something gold was glimmering above the brute's head. There was an ugly thump. The pressure on Herman's neck began to subside and Herman realized that a brass club was descending on the giant's head a second time. There was another thump and the monster's grip loosened. He went to his knees, wavered, and rolled over.

"Don't," Herman croaked. "Don't do it." He wrestled the heavy brass club from Angelina's hand—a table leg—and tossed it aside. He slid to the floor, holding his throat, and she dropped beside him. Propped against each other, they sat silently for a time, breathing hard. Then Herman put his arm around her. "Are you okay?" His voice was still a croak.

Angelina winced at the sound of his voice, and sobs shook her body. "It'll never end. I'm being punished!" she cried. "And everybody with me is being punished!"

Herman pulled her head to his chest and gently ran the tips of his fingers through her hair. "It's over, Angelina." But his body was trembling, too, and he was struggling to breathe.

She sensed his turmoil. Tears flooded her eyes.

Seeing her tears, Herman started to regain control. He gestured at the lifeless Giulio and said, "He won't do any more harm." He held her face in his hands. She watched his eyes brighten like stars coming out from behind a cloud. He was grinning.

"You fought like a wildcat!" he told her, husky-voiced.

His grin more than his words brought Angelina back from hopelessness. "I did?" Then less timidly: "I really did?"

"I'd say you saved the day, sweetheart!"

Angelina took a deep breath and let it out with a long sigh. The trembling slowed as she was regaining control. With the back of his hand, Herman wiped away the last of her tears.

A door opened timidly in the back of the store. Herman raised his head and pointed. "There's a young woman . . ."

Angelina turned and jumped up. "Sabrina! Oh, my dear Sabrina." She rushed to the woman. "Oh, I'm so sorry, my dear Sabrina. Are you all right?" She took the girl into her arms and kissed her on the cheeks.

Sabrina broke into tears. "O God, you're back. I've never been so scared."

Angelina patted her back, gently. "It's over, Sabrina. Everything's going to be all right. I'm here to stay. I should never have left you alone. I'll never do that again." She caressed Sabrina's hair. "Have they harmed you?"

"No," sobbed Sabrina, "they didn't hurt me. But one of them, the one with the gun, was furious because you weren't here. He ripped the phone line from the wall and . . . and he threatened to cut my face if I screamed or if I left the office. But he was very nervous, I thought, anxious to get out of here. I overheard him say they'd better skip Milan while they still had a chance—then, right after they left the office, I heard the commotion and a shot . . . I was scared to death, unable to move . . ."

"My poor thing. But—but how did the men get into the store?"

Sabrina shook her head. "I don't know. They must have been hiding in a dressing booth before I locked the doors. Suddenly, they walked into the office just as I was closing the safe."

Angelina bit her lip. "Where were the police?"

Sabrina raised a shoulder. "There was a phone call for them just before we closed up and they rushed out the front door. They didn't say why."

Herman was searching for the revolver. He found it behind a rack of garments almost at the spot he thought it would be. The cylinder was fully loaded except for the one spent round. He pushed the gun into his belt. He checked on the two men. Giulio struggled to breathe and his eyes had an empty gaze. Herman unplugged electric extension cords from an illuminated display, and Giulio's hands were deftly tied behind his back. The Giant, still out and bleeding from two wounds on his skull, was next.

Angelina tapped Herman's shoulder. "Herman, this is Sabrina, my partner," she said.

He looked up, straightened, shook Sabrina's hand. "Angelina has told me about you. So nice to meet you finally," he said in German.

To his surprise, Sabrina answered him in perfect Swiss dialect. "I feel I know you already, Herr Schuller," she said, still jittery. "Angelina has spoken of you often."

"You speak Swiss!"

"My father is Swiss," she said, still trying to calm herself. "I've been speaking the dialect since childhood. My father would be delighted to meet you."

"Sabrina," Angelina cut in, "please look up the precinct's phone number and call officer Gianotti. Tell him to hurry."

Sabrina nodded, excused herself, and walked toward the office.

Generale Gianotti was leaning back in his wooden desk chair, legs crossed. He removed a cigar from an ivory box, poked the rounded end with the awl of his pocketknife, and lit the flat end with a match. He sucked fiercely to get it going. He was the captain of the *Polizia Municipale*, but his men saluted him as generale, his former military title. The cigar failed to bring about the calm he sought, and after a few puffs he rubbed it out in the ashtray. He leaned back in the seat and stared at the ceiling. Things had not been going as they should . . . Giulio, evasive as a snake, was still at large. This wouldn't have bothered him quite as much, except—Signorina Bianci was a close friend of his wife, Barbara, and the protection of the Fashion House had therefore become the precinct's highest priority. But patience was growing thin—the use of extra detectives and policemen at the Galleria was putting undue strain on his understaffed police force. Then a robbery of a jewelry store a mere block from the Galleria occurred during the early evening hour . . . and his overanxious officer on duty took it on himself to dispatch the two patrolmen from the Fashion House . . . and . . .

The phone rang. Uncrossing his legs, Gianotti bent forward and lifted the receiver. "Yes!" he shouted, but quickly changed his tone . . . "Okay, okay—put her on!"

⊰⊱◆⊰⊱

Giulio's arms began to strain against his bonds; his eyes blinked open. He raised his head, uncertain where he was. Angelina noticed him coming around.

"Hurting, Giulio? Huh? What do you know—he's hurting!" Angelina cried piercingly. "Well, get used to it, Giulio, it's not the last pain you'll feel. Where you're going you'll be tormented for all eternity!" She was bent over Giulio's prostrate form, her eyes blazing. "Herman, give me the revolver!"

Herman turned his back on Angelina as if he didn't hear and fiddled with the gun.

"Herman! I want that revolver."

He handed her the gun, and muttered, "Be careful with it."

Angelina pushed the long barrel into Giulio's face. "Can you hear me, Giulio?"

He nodded.

"Good, then listen." Her eyes showed no pity as she cocked the hammer with both thumbs. Giulio panicked. His eyes begged Herman to intercede. But Angelina was not disturbed by his pitiful looks. "I'm going to say this only once. If you so much as put a foot in my place, or ever threaten any of my friends again, I'll hunt you down like a rat and kill you!" In a rage, she whipped the gun barrel across his forehead.

What had come over her? Herman took back the revolver. "Well spoken, *mi' amore*," he said good-naturedly, "but leave something for the *polizia*."

Her face still showing her torment, Angelina began to laugh, louder and louder, until she was roaring. The laughter was a huge release of some kind. Soon Herman was laughing along, holding his sides.

The glass door swung open with a bang. Three policemen—guns drawn and faces taut—charged into the showroom.

"What's going on in here?" cried the stout officer up front. His cap askew, his necktie loose, and the first button of his shirt open, he stared at the two figures on the floor with the frozen smiles. He shook his head. "Signorina Bianci! Are you all right?"

"I'm fine, Generale Gianotti," she said, slightly baffled.

He coughed. "Now tell me what the hell is going on."

Angelina managed a smile. "As you can see, General, things are under control. But thanks for getting here so fast." She pointed to Herman and said in French. "This is Monsieur Schuller; he's a friend."

"I'm Guiseppi Gianotti; it's a pleasure to make your acquaintance," the general said in French. He shook Herman's hand. "So—you are the young man I've been hearing about? Zanardelli has plenty to say about you. All good, though."

"I'm Herman," Herman said. "I've never met a general."

"Forget that general business, Herman. To friends of the signorina, I'm simply Guiseppe."

The giant groaned and moved. He tried to stand up but fell back down, shaking badly. The two policemen helped him to his feet and replaced the electric cord with handcuffs. The blows from the rugged table leg had left grooves that had swollen to sickening bulges.

Gianotti pulled Herman to the side. "My French is a bit rusty, and I've never cared much about German. I'm married to an Australian, so my English is quite good. Do you speak English?"

Herman nodded. "I'm learning," he said in English. The general's simple manner put him at ease. He pulled the revolver from under his jacket and gave it to the general, then reached into his pocket and retrieved the five unspent shells he had removed from the cylinder. "I took it from him," he said pointing to Giulio. "I'm sure the French Police will be interested in this gun."

The general nodded. "I learned about that from Zanardelli," he said. "What a mess. Could become complicated! Now, Herman." He pulled two chairs from a table. "Sit down and tell me what's going on. Keep it brief. There's plenty of time for details at the precinct." Gianotti pulled a notebook and a pencil from his pocket. He listened intently, his expression switching from bewilderment to disbelief to astonishment.

"You two could have been killed . . ." when Herman was done. "Look, I'll need you and Angelina to come to the station and make an official report. Tomorrow morning? Barbara will never forgive me if I come late for supper again. Shall we say at—at nine? And bring your passport."

Herman nodded. "You can count on us. I'll tell Angelina."

"She's quite a woman, isn't she?" the general asked absently. He put the booklet back into his breast pocket. "My wife drags me to Angelina's every fashion show. Not that I mind it all that much—the models are cute—but at the end I'm stuck with the bill." He chuckled.

The glass door swung open again, and all eyes were on another giant as he entered the room. Angelina's face went cold. "Aren't you just a little late, Colonnello Zanardelli?" she asked caustically. She pulled Herman to her. "You do remember the corporal, don't you?"

Vitt Zanardelli reddened.

Herman was startled by the colonnello's sudden appearance, but he came forward and put out his hand. "It's been a long time, Colonnello."

"Yes, it must be a year. We seem to be meeting under all kinds of circumstances." He shook Herman's hand. Zanardelli tipped his hat toward Angelina. "I'm glad you're safe," he said, collected now.

Angelina nodded frigidly and left the office.

Zanardelli shrugged. "Looks as though things are under control."

"Yeah," said Herman.

"Angelina seems upset."

"It's been a long day. She's tired and a bit confused."

The general stepped up. "Vitt, you might want to have a talk with this renegade before we haul him off to jail." He put his hand on Herman's shoulder. "I'll see you in the morning. Nine?"

Herman nodded. He glanced at the captives as the policemen were taking them to their van. All life had drained from Giulio's face. His eyes were empty, lacking any trace of will. He was a broken man.

Angelina waited for Herman at the reception room until the police had left. She closed the door behind him. "I need to know something, Herman," she said in a slightly annoyed tone.

Assuming it was about the colonnello, Herman said, "I'm sorry."

She seemed to look right through him. "Why did you remove the shells from the gun before you gave it to me?"

Herman shrugged. "I always unload a gun before giving it to someone else." He couldn't help blushing.

"You don't trust my judgment!"

"Of course I do, Angelina."

"Herman!"

"Okay, okay," he said. "You know I trust you, Angelina. But we all have weaknesses now and then, and I hope that some day you will act toward me with the same concern."

Angelina stared at him, bewildered. She felt stripped by his keen mind. She couldn't fool Herman—he knew perfectly well that her outburst had nothing to do with the empty gun—it was all about the colonnello. The mere saying of his name could release a flood of rage.

Sabrina walked into the office. She sat on the chair closest to the door. "Weren't you a little harsh with the colonnello, partner?"

"Harsh? I wasn't harsh, was I, Herman?"

He shrugged. "To each his own."

"Maybe I had my reasons. I—I'm going to change into some clean clothes. Then we should hurry to the restaurant and grab a bite before they close."

"I'm done in," said Sabrina. "I'm going home. We can talk in the morning."

"Of course," said Angelina. "We've got a lot of catching up to do. Forgive me for being so wound up: I haven't felt this safe in a long time!"

Angelina gave Herman directions to the lavatory and then headed for her dressing room.

Herman used the bathroom and washed up. On the way back to the office, he took a wrong turn and found himself in the middle of the showroom, surrounded by life-sized mannequins and a sea of garments of every design and color. Full-length mirrors added life to the deserted showroom, making it look twice its size. But Herman's gaze was on the large, black-and-white posters pasted on all four sides of the massive center columns, which showed life-sized poses of Marie Theresa and Angelina dressed in haute couture. The models looked so much alike, yet each had her style. Angelina was vibrantly elegant and imposing, yet conservative. Marie Theresa, on the other hand, exposed her bosom generously, unafraid and shrewd. Herman couldn't take his eyes off her.

"Do you like her?"

Herman spun around, turning red. Angelina quickly put him at ease. "Do you like my outfit?" she asked, turning around twice. She wore a pantsuit as red as her fiery hair, with matching high heels, gloves, and a hat that would make a Spanish *caballero* proud. A snow-white blouse with an extended collar created a stunning contrast. Fresh lipstick made her lips shine and stand out from her silk-smooth skin, and dark-blue mascara brought out the blue in her eyes like no other blue on earth—her tresses flowed across her shoulders like a raging fire.

Herman exclaimed about her beauty and meant every word. It was the first time he'd seen her made up. "How did you change so quickly?"

She smiled. "I'm a model, remember? We're used to quick changes. So you like it?"

"You're striking!"

"Not me, the poster of Marie Theresa in that revealing evening gown; the one you almost swallowed with your eyes."

"Oh—yes. She's—well, she's out of this world!"

His uneasiness amused Angelina. "Just say it, darling: she's sexy, isn't she?"

"More than that. She's simply gorgeous."

Angelina smiled. "Yes, Marie Theresa was one of a kind." She opened the first three buttons of her blouse and folded the collar to the sides. "What do you think, Herman? Should I show more?"

Herman coughed onto his closed hand. "What do you mean?"

"Just what I said. Should I expose more of my bosom, like Marie Theresa?" He didn't say anything, just stared. "Don't be shy now, tell me. Would I be more desirable to men?"

"I don't know. You're plenty desirable in all your pictures."

"Maybe. But men *are* attracted to women who show more of themselves, and Marie Theresa made the most of it. Now tell me, what should I do?"

"Sweetheart," he said, almost as if rehearsed, "you should always wear what feels good and comfortable to you, not what others want you to wear. You're beautiful and exciting as you are. Besides, the women, not the men, wear your clothes, and the last thing you want is to spread jealousy among your female clients. No other woman could measure up to you."

Did he say that? Angelina was floored. "Thank you, darling! But then—I should have expected you to say something like that." She embraced and kissed him, leaving traces of her lipstick.

The restaurant Puccini, located on the mezzanine above the hotel lobby, would close in fifteen minutes. Angelina, her arm wrapped around Herman's, rushed him through the lobby along massive marble columns, and across a marble floor so shiny Herman thought it was wet, to a brass elevator beyond the registration desk. The elevator cab stopped at a waiting room that was furnished with brass tables, two lavishly upholstered sofas, and matching easy chairs. The wall adjacent to the restaurant was covered with a huge mirror, on it the etchings of seagulls and cattails, and a sailboat slicing through lively waves.

A young hostess, reservation book under her arm and a pencil in her hand, greeted the unlikely couple. She took the lead between tables set with pink damask, sparkling silverware and crystal, and mauve napkins folded like oriental fans. Antique posters, mounted in gilded frames along the walls, announced the works of composer Puccini at Milan's *La Scala*, at the turn of the century. The hostess stopped at a corner table and pulled the chair out for Angelina. Herman hesitated then sat down in the chair across the corner. As usual, he was a little tense. He had yet to get accustomed to such elegance and, as usual, he was looking for something he could associate with.

On the wall behind Angelina was a poster of *Madame Butterfly* depicting the young Japanese woman, her eyes begging, her face torn by pain; her left hand was reaching out, and in her right hand was clutched a pointed dagger. Herman's eyes moved on to an oil painting, an original portrait of Giácomo Puccini. Herman studied his features—his wide forehead, the abundant hair neatly parted on the left, his bushy eyebrows beetling out above an aquiline nose, its nostrils almost hidden by his furry mustache. Above were his wide-set eyes filled with a strange passion, almost sadness.

"Darling." When he didn't respond, "Herman darling!" She pulled on his coat sleeve. "Are you in a dream world, Herman?"

"I—I'm sorry," he said slightly embarrassed. "I was fascinated by Puccini's portrait, wondering what made him so awesomely popular."

"He's Milan's pride. Do you like going to the opera, Herman?"

"I once saw *Madame Butterfly*, my father's favorite. I couldn't follow the Italian lyrics, though, so I studied a German translation afterward."

Angelina pointed to the poster behind her. "A sad ending, wasn't it, Herman?"

He raised an eyebrow. Was Angelina probing him? It wasn't so much what she said but the way she said it, the tone of her voice. "Yes," he replied uneasily, "it was a sad ending indeed."

"She was a beautiful woman inside and out."

"Cio-Cio-San? She was but a child of fifteen."

"She was a mother and didn't deserve her fate."

Herman agreed.

Angelina continued. "What do you think was the real reason for her senseless death?"

Herman pondered her question, then quoted from the story he had read: "To die with honor when one can no longer live with honor." He paused. "It was her upbringing that instilled such thoughts in her; her father too had died of suicide."

Angelina threw him a surprised look. "That's true, Herman, but—but she was driven to her action . . ."

"By Pinkerton, the American naval officer?"

"Yes. His betrayal and self-centered taking of her child was too much for Cio-Cio-San to bear."

Herman nodded. "I would agree . . . except one could hold her religion largely responsible for her death."

"Her religion? No, Herman, her baby and her love for Pinkerton were all Cio-Cio-San had in this world. With both taken from her, she had nothing left to live for."

They sat in silence, and silence stretched on after they had ordered their food, he shifting his gaze to the poster and she keeping hers steadfastly on his face.

Herman felt uncomfortable—felt her stare at him waiting for his comment. He chose his words thoughtfully. "Cio-Cio-San was seeking death, yet, when the last glimpse of consciousness was leaving her, just moments away from death, she wanted to live."

Angelina had read a biographical writing of the final act but had not interpreted it quite like Herman did. Her cheeks were flushed. Then she smiled. "Bravo, Herman," she said pretending clapping, "I couldn't agree more." She quoted: "Her faith taught her how to die—*he* taught her how to live."

Angelina drove up Corso Buenos Aires, turned into Via Ulisse Aldrovandi, and after two short blocks stopped at a massive gate of steel bars with ornate brass tips. Beyond the gate and a tall wrought-iron fence was a five-story apartment building. Unlike the neighboring buildings, which were parallel to the street, this was set back at an angle that left a small, triangular garden between it and the street. This was illuminated by electric lamps and landscaped with a hibiscus hedge, a gnarled old camellia tree, and a lawn so perfectly tended it begged not to be trod upon. In the middle was an octagonal fountain with a life-sized cherub pouring water from a narrow-neck vase. The building was in perfect repair. Balconies with scrolled steel rails looked freshly painted, and the walls behind them had been newly plastered, in contrast to its neighbors, which were in need of restoration.

Angelina took the lead along a path of solid stones that wound around the fountain, moist from wind-blown mist, between a gap in the privet hedge, to a carved wooden door.

"Welcome to Number Ten Aldrovandi, darling, and our home." She unlocked the massive door and stepped onto the rich mosaic tile of the parlor floor. A handcrafted chandelier, hanging on a long chain that disappeared into the vast darkness of the stairwell, was lit with scores of decorative bulbs. The hallway looked almost too elegant, which only increased Herman's curiosity to know what lay beyond the next door. It was deftly unlocked and opened wide.

Angelina pushed Herman onto the threshold, put her hands on his shoulders from behind, and pressed against him. She flipped a switch, and a hundred tiny bulbs on an immense chandelier sprang to life. A motif of acanthus leaves, attached to elaborate scrollwork arms, formed a grand neoclassical basket interwoven with brass blossoms that held the electric bulbs. Their reflections shone in the marble walls and brightly polished marble floor like silvery-blue comets. Under the chandelier was a round Persian carpet, and on it a marble-trimmed glass table with cut flowers in a hand-painted Venetian vase.

The rooms of the lower floor had been transformed into an open space with marble columns. A heavily ornate credenza set apart the cozy sitting room. The kitchen was divided from the formal dining area only by a counter, like a little bar. An open spiral staircase, its steps made of black marble and its railings of polished brass, led from the octagonal foyer to the upper floor. A light marble pedestal flanked the staircase on each side—the bronze bust of Giácomo Puccini on the left and the bust of Guiseppe Verdi on the right.

Herman had never been so overwhelmed by an artistically designed interior. He was subdued. This was not his world.

Angelina watched him expectantly. *He hates it, I can tell.* Nobody ever liked her decor. "Do you like my flowers?" she asked finally. "Delia cuts me fresh flowers from her garden once a week."

"Delia?" he asked absently.

"My maid; she keeps my place in order. She's been with me almost a year now." Herman hadn't reacted as she had hoped he would. She pulled a rose from the vase and held it under his nose. "Isn't it a wonderful fragrance?"

As if awakened from a spell, he said, "It smells wonderful. Everything's wonderful; I'm simply not accustomed to such glamour."

"Thank you, Herman. I kept it exactly as Marie Theresa had it before she left me. It takes getting used to, I know." Angelina pulled him through a column-flanked Gothic arch to the sitting room. A silk Persian rug covered much of the marble floor. Beyond, there was a large silk-upholstered, deep-carved cherrywood divan with six overlapping, sinfully red pillows. A large equally-rich chair, with an ottoman, was angled on each side of the crystal coffee table. To the side was a rococo buffet console ornamented with flora and ribbons.

The dining table was glass-topped with six high-backed, armless chairs. On the console was a bronze Louis XV clock flanked by sconces that had been converted to electric lamps. On the wall beyond the dining table was a mirror boasting red marble insets and gilt feminine masks framed by ivy swags.

But Herman's eyes were on a watercolor portrait mounted in a gilded frame adjacent to the mirror. The artist had chosen soft colors and short brush strokes to achieve an amazing likeness of Marie Theresa clad in a translucent veil that hid little. At the lower left corner, a photograph was stuck into the frame. Herman bent forward, not believing what he saw—Herman Schuller in uniform the day he made corporal.

"How did you get this?" he asked, astonished. "It's the worst picture ever taken of me, it's—"

"Lieutenant Stucki sent it to me for Christmas. Wasn't that nice of him?" She smiled mysteriously. Without waiting for his response she pulled him across the Persian rug and up the arching staircase. She opened a heavily decked French door with a hand-painted inscription: *Tranquility.* Angelina dimmed the lights to a soft glow. "This is my . . . our bedroom, Herman," she said with barely hidden excitement.

He was not prepared for the glamour. Silk sheer curtains between scrolled bedposts supporting a canopy of flowers and butterflies shrouded a quilt of a thousand hearts. Stacks of pillows were embroidered with more flowers and butterflies in ruby, cerulean, and emerald.

"This was Marie Theresa's bedroom," said Angelina quietly. She dropped her head against his shoulder and wrapped her arms around his waist. "I did not have the courage at first to sleep in her bed. I changed the quilt and the canopy and all the furniture in the room, but it didn't help. One day, I put everything back as it was, and that night I slept so soundly I didn't wake up until noon."

Angelina took a step away from him and held him at arms' length, her voice not much above a whisper. "No man has ever set foot in this room, darling; you're the first and shall be the only one."

Herman brushed aside the silken shroud, lifted her and lowered her onto the quilt of a thousand hearts. He undid the buttons of her blouse, one at a time, slowly, then slipped the fabric from her arms. Angelina looked at him steadily as he unhooked her bra and freed the loveliness of her breasts.

"Oh, Herman." Angelina reaching behind his neck and pulling him to her, kissing his eyes and nose, his cheeks, his ears, his lips. "Oh, Herman darling, please . . . please love me . . . oh, my wonderful darling."

Herman twisted and turned. The long-barreled, blue-steel gun was aimed dead-on at his chest. He leaped forward—there was a blinding flash.

Herman bolted from bed. He was alone in a sea of pillows. The sunlight streaming through the open window blinded him.

"Angelina?" he called lowly. Then more strongly, "Angelina?" He slid from bed.

The door to her bathroom was ajar. He opened it with bated breath and flipped a switch. Two dozen light bulbs around a large round mirror lit up, brightening the stylish marble vanity of soft salmon. A note was scribbled with red lipstick on the mirror. "Darling! Your sleep was so deep—I'll wait for you at the office. Love!" Herman smiled and wiped the mirror clean with a paper tissue.

A beveled crystal shelf was running between the vanity and the mirror. On it was an ivory bowl with rose-shaped soaps, pearl jars with makeup creams, lipsticks, and purple heart-shaped bottles with perfume. He unscrewed a bottle, inhaled its heavenly scent . . . He pictured Angelina on the silk-embroidered stool, her legs crossed in utter relaxation, putting dabs of attar behind each ear and a few drops onto her breasts. He imagined her brushing mascara on her eyelashes, makeup on her cheeks, rouge on her lips, her hair crackling as she combed her red tresses draped across her naked skin. He fantasized—he could almost see it—her selecting a black bra trimmed with lace and molding her breasts into it, lifting and shifting until it fit just right, and slipping black stockings over her slender legs.

Herman showered and shaved in the guest bathroom on the lower floor then followed the scent of freshly brewed coffee to the kitchen. He poured a cup from the drip pot and added some milk from a blue, porcelain-coated steel bucket in the cooling cabinet. Here in the kitchen, at the simple window table where overwhelming luxury was distinctly absent, Herman felt less intimidated. He took time to ponder. Things were so different here in Milan, so unlike the lifestyle he had known at home. He had tasted such glamour at hotels where he worked, where he met the people that go with such elegance. But he had never pictured himself as fitting in with them, and these surroundings were so much like it—the very thought of it made him feel almost physically sick with frustration and envy.

Herman had never shied away from a challenge, but while this challenge was in plain sight it was invisible, close enough to be touched yet unreachable, palpable but intangible. Angelina was so very close . . . yet so unattainable. He finished his coffee and began to rinse out the cup.

"*Buon giorno*, signore."

Herman turned. She was young and pretty, eighteen at most, and she talked her head off in Italian. He understood not a single word. She smiled and put her hands to her braided hair, as women do when uneasy. Her black hair and eyes and her dark complexion were in stark contrast with her large, naturally pink lips. At last she stepped to Herman and took the cup from his hand. "No, no, Herman!" she said sternly as she finished rinsing it. Then she pointed to the door in an unmistakable gesture that she wanted him out of her way. Herman grumped a, "*Mille grazie*, signorina," snapped his heels, threw his hand to his temple, and hurried out of her kitchen.

Milan awakened to a sunny day. On Corso Buenos Aires, mid-morning traffic was a mélange of wheels: aggressive Fiats, a Ferrari firing its engine, fleets of bicycles, Moto Guzzi motorbikes and scooters zigzagging, dashing ahead, and Goggomobiles like a horde of panicked bugs fleeing a lizard's tongue. And above the cacophony of horns and engines were the whips, shouts, and whistles from the drivers of two-wheeled, mule-drawn carts loaded to the hilt with fruits and vegetables for the market.

Dodging the lively traffic, Herman crossed Corso Buenos Aires and headed straight for the green canopies and showcase windows of the Masoni Fashion House. A green-striped awning jutted out over the main entrance, and just below it, a marble plaque, embossed with the Gothic letters *Moda Masoni* was prominently displayed. Women, most of them advanced in years, wearing fancy gowns with matching hats, gloves, and high heels, and large leather purses on their arms, entered the showroom through the rotating brass door. Herman, his foot already on the threshold, decided he was out of place and used the Galleria side entrance instead.

An elegant young man, dressed in orange uniform trimmed with black velour, greeted Herman and directed him to Angelina's office. The door was ajar.

"Good morning, darling," Angelina said affectionately. She rushed from behind her desk, and embraced Herman and kissed him. She pushed an upholstered armchair closer to the desk. "Make yourself comfortable, Herman." He did. Angelina closed the door and embraced him from behind. "How was your sleep, darling?" she asked. "You looked so innocent, so content, I didn't have the heart to wake you. I left you a note. Did you see my note?"

"I did," said Herman. "I also met Delia."

"Isn't she something? A little rough on manners and likes to talk too much, but she has a heart of gold. I told her to have your coffee ready."

Angelina loosened her embrace. "This is the heart of my operation," she said proudly. "Nothing major happens without it first passing over my desk. Even Sabrina, who enjoys my full trust, observes that rule."

Herman admired the desk, a masterpiece of Italian workmanship. The rosewood frame was bordered with solid brass, including figurines of maidens supporting the swagged Louis XIV legs. The top was made of leather; it was tanned a touch lighter than the reddish wooden frame. A boat-shaped, brass cradle held two gold-plated fountain pens, and beside it were the framed portrait of Marie Theresa, an ivory telephone, and an engraved plaque with block lettering—*Vietato Fumare*.

The desk chair was an elegant wingback, straw-white tapestry with green leaves and red roses, and it was definitely too large for Angelina's slender build.

"Do you like my office, Herman?"

"I love it! It's elegant. I especially like your desk. But . . ."

"But—but what?"

He raised a shoulder. "The chair's too big for you."

Angelina smiled. "It's just right and very comfortable; you'll see."

"It swallows you. Anybody can see that," he insisted.

Angelina burst into laughter. "What an imagination! No, it's comfy. Go ahead, Herman, sit in it and try it out."

"I wouldn't dare."

"I mean it, darling. Go ahead. I want you to," she said, and laughed.

Herman walked behind the desk and dropped into the seat. The upholstery wasn't soft, as he had expected, but firm and solid. This chair was for work, not relaxation.

Angelina brought out a camera with a large flash disk and put it to her eye. The unexpected flash blinded him. Angelina popped the burned-out flashbulb into a brass wastebasket, took a new bulb, moistened its base with her tongue, snapped it into the fanned flash. She rewound the camera and focused. But Herman had disappeared from the viewfinder.

"It's my turn to take the picture," he teased, coming around the desk. "Sit in the chair, sweetheart." When Angelina stalled, he said, "I want a permanent record to show to the world that the chair swallows you."

Angelina giggled. "All right." She sat in the chair. It didn't swallow her; actually, she filled it quite elegantly. Crossing her legs, she put her right hand on her knee, the tip of her fingers leisurely to her cheek, her left arm on the armrest, her lips parted slightly to show her flawless white teeth. *Like a pinup girl*, Herman thought. He aimed the camera.

Angelina winked. "Count to three," she said.

"Okay, get ready. One, two—"

The camera clicked and flashed.

"You didn't say three!"

"I didn't intend to. Poses are more natural that way."

"Do you always have to be different, Herman? I had my eyes closed."

"No, you didn't."

"I know I did," she insisted.

"No, your eyes were wide open; trust me—you looked lovely, beautiful, spunky, out of this world, seductive—"

"Stop, darling; don't always try to make a point." Angelina laughed a carefree laugh. "Come, it's time to visit the generale at the precinct. When we're back, I'll introduce you to my staff before we have breakfast at the Puccini."

Herman found a world very different from what he had imagined. As Angelina walked with him from department to department, chatted with the people in sales, critiqued with the seamstress a mockup on a dressmaker's dummy, adjusted the collar on a model on the run, advised a client of her rights when the dress she had bought didn't fit, Herman began to understand the enormity of her business. He was taken by it, and as he began to sort things out, he realized that Angelina's success was not the result of chance but of careful planning, knowing what the client wants. It came from putting the job before all personal needs, spending long hours, committing to damned hard work. The fashion house was more than just a job—it was a love affair—it was Angelina's life. As impressed as Herman was, a strange jealousy emerged—would he be playing second fiddle?

In the middle of the showroom was the Fashion House crown jewel: a marble staircase arched like a scimitar. Its solid brass rails glistened under countless spotlights suspended from various heights throwing bright circles on the polished marble steps. Hollywood could not have produced a better ambiance, which reminded Herman of a movie he had seen of Dorothy Lamour tap-dancing in a like setting with charmers Hope and Crosby at her side.

"Isn't it magnificent?" asked Angelina expectantly. When Herman just shook his head, "It's our pride and joy."

Herman was deprived of words.

"Say something, darling; what do you think?" pressed Angelina.

He swallowed. "I just don't know what to say. All this is so stunning, so unexpected. I—I'm overwhelmed. I had no idea of the enormity of your business, and everything is so skillfully arranged and organized." Herman felt small, insignificant, and the more he thought of his role in Angelina's life the more he thought of himself as a despondent passerby.

On the second floor, a modeling stage looped around the staircase cavity, and beyond it were tables with small mirrors and crystal candelabras. Folding chairs were upholstered in ruby-red fabrics that matched the carpets and silk-covered walls, and crystal chandeliers reflected elegantly in gild-framed antique mirrors—the room gave the feeling of a fancy nightclub.

"Is this the room for the fashion show you said was Sunday night?" Herman asked.

"The event used to be held here in its early stages, but some years ago, the facility grew too small for it," Angelina explained. "The Fashion Soirée is now held at the Puccini Ballroom—it is an exceptional facility, and the organizers spare no costs putting on the Ritz. You'll enjoy the spectacle and—" The sudden ring of a wall phone interrupted her.

Angelina picked up the handset and quickly put her hand over the mouthpiece. "I'm sorry, darling, but I'm needed at my office and this may take a while." She shrugged and smiled regretfully. "Can you forgive me? This just can't wait. As soon as I can, I'll meet you at the Puccini dining room for breakfast. There are newspapers and magazines in the anteroom, I won't be long, darling—I promise."

Herman was disappointed. He stepped from the elevator into the anteroom at the Puccini dining room. He chose the London *Evening Standard* from the newspaper rack and dropped into the soft cushions of one of the two wingbacks. *A perfect moment to polish up on my English.* He crossed his legs and flipped through the pages. He had barely begun to read.

"May I join you?" The English voice was pleasant.

Herman looked up. He was an older gentleman dressed in a black suit, white shirt, striped tie, with a fresh daisy in his lapel. His black shoes mirrored the chandelier, and he held an ebony cane with a large, shiny silver knob. Neatly folded under his arm was a copy of the *Corriere Della Sera*, Milan's leading evening paper. He was a picture-book gentleman and could have doubled as Uncle Bob in Geneva, except he walked with a distinct limp.

"Well, of course, I would be delighted," said Herman in English, trying to pronounce the words perfectly. "I am Herman Schuller."

"My name's Carlo Alfonso Verdiccio." There was a long pause, to let his name sink in, Herman thought. The gentleman continued, "but—my friends call me simply Carlo." He stretched out his hand. "Welcome to Milan, Herman." He leaned the cane against the brass table and sank into the chair on the other side, pushing against the armrests for support. His leg stuck out straight, and he pushed it down with his hand.

There was judicious silence. The two men scrutinized each other discreetly above the newspapers.

Signor Verdiccio put his head down and read. He chuckled, almost like a short cough. "Quite a fellow, this Dino Buzzati," he said. He kept reading, then chuckled again. "His column is the only reason I read this, or any, newspaper."

He didn't look up, but Herman had the distinct feeling of being watched. He was not all that sure however if the old man was talking to him or to himself. Herman glanced over the edge of his paper. The old man, slightly taller than Herman, appeared to be in his mid-sixties. What stuck out most was his white-as-snow hair, waved and combed back with every strand in place. His bushy eyebrows and trimmed mustache were also of the same whiteness. He was slender, and his shoulders were wide and squarish—*with the help of shoulder pads*, Herman thought. The signore gave the impression of living a carefree life, were it not for that twitch in his eyes, unnoticeable at first glance but more defined in time, hinting at some great tragedy in his life. Whatever his past, Signor Verdiccio seemed a most interesting individual.

The old man looked up. "Don't let this white hair fool you," he said. He was visibly amused by Herman's stare. He dropped the newspaper onto his lap. "I'm much younger than I look, and if you have the time to listen to my story, you'll understand why my hair turned white so early on in life."

Herman nodded politely.

The old man continued. "But young man, if I may, let me ask you first," he said twisting his mustache, waiting for Herman's nod. "You speak English quite well but not good enough to be English." He paused. "May I ask where you're from, and what brought you to Milan?"

His ego slightly bruised by the critique, Herman said, "I live in Zürich. I'll be in Italy but for a few days."

The old man shook his head. "Why would you—why would anybody—want to leave this gorgeous place? What a pity, we need good young men in Milan."

Herman smiled at the compliment. "How about you, Signor Verdiccio? Do you live here in Milan?"

"All in time, young man." This time he spoke in perfect German with no noticeable accent. Herman couldn't hide his surprise, and the old man couldn't help a small smile. "Amazed about my German?" he said. "Well, that too will come in time." He seemed to enjoy the young man's growing curiosity. He leaned farther into the wingback. "Isn't it a gorgeous day, Herman?" he asked, waiting for his nod. "Well, I live in a villa south of Rome." He paused. A slight blush brought some life to his pale cheeks. He took a deep breath, exhaling slowly. "I love this city, but my visit to Milan is solely to see a beautiful signorina." He chuckled. "Yes, my young friend, I still have a bit of spunk in me spite of my age." He twisted the ends of his moustache, then let them snap back. "She's an old acquaintance, or more precisely, I'm in love with her." The amused twitch on his lips widened. He added, all but talking to himself, "But then, who wouldn't be in love with such a beautiful woman?"

"Yeah, any woman must look beautiful at your age," murmured Herman under his breath.

The old man didn't hear the remark, obviously. He continued. "You wouldn't know the signorina. She's not only gorgeous but also exceedingly successful in her own business. Besides, she is one of the most adored fashion models of all Milan—her name's Signorina Bianci."

The burst of a grenade could not have hit harder. Herman paled. He was unable to think or move, even the pathetic smile was frozen to his face.

Signor Verdiccio looked up. "Do you know the signorina?" he asked suspiciously.

Herman buttoned his lips and struggled to keep in control. Life came back to him slowly—a tickling in his legs, a biting in his arms—then blood rushed to his face. "I have met the signorina," he said, knowing that his face was turning red.

The old man waited for more, but his young friend stayed mute. "So, you have met the signorina, Herman," said Verdiccio thoughtfully. "What do you think of her?"

Herman was back in command. His cheeks returned to their natural color and his lips recovered their normal heart-shaped line. He even managed to put on a smile. He said, "She is a beautiful model—"

"Beautiful? Ha, she's more than that; she is the most beautiful woman in the entire universe. I have never met anyone like her, except—but that, too, shall come later."

Herman, still jittery inside, shook his head; the old man was full of mystery. Silence fell between them. But curiosity soon plagued Herman. "How long have you known the signorina?" he asked, troubled.

Carlo pulled himself away from his own reverie. "I met her a few years ago at a fashion soirée for charity; it was right here at the Puccini Grand Hotel." He paused and watched his new friend through narrowed eyes. "It is time again for the soirée, and that is why I'm here——to watch her performance on stage." He cleared his throat. "You should see her, my young friend. She's absolutely sensational, steals the show every time."

But Herman's calm was only temporary. His breathing quickened. His hands tightened to fists. Jealousy grew in him. His throat closed, a pain shot to his side, and something pressed on his chest.

Verdiccio was unaware of the struggle going on inside the young lad, who to him seemed unconcerned. He leaned back into the chair. "I promised you my story, Herman," he said, "that is, if you're still interested?"

Herman nodded impassively—the old man had suddenly lost his allure. Right now, Herman felt like taking the next train back home. But he stayed put.

The old man sank back into the cushions and stared at the ceiling. "My family," he began, "had made its fortune back in the seventeenth century with shipping lines around Cape of Good Hope to the Far East. We—by that I mean the Verdiccio family—consider Bartholomeu Dias, the Portuguese navigator and explorer, a hero and provider of fortunes. His portrait still hangs on every vessel we own and in our place of business. I have an original in my study. Across the centuries, my ancestors have kept those fortunes intact by turning excess currency into gold bullion and real estate. After every war, especially after WWII, many rich Italians lost everything to the industrial collapse and devaluation of the lire." He chuckled. "Rumors have it that I hid a fortune in gold in my backyard."

The story began to interest Herman. He smiled as he visualized bars of gold buried in dirt. He asked, "Did you?"

Verdiccio laughed. "Sorry, my young friend but if I'd spread the word, I couldn't stop the flow of prospectors digging up my backyard—probably including you." He twisted his mustache, an obvious habit when distracted. "Uh, let's see. Oh yes. I grew up rich among the rich. I met my wife, Joséphine, in 1921 at the Université Sorbonne in Paris where I studied art and music. She was the most beautiful woman in all of France, and it was love at first sight. Joséphine was from an old aristocratic family with no wealth. I was no viscount but had plenty of what she lacked—it was a perfect marriage. We moved to Italy where I built her a mansion on an estate just west of Frosinone. I called it Villa Joséphine Verdiccio. It is but a short bike ride from Monte Cassino, a ride we would take every Sunday after church."

Herman cut in with sudden interest. "Monte Cassino, the famous monastery? Where all that fighting was about?"

Signor Verdiccio nodded. "Yeah, the beautiful monastery that was leveled by the Allies during the war. Unnecessary, too, I might say." He closed his eyes shortly. "Anyway, we raised one boy and four girls. We were a happy family, and the house was filled with art and music. Joséphine played the harp, and our son accompanied her on the piano. Heavenly tunes vibrated through the mansion, and Josephine and I renewed our love each year at the Church of Sorbonne in Paris, where we were wed.

"Because of my foreign language skills—I'm fluent in German, French, Latin, and English, but also have a good knowledge of Portuguese and Spanish—the then-dictator, Mussolini, sent me to Argentina as ambassador. Before I left, I moved my family to Lake Como at the Swiss border, as far away from the war as was possible— that is, for the boy, who became a pilot in our army. But Joséphine missed her mansion more than safety or family. Alone, without the girls, she moved back south, 'to live or die at my beloved home,' she wrote later in a letter.

"On September 3, 1943, Maresciallo Badoglio signed an unconditional armistice with the Allies, and a month later, Italy declared war on Germany. The Allies had invaded Sicily, but were stopped by the Germans at Cassino. I was devastated by worry for Joséphine—it was time to come home. I landed in Rome in one of the last JU88 Junkers that made it safely across the Atlantic from South America. Rome's infrastructure was surprisingly intact—I still remember the silk nightgown I bought on the black market. A military convoy took me as far as Frosinone, and I walked to the villa from there. But when I arrived at the estate I found only smoldering ruins. An ill-placed Allied artillery barrage had destroyed the mansion and its gardens and the fountains—it was all gone." Verdiccio closed his eyes and bit his lip. When he reopened his eyes, they were shrouded by moisture.

"With my bare hands, I ripped apart concrete and mortar, and I found my Joséphine. Her face was untouched, but her body was crushed by a steel beam." He wiped his eyes with the back of his hand. "She was clad in her white morning robe. She looked so beautiful, so peaceful—Joséphine was all I ever wanted, all I ever loved. I carried her to the highest point of the estate. There I knelt at her side all night, whispered to her as though she could hear me and wake up again. The spot became her burial place, a shrine I would visit relentlessly to this very day. It has been over ten years, but I was never able to put my grief behind." Signor Verdiccio looked at the floor, his face twisted by the emotions pushing to the surface.

Herman was taken in. He felt like patting the old man's shoulder, holding his hand, expressing sorrow—he did neither. Instead, he watched him from the side.

Slowly, Signor Verdiccio looked up and then at his wristwatch. His face lightened. "Gee, it's time for lunch," he said with unexpected cheeriness. "Care to join me, Herman? The Puccini has a great daily special."

"I'd be delighted," said Herman, surprised by the old man's sudden change of mood. Herman, too, had had a change in mood—his misplaced feelings toward the signore had turned to fond respect.

They walked the few steps to the restaurant. Signor Verdiccio ordered the special, piccata Milanese, while Herman decided on a bowl of spaghetti *al dente* with freshly grated Parmesan.

"You must be bored with my story," the signore said, testing.

Herman shook his head. "No, not in the least," he said. "I'm really sorry about Joséphine, but I'm also fascinated. I assume that your children were safe from the war?"

"Yes and no." He twisted his mustache again. "Mussolini's government had fallen earlier that year, and he was under house arrest at the Gran Sasso Mountains, guarded by a company of *carabinieri*. The daring aerial attack of German paratroopers led by Colonel Otto Skorzeny is well documented. After a hazardous takeoff down an almost sheer mountainside in a Fieseler Storch, Mussolini was liberated and flown to Germany. After setting up the so-called 'Rebublica Sociale Italiano' the 'RSI,' he returned to Milan. My country was split in two. For whatever reason—I knew it was irrational—Mussolini ordered me to fly to England to explore a possible amnesty for him and his family." Verdiccio shook his head as though still questioning that request.

"I petitioned Alfonso, my son, to fly me to England. On a foggy morning, my son and I left Linate Airfield in an unarmed, twin-engine BF110 Messerschmitt under thick overcast. After crossing the mountains, we flew through France at treetop level to avoid radar. We were shot at repeatedly but somehow reached the English Channel unharmed. The weather had cleared by then, and the English coast was visible in the distance. We were already celebrating our success when a Spitfire appeared out of nowhere. Without warning, it blasted us with all its cannons. One round smashed the canopy and instrument panel in the rear; another went straight through my son's body. When I close my eyes I'm still haunted by his expression of total disbelief." He wiped his eyes.

"Alfonso still had the strength to land the aircraft in the ocean close to the rocky beach. The impact was terrific, and I felt a terrible pain in my left leg. I managed to pull my son from the sinking craft and keep him afloat. But I knew he was dying, and decided that when that moment came, I, too, would let go of life." Carlo sighed deeply. "His last words almost broke my heart: 'Sorry about Mamma—I love you, Papa.' Then his eyes grew empty, and he was gone." Verdiccio pulled out his handkerchief, wiped his eyes, and blew his nose. Almost apologetically, he said, "As you can see, Herman, I didn't die. Instead, I had the sudden urge to bury my son beside his mother on the hill."

The ensuing silence became painful to Herman. He took a deep breath and asked quietly, "What happened to your leg?" the only thing he could think of saying.

The signore raised his head. "Oh yes, my leg. It was crushed beyond repair, so I was told at first. But a surgeon in London did an outstanding job with it. When I looked into a mirror for the first time, I was as white as the ivory keys on my son's piano—hair, eyebrows, and mustache, even the hair on my chest. The mission, of course, was a total flop. I was reunited with my daughters after Germany capitulated."

"And the mansion?"

Verdiccio sighed. "I was going to plow it under but knew in my heart that Joséphine would want me to rebuild it as a memorial to our love. The villa's red tile roofs and marble columns, the gardens with palm trees and bougainvillea, the gazebo with the hanging baskets, and the ponds stocked with goldfish and water lilies are exactly as before." He paused, and added softly, "With the exception of the two graves on the hill above."

Herman was shaken. He hadn't misjudged the old man after all, and the twitch in his eyes suddenly had new meaning. All traces of jealousy were gone, and he looked upon the old Verdiccio with new respect.

"However," continued the signore with fresh enthusiasm, "life goes on, and I started to look for a companion for my old age. And I found her right here in beautiful Milan; it is as though God sent her to me." His expression had changed back to an amusing carefree smile.

Herman asked almost fearfully, "Have you dated the signorina?"

Verdiccio nodded. "I did indeed, on several occasions," he said proudly. "We have visited museums and dined in fabulous restaurants, and we went to the opera to see *Tosca*—or was it *Madame Butterfly*, the signorina's favorite? Hell, I even gave up my priceless cigars because she had no taste for it." He shrugged. "On our last outing, just a year ago, I proposed to her. But she turned me down, saying something about being in love with a young soldier, and a corporal of all things. I'd understand it better if he were a general or admiral. Nonetheless, the signorina is the only woman I have found to be an equal to my Joséphine." He stared back at the ceiling, his gaze lost somewhere in the chandelier. Then his voice turned to a mere mumble.

"I'll wait for her for as long as I have to. Someday, she'll be my wife."

Herman stood and said goodbye to Signor Verdiccio. Fascinated, yet still shaken by the story, he strolled back to the fashion house.

Angelina was still bustling around the office. "Santo cielo! " she exclaimed guiltily. "I've been so busy that I forgot all about you. Oh, Herman, I'm so sorry. You must be starving. Let's go to the dining room while they still offer the luncheon menu; after that I'll take you shopping for a suit and appropriate shoes for the Sunday evening Fashion Soirée."

Herman smiled. "I already had lunch, with a most interesting old chap—but I'll have dessert with you."

Herman entered the fashion house dressed in his new, dark-blue double-breasted suit, starched shirt, striped necktie, and mirror-polished black shoes Angelina had bought for him. He had felt uncomfortable when she paid for it.

Sabrina whistled. "Wow, what a handsome guy! That suit brings out the blue in your eyes!"

Herman turned to Angelina. "I'm very grateful, but it might be a while before I can repay you."

"Don't you worry about that, darling," she said warmly. "It's the least I can do after everything you've done for me!"

The two models were having a dress rehearsal for the Fashion Soirée. Sabrina placed a folding chair at the bottom of the staircase. "Front-row seat, Herman," she said with a giggle. "It's the most dangerous seat in the house, so enjoy the show." The women walked to the elevator. Moments later, Angelina appeared at the top of the staircase.

"What do you think, Herman?" she said as she whirled around. She wore a full-length cocktail gown of black satin adorned with a scarlet ribbon wrapped snugly around her neck. The fabric hugged her body so tightly that she looked like an exclamation point. With every step, her wide-brimmed hat flapped like butterfly wings, as her gloved right hand swung the other full-length scarlet glove. On her belt was a diamond-dotted sterling-silver clasp that reflected the spotlights like shooting stars.

Herman was electrified. Angelina's eyes were sparkling, her smile mysterious.

By turns, the two women modeled their stunning creations, adjusting a collar here and a belt there, adding a pin to a shoulder pad, or opening an extra button on a blouse. Sabrina's outfits were always more revealing, Herman noticed. Tinted spotlights made their skin glow, as if they'd just acquired a healthy, all-over tan.

Herman was flattered to be an audience of one, but he couldn't ignore an inner voice of caution. *You have no business here . . . forget all this . . . wipe this illusion from your mind.*

"Darling," Angelina said lovingly. Herman seemed preoccupied, and she shook him gently. "Herman? There's one outfit you won't see until the fashion show. I'll end the show with it, so it's very special . . . And I created it with you in mind!" She bent down and kissed him.

A sulfurous smell hung heavily above Corso Buenos Aires after an afternoon thunderstorm. As the clouds dissipated, the sun, magnified by the thinning mist to a giant fireball, hovered weightlessly above Milan.

Herman walked to Verziere, the ancient fruit and vegetable market at Largo Augusto. Its sheer size amazed him. He had bought a German-Italian dictionary and began memorizing the most important words for his shopping trip: Belgian endive—*indivia belga*, mushrooms—*funghi*, asparagus—*asparagi*, shallot—*scalogno*, raspberry—*lampone* . . .

Soon he was bargaining with the women tending the stands. He stored his purchases in a bow-handled wicker basket he had bought at a wicker shop. He bought rice at a grocery store, vegetables at an open stand, and half of a veal filet at the meat market. He stopped at the wine handler and made his selections, including a sweet Port for dessert. The dealer gave him directions to the metro. With his full basket on his arm, Herman walked up Via Cerva to the station at Piazza Babile. It was his first trip on the underground, but he quickly acquainted himself and took the Red Line to Stazione Mila, a mere block from Aldrovandi. He went into a flower shop at the corner of Buenos Aires and Ponchielli and bought a bouquet of fresh carnations.

Herman had insisted on cooking dinner at home. "It's the least I can do for you," he had said jokingly. "Besides, I want to prove that I'm a master chef!" Angelina had finally agreed to meet him at 10 Aldrovandi after work. Herman got busy. He cleaned the white leaves of the Belgium endive and forced fresh raspberries through a strainer for the vinaigrette. He made stock from split veal bones the butcher had thrown in for free, reduced and cleared it with egg whites and chopped beef, and strained it gently through a cheesecloth for his consommé Diablo.

Delia poked her head into the kitchen but quickly retreated when she heard Herman whistling. He sautéed the shallots and the chanterelles, deglazed them with dry Sauterne, and added stock and roux and heavy cream to make the paprika sauce for the Hungarian veal. He added roasted almond slivers, fresh pimento, chunks of pineapple, and plump raisins for the oriental rice, then peeled and bundled the stalks of white asparagus before boiling them. When the water came to a simmer, he blanched fresh peaches to remove the skin and boiled the halves in tart lemon-sugar water. He crushed currant berries and reduced them with limes and simple syrup for the tangy Melba sauce.

Delia walked into the kitchen with an expression of: *What are you doing in my domain?* But one look at Herman left no doubt in her mind as to who was in charge and she quickly disappeared. It was the last he saw of her. Finally, Herman mixed the ingredients for the ladyfinger batter, squeezed it onto a baking pan, and shoved the pan into the pre-heated oven. He intended to serve the sweets with his Peach Melba Coupe for dessert. He washed the pots and pans and cleaned the kitchen so neatly that no one could tell he had been at work.

Herman pulled the smaller kitchen table into the dining room. He folded napkins into fans and set the table with the sterling silver from the buffet drawer, the wineglasses from the cupboard, the carnations, and a single candelabrum with a red candle that he found in the silver cabinet. He took his ladyfingers out of the oven. Now there was nothing to do but wait.

To pass the time, he browsed through Angelina's library and chose the Dumas classic, *The Three Musketeers*, in French. But he couldn't concentrate. Finally, he put the book down, turned on the short-wave radio, and searched the dial for a local music station. It was getting dark. He sat down on the divan and waited.

Angelina opened the door. *Hmm, it smells wonderful.* She smiled—Herman was asleep on the divan, leaning back on the cushions. After hanging up her coat she fixed her hair and retraced her lipstick. The table was lavish, the red wine had been decanted—*a bottle of Barbera, how thoughtful!* Angelina tasted the wine and partly filled their glasses.

She tapped Herman on the shoulder. "Darling?"

Herman opened his eyes as if awakening from a dream. He blinked. "Hi!"

"Hi!" Angelina bent down and kissed him on the lips.

"I must have dozed."

"You deserve the rest." Angelina handed him a glass. "Cheers!"

"Cheers!"

She kissed him again. "Was I in your dream?"

Angelina switched on the low lights in the dining room, and the table was fully revealed, set with crystal and shining sterling and the centerpiece of red carnations. The candle flickered.

"Oh, Herman, this is all so lovely."

They ate in silence, broken occasionally by Angelina's flattering remarks about the meal. Then the silence grew uneasy as it does when someone lacks the courage to speak a significant thought. Angelina felt the tension in the air but remained silent.

Herman swallowed and put down his knife and fork. "Remember," he said nervously, "my train leaves Sunday night."

Angelina did not react. She poked her fork into the filet, cut off a slice, scraped paprika sauce on it with the knife, pushed it into her mouth, and chewed it slowly.

"Sunday, at midnight," he repeated.

Still Angelina did not respond but kept on eating.

The silence hung heavy. "Did you hear me, Angelina? I'm taking the train Sunday night."

She put down her knife, eyes glued to her plate. "You can't leave—the Fashion Soirée!" she said sharply. Then she looked up, eyes hazy as if seen through tracing paper. Her voice was panicky. "You can't leave me, Herman—not now! We made plans—I made plans for us."

Herman frowned, pressing his eyelids together hard. He wanted to drop it right then, but couldn't. "It's the absolute last train, the last chance for me to get back home in time to beat the military deadline."

She shot him a stern look. "What about me, what is *my* chance?" she asked with increasing urgency. Surprised by the tone of her voice, he forced himself to look at her but didn't answer. His silence made her cringe. "You don't care for me," she rasped. "I knew it from the start. You're only thinking of your own selfish good—you men are all alike!" She threw down her fork, almost breaking her plate.

They had been talking without raised voices. When she came out with this, however, Herman lost his temper. Hadn't he proved how much he cared? "How can you say this so harshly? Can't you see that I'm torn apart? Or are you too ignorant, or too busy with the Fashion House? Hasn't it occurred to you that I can't sleep—can't think—can't make sense of our relationship? That I have responsibilities that are beyond my control? What if I asked you to come with me to America?"

"And give up the Fashion House? My modeling career? How can you even think such an absurd thing! Never! Never! I can make a living for both of us—you can't!"

Herman recoiled. "That's not fair!" he said in a strangled voice. "You make me look like the worst sort of man, a sponger—a dependent sleaze unable to care for himself. I may not have anything—not yet—but there's more to life than slaving for money. Things like career and learning, pride in oneself, dignity."

Angelina felt suddenly ashamed, wishing the angry words unsaid. She stood up. Her napkin dropped to the floor and she ran to the staircase.

For a moment, Herman was paralyzed. How could they have said these things? He raced after her and caught her before the top step. He put his arm around her waist to restrain her. "I'm so sorry. I had no right to raise my voice. Oh my sweet Angelina! Please come back down. I don't want to leave you. I want to stay right here in Milan, but I have obligations—the military, my dear parents. Please understand."

Angelina stared at him with fear in her eyes. She looked almost lost. They had disagreed before, but had never quarreled or raised their voices. His sincere plea quickly reassured her. With a deep sigh, she leaned her head on his shoulder.

"I'm so sorry, Herman. You, of all people, don't deserve this. You know I didn't mean those things." Her hands gripped his. "It's just . . . oh Herman, I love you so, and I'm so afraid of losing you!" She ran her fingers through his hair. "Darling," she said tenderly but with a touch of realism, "I didn't mean to spoil this wonderful evening." She grabbed him by the arm. "Shall we?"

Back at the table, she raised her glass. "*Salute!*"

Herman picked up her napkin and draped it over her lap. Then he raised his glass. "*Salute!*"

A sudden change came over Angelina. She chatted lightheartedly about fishing for trout in the Toce River and cooking them over an open fire, hiking the trails of the Aosta Mountains, watching Puccini operas at La Scala, listening to the melodiously rushing waters of the Fountain of Trevi in Rome, and strolling through the Capitoline Museum studying the busts of philosophers and poets—all experiences she wanted to share with Herman soon. She barely took a breath in between and Herman had to slow her down while they had dessert. The sweet Port wine had them back in a laughing mood while they stacked the dishes in the sink for Delia in the morning.

Angelina brought the candle to the coffee table in the living room and turned off the lights. She sat on the divan. "Join me, darling." Her eyes were sparkling. She pulled Herman onto the pillows. "You're truly a great chef, Herman. Your food was as good as any I ever tasted. That paprika sauce—how can you bring about such flavor?" She pulled his head into her lap.

It was suddenly very quiet save for the ticks of the Versailles clock. Somehow their argument had left Angelina's heart bursting with love for him. "You have such pretty hair, darling." She picked up a curl, pulled it out straight, then let it go and watched it bounce. "How come you boys get all the curls, and we girls don't?"

Herman grinned. "Mother Nature favors us boys, I guess."

Angelina pouted. "It isn't fair!"

Herman cocked an eyebrow. "I don't believe what I'm hearing. Someone with your physical assets talking about fairness? Besides, you have the most beautiful red hair."

"But no curls," Angelina insisted. She pulled on a lock of his hair.

"Ouch! That hurts!"

"Angelina laughed. "I like the way your curls snap back, darling."

"And I like how your lips feel, sweetheart."

"You do?" she bent down and kissed him. "This way, darling?"

"Kind of. I'm not sure."

She kissed him again. "How's that?"

"That's better, a lot—"

Her lips smothered his words. They were up late into the night.

❦

Herman slipped in and out of sleep. Guilt threatened to crush him. He was sure now that he had failed to convince Angelina of the necessity of his departure. But all the twisting and turning could not bring relief, and he decided to skip it until morning. But trying not to think about it simply meant that he thought of nothing else.

Herman woke up late. Angelina had scribbled another message on the mirror. He showered and shaved. Delia had already cleaned the kitchen. He enjoyed a cup of her fresh-brewed coffee, then went straight to Angelina's office at the Galleria.

The door was ajar, and he could see her through the crack, bent over an easel. She had a charcoal marker in her hand and was gesturing to Sabrina, who was behind her. Herman knocked timidly and opened the door a bit more, but the women were too preoccupied to notice him. Their voices were excited, almost childish, as they discussed a sketch on the easel.

"What do you think about enlarging the collar just a bit?" suggested Sabrina.

Angelina nodded agreeably and with a few strokes of the marker quickly changed the image. "Is that better?"

"I love it."

Angelina shrugged. "I think I'm going to fluff up the sleeves some more, give them more body. What do you think, partner?"

As the sleeves took shape, Sabrina nodded. "That's it—that gets it!" She stepped back. "Yeah, that's it. You're still the genius around here."

Angelina saw Herman at the door. "Oh, here you are," she said warmly. She came to him and gave him a hug and a kiss. "We're working on a new design. What do you think?" She took the drawing from the easel and held it in front of him.

He was impressed, of course, but what could he say? "Hmm." He managed an approving nod.

"Say something, Herman," smiled Sabrina. When he stayed mute she added, "It's nice seeing you again." She shook his hand and then tore the sketch off the pad. "I'll take it to the seamstress; she should have a mock-up ready by noon." Sabrina left the office.

The telephone rang. Angelina answered and hastily put her left hand over the mouthpiece. "Herman, I—"

He broke in quickly. "I know; I understand," he said. "I'll be at the Puccini waiting. You *will* join me for lunch, promise?"

Angelina nodded. "Of course I will, Herman; I'll see you at noon at the latest—you have my promise."

She'd been late yesterday, so he already knew that she couldn't back up such promises, but the last thing he wanted was to be in her way. He bent down and kissed her forehead. "*Ciao.*"

"*Ciao,* darling." She kissed his hand.

Herman was heavyhearted but not surprised. He strolled to the Puccini Hotel lobby and stopped at the reception desk. "What street will take me to the train station?" he asked the young male clerk.

"I assume you're looking for Stazione Centrale," replied the clerk in broken German.

"I'm going to Zürich."

"That would be the station." He cleared his throat with a short cough. "It's simple." He played with a pencil, twirling it around his fingers. Then he pointed it to his left. "Go left on Corso Buenos Aires to Via Vitruvio. The Metro's on the right. Take the blue line—"

"I thought I would walk. Is it far?"

"Not really. I have a street map." The clerk bent down and brought up a map that he spread over the counter. He pointed with the pencil. "Here is Stazione Centrale."

Herman switched the map around and measured the distance with spread fingers.

The clerk said, "It's less than a kilometer, eight hundred meters from here to be exact. I have walked it many times."

"Thank you so much. May I—"

"Yes, you may keep the map. *Arrivederci.*"

"*Arrivederci,* signore." Herman glanced at the map once more, folded it, then put it in his jacket.

The sidewalk was crowded with morning shoppers. Absentminded, Herman bumped into a woman holding two large shopping bags. She dropped one, and cans of vegetables and tuna fish, and a cylinder of spaghetti rolled over the curb onto the street. Herman was embarrassed. He responded to the woman's outburst, of which he couldn't make out a single word, with profound apologies, dropped to his knees, and quickly scooped up the groceries. But even as he returned the bag to the woman, who was now grateful and smiling, he was thinking of Angelina, about the men in her life—tall, handsome men, successful men—and where he would fit in, if at all. And he thought of Angelina's busy schedule and of all the things that stood between them.

Buying the railroad ticket was a first step toward separation. The thought wrenched his chest with every painful step, yet he couldn't change his course any more than a hatchling turtle could turn away from the sea. Also, he knew that his feelings were going to get even more intense.

Herman turned left on Via Vitruvio. Breathing was becoming difficult. The side of his head began to hammer, and a sickening pain crept up from deep within. Though he had no choice, leaving Angelina felt like running away. But this train was his last chance to honor his military commitment. He'd have a few more hours with Angelina and, upon arrival, just enough time to report for muster.

Would I take that train if it were not for the military? Would I return to Milan if it were not for hotel school, if there were no America? Herman usually was able to examine his emotions objectively. But today his mind was dulled, and no matter how much he wanted to make a cut and dried analysis, he was mired in indecision. What Herman had taken lightly, even made fun of occasionally, now became painful. With sudden clarity, he realized he had foreseen it from the very start: he was no match for Angelina. But he loved her! Love, oh, love! What joy it brought, what pleasures, and yet what dread at the mere thought of it dying.

The distance to the station seemed infinite. He dragged his heavy feet. His head pounded, and the bittersweet sickness pushed to his mouth and nose. He couldn't hold back and vomited next to the curb.

At Via Marcello plaza, he dunked his head in the fountain and rinsed his mouth with water from the bronze spout. Sitting on the rim, he submerged his hands in the coolness and time was lost to him.

He found himself in a bitter duel, *épées* crossed. On the one side, his love for Angelina, on the other, logic. There couldn't be a victor—only death for one and sorrow for the other. Still, there had to be an answer.

The wind picked up and ruffled his hair. Shivering, he got off the rim of the fountain and continued along the sidewalks, his mind in chaos.

From the I*stituto Gonzaga* compound, he could see the dark domes of Stazione Centrale. He crossed Via Vitruvio at an angle, dodging cars and motorbikes. The traffic distracted him from his thoughts, then they emerged again when he stepped onto the center island. He stopped abruptly. An answer had finally occurred to him. By separating, nothing could come between him and Angelina. No feeling of inferiority, no busy schedules, high society, or fancy strangers; no waiting at the lunch table, no staying up late at night wondering where she was; there would be no heartbreaking quarrels— nothing could destroy their love . . . it could be preserved forever. The thought was weird, but then, in Herman's twisted state of mind, it made perfect sense. He was so excited that he shouted, "O God, *help me; help me preserve our love!*"

The blackened domes of Stazione Centrale were in plain sight now. As he set out on the last stretch, there was a spring in his step. At the station, he swapped Swiss currency for lire and bought a one-way ticket to Zürich. Then he headed back to the Puccini, his head on straight, walking fast.

Back in the waiting room, Herman picked up the Evening *Standard* from the rack and dropped into his favorite wingback chair.

"How about joining me for lunch?"

It was Sabrina. He jumped to his feet and stretched out his hand. "I'm waiting for Angelina," he said. "She should be here shortly."

Sabrina grabbed his arm. "Angelina is delayed, like always, but she'll join us later. How about it, Herman?" She pulled him into the dining room without waiting for a response.

He followed hesitantly. "This is the second day in a row she's been late."

"Maybe it's just as well, Herman. You and I need a private chat."

Her serious tone worried him, because he couldn't imagine what he and Sabrina needed to talk about. The hostess seated them at the window overlooking Corso Buenos Aires, busy with lunch-hour traffic. The convex mirror on the wall reflected the portrait of Puccini. The waitress removed the extra table settings.

"Uh, you may leave one setting," said Sabrina, "we expect Signorina Bianci to join us." The waitress quickly put back one napkin and the silverware.

Herman was nervous, as he would have been around any woman so beautiful that he didn't know that well. Herman's nervousness was apparently contagious. Sabrina lined up her fork and spoon, folded and unfolded her napkin. The corner of her lip had begun to twitch.

"It's bad enough that I am nervous, Sabrina, but not you," he said, smiling.

She blushed slightly. "I'm not nervous. Well—I might as well say it: it's not my nature to mix into someone else's business."

"So you want to tell me something about Angelina," said Herman.

Sabrina only smiled in reply. She was wearing a white lutestring blouse over a pleated skirt with an open collar that showed almost as much as it concealed of her rounded breasts.

Sabrina was amused by the way he stared. "Do you like my tan, Herman?" she smiled. "I sunbathe a lot. Angelina and I visit the local spa often, and in the winter I spread out on the rooftop terrace where we hang the laundry."

"You've got a great tan," was all he said, but it felt like too much.

The waitress took their order of fruit and yogurt for Sabrina and the lasagna special for Herman.

"I still can't get over your Swiss dialect," said Herman, clearing his throat. "I've never been more surprised. I was hoping to meet your father."

"And he would like to meet you, I'm sure. Unfortunately, he is in Switzerland at the BBC plant to work out a new contract. He won't be back for two full weeks."

"He works for Brown Boveri Company? That plant is not far from my hometown."

"He's no longer with BBC, but he was with them during the thirties, when they were building the hydroelectric plant northeast of here. That's when he met my mother."

"Your mother's Italian?"

"Yes. They met while she was employed by the housing project for the construction engineers. She was their cook and kept things tidy for all the hardworking men." Sabrina grinned. "Mom would tell me how lonely my father would get and how he refused to join his friends in search of short-term romance. Then the project was completed ahead of schedule and my father moved back to Switzerland." She paused.

"And?"

"Through a buddy of his, my father learned of my mother's pregnancy, which she had kept from him. As it worked out, BBC needed an onsite engineer to fulfill warranty commitments, and my father returned to Milan. They married shortly before I was born, and they made Milan their permanent home.

"He was the best father anyone could have. He enrolled me in piano lessons and sent me to ballet." Sabrina laughed. "He wanted me to become a ballerina, but things did not turn out as he had planned."

Herman had no intention of revealing what he had heard about Sabrina from Angelina, but her next comments made it easier for him to hold his tongue.

"I became pregnant. Only fifteen years old!" She glanced at Herman, who seemed sympathetic—smiling and shaking his head. "It wasn't the proudest moment in my life, but I wasn't entirely to blame. I was raped by a carpenter's apprentice when we went swimming at a remote spot of the *Lambro River*." She shrugged. "I actually liked Maurice and I forgave him quickly. I was way ahead of my school friends physically. They were all still straight as planks." She chuckled. "I was provocative, in other words—Maurice was pro-voked." She still seemed amused by the memory. "You should have seen his face when the judge said: 'Marry the girl or go to prison.' It was not until later that I learned that my father had conspired with the judge, and when I came of age, Maurice had no choice but to marry me. Meanwhile, my mother helped me to take care of my little girl.

"But I was quickly fed up with marriage. I couldn't accept that it was my destiny to stay home and raise a kid. On the morning of my seventeenth birthday, with my mother's assurance she would care for my baby, I went in search of a job. Without asking my age—

I looked all of twenty-one—the Puccini manager hired me for the dining room." Sabrina sighed. "It was the high point of my life till then. Not only was I a terrific waitress, but I quickly learned that I could increase the size of my tips by flirting with the men."

"I'm a chef, Sabrina. I know something about the restaurant business. Anyway, my parents own a restaurant."

"Angelina told me. Maybe that's part of the reason I'm telling you all this. Anyway, starting out, I fantasized about dating those guys, especially my wealthier customers. I couldn't help it. There was a drive in me I could not understand at first; a drive to explore life, explore the world, and to date men who could show me that world. There's excitement in it, an almost uncontrollable desire to get things without—"

"Having to earn them?" Herman shook his head. "You wouldn't want to go there, Sabrina—there's a fitting name for that kind of woman."

Sabrina sighed. "But that's where my life was headed when I got to know Angelina. I owe a lot to her. Not only did she introduce me to an exciting life, she also paid for my classes at the university where I studied business. Then she made me a partner, and all seemed well." She inhaled sharply through her nose, then emptied her lungs with a frustrated sigh. "Except—"

"You still have that desire to play out your fantasies—exploiting those affluent men?"

Sabrina shot him a stern look. *How dare you!* "Not at all!" she said, almost too quickly. "But sometimes I do feel that I didn't earn all my good fortune. A lot of the women I used to work with are still waitresses here—I wouldn't trade places with them, not anymore, not for anything in the world. I know that most of them are happy for me, but some are resentful."

Their waitress was approaching with the food they ordered and wearing a big smile that seemed entirely genuine to Herman.

"Will there be anything else?" she asked.

Sabrina glanced at Herman, and when he shrugged, she shook her head. "That'll be all for now, Rebecca," she said. The color had drained from Sabrina's cheeks. She turned back to Herman. "I must be boring you with my twaddle."

"Not at all," he said, laughing, "but I guess we should begin eating. Maybe the only way we're going to have Angelina at this table is as a subject of conversation." He cranked the cheese grater and spread fresh Parmesan over his pasta, and Sabrina spooned up some yogurt.

While they ate, Herman considered how different Sabrina was from the woman he had pictured when Angelina described her, from the day he met her. He now saw her as an aggressive woman who would do whatever it took to reach her goals. But then, Herman thought, life was not really a series of stark alternatives: good and bad, right or wrong—there had to be more to Sabrina's ambitions. Herman decided to find her core. At some point while his mouth was empty, he let the following remark drop: "When Angelina told me about you, I didn't picture you as a hustler."

Sabrina turned red through her makeup. She leaned out of her seat. "To hell with you, Herman. What's wrong with wanting excitement, wanting wealth and glamour, a castle in the sky? What's wrong with wanting to be rich, to be on top of the world, to wear jewelry and furs fit for a queen, and drive a Ferrari and live in a villa with a heated swimming pool surrounded by water gardens and ponds with goldfish and graceful swans?" She pulled wildly on his sleeve. "Tell me, Herman, what's wrong with that?" She took a deep breath and then snorted with laughter. "Say it Herman; tell it like it is! I'm awful—awful—awful!" She dropped back into her seat.

Herman was astounded. "Angelina has told me how hard you work and how much she depends on you. It sounds like you're trying to trick me into judging you! But no matter how hard you work there will always be people who think the only reason for your success is your beauty. Still, if you had succeeded in finding a rich man back when you were a waitress, I doubt you would have been happy with your lot. I've met a few such women in the hotel business, where they spent much of their time in bars, and none of them were really happy. Those who were lucky enough to marry their man wondered just who eventually was going to fill the void they'd left behind."

Sabrina shrugged. "You're right, of course! I've become a convert to hard work, to doing things Angelina's way. But there's something in me crying out . . . I want to have those things now—

not tomorrow, or at some unforeseen future. I'd gladly sacrifice some principles to get there—how else, tell me, Herman, how else can a woman achieve such riches?"

"I don't know, Sabrina. It seems to me that you and Angelina are right on the brink of fulfilling the most impossible desires. When I think of my own parents during World War Two, and their struggle to succeed afterwards . . . But their hard work and patience finally paid off."

Sabrina raised her eyebrows. For a simple, down-to-earth man, which was how Angelina had portrayed him, Herman seemed to have plenty of astuteness. "You make lots of sense from nonsense," she said.

Herman took her remark as flattery. "Even so," he moved on, "it might take more than hard work to make it today. It was different when everyone was starting with nothing. Your goals and standards need to be very high, but to really succeed in today's world one has to find new ways of doing business."

"New ways to do business?" She sank deeper into her seat. She pondered. "That sounds interesting, Herman. But . . . but what are you getting at?"

Herman was as surprised by her reaction as he was to find himself lecturing her. He had been thinking of Lady Marvel and John's business dreams. "While in Geneva, I met a couple from Texas. The woman's name was Marvel and she taught me English. His name was John and he lectured me on American business customs."

Sabrina leaned closer. "I heard that Americans do business differently, that they're more organized," she said.

"That's what John used to say. But he mostly talked about a new idea called 'franchising'; a frenzy that is sweeping America. He could talk about it an hour at a time."

"Franchising," Sabrina said. "I've heard of it, but I have no idea how it's done."

"It's quite simple, according to the Texan," said Herman. He closed his eyes trying to quote the exact words John had used. "A company or individual gives the right or privilege to others to use or sell their products or services under an established trade name." Herman paused, amazed at all he'd remembered.

"Tell me more."

Herman pulled his chair closer to the table. "Let's say you own a successful pizzeria—that's the example John used—and you want to expand your operation to another city. Instead of taking all the risks of financing and managing, you take in a third person—"

Sabrina broke in, "Like a partner? We do that already."

"No, not a partner in that sense, but working within a specific contract. The franchisee—that's what John called him—is permitted to use your trade name, your recipes, and your method of doing business, anything that makes you a success. In return, the franchisee pays a commission on gross sales, usually a fixed percentage."

Sabrina leaned forward, elbows on the table and chin in her hand. "In other words, they work for themselves, profit from your trade name and trade secrets, and you collect a share?" She shook her head very slowly. "Sounds great, exciting," she exclaimed as she dropped back into her chair. If the gears of the mind were audible to the human ear, thunder would have been roaring from Sabrina's head. Her jaw tensed, her eyes grew narrow, and her fingers tapped the tabletop. "So you think . . . you think this concept could be applied to the fashion market?"

As they discussed the details of such an adventure, Sabrina's face changed from that of a beautiful but bored model to that of a determined businesswoman. She looked at Herman and her expression changed once more. "I heard you were leaving town?"

Herman nodded.

"If you do, it will break Angelina's heart. I have never seen her so wrapped up in a man. She truly loves you." Sabrina waited for his comment. He said nothing, just looked at the table. Sabrina persisted. "Surely you've made plans for a life with her . . ."

Herman shook his head. "There is no plan other than my departure Sunday night." Tears came into his eyes. "I have no choice, Sabrina; I have to go back home. Besides, could you imagine a man of my status with a woman like Angelina? You of all people should see this. It wouldn't make sense!"

There was a heavy silence.

Sabrina glanced at him. As much as she empathized with Angelina, she also knew perfectly well that a man in her partner's life would be disruptive. "So you're not coming back?" she asked with barely hidden anxiety.

Herman shook his head. "I won't be back."

Sabrina wasn't sure why, but she felt sudden sorrow for him and reached for his hand across the table. "Herman, I can't say this to you. I can't be the one to persuade you. And I'm late . . . I've got to get back to the shop." She let go of his hand and pulled a pencil from her purse, tore a blank page from an appointment booklet, and scribbled on it. She stood up abruptly, folded the paper, and pushed it into his shirt pocket. "Read this when you have a moment to yourself," she said, "and please think about it. Now I've got to go—*ciao*." She left money on the table, patted his shoulder, and was gone.

Herman watched her disappear into the elevator, a belated "*Ciao*" on his lips.

Angelina walked up to the table.

"I saw you holding hands with Sabrina," she said with what Herman thought was a jealous smile.

Later in the afternoon, Herman remembered the paper in his pocket and read it: "Angelina doesn't think you'll really leave Sunday. Telling her could ruin the success of the Fashion Soirée. Will you please not mention it? I know you'll understand. Sabrina."

The rising moon shone on the great Duomo dominating Milan's central square, illuminating a thousand statues and putting a magic glow on the *Madonnina* at the cathedral's highest spire. Brutally damaged during the war by Allied bombs, the Duomo was still under reconstruction, but Angelina knew her way around the barricades and was familiar with the steps and corridors that led to the rooftop terrace. There they sat, surrounded by ornate spires and Gothic figures that Herman found vaguely disturbing.

"Oh, darling, this is so romantic," said Angelina, lost in the space and quiet. "I wish the world were standing still."

Herman smiled mischievously. "You want to stop time? Think of the consequences: if someone stopped time when you were a little girl, sweetheart, you'd still be sucking your thumb."

"Watch your tongue, darling," said Angelina, "and don't spoil my beautiful thoughts! Instead of smart remarks you should be a gentleman and stop time."

"Okay, okay," he said quickly. "I'll stop time just for you!" He held her face between his hands. "Close your eyes, sweetheart."

She squeezed her eyes shut.

Herman rocked her head slowly back and forth humming a monotonous tune: "Almighty Atlas, distinguished of the gods, keeper of the world, please stop the world from spinning. Take it from your mighty shoulder and set it on the nearest star. Relax a bit while lovers throughout the world enjoy that extra special moment. I can tell from the sweat on your forehead, Atlas, that you're tired from carrying us around, so take all the time you need."

He gently kissed Angelina's eyes and then her lips.

She opened her eyes then and looked at him as if it were his first kiss. "Oh, darling, it's working!" she said, charmed. She returned his kiss. "You did it—oh, Herman, time is standing still." She threw her arms around him and kissed him, and time truly did seem to be standing still.

Then a shiver went through Angelina. She pulled away, took his hands and looked at him wide-eyed. Her voice was as clear as a chapel bell. "You are Lutheran, aren't you?"

Herman nodded. "Actually, Zwingli—same thing."

A slight tremor shook her voice. "Could you—Herman, oh my darling, could you marry in a Catholic church?" The tremor in her voice made her even more beautiful.

Herman was at a loss for words. Angelina couldn't be serious, could she? He swallowed hard. "If I were to wed the woman I love, my dearest," he said warmly, "I'd marry her in any church."

Angelina threw her arms around his neck and kissed him. "I knew you would say that, Herman. Oh, you're so predictable, but thank you for saying it so nicely. Do you love me as much as I love you?"

"Of course I do, sweetheart," he said. "But I'm also starving—when are you going to take me to Ruffino?"

"Right now, darling." She jumped to her feet. "Come, it's an easy walk from here."

They descended the twisting stairs, replaced the barricades, and walked across the plaza to Ruffino. There Herman had his Campari and his Ossobuco Milanese with *risotto zafferano* and fine Italian wines, and Cassata Napoli with Asti Spumante for dessert.

It was getting late, but the night was clear and crisp, and they walked all of two kilometers to Angelina's apartment. She made caffellatte, lit a candle in the living room, and turned off the lights. They sat on the divan, held hands, and watched the candle burn.

Angelina was in a romantic mood, but Herman was getting depressed. He thought of the scribbled note Sabrina had pushed into his shirt pocket. The words still engaged his mind—he felt he had read it a hundred times.

Angelina pulled Herman's head to her bosom. "I have never been so happy, darling. I never had a happier day."

Herman nodded.

Angelina pulled on his earlobe. "Say something, Herman. Tell me, can such happiness last?"

"Nothing lasts forever, my love," he said somberly. "Sooner or later, all things come to an end."

Angelina shook her head. "Not this happiness, darling. It's not going to end. Tell me it won't."

Herman put on a good-natured smile. "Look at the candle."

"What about it?"

"It'll burn down after a while."

"So? What has that to do with our happiness?"

"It will be dark."

Angelina shot him a bewildered look, then something clicked. "Maybe I do understand: it will be dark unless we light a new candle, as love has to be renewed from time to time." She kissed him. "We'll have to do this very often so our light won't go out." She kissed him again. Then she pulled away. "I'll get another candle."

Herman held her back. "Wait," he said. "Sometimes we need the dark to rejuvenate our thoughts, strengthen our soul, like letting a field lie fallow before planting a new crop. Besides, it's bedtime anyway."

He lowered her onto the pillows and leaned upon her and kissed her long and tenderly. The candle gave its last flicker and died.

Angelina was tossing in her sleep and moaning. Suddenly, she sat up. Her voice was tender. "Darling, why are your eyes wet? Look, your pajama collar is all soaked. What is it?" She wiped his cheeks with the tip of the sheet and pulled him to her. "Is it something I said? Have I hurt you in some way?"

He wanted to say something beautiful; instead, he buried his head in his arms and cried.

He sensed a nibble at his neck. Then the nibble was at his earlobes, gently, barely touching him. He turned his head, and the nibble was at his eyelid. He opened his eyes. Angelina was bent over him. The draw-string dangled from her nightgown, and her precious breasts pushed against the silk. The moon shone softly through the open window, transforming her lovely features to those of a marble statue.

Herman reciprocated, slowly kissing her neck and ears. His lips slid to her chin, down her throat to her shoulders, to her breasts, and beneath.

Herman was so full of delight and deep love he couldn't think of leaving. *I can't leave you; oh, my sweet Angelina, I can't be without you.*

It was a long night.

In the morning when the first rays of sun were kissing the nearby rooftops, he felt Angelina's breasts pressing against his back. She sensed his movement.

"You're awake early, my sweet darling—it's not even seven," she said.

He turned around and kissed her.

She shuddered and closed her eyes, letting his sweetness come to her, accepting his love with unreserved delight.

The sun rose higher and engulfed the bed with its warmth and brightness.

"Herman." Angelina released her tight embrace. She lifted her shoulders from the sheets. Her eyes glowed with love. "The night at the cabin was the happiest, most gratifying in my life. But last night was so—so different, so full of tenderness. Oh, Herman, you were so gentle, so concerned about my pleasure. My sweetest, my all, tell me that it will never end."

Herman closed his eyes as new pity swept through him. *It has to end, my dearest love.* He couldn't say it. Instead he said, "I have an idea, sweetheart. You will be so busy with the fashion show today you won't have any time for us. Why don't we have breakfast at the Puccini restaurant before you go to the office, just the two of us?"

Angelina perked up. "What a wonderful idea, darling! That way I won't be distracted at work! I'll be dressed in no time." She left for the bathroom. Herman stripped off his pajamas and went downstairs to shave and shower.

He had just finished putting on his shirt and tie when Angelina walked in from her dressing room.

"Wow!" he said. "What a beautiful dress!"

Angelina modeled her new outfit for him. In a hundred pleats, the lilac fabric dropped from her hips onto her shoes, and as she stepped toward him, the pleats parted, exposing her miraculous legs. As inconspicuous as a watermark, the embroidered Roman initials "AH" adorned the spot above her left breast.

Angelina twirled around. "Do you like it, darling? I designed it just for you."

Herman's mouth had fallen open. Then he bubbled over with excitement. "The drawing—it's the dress from the drawing you showed me. It's the most beautiful dress I have ever seen, and you're the only woman beautiful enough to model it."

"Thank you, darling. Do you like the initials?"

"Yes, of course I do." He walked to her, traced the embossed letters with his fingertip. He smiled sheepishly. "Uh, what do they mean?"

Angelina giggled. "Guess, darling."

"Uh, do they mean—uh, Athena and Hermes?"

Angelina burst out laughing. She dropped her head onto his shoulder and pulled his earlobe. "I know Hermes—but who's Athena? Some former girlfriend?"

"I don't know," he shrugged. "The virgin goddess of wisdom? Yeah, that's it. The daughter of Poseidon, supreme god of the sea—or was she of Zeus?"

"How do you remember all that stuff?"

"Things just pop up sometimes."

Angelina pulled his head to her and gave him a quick kiss. "She was the daughter of Zeus, silly." She adjusted her hair. "I'm ready."

They left then, feeling sad.

Enrico, the Café Puccini's morning waiter, seated them at Angelina's usual corner table. "People don't get up early on a Sunday," he said, apologizing for the empty dining room. He pointed to the skirted table along the mirrored wall. "I just put the finishing touches on the buffet. You'll find just about everything: Try our Danish pastry this morning. And there's juice from freshly squeezed blood oranges." He caught his breath. "Can I fix you some eggs?"

Angelina shook her head. "Thank you, Enrico, but I'll stick to café-au-lait, fruit, and yogurt. Herman, do you want him to fix you an egg or two?"

Herman nodded, and the sizzling smell of frying butter in a silver skillet soon filled the air. Enrico cut a slice of ham into quarters, stuck the wedges on each side of the sunny-side-up eggs, and put crisp zwieback in between. The plate looked like a morning star.

But Herman couldn't take his eyes from Angelina. They ate quietly, involved in their own thoughts. She reached across the table and took his hand, and a harsh sensation shot through his body. The thought of holding her hand for the last time was too much, and his eyes filled with tears.

Angelina looked at him, saddened. "What's bothering you, Herman?" she asked, concerned. "You seem so happy, yet I sense a deep sadness."

He wanted and needed to tell her, but couldn't. He stirred the fork around in the eggs and took a sip of the orange juice before he pulled himself together. "The fashion show," he said, "it seems so terribly important to you. How did it come about?"

Angelina's face showed her pride. "Marie Theresa had the idea almost fifteen years ago as publicity for her fashion shop," she explained. "After the first show, she donated entry fees to an orphanage for war victims. The response from Milan's upper crust was overwhelming, and the show grew. Fame came finally with an endorsement from the *Corriere della Sera*. As the show grew into today's Soirée, a local charity group headed by Signora Palma—a direct descendent of the renowned painter Jacopo Palma, so she says—took the lead. Signora Palma developed the silent auction as it is held today."

Herman reached to the back of his neck and scratched it. "What's a silent auction?"

"Pledges are written down for each modeled dress," Angelina explained. "All the pledges are collected, but only the highest bidder gets the garment. Fashion shops throughout Milan sponsor models and garments free of charge. The charity collects vast sums of money and all of it goes to an orphanage. So not only is the Fashion Soirée, as it is referred to today, the main source of support for the orphanage, it has made Moda Mosani, our fashion house, the household word in moderately-priced high fashion."

They finished breakfast.

Angelina reached across the table and put her fingers to his lips. "I'll never forget that beautiful Sunday afternoon when we first met," she said. "The simple tavern, you a proud soldier, sharp as a tack in your corporal uniform. A church bell was ringing in the background." She came out of her reverie and withdrew her hand. "What were you whispering at that table, anyhow?"

"We tossed a coin about you."

"You did—what?" Then she giggled. "Who won?"

Herman laughed. "We didn't, really. I was too absorbed in your beauty to let any gambling snatch you from me."

"Now I know you're teasing!"

"Not in the least—cross my heart." His voice became more serious. "Someone like you coming into a soldier's life—you were too good to be true."

"I knew you liked me when I saw you blush."

"I did? You blushed, too."

"No, I didn't; I never blush for a man."

"You did, too!"

"Well, maybe just a little. But you were going out of your mind when I waited for you up the road. I wish I'd had my camera."

"Oh," he said, breezily, "I knew you'd be waiting for me. You had it all figured out—just wanted me to sweat a little longer."

"Come on, darling, admit it—it was a surprise, wasn't it? You didn't expect me at that curve, did you?"

"Maybe I did. Maybe I knew my woman."

"Ha! Stop the bragging. You just said that I was 'too good to be true.' How does that add up, Herman?"

"Well, it doesn't." His eyes softened. "Nothing added up. You were on my mind from the moment I got into your Topolino. I couldn't sleep that night, and when I closed my eyes, I dreamed about you and your blue eyes. I wasn't sure of anything, except—I knew I would see you again."

Angelina smiled. "I never thought you cared for me so

deeply," she sighed. "Then you were lying at the bottom of that ravine, your face covered with blood and bruises. Oh, darling, my heart was breaking. I held you, prayed for you, but there wasn't much else I could do."

"I thought you were my mother," he chuckled.

"I know; you mumbled something about her." She smiled. "I would have loved to be your mother."

"My mother?"

"Then I could have taken care of you permanently."

He chuckled. "We couldn't have made love then."

"Is that all that's on your mind?" she scolded. "You never miss an angle, do you?" She lowered her eyes. "I still see your naked feet come down that flimsy rope, going in circles trying to make contact with the ledge. I instantly knew it was you even without seeing your face."

Herman sighed. "All I could think of was getting down to you and holding you." He paused. A gray shadow veiled his eyes. "Then there was the colonnello . . ."

An uneasy silence fell.

Angelina stirred her spoon in the empty yogurt bowl. "Please, Herman, don't bring it up again. I want to forget that there was such a man and pray that you, too, will forget."

Guilt seized Herman. He said quickly, "But the night at the cabin made up for everything."

"I'll never forget that cabin," she said dreamily. "It was the happiest moment of my life." She pressed his fingers to her lips. "Herman." She kissed his fingers. "I love you, oh, so much. I never want to let you go."

But time was running out—Angelina was needed in her office, and the phone would soon be ringing off the wall. Leaving, Herman wrapped his arm around her waist, and she put her hand on his shoulder. He made every step count as they strolled through the Puccini lobby, along the Galleria's showcase windows to her office.

The time had come to say goodbye. He was tied up in knots. There would be little time after the fashion show to say goodbye, to say a last farewell to someone he loved more than life itself. He gave Angelina one last squeeze. He let go of her and held her at a distance to see all of her just one more time. Soon, she would be in the past, just a dream—too good to dream about.

"You're so beautiful, Angelina." He pulled her closer, looked into her shining blue eyes, his voice a whisper. "Whatever happens, my sweet love, I'll love you for all eternity." He kissed her one last time and walked briskly away.

Depressed and holding back tears, Herman sank into his favorite wingback in the Puccini anteroom.

"What happened to you, Corporal? You look crushed."

Herman looked up at the familiar voice. Signor Carlo Alfonso Verdiccio in an immaculate suit, with another daisy in his lapel, was pointing his ebony cane at Herman's chest.

"Does it show that much?"

Carlo nodded. "It does, and you can't hide it. Come, let me buy you a drink."

Herman hesitated, then nodded. "I suppose I could use one."

"There's a sidewalk café a couple of streets over," Carlo said. "Nothing fancy, but it has charm."

The two men left the Puccini and strolled up a side street past shops full of gossiping people.

Herman broke the silence. "When did you figure out who I was?"

"That you're Angelina's lover?" He grinned. "I thought of it when I first talked of her in the anteroom. Your face lost all color. You looked like you'd seen a ghost! I took you for a powerful rival, but I wasn't as troubled as I thought I would be. I liked you from the start—in a strange way." He pointed ahead to a small café with two outside tables shaded by Cinzano umbrellas.

"Here we are." He snapped his fingers. "Uh, signorina, bring us two *Campari sifone*."

It was an uneasy truce: two men in love with the same woman. But what one man sought the other was about to toss aside.

"Am I out of line asking why you look so bad, Herman?"

"I'm leaving Milan." He took a deep breath. "I'm leaving Angelina."

"But—why?"

"It just won't work between us. She has her business; I have to think about my own career."

"You'll quit her just like that?"

"Just like that," parroted Herman, flustered.

Carlo wasn't sure how to take the news. A part of him was jubilant—here was his chance!—the other felt compassion for his young friend. He had to force himself to look humble as he said with a slightly unnatural voice, "You know how I feel about Angelina. I adore her. So, forgive me my young friend if I sound insensitive. But how could Angelina, a woman of such charm and beauty, fall in love with someone as young as you? She could choose any man. Why you?"

Herman leaned back in the chair and let out everything that had been building up in him. And as he talked, Carlo learned of a story of love and courage such as he had never heard before.

When Herman finished, the ensuing silence swallowed the sounds of traffic on the narrow street. Finally. Carlo snapped his fingers: "Bring us two more Campari, *piacere.*"

When the waitress brought their drinks, Carlo raised his glass. "A salute to you and our Angelina, the most beautiful woman in the universe."

"To Angelina."

"Strange," said Carlo. "Here we are, saluting one another, yet we're in love with the same woman. Hell, we're supposed to be dueling with épée and pistol." His remark made Herman chuckle. Carlo slapped his shoulder. "That's better, Corporal. I want you to know that I'm growing more jealous of you by the minute—but I also have a soft spot for you. After all, you're young and in your prime and you have her love—there's no contest there. Yet . . . I can offer Angelina more than any other man, even you, my young friend. I can cover her with furs and diamonds, and I can build her a mansion that will rival a king's palace. I can place the world at her feet. Yes, my friend, I can and I *will* give Angelina that which no other man can give, and in time, I shall win her heart."

Herman nodded, though he was only half-listening. But Carlo had lain out precisely what Herman thought was needed to make a relationship with Angelina last. He pushed his chair onto its back legs and gazed at the narrow strip of sky between the roofs.

"Tell me, my young friend," Carlo said when Herman failed to respond. "If you love her as much as you say you do, why are you abandoning her? You're a fool. You'll never again find her equal."

Herman brought the chair back down. "That's just it, Carlo," he said. "It is for that love I have for Angelina that I'm leaving her. We're too far apart. I could never offer her the things she needs; and I don't mean material things but character, business acumen, a success of my own. Maybe some years from now I could, but the possibility is so remote—" He looked back at the crack of sky. "I had another dream. The same premonition that has brought us together is the one that is pulling us apart."

Milan's high society arrived in swarms, and the second floor ballroom at the Grand Hotel Puccini grew lively. Carlo Verdiccio was pleased to see his young friend at his table at the end of the stage. Most of the men were in tails. The women wore revealing gowns with furs over bare shoulders, and platinum chains with diamonds the size of olives dangled from their synthetically tanned skins. The air was thick with prosperity and sweet perfume. Giant spider-web chandeliers hung from the high ceilings. The sound of violins and a thousand candles flickering in crystal mirrors brought elegance and beauty to the festivities.

Carlo Verdiccio, clad in black tails, vest, and top hat, and carrying the ebony cane with the silver knob, fit right in with this crowd, whereas young Schuller felt completely out of place. He longed for Angelina, whom he had not seen since breakfast.

Unexpectedly, the chandeliers went out and the guests were at the mercy of flickering candles which cast ghostly shadows. The chandeliers brightened briefly only to go out again. The MC tapped her glass to get attention and raised her voice over the concerned chatter and the clatter of high heels on the parquet floor.

There would be a slight delay until the electricity came back on, said the stately woman with considerable charm. The chandeliers stayed dark. She repeated her pledge. But as the room grew warm from the lack of air, the crowd grew unruly and expressed their displeasure with shouted slurs. "Why don't they get their act together!" complained a hefty woman waving her oriental fan. "Don't blame the hotel," said the man beside her, opening the button on his stiff shirt collar, "some drunk ran into the electric pole—happens every time."

It was almost an hour before the chandeliers sprang back to life. The MC thanked the patrons for their patience as she declared the 1956 Fashion Soirée open.

Rules for placing bids were announced, the chandeliers dimmed, and bright spotlights spilled over the lengthy stage. The first model took to the platform. She was young and sexy, perfectly suited for the opening act, as she claimed the attention of every man. The other models appeared by turns. Some were alone, some in pairs, and others in small groups. Sabrina, in a low-cut yellow chiffon gown, held her head up high and stepped smartly in her high heels. Her tan glowed richly under the bright spots.

A mumble rolled across the room as Angelina stepped onto the stage. With verve and charm, dressed in a black dress that hugged her like a glove, she twisted and turned—distinctly different and very sexy. Her eyes sparkled like stars, and her red hair flew behind her like the mane of a stallion. Men jumped to their feet and clapped. Angelina reached the end of the runway. She paused, smiled at the men at the table in front of her, and with a blush turned and finished her run. A second round of models took to the stage.

The chandeliers brightened for the mid-show break. Young ushers rushed to the tables collecting bids, and waiters carried loaded trays with aperitifs, wineglasses, and magnum bottles of champagne. Carlo ordered Campari for both, but Herman barely touched his. Nothing would dispel the sorrow that was building within him. Tears were ready to flow, threatening to drown him in self-pity.

The second half of the show started. The models, more beautiful and more exciting, took to the stage, with Sabrina scoring the highest cheers. The MC announced the last model and allowed final bids.

Herman looked at his watch—he had to leave. He leaned toward Carlo Verdiccio. "I can't wait any longer, Carlo," he said, his voice full of emotion. "I'll barely make the train." Tears ran down his cheeks and onto his new suit. "*Arrivederci*. Please—please take care of my Angelina."

Carlo couldn't speak the words he had prepared. He stood up and shook Herman's hand. In a moment of passion, the two men embraced.

Herman made his way between the crowded tables to the double entry door. He leaned against the doorpost and waited for the last model to arrive.

And there was Angelina, his love, his everything, in her surprise attire—a silk wedding dress, its veil trailing in the hands of six bridesmaids, dressed in white silk also. An unorthodox slit exposed the cleavage of her bosom. Angelina looked like the angel he thought she was.

She reached center stage. The girls removed her veil and dashed away.

To sudden drumbeats, Angelina ripped off her dress. In hotpants and skintight top, with a translucent, red silk veil in her hands, she swayed gracefully, gyrating on outrageously high heels, her striking figure silhouetted repeatedly by strobe lights, her hair blazing about her in wild eddies. The guests shot to their feet, applauding and stamping. Angelina was at her best doing the unexpected . . . and only she could have pulled it off, arousing the enthusiasm of men and women equally.

She was at the end of the runway. She shaded her eyes with her hand—and her face froze. The corporal's chair was empty. Something was terribly wrong . . . her worst fears had come true. She sank to her knees and covered her face as tears dripped between her fingers. The applause grew even wilder as the crowd evidently thought she was humbly expressing her gratitude . . .

The spotlights went dark and the brightening chandeliers signaled the end of the show.

Carlo rushed to Angelina. He snatched the gown from the stage and draped it over her shoulders. Instinctively, she closed the buttons. She grabbed Carlo's arm and looked at him bewildered. "Carlo," she asked, her voice trembling, "where is the young man who was sitting beside you?"

Carlo pulled her to him. He smoothed her hair. "The corporal's gone, my dear Angelina," he said softly. "He has left for Zürich."

Angelina was paralyzed; then cried out, "No—it can't be!" She broke loose and ran through the crowd. People turned and shook their heads, but Angelina didn't see or care. The curb was packed with the soirée crowd waiting for cars and taxis. Her Porsche was out of reach. She ran across Corso Buenos Aires to 10 Aldrovandi and up the stairs to her bedroom, the room of tender love. He wasn't there. But neatly folded on the wingback chair was his new suit, and on the floor below the chair his new shoes. On top of the clothes was a note. She read it with shaky hands.

> My dear Angelina,
> By the time you read this note, I will be on the train to Zürich. We may never understand why God has brought us together and why He is keeping us apart. My heart bleeds and my eyes weep as I crave your warmth. But while there is emptiness, we will have our memories and everlasting love.
> Goodbye, my darling. Your corporal

Angelina collapsed onto her bed, tears wetting the comforter of a thousand hearts, the note clutched in her hand. "No, Corporal, you can't leave me! I need you!"

With sudden determination, she jumped to her feet. *I have to catch that train!* She rushed out the door.

In the street, she waved at a taxi but it didn't stop. She crossed Corso Buenos Aires and ran along Via Vitruvio—*eight hundred meters to the station.* She ran as fast as her feet could go, unaware of onlookers, unaware of her attire, a determined woman in her wedding dress. *Five hundred meters to go!* There was a taxi. "Taxi! Taxi!" It continued on its course.

At Istituto Gonzaga, she crossed Via Vitruvio, dodged cars, and ignored the blaring horns and shouted curses. *Two hundred meters to go!* "Taxi! Taxi!" None stopped.

Stazione Centrale, black and massive, rose beyond Piazza Duca d'Aosta. She rushed across the piazza to the station's giant entry hall and up the first flight of granite steps. She kicked off her shoes, taking two steps at a time. *One more flight of steps.* Her knees buckled, and she fell and scraped her knees and elbows.

I have to make that train! She struggled up and took on the second flight, two steps at a time, then ran through the coal-blackened, vaulted hall to the display board. "Zürich—Linie 6!"

"One gate to the left!" she shouted, while more and more onlookers followed her with their eyes.

She ran.

The train was moving. There he was, standing at the open window, a bewildered look on his face.

"Corporal, wait! Please wait!" she cried. "You can't leave me! You can't leave!" She ran alongside the train, her eyes dry now. "Please, Corporal!"

The train muffled her voice. She reached for his stretched-out hand. Their fingers touched. Her legs gave out. Exhausted, she fell to her knees, unable to go another step.

Herman was torn apart inside. He wanted to jump—but he was paralyzed with pain. And the train kept rolling.

The crouching figure got smaller. A woman knelt beside Angelina and held her in a tight embrace. Sabrina, alerted by Carlo Verdiccio, had caught up with her partner, having left for the station directly from the Galleria Puccini. The two friends watched the train vanish into a snarl of tracks and signals.

EPILOGUE

FRIDAY, OCTOBER 16, 1959

Lightning and thunder dominated the sky, and torrential downpours drenched the flatlands north of the Alps. In the southern part of the range, however, across St. Gotthard Pass and across the Ticino valley all the way to Milan, the sun shone brilliantly from a clear blue sky.

In an aisle seat of the Swissair DC-6, eight rows back, sat a young woman with her infant son napping on her lap. She was not comfortable, obviously, as she closed her eyes and gripped the armrest each time the airplane banked into a turn. She was a striking woman with delicate skin, light blond hair, and wide-set eyes, though she had modest ways and wore a self-effacing smile. She was smartly clothed in a flowery dress tight at her waist that emphasized the loveliness of her slender body, and when she rose from her seat, her high heels made her appear exceptionally tall and elegant.

Sonja Schuller adjusted the air-conditioning nozzle above her seat then sat back down, the baby clinging to her chest. She glanced at her husband leaning halfway from his seat with his safety belt loosely against his thighs, face pressed against the oval window. Sonja admired Herman's confidence. That, along with his youthful dreams and appetite for adventure, had exerted an irresistible attraction.

Herman and Sonja had met at the hotel school in Zürich, where Herman had attended the first week of classes in his military uniform. Though engaged to a man before she went there, Sonja had felt an instant attraction to the young corporal—drawn to him by a force she could neither understand nor overcome. As the months passed, it became evident that he returned her interest. Yet his eyes had often spoken to her of a loss of some kind, a sad experience that he kept at a distance. It was a sadness he hid in words, as if covering something up.

Unexpectedly, toward the end of college, Herman seemed to undergo a change of heart. Out of the blue, he asked Sonja to dinner and they began courting. The shadow in his eyes remained—until they were married six months later in the tiny Catholic church in Glattbrugg, a suburb of Zürich. Then, with his vows of love, his eyes became as clear as crystal.

In many ways, Sonja was different from Herman. She liked an orderly, organized life, with no surprises. Yet when he revealed his plans to emigrate, she never questioned him. And now, one day after her twenty-fourth birthday, they sat in the DC-6 that would take them to a new home—America.

The intercom crackled. "Ladies and gentlemen," the message came, repeated in French and German, "this is Captain Keiser." He cleared his throat. "It is an unusually clear day, and the Alps have never looked more beautiful. I'd like to call your attention to the St. Gotthard Mountain right below us now to your left . . . ."

At the Puccini Galleria in Milan that Friday morning, the Masoni Fashion House was dark and only the safety lanterns in the Galleria and the glare from the Puccini hotel lobby lit the desolate place. Angelina Bianci drove up at the curb. She wasn't sure what she was doing at her business at this early hour, but she had barely slept for the second night, kept awake by a startling dream. She was on a bank of clouds above the tallest mountain peak held there by a force she could neither see nor feel, almost as if sitting on God's invisible hand. Then there was a manly voice, pleasant yet frightening, calling her name, and though she did not recognize nor understand the words being spoken she knew with utter certainty what the voice wanted of her, what she had to do. A similar dream repeated the second night had shaken her almost pathologically. Angelina, always ready to find a portent, saw in the dreams a calling, a premonition. And as she dwelt on the strange phenomenon at work in her subconscious, her thoughts began to focus on—the corporal.

Settled deep in her office chair, Angelina gazed aimlessly around the dim room illuminated only by her desk lamp, a Tiffany, with its colorful inlaid glass. Sighing, she took a framed picture out of the center drawer of her desk—one she looked at often when distressed: Herman Schuller sitting in her desk chair with his disarming smile. His farewell note, crinkled and smeared by tears, was tucked into the frame.

It had been three very long years. She wiped the tears from her eyes with the back of her hand. Her thoughts touched on the Fashion Soirée that fateful Sunday, which had begun so beautifully and ended so heartbreakingly, imagining the empty chair at the end of the stage. The initial shock was still painfully real to her, though Herman's sudden departure hadn't brought about the severe reaction she and everyone around her had expected. She had gone about her business as before, working hard, putting in long hours. But the calm hadn't lasted.

One night, almost a month later, she was awakened by a painful chill. It was a stabbing pain, not unfamiliar—a nauseating pain that scurried up from her stomach across her spine as though a huge hand had yanked the two apart. It didn't last very long, but while it went on, it felt like a struggle inside her body.

"You're stressed, slow down," her physician had said. But the struggle inside her continued, and as it went on, a new and almost unbearable desire for Herman sprang up in her, and she found herself repeatedly at the anteroom of the Puccini restaurant, staring at the empty wingback, imagining him there, waiting for her.

One day, to conquer desire and loneliness, Angelina drove to Switzerland in anticipation of the valley and the Bedretto tavern. But when she reached the Airolo crossroad, she couldn't make the turn. Instead, she continued up the mountain toward St. Gotthard Pass, to a lookout where the Bedretto Valley could be seen spread out below. She parked the Porsche and sat on the safety wall. The view was inspiring. The tiny town of Bedretto lay at her feet, and in the background at the end of the valley, peaceful and strangely remote, All' Acqua was barely visible against the setting sun. She sat until night fell, absorbing the quiet and listening to Airolo's church bell announce the hours and the half hours with its deep, penetrating ring. As Angelina remembered, she felt a gentle awareness, as though

Herman were sitting beside her, talking to her in his gentle way.

She stayed until the lights of the tiny hamlet at the end of the valley faded. From then on, on the second Sunday of each month, Angelina journeyed to the lookout where she found peace and calm. When she returned to Milan, the struggle inside her continued.

Now at a knock on the door, Angelina tore her eyes from the framed note. "Come in," she said.

A young woman entered. "Good morning, signorina," the girl said with respect and fondness. She left the door ajar and added, "Is that a new dress? It is gorgeous; it becomes you well."

Angelina was flattered. "Thank you, Nora, but it is really not new; I designed it three years ago." She stood up and stepped from behind her desk. She turned around letting the skirt fly, and the pleats opened up, exposing her slender legs.

"How beautiful! And only you are beautiful enough to model it," gushed Nora.

Angelina turned away and closed her eyes—someone else had said those very words three years ago.

Nora sensed the emerging shadow and asked quickly, "What do the initials 'AH' mean, signorina?"

Angelina, her back turned to her, wiped away a tear. She said lovingly, "It's a long story, Nora; I'll tell you all about it someday." Instinctively, Angelina pressed her right hand over the initials.

"Anything I can do for you, signorina?"

Angelina faced the girl. "Yes, Nora. Please bring up the Porsche, I'll be leaving shortly."

"Will you be gone for long?"

"Only a few hours. I'll be back long before we close."

"Yes, signorina," said Nora, leaving the office.

Angelina let herself sink into the large desk chair and closed her eyes. She smiled, remembering how he'd said it swallowed her.

"Are you going somewhere?"

Angelina came back to reality. Carlo Verdiccio, immaculate in a black suit, with a fresh daisy in his lapel, was gently tapping at her desk with his ebony cane, wearing his usual bemused smile. Carlo had helped her overcome her sorrow with keen advice, and he knew when to keep his distance.

Two years before, he had moved into the Galleria Vittoria Emanuale adjacent to the great Duomo and turned the second-floor office space into stylish living quarters. His windows overlooked the giant shopping hall with the fashion stores, cafés, fine restaurants, and fancy jewelry shops. He watched shoppers haggle with merchants and diners argue with waiters as he longed for Angelina's love. He took her to fine restaurants, to La Scala and the museum, the park, even to the zoo. When he had asked for her hand in marriage, Angelina had turned him down, saying, "He'll be back; you'll see." Carlo never brought it up again, nor did he change his ways.

Angelina stepped from behind her desk and greeted Carlo with a kiss on each cheek. "I'm going to Switzerland," she said.

"To the Pass? But my dear, you were there last Sunday." Carlo couldn't hide his puzzlement, though he had learned to cope with Angelina's caprices.

"I know, Carlo, but I've had this strange anxiety for the past few days," she said. "I saw him in my dream sitting on the retaining wall at the lookout, beckoning with his stretched-out hand. He stared at me, yet his eyes were empty; he moved his lips, yet he made no sound—but there was a voice and it made me understand that I should meet him there. As much as I wanted to reach out to him, I was frightened. It was not until last night that I began to understand what the dream was telling me. I have to go to the lookout today!"

Carlo shook his head, bewildered. "Are you all right, Angelina? Perhaps I should go with you. I could do the driving while you relax and think things over."

Angelina shook her head. "I know it sounds strange, my dear Carlo." She stepped closer to him and her voice was kind and soft, her breath gentle on his face. "You're a fine friend and you mean well, but please understand, I must do this on my own."

"You just can't put him behind you, can you!" He sounded harsher than he intended and bit his lip to control the rancor that had been building up.

Angelina put her hand on his shoulder. "I can't forget him, Carlo, not yet. He's still in my heart." She pressed his hands to her cheeks. "You've been a wonderful friend to me." She closed her eyes. "Something special is happening today, and I have to find out what it is." She faced him straight on and said passionately, "I'll know tonight, Carlo, whether I can marry you."

Sensing a turn of events, Carlo snapped to attention like a soldier getting his first whiff of a promotion. "I'll pick you up at the apartment for dinner at eight sharp," he said with a smile. He kissed her forehead, picked up his cane, and walked from her office, limping slightly, as always.

Sabrina came in with a coat over her arm and a suitcase in her hand. "Good morning, partner," she said cheerfully. She dropped the suitcase by the door, folded her coat over a chair, and removed her gloves. She walked up to Angelina, who had risen from her desk, and kissed her on both cheeks. Sabrina had left Génova, on the Mediterranean coast, with the early morning train, anxious to bring home the news. "But tell me," Sabrina said amiably, "what's with your outfit—it's the nicest dress you've ever designed."

"Welcome back," Angelina said. "You must have left in the wee hours to be here this soon. How did everything go with the grand opening?"

Sabrina pushed the brass penholder aside, sat on the edge of the desk and crossed her legs. "Exceptionally well, partner," she said with glowing eyes. "It will be a good franchise, but there's much to be done yet—opening day all but emptied their shelves. We have come up with some new ideas, too, and I want to implement them right away. I'll have lots to do during the next few days."

"How's the franchisee holding out? She must be exhausted."

"Actually, she is in great spirits," Sabrina said. "You were right when you said she'd have the stuff to pull through. She is not only smart and beautiful, but she's an exceptionally effective model. You should see her take the stage, knowing and feeling that it is her business."

Angelina listened while Sabrina gave her the complete rundown on their latest business venture, yet her mind wasn't there, and her occasional nods were not convincing.

"Now tell me, Angelina, what's the occasion for the dress?" Sabrina asked, sensing her partner's inattention. "You haven't worn it in years."

"Oh, it's nothing, Sabrina. I just had the urge to wear it," Angelina said with a smile. "By the way, I'll be leaving in a little while."

"Where to?"

"Switzerland."

"To the Pass?"

Angelina nodded.

"Weren't you there last Sunday? I know—it's none of my business," she said, waving her hand. "It's been three long years. Don't you think it is time to put this thing behind you? No man, not even the corporal, is worth that kind of loyalty." Sabrina regretted her outburst. On the other hand, she knew that precisely this fruitless belief in the corporal was what kept Angelina going, giving her the strength and energy to succeed in business.

And what a success they had become. It had taken six sleepless months to perfect the franchise idea Sabrina and Herman had discussed at Puccini's. When Sabrina finally presented it, Angelina not only approved, but jumped in with her relentless energy. Within a year, they had opened a pilot store at Via Monte Napoleone, Milan's leading fashion street, and now competed with fashion giant Paola Fendi's minks and Fernanda Gattinoni's wedding dress designs. They gave Mariucia Mandelli's Krizia a run for its money, and their in-house-designed belts and purses even rivaled those of the incredible Vasco Gucci. Then came their first franchise store in Torino, followed by stores in Firenze, Como, and now Génova.

Sabrina looked at Angelina kindly. "I'm sorry, partner; I didn't mean to be critical of you. It's just, well, I love and respect you so."

Nora entered. "The Porsche is ready, signorina."

The Swissair DC-6 continued its turn while the passengers gloried in the breathtaking, snow-capped mountains.

Herman, his face glued to the window, had a lump in his throat as he followed its curving road to All' Acqua, his mind filled with remembered joy and sadness and love. *Angelina, my sweet Angelina*—he would never forget her kind blue eyes, her inviting lips, her fiery hair, her sweet, soft skin. As he looked over the valley one last time, dreaming of a cabin filled with happiness and love, his heart threatened to burst.

Then, inexplicably, calm took over. The lump in his throat subsided, his murky mind cleared, and he envisioned Angelina far below, waving to him, wishing him a pleasant journey. He raised his hand and beckoned with his fingers. "Goodbye, Angelina. Farewell, my love," he whispered. And as he wiped the last tear from his cheek, he felt new warmth coming into his mind and heart.

He turned in his seat toward his son and looked into his blue, blue eyes and ran his fingers through his curly blond hair.

Angelina parked her Porsche by the lookout and turned off the ignition. It was so quiet and peaceful.

She heard the faint noise of aircraft engines coming from the Pass. She looked up and saw the airliner in a shallow bank above the lookout. Angelina had seen other planes crossing the mighty San Gotthard, but something was different. She felt a quiver of excitement as if at the vibration of someone's love. Her heart pounded louder and stronger; her chest tightened and robbed her of her breath. Angelina rose from her seat breathing deeply, holding in the precious air.

A small cry from the seat beside her pulled her from her thoughts. "Oh, my bambino," Angelina cried softly. She picked up the two-year-old toddler from the seat and pressed him to her chest. "Come to Mammia—come watch the plane," she whispered. There were tears in her eyes. She and the infant followed the airplane as it finished the turn and continued in a westerly direction. As Angelina followed its course, thoughts of the corporal intensified as never before. She saw him clearly before her, smelled his breath, felt his arms about her and his tender lips against hers. She wanted to touch him, to love him, to hold him one more time and never let go. Her thoughts turned to the cabin above Losanche. *Oh, Herman, oh darling.*

Then, peace came to her like the calm after a wild summer storm. The engines could no longer be heard, the plane was lost beyond the horizon. Herman had slipped from her as quietly as he had entered her heart on that glorious Sunday afternoon so long ago. "Goodbye, Corporal," she whispered. The pool of tears overflowed her cheeks and fell into her baby's hair.

Suddenly, yielding to a strong impulse, she shouted, "Yes, Carlo—yes! I will marry you!"

She turned toward her son and looked into his blue, blue eyes and ran her fingers through his curly blond hair.

THE END

ABOUT THE AUTHOR

*H*ansueli Schlunegger, always had a creative streak even as a child growing up in Switzerland. He dreamed of becoming a master chef, catering to the in crowds and upper crust of society. After completing his culinary education, his early career led him to some of the great European cities, including Basel, Zürich, Geneva, St. Moritz, Oslo, and Stockholm. In 1959, he moved his young family to the United States and became Chef de Partie at the Western International Olympic Hotel in Seattle. They eventually relocated to Houston, where Hans wowed the Texans with his culinary skills at the Rice Hotel. Hans directed the dinner preparation for President and Mrs. Kennedy on November 21, 1963. Hans later became Executive Chef at Houston's renowned international hotel, The Warwick, which catered to the rich and famous.

Hans and his wife, Annemarie, began their entrepreneurial career in the Texas Hill Country in 1969, buying several hotels, including the plush Inn of the Hills Conference Resort in Kerrville, Texas, where they enjoy entertaining and hosting people from all over the world.

Entrepreneurship has allowed Hansueli to branch out into other creative endeavors, and this is his first novel. He is currently busy working on a sequel.